THE ART OF EXILE

THE ART OF EXILE

ANDREA MAX

MARGARET K. MCELDERRY BOOKS
New York Amsterdam/Antwerp London
Toronto Sydney/Melbourne New Delhi

TO THE TEACHERS,
who, despite countless odds, are still fighting
to teach the importance of art, the integrity
of science, and the truth of history

MARGARET K. McELDERRY BOOKS
An imprint of Simon & Schuster Children's Publishing Division
1230 Avenue of the Americas, New York, New York 10020
For more than 100 years, Simon & Schuster has championed authors and the stories they create.
By respecting the copyright of an author's intellectual property, you enable Simon & Schuster
and the author to continue publishing exceptional books for years to come. We thank you for
supporting the author's copyright by purchasing an authorized edition of this book.

MARGARET K. MCELDERRY BOOKS is a trademark of Simon & Schuster, LLC.
For information about special discounts for bulk purchases, please contact Simon & Schuster
Special Sales at 1-866-506-1949 or business@simonandschuster.com.
Simon & Schuster strongly believes in freedom of expression and stands against
censorship in all its forms. For more information, visit BooksBelong.com.
The Simon & Schuster Speakers Bureau can bring authors to your live event. For more
information or to book an event, contact the Simon & Schuster Speakers Bureau at
1-866-248-3049 or visit our website at www.simonspeakers.com.
The text for this book was set in Adobe Garamond Pro.
Manufactured in the United States of America
First Edition
2 4 6 8 10 9 7 5 3 1
CIP data for this book is available from the Library of Congress.
ISBN 9781665959841 (hardcover)
ISBN 9781665959865 (ebook)

GENESIS INSTITUTE GUILDS

Sophists—social sciences and humanities
Guildstone: sapphire
High Material: sense

Artisans—fine art and performance art
Guildstone: amethyst
High Material: loam

Alchemists—chemistry and earth sciences
Guildstone: emerald
High Material: glace

Ciphers—mathematics and physics
Guildstone: pearl
High Material: spidersilk

Bioscience—biological sciences and healing
Guildstone: amber
High Material: sap

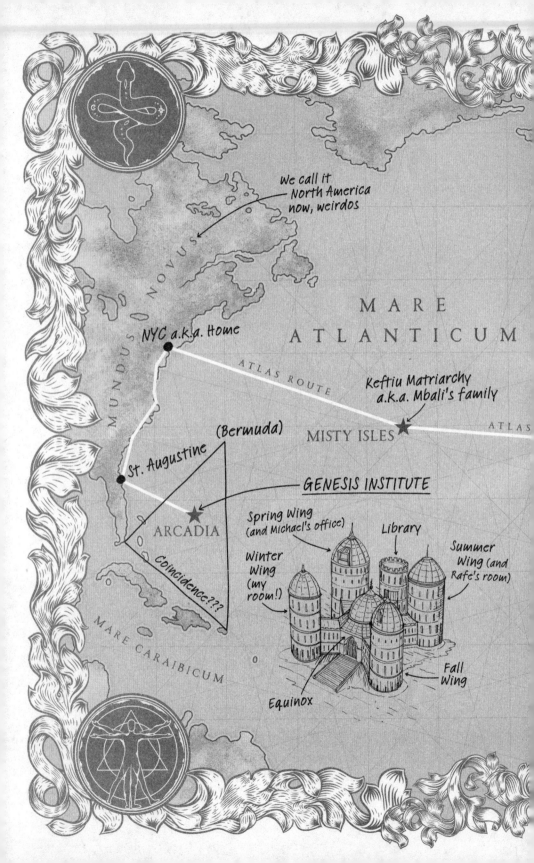

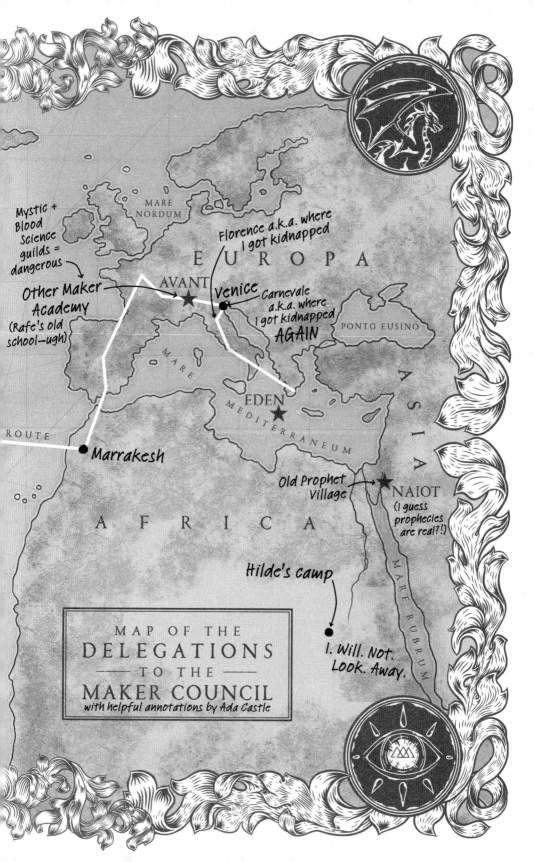

MARE
NORDUM

Mystic +
Blood
Science
guilds =
dangerous

Florence a.k.a. where
I got kidnapped

E U R O P A

Other Maker
Academy
(Rafe's old
school—ugh)

AVANT

Venice Carnevale
a.k.a. where
I got kidnapped
AGAIN

PONTO EUSINO

MARE

M E D I T E R R A N E U M

EDEN

A S I A

ROUTE

Marrakesh

A F R I C A

Old Prophet
Village

NAIOT
(I guess
prophecies
are real?!)

MARE RUBRUM

Hilde's camp

MAP OF THE
DELEGATIONS
— TO THE —
MAKER COUNCIL
with helpful annotations by Ada Castle

I. Will. Not.
Look. Away.

1

It figures that when I'm finally chosen for something, it's to be kidnapped.

I'm trapped in a box. My knees are pulled to my chest, my whole left side numb from lying here for so long. My head throbs from the blow that knocked me out earlier, and metal gloves restrain my hands behind my back, painfully burning my skin. The burning subsides when I relax, but that's difficult under the circumstances. If I ever get out of here—please, please let me get out of here—I expect to find my palms burned and blistered like over-grilled cheese.

A sob escapes, and in the cramped space, there's no room for my breath to go except back to me, warm and cloying against my cheek. Strands of my wavy brown hair stick to my face and tickle my eyes, forcing me to keep them shut.

Maybe if I'd received some training before this ill-fated trip, I'd know what to do. Instead, I'm utterly helpless.

I have no idea what's going to happen to me.

The allegro of my heart beats faster, and my throat tightens. My palms prickle with a familiar warmth. *No.*

Breathe. Don't panic.

I had a glass of wine before I was taken, which, at first, helped subdue my hysteria. But now it's worn off and traveled from my head to my bladder, where it sits with an uncomfortable, building pressure. I won't be able to hold it in for much longer.

Inhale.

Exhale.

Think of puppies and guys with dimples.

I was with a guy with dimples when I was captured. A guy who is clearly not who he seemed to be.

Tsss. I gasp as the glove scorches the flesh of my palm near the base of my thumb.

Don't think about him.

Inhale.

Exhale.

Don't panic.

Who knows how many hours earlier . . .

When I was planning my trip to Italy, I daydreamed about falling for an Italian, so this should be no surprise. However, I hadn't expected him to be over five hundred years old. I also hadn't expected to cry. Yet here come the tears, blurring my vision as I look up at him.

David.

The veins in his hand pulse with tension. I can almost feel him breathe, can almost see the blood orchestrating the life under his skin of cold, hard marble as he prepares to face his much stronger foe. I've heard his expression described as determined, but as his gaze bores into me now, it seems more . . . unsure, self-conscious.

Same, babe. Same.

I can't believe I almost skipped coming to the Accademia Gallery where

Michelangelo's *David* stands ready to sweep unsuspecting tourists off their feet.

I've seen enough naked male bodies (only one and a half up close and personal, but who's counting) to realize how incredibly lifelike he is. Though I haven't ever seen, uh, anyone uncircumcised, so I can't comment on that particular bit of artistry. Not that I'm looking.

But the fact that a person could hew this man out of stone absolutely boggles my mind.

My dad often quotes that "Man was created in the image of God." Having a Jewish father, an agnostic mother, and a Catholic grandfather, I've always found the concept of "god" to be pretty abstract. But for the first time, I maybe understand what that quote means. The ability to create something as beautiful as *David*, to craft flesh and bone from mere marble, is surely some kind of divinity.

But this realization of the heights of human potential kinda sucks.

Because how do I use *my* potential?

This question settles over me, and for a moment I hate myself. For every unfinished painting, every half-written song, every abandoned story. Every attempt that was never quite good enough. Even this trip, which is almost over, and I have yet to accomplish what I was sent to do. I'd come knowing it was a long shot, finding one man in all of Florence, but I'd hoped to finally prove myself to my family. And the door's about to close on my one and only chance to do so.

I look up at *David* again; his intense gaze now seems to be one of accusation.

It's a familiar feeling. Growing up as the least talented member in a family of artists and scholars, I'm accustomed to being judged. I know I have talents, but they often feel more like expectations.

And I always fall short.

I sniff and glance around to see if I can get away with wiping my nose on my sleeve, but somebody's watching me. A very handsome somebody. And this handsome body has an actual heartbeat, and, though quite tall, is still within the realm of human size, unlike my new boyfriend towering above us. Now I'm even more self-conscious of my tears.

I look back at the boy—the living, breathing one, that is—and he's still watching me. When our eyes meet, he smiles, and he has dimples that are so charming that I decide to break up with *David* on the spot.

Sorry, my love. I'll still buy a postcard with your face on it.

Mr. Dimples is moving toward me now, or maybe he's just trying to see the sculpture from another angle. He's even cuter up close, all long limbs and floppy brown hair. A blue gemstone hoop hugs his right earlobe. I've been on the hunt for someone wearing a sapphire earring but . . . no. He's nothing like the recruiter I've been told to look for: a Black man in his fifties with an eye patch or sunglasses and three piercings in one ear of sapphire, emerald, and pearl. This guy might have a blue earring, but he's white, looks like he's in college, and has nothing obscuring his twinkling brown eyes and too-long lashes.

The T-shirt he's wearing has a picture of da Vinci's *Vitruvian Man* playing an electric guitar.

Be still my beating heart.

I pretend to scratch my nose so I can deal with the snot situation as inconspicuously as possible. Then I too decide to see *David* from another angle, wandering close enough to give Mr. Dimples an opening to flirt with me. Though the fact that he just watched me cry over a statue might reduce my chances.

He smiles in a way that shows he sees right through my ploy, and now he's close enough for me to see that the dimple on his left cheek is deeper than the one on the right.

"Nice shirt," I say.

"It's refreshing," he responds, "to watch someone truly appreciate a masterpiece."

Heat rises in my cheeks. "Isn't it rude to come in here flaunting a rival's work?" I ask, eyeing his T-shirt meaningfully.

"Da Vinci and Michelangelo weren't rivals," he says with complete assurance.

Considering that I don't know nearly as much about the Renaissance masters as I wish I did, I'll take his word for it.

He extends his hand to me. "I'm Michael."

I awkwardly shake his hand. It's warm and calloused, but his nails have been chewed to the quick.

"I'm Ada," I reply as I pull my hand from his, though I can't say I want to.

One of his dark brows arches. "Like Ada Lovelace," he says.

This takes me by surprise. Only a certain kind of person immediately associates my name with Ada, Countess of Lovelace, the first computer programmer.

"The inventor of poetical science," he continues, amused. "My very favorite kind of science."

"Theoretical physics is my favorite kind of science," I respond. "Too bad I suck at math."

"Theoretical physics is definitely in my top three," he says.

"For the time travel, right?" I ask.

"How did you know?"

I should stop grinning so hard; I don't want to appear too eager. But he's grinning too.

"So, you're a fan of sculpture?" he asks.

"I didn't know I was until today." No other sculpture has ever hit like this one.

"Ah, yes, the *David* can have that effect on people."

I feel the easy flow of the conversation settling to a natural conclusion, see the polite shift in his manner as he prepares to move on. But I dumped *David* for this guy, so I can't let him slip through my fingers just yet. I say, "If you know so much about its creator, what else can you tell me about my new favorite piece of art?"

"Ah, so I've been unsuccessful at hiding the fact that I'm an insufferable know-it-all." Michael runs his hands through his thick brown hair, pushing it out of his eyes, and his forearm flexes in a way that makes me want to inspect his form as closely as I just did *David*'s.

"You say know-it-all. I say kind educator of ignorant, helpless tourists."

"Ah, yes, ignorant and helpless, the exact two adjectives I would use to describe you," he says with a dimpled grin. "Well, did you know that in order to familiarize himself with human anatomy, Michelangelo dissected cadavers?"

"I did not know that."

Michael mimics the position of *David*'s hand with his own. "So much of the realism is because Michelangelo was as knowledgeable about the human body as any physician."

I add, "And he was also a painter, architect, and engineer. Talk about a know-it-all." I roll my eyes dramatically.

"You say know-it-all. I say true embodiment of the Renaissance ideal." He lowers his hand.

"The epitome of a Renaissance man," I say wistfully and perhaps with an edge of bitterness.

The concept of a Renaissance man—someone who's an expert in multiple fields—is an ambition I'm all too familiar with. It's the very ideal that's been hammered into me by my family ever since my hands were big enough to hold a paintbrush and plink at the keys of a piano. But I couldn't keep up with those expectations. So while my brilliant best friends, Kor and Izzy, spent years training in all sorts of disciplines, I was left home to merely dabble in various hobbies just long enough to start to get good at them and then get bored and move on to something new.

"And here's another fun fact," Michael continues. "The piece of stone used for the *David* had been discarded by other artists for being too flawed. But Michelangelo saw its potential. He carved it freehand, with no model, claiming that he was revealing the form that was already inside as opposed to designing it himself."

I look up at the statue of an underestimated boy about to fight a giant with nothing but a slingshot. The knowledge that the stone he was created from was equally underestimated adds an additional layer to my appreciation.

Am I underestimated? Or do I just suck?

Considering that many people are relying on me to accomplish a crucial task, but instead I'm getting my flirt on—I'm leaning toward the latter.

"That's really cool," I say. "Seeing something's truest potential instead of its most negative outcome. Unfortunately, I'm a chronic cynic."

"Is that so? Then what's this interaction's most negative outcome?" He motions his hands between us.

"You turn out to be a kidnapper who's hoping to add my teeth to the collection hidden behind your bedroom mirror?"

His eyebrows shoot up, and his eyes widen. "Okay. Thank you for reminding me of the realities of being a woman alone in a big city. My answer was going to be you leaving before I get the chance to ask you out. But you're right, molar harvesting is a lot worse."

I tuck escaping waves of brown hair behind my ear. I heard correctly: the hot, smart dude wants to ask me out. "Well, I can't possibly go out with you now that I know what you keep behind your mirror!" I say.

Michael steps closer. "Or instead of planning for the most negative outcome, you could consider the positive potential."

My breath hitches. "Well," I say. "What do you think the most positive outcome of our interaction could be?"

"I have a few ideas."

"Is that so?"

"Indeed." He winks. "Starting with more titillating discussions of sculpture."

"You think you're joking, but that sounds excellent to me."

He grins. "In that case . . ." He motions for me to follow him as he heads away from *David* and down the corridor. It's lined with statues of men. But they're incomplete, their shapes emerging from rough, unfinished stone.

"These are Michelangelo's Prisoners," Michael explains. "He deliberately left them unfinished to represent the struggle of humanity."

Prisoners. Like they're trapped in the rock, trying to escape. God, don't I feel just like that sometimes. Like I could just *break free* if—

"Sometimes I feel just like that," Michael says. Our eyes meet, and I'm flooded with the warmth of shared experience.

"I know what you mean," I say, finding it hard to break his gaze. I blink and clear my throat. "So, where does all your sculpture knowledge come from?" I ask. "Do you read up on art trivia just to pick up tourists?"

"I do, actually," Michael replies.

"I *knew* it." I'm grinning too big again. "Okay, but what's the real answer?"

"Well, I have a vested interest in Michelangelo because I was named after him."

It takes me a moment for it to click. Michael, Michelangelo. My eyebrows rise.

"I applaud your valiant effort not to make fun of me," Michael says.

I scrunch up my nose. "No! I was just . . . thinking about what kind of parents you must have."

"Ha. The kind who read Machiavelli and Maimonides to my sister and me before we were old enough to read on our own."

"I see. I was only getting Shakespeare at that age. My grandfather didn't graduate me to the philosophers until middle school."

"A kindred spirit! Have you too been raised constantly terrified to fall off the pedestal you've been placed on?"

"Oh, no. I fell off my pedestal long ago. I'm now officially 'the disappointing one.'"

"You? Disappointing? The standards must be high."

I feel a blush creep up my cheeks. "You have no idea." He really doesn't. The standards I'm compared to are ridiculous. Kor is at Columbia with a growing collection of honors, has his artwork displayed in various prestigious galleries around New York City, and have I mentioned his recent Grammy nomination? Izzy's in her first year at MIT, and an app she designed was just bought by one of the world's most successful companies, Ozymandias Tech. Meanwhile, I—though I've been aggressively avoiding thinking about it—have already missed the deadlines on some of my (very mid-tier) college applications.

I brush my bitter thoughts aside and ask Michael, "What has you worried about falling from your pedestal?"

He looks away, talking to the statue instead of to me. "Sometimes . . . I want to question the status quo. Do what I think is right instead of what I've been taught is right."

"What's the worst that could happen if you do?"

"I'll let people down, lose their trust." He pauses and then adds, "Not know who I am if I'm not who I'm expected to be."

It scares me just how well I know what he means. I don't think I've ever felt this connected to someone this quickly. And that's scary too, like holding something impossibly delicate, just waiting for it to fall apart.

"And what's the best that could happen?" I ask.

He looks at me contemplatively without answering.

I teasingly poke his arm. "What happened to seeing the truest potential instead of the most negative outcome?"

He cocks his head, watches me for a moment, then says, "I needed to hear that. I feel like meeting you today was meant to be."

Meant to be. It does feel that way. But I'm not about to admit it. "I don't know. That sounds an awful lot like something a kidnapper would say." I jokingly back away.

He lifts his fingers toward his mouth as if to continue the decimation of his nails, but he catches himself, lowers his hand, and instead says, "Come out with me for a drink."

My heart is thumping so fast. I want to say yes. But there's a small tug at the back of my mind telling me that he's too handsome, too sophisticated to actually be interested in very average *me*. I can't help but wonder if he's taking interest for another reason. He does know an awful lot about Renaissance history. . . .

No. I've given him no reason to suspect who I am. He's asking me out for real.

"A drink sounds lovely," I say.

★ ★ ★ ★ ★

When we exit the museum, the sun has mostly set. The days are short during these winter months.

Mom would not be happy. Me going out with a boy was definitely not something she had in mind when she agreed to let me go on this assignment during my winter break. To alleviate my guilt, I send her a quick message saying that I'll call her before I go to bed. I've been good about calling her daily, though I don't know why I bother since she's always too busy to talk. I also text my aunt who I'm staying with to let her know I'll be back late.

Apparently, in addition to art, Michael is also extremely knowledgeable about Florence, and as we walk to a restaurant he recommends, he tells me about the different churches and piazzas we pass. We stop a few times to listen to buskers filling the squares with their crooning covers of every generation's greatest hits. I even hear a rendition of "Mona Lisa Smile," the single that skyrocketed Kor from playing the underground Columbia University music scene to the top of the Billboard charts last year. He's still pissed about it, considering that everyone thinks it's a love song, and he insists that it is *not* a love song.

But even though I know Kor's intention with the song, I can't help but find it romantic when the lyrics *You'll see whatever you want to see, her truth is whatever you want it to be* pull Michael's gaze to mine. And when the line *If that's what you seek, then she's sure to beguile, but don't lose yourself in her Mona Lisa smile* draws his gaze down to my lips, I don't think I'm reading this wrong. I'm pretty confident I'm getting kissed tonight.

Michael leaves a jangle of coins for each busker before we move on. I like that. I like a lot of things about him.

When we're not talking, there's a comfortable quiet between us that buzzes with possibility. I watch his hand, which swings beside mine. It's constantly animated, stretching, tapping, emphasizing his words. If I shift just a little, our hands would inevitably brush against each other the next time he swings his arm. I imagine the thrill of the contact, but I don't step closer.

We arrive at the restaurant, and it's crowded with people enjoying their meals, nursing glasses of wine and plates of decadent carbohydrates. The room is small and echoes with the sounds of live piano. Really good piano. I breathe in the smells of crusty bread, simmering sauces, and melting wax.

Michael is familiar with the necessary choreography to get us a cozy, candlelit table with a bench facing the music. He slides in next to me and asks me if I want anything to eat or just a drink.

"Just a glass of red wine," I say, trying to sound like the type of girl who might actually have a preference between red and white grape water. It must work well enough because no one asks to see my ID.

While we wait for our drinks, Michael asks, "What instrument do you play?"

"How do you know I play an instrument?"

"I can tell," he says. "I have a sixth sense when it comes to pretty musicians." Grin. Dimple. Eyebrow raise. His eyebrows have more expression than my entire face. "Also, you're tapping your fingers along with the music in a very telling way."

My cheeks warm. "I play guitar, but I'm hardly a musician. I'm really bad at it." Despite growing up surrounded by multiple musicians, this is true. I'm even worse at the other instruments I've dabbled with. I try to hold off the descending wave of mediocrity and focus instead on the part where he called me pretty.

"I play guitar too," he says.

"Yeah, I had a feeling." His hand is resting on the table next to mine, and deciding to be bold, I trace the callouses along the tips of his fingers. The kind earned by the intimacy of stringed instruments.

He swallows, his Adam's apple bobbing. "I'm . . . not bad at it."

"I bet." Who knew I had a thing for Adam's apples? I very much do.

My fingertips are still touching his, and he gently twines our fingers together. His hand is strong and warm, and everywhere our skin touches feels sensitive, like the nerves are directly connected to my tightening belly.

The waiter arrives with our wine, and Michael raises his glass while keeping one hand linked with mine. "To seeing the true potential despite the flaws." We clink our glasses. In the candlelight, his brown eyes look almost amber from beneath his thick, long lashes. His thumb is tracing circles on my palm, spreading heat along my skin. My breathing starts to go wonky.

It feels a little too intense, so I pull my hand away. I also instinctively work to calm the tingling sensation in my hands. The tingling is something that often happens when I'm nervous or excited, but I don't want to worry about that right now, even though it has everything to do with why I'm in Florence in the first place.

I take a sip of wine. It's tart and, honestly, not very tasty. But definitely better than the craft beer that Kor likes (and that I pretend to like to impress him). I take another sip and feel it warm my empty stomach and my excited nerves.

"You seem really familiar with the area," I say to Michael. "Do you live here?"

"No. I live quite far away." He doesn't elaborate, and his expression tells me I have reason to be curious.

"Where's far away?"

"I doubt you've heard of it," he says with a smile that doesn't reach his eyes.

Why is he being cagey?

The gemstone in his earring glitters in the candlelight, and I feel a fizzing in my blood, a return of that nagging feeling from earlier. He approached me first. He won't tell me where he's from. He knows more about Renaissance history than the average college guy.

No. I'm being silly. He asked me out because I shamelessly flirted with him. Do I really find it so hard to believe someone would want to go out with me without ulterior motives?

"What about you? Where are you from?" Michael asks, diverting the attention away from himself.

I shake off the feeling that this is anything other than what it is. "New York City," I respond, and take another sip of wine. "How did you know about this place?" Maybe it's the alcohol in my blood that encourages me to shift closer to be heard over the rising noise in the room, so close our thighs press together.

Michael leans even closer to answer. His breath tickles my ear. "I've been coming here for the pianist. We're considering recruiting him to the school where I work." His nose is so close that it brushes against my cheek. But I don't respond to the physical touch because I'm confused by what he's said.

Recruiting for a school? It's too much of a coincidence.

But also, if he's not a college student, how old is this guy?

I'd assumed around nineteen. The fact that he was clearly older than me had felt exciting, but how much older is he actually? I try not to stare as I reassess. Full head of dark hair. Crinkles around his eyes, but only because he's smiling. There's certainly a maturity about him that I hadn't noted before. Suddenly, he seems kind of ageless, and I feel panicky. How old does he think I am? Will it matter? I really don't want to ruin this.

"So, you're a teacher?" I ask.

"I guess you could call it that. What do you do? I'm guessing you're still in school." His smile is wide, and by the way he says "school," I know he means college and that he's not going to be comfortable when he realizes I'm only a senior in high school.

"Um . . . yeah, still in school. I'm on winter break," I respond.

"What are you studying? Wait, let me guess . . . art history?" Still with that smile and those oh-so-playful dimples. I really don't want to, but I know I need to tell him.

"Actually, um, Michael, I'm still in high school."

His thigh that is pressed against mine tenses. His eyes widen, and he assesses my appearance much like I did his a moment before.

"How old are you?"

"Almost eighteen." Depending on what constitutes as "almost."

"Oh." He sits up straight, shifting over so none of his body is in contact with mine. I feel cold air replace his warmth. "I should've . . . I just assumed . . . I mean, a smart, beautiful—uh, traveling on your own . . ."

The bench is small, and we're still very close, and the music is loud, and it's just too much for me. I stand, my napkin fluttering to the floor. "Maybe let's go outside and get some air?"

"Good idea." As Michael leaves some euros on the table, I rush into the cool night. He follows behind me tentatively. We dodge a couple of smokers and lean against a stretch of the cast-iron gate. The leaves of a dying potted plant sag along the rails, crunchy and brown. I busy my fingers by massaging the stem of the plant. Michael starts to nibble his nails, then catches himself and instead pulls a Swiss Army–style multi-tool from his pocket. He flips the bottle opener open and shut, open and shut. We both look at the ground instead of at each other.

He called me smart and beautiful.

I'm too soft, too frizzy to meet the standard definition of beautiful. I have some nice features: large brown eyes and a button nose, a butt that's too big, or just right, depending on who you ask. Average pretty. But I understand that there is a distinct difference between pretty and beautiful.

Unfortunately, "average pretty" has never been good enough for Kor, but Michael seems to like it.

Not that it matters anymore. The disappointment burns deep. I guess I should have known Michael was too good to be true.

"So how old are you?" I finally ask him.

"Twenty-one."

Okay, that's not *that* bad. I went out with a senior during my freshman year of high school, and he must be about twenty-one by now. Kor's already twenty. But the active distance Michael is keeping between us makes it clear that my age is a hard no for him.

I continue fiddling with the plant, wrapping it around the bars of the gate. It brings that tingling warmth to the skin between my fingers, a feeling I'm so used to suppressing that I immediately remove my hand from the leaves. I don't quite know where to look or what to think as the silence descends between us, the buzz from earlier now completely unbuzzed, doused with a cold bucket of awkward.

The easy thing to do would be to walk away. But I can't. No matter how disappointed I may feel right now, the fact that Michael is here to recruit students is not something I can ignore. I need to establish whether he's who I've been sent to find.

Despite my instincts warring against the action, I reach out to touch the plant again; I can use it to help confirm my suspicions. I normally try to avoid the tingling in my hands at all costs, but now I do the opposite and let it flow freely. As I do, I pry for more information.

"Twenty-one seems pretty young to be a teacher at a graduate level," I say. There's no way he's teaching anyone younger; that piano player had been a full-on adult.

Michael blushes at this and looks down as he says, "I was the youngest, uh, graduate in my field in the past two decades."

Handsome, sweet, and a prodigy. Figures.

I'm itchy with nerves as I feel the warmth still flowing from my hand into the plant. I can't help but hear my mother in my head warning me that someone is watching, my father telling me to take deep breaths and hide it.

But when Michael glances at the plant curling around my fingers, his eyes light with wonder.

"What are you doing?" he asks.

"Just adjusting the stem so it will have better sunlight in the morning."

"Ada, look at the vine. It was practically dead a few moments ago. Now it looks one sunny day away from pollinating."

"I've always been good with plants," I say. It's true, but that's not all this is.

This is me using the abilities that make me different. The abnormality that, if I play my cards right, could get me the invite I've been sent across the globe for. The curse that, until recently, I was convinced no one must know about but now may finally prove useful for something.

Michael's eyes are rapidly roving over me, but not in a suggestive way; it's more . . . clinical.

"Do you heal easily?" he asks.

Alarm ignites in my gut. This line of questioning practically confirms my hunch. The answer to his question is "yes." Though I've injured myself many times, it's never been serious. Like the first time I went snowboarding and crashed into a tree but was completely fine, or when I cut halfway through my finger with pruning shears and didn't need stitches.

When I don't answer, he presses on. "Does your hair grow fast?"

Yes again. My wavy brown hair, and my nails too, no matter how often I cut them, constantly seem to grow, grow, grow. I have always suspected that these traits are symptoms of what makes me different, but the only way Michael could guess these things is if this rendezvous was less of a coincidence than I thought.

I still haven't responded, but he senses the affirmative in my gaze.

"Eureka," he says in a quiet voice. His playfulness has been replaced with seriousness, and now he looks older. More his age. "I've been coming to this place every night this week to recruit a pianist when I should've been looking for you all along."

I should be excited by this; instead, my stomach is heavy with disappointment. I just wanted to go on a date with a cute boy.

Not a boy, I remind myself. A man.

And over the course of our flirtatious banter, I have learned almost nothing about him. I don't know where he's from or what he's really doing here in Italy.

Which probably has to do with why *I* was sent to Italy.

My pulse picks up. I'm so close to what I came here for, but I'm also scared. I'm alone at night with an older stranger, who I accepted a drink from, who's watching me like I'm a science experiment. I need some space.

"I need to use the bathroom," I say.

"Oh, okay. I'll wait here for you."

I reenter the restaurant and wind my way through the throng of people to the hallway in the back. A draft from the service entrance to the parking lot chills me as I push through the bathroom door.

I go to the sink and press cool water to my flushed cheeks. The door creaks, and I twist around, but no one's there. The hair on the back of my neck rises, and I turn off the water. The faucet continues to drip.

Drip.

Drip.

I see movement in the mirror, but when I whip around again, there's still nothing. I reach into my pocket for my phone, fumbling to unlock it, too scared to even breathe.

A large arm snakes around my torso. Panic jolts through me as my phone drops and skitters across the tiled floor. I push against my attacker and almost manage to slither out of his grasp, but then pain explodes behind my eyes as I'm struck on the back of my head. Everything goes fuzzy around the edges.

That's when I'm shoved into a box.

2

I'm considering peeing my pants.

I've spent all my time in this box calming my fears to prevent that tingling in my hands, which seems to trigger the gloves to burn me, but now my anxieties have been reduced to one thought:

Hold in the pee.

But who knows how much longer I'll be in here?

Izzy had said she had a bad feeling about this trip, and now I wish I'd taken her more seriously.

Maybe I should just . . .

Is this really what it's come to? I finally get to become part of my family's historic order. I finally get the chance to do something meaningful with my life. And I fumble it all so bad that it ends with me peeing my pants? Am I actually doing this?

Cons of just doing it:

1) My clothes will be wet.

2) I'll be stuck in a box that smells like pee.

3) I will have peed my pants.

Pros of just doing it:

1) The glorious lack of pee in my bladder.

Yup, I'm doing it.

But before I relax the necessary muscles, I hear movement outside the box. There's no way I'm facing my captors covered in pee.

My bladder is a steel fortress. It will not yield.

The walls of the box are creaking and shaking. Someone is finally opening this thing. My fear returns, and with it, the painful burn of the gloves. I'm still acutely aware of the pressure down below, but with the knowledge that I'm about to be out of here, and possibly on to some new kind of horror, letting it flow no longer feels like an option.

My bladder is a concrete dam. The floodgates will not fail.

There's a lot of bumbling and fumbling. These guys don't sound particularly well orchestrated.

Not guys plural, only one guy. Or so I see after my eyes recover from the light that streams in once he manages to pry open the crate. The face that greets me is the same one that's been on my mind most of my intolerably long imprisonment. Disappointment mingles with my fear; I had really hoped he wasn't involved.

Michael helps me up, and I immediately stumble and end up flat on my butt on the floor of what looks to be a conspicuously empty garage. I have no sense of balance with my arms still restrained and my legs cramped. Michael helps me back up again. There's a large gash on his forehead with blood crusting over a blossoming bruise.

He gives me a tired smile.

I trusted that smile. It makes me so angry that I forget to be afraid. So angry that despite the risk of accidentally losing control of my bladder, I knee him squarely in the groin.

His eyes go wide as he folds over clutching himself. Lucky for him, my legs are still pretty noodley, and there wasn't as much force behind my strike as I would have liked.

"What was that for?" he chokes out.

"You put me in a box!"

"Of course I didn't!" He's recovered somewhat, though he's hopping around awkwardly. "I'm here to rescue you!" His hands remain protectively over his crotch. "I knew you might be in danger, so when I saw two guys loading a girl-size crate into a truck and then saw your phone on the bathroom floor, I went after them. I actually stole a kid's bike to tail them. Stole a bike. From a child!" He finally drops his hands, then sighs. "I've been waiting for hours for a chance to sneak in without being seen. Now here I am"—he levels an accusing glare at my knee—"the lucky recipient of your gratitude."

The gash on his forehead is seeping fresh blood, and it looks pretty bad.

"What happened to your face?" I ask.

He looks away and mumbles something about not having a lot of experience riding bicycles.

Ouch. "Well, what do you mean, you thought I was in danger?"

"Once I realized that you're a Sire," he responds.

"A what?"

"A Sire. It was obvious once I saw you revive the plant."

My mostly-a-mystery-to-me abilities have a name, and this can't-tell-if-he's-safe-or-not stranger knows what it is. Which only strengthens my suspicions about who he must be.

"I'll explain more once we get you out of here," he says.

"No. Why does me being a, um, Sire mean I'm in danger?"

"There's been a slew of Sire abductions recently. Which is why my school has been recruiting Sires—to bring them somewhere safer."

Abductions. I wasn't prepared for any of this.

Granted, this whole trip came together very quickly.

Despite my family's generations-long participation in a historic order, I was never able to be a part of it. I'd grown up with all the stories, heard so many of their wild, secret theories, and I couldn't wait to be trained to take part in their important work. Kor and Izzy were both initiated into the order on their thirteenth birthdays, but then my own birthday came and went with nothing. My mother said I probably just needed to wait until they considered me ready. I worked so hard the next few years, hoping to impress whoever needed to be impressed, but nothing I did ever seemed to be good enough. Eventually, I stopped trying.

Until last month, when the Families discovered the condition I'd been hiding for so long. And it turned out they needed someone exactly like me for this job. I was given an itinerary, basic explanations of what to look out for, and that was it. I knew there were some risks, but no one had said anything about any *abductions*.

I feel my panic rising, but I'm still wearing the gloves and am not in the mood to have my hands cooked again. At least I'm out of the box.

I was in a *box*.

The reality of what I've just been through floods through me. I've been damming up my emotions as much as my need to pee, but now they're breaking through.

"I was trapped for *hours*." I choke on a sob. "Why didn't you call the police or something?"

Michael is immediately at my side, laying a comforting hand on my arm. "Ada, I'm sorry, but these are not people that the police can protect you from. Hopefully I can. I promise that I'm here to help you, but we need to move quickly. The guards are gone for now, but I don't want to take any chances. We've been incredibly lucky so far."

I swallow past the lump in my throat and try to regain as much control as I can. "Well, if you're here to help, can you get these off." I shake my hands behind my back, the metal clanking loudly. "They really hurt."

"They're causing you pain?" He looks confused by this.

"A lot of pain," I say through gritted teeth.

Michael circles me and crouches to inspect the gloves. He winces as he bends, and I feel a twinge of guilt for my testicular assault. He prods the gloves, then sniffs them. "By the Conductor," he whispers in awe.

Who the hell is the Conductor?

I crane my neck to watch what he's doing. He flips through the different functions of his multi-tool and uses one to tinker with the locking mechanism. "Are you still able to conduct?" he asks me.

"What?"

"Sorry, I mean like you did with the plant. Can you push energy through your hands?"

I stare at him blankly, but my mind is the opposite of blank. Push energy through my hands? Is that what I have been doing all my life?

"Never mind," Michael says in response to my clear confusion. "Are the gloves still hurting you? Right now?"

They're not, actually. My current discomfort is from the preexisting burns. I shake my head.

He bites his lips and continues to work at the lock, now with more urgency. He swipes at his brow, irritating the messy wound, which starts to bleed again. Seeing his panic causes my own to rise, and with it, my hands begin to sting against the metal.

"Ouch!" I gasp, jerking my hands away from him.

"Good," he says with relief. "If they're burning you, then it means you're still conducting, and the compound probably hasn't done any permanent damage to your abilities."

Whatever that's supposed to mean.

He finally gets the lock open, and the gloves fall away, hitting the floor with a metallic clack. Still crouched behind me, Michael gently inspects my hands. His rough callouses ghost over my sensitive burns. My palms flare with that familiar tingle of warmth, but this time, instead of pain, most of the lingering soreness fades completely.

Michael lets go of me and rises. "Looks like your abilities are functioning."

I stretch my arms up, working out the stiffness before I finally look down at my hands. They're not the blistered mess I expected. In fact, they look almost normal, except that each of my palms has a scar along the slope connecting my thumb and pointer. Twin half-moons of pink, new flesh. I've never had a scar before. What did the gloves do to me?

I think about the healing warmth I just felt. I've always healed quickly but never instantaneously.

What did I do to myself?

"Okay, let's get out of here," Michael says. He uses the hem of his T-shirt to wipe his bloody forehead, exposing quite a bit of too-old-for-me abdomen.

My gut says I shouldn't go anywhere with him, but the sound of a door slamming followed by threatening footfalls has my gut changing its mind in favor of any option that will get me out of here fast.

"Quickly," Michael urges, tugging me by the arm, and I follow, every cell in my body wanting to flee from the people on the other side of that door. The ones who knocked me out and put me in a crate.

The interior doorknob rattles with the sound of a key as Michael lifts the garage door—the lock has already been busted open—just high enough for us to scuttle through into the cool night. He pulls the door down with a bang and then takes my hand and starts to run.

"I'll bring you somewhere safe," he says over his shoulder. "I'll explain everything once we're there."

His long strides are too fast for me to keep up, but the mechanical sound of the garage door rising behind us convinces me I really don't have a choice. I clutch tightly to his hand and run until my chest is heaving, my thighs are burning, and my bladder feels like an overfilled water balloon.

This safe place better have a bathroom.

Earlier in the evening, the thought of us ending up at Michael's place, panting and hearts racing, had been a tempting outcome.

Fleeing kidnappers isn't quite what I had in mind.

We'd kept running long past when Michael thought we'd lost our pursuers. Now we fumble our way into his building. I'm sweaty and shaky and still trying to catch my breath as I follow him through a cramped hallway to his door. My eyes dart around, and it sinks in how very alone we are and just how difficult it would be for me to escape if I've made a terrible error in judgment.

We enter a cozy studio with only enough room for a kitchenette, a desk, and a bed. I do my best to ignore the intimacy of the space as I dart into the tiny bathroom.

Finally peeing is oh so satisfying, but the walls feel too close. The drip of the sink causes my gut to clench, and I want to get the hell out of here.

Breathe in. Breathe out.

It's just a bathroom.

Once the panic has subsided, I feel around my head with my fingers. There's no pain where I was hit, but there is some dried blood. The lump must have healed along with my palms. My long brown hair is wild and full of snarls. I comb through it with damp fingers and twist it into a knot at the base of my neck. I splash my face with water and wipe off the bruises left by tired makeup.

No, I don't care that the handsome stranger on the other side of the door saw me looking like the Picasso version of myself. Or that he probably just heard me pee. I can't care about any of that. Because I need to focus on not letting anything slip that could alert him to why I'm actually here.

Breathe in. Breathe out.

I have a job to do.

I can't get distracted by fear. And I definitely can't get distracted by Michael's dimples. Especially now that I know who he must be.

I'm here to do what I've always wanted: to be a member of the Families, the historic order that my ancestors have long been a part of. That I too am *finally* a part of.

The Families have spent generations passing down the secret history of a group of exiles rumored to be in hiding. They supposedly have artistic talents and scientific knowledge far beyond anything we know to exist in our own society. I've grown up on stories of the exiles' incredible innovations and their tragic disappearance, and I've heard countless fantasies of what the world could be like if we ever found them again and could share their knowledge.

And I'm pretty sure Michael is one of the exiles.

I take a few more calming breaths, ready to face whatever happens next.

When I come out, Michael is sitting at the desk chewing his nails and inspecting the gloves. His face is illuminated by the strands of dawn peeking through the window; his wound has been cleaned up, and there's little evidence that it was ever there at all.

There's nowhere else to sit, so I perch myself on the edge of the bed. I cross one leg over the other, then awkwardly uncross them.

"Here's your phone," Michael says, handing it to me.

"Thanks." The screen is cracked and the battery is dead. No one knows where I am, and I have no mode of communication. Great.

Michael continues to tinker with the gloves. He lifts his multi-tool and uses a tiny magnifying glass to peer at the metal. "How did they get ahold of antimatter?" he mutters. "I can't wait to bring these back to Genesis; they're incredibly valuable." He looks up. "And so are you."

No one has ever called me valuable.

As his gaze locks on mine, his floppy hair a wayward mess, I remind myself that I have no reason to trust him. But I really need to convince him that he can trust me.

He blinks, looks away, then looks back at me. "Uh, what I mean is that we need to get you to the institute as well."

I swallow. "What institute? Why?" I don't have to fake my curiosity, even if I may not be quite as clueless as Michael believes me to be.

Finding out about this supposed institute is the whole purpose of my mission. Over the years, the Families have come closer and closer to tracking down the exiles. Recent intel led them to believe that someone with my abilities could make contact with them at the right place and the right time and could maybe even be invited to join them. I'm not sure whether I ever truly believed it was actually possible. But here I am. And it's suddenly seeming very, *very* possible.

"You're a Sire. You need to be trained and protected."

Mission aside, I can't deny that I'm desperate to know what it means to be a "Sire." These people understand this part of me that has been a mystery—and a weight on my shoulders—for so long. It might not be my main purpose for being here, but a little more probing would only be natural from a girl who's supposedly never heard about any of this.

"So, what, I'm some kind of scientific anomaly?"

"What? No. Not at all. Having Sire abilities is a normal recessive genetic trait. Just like blue eyes or red hair."

Normal. I feel so much relief in that one word.

I'll never forget the time my parents first saw evidence of my abilities. I accidentally revived some wilted roses at our dining room table, and they freaked out like I'd gotten a face tattoo. My mom threw the flowers out immediately, and my dad's hands were actually trembling. It's a horrible feeling, seeing fear on your parents' faces and knowing they're terrified of you.

I could never understand what made them so afraid, until I saw the book.

I was in middle school, and Grandfather had brought me to visit Mom at her office. As I was waiting for her, I could tell the big, gilded book on her desk was the kind of thing that those not yet initiated into the Families were definitely *not* allowed to see. Of course, I couldn't stop myself from looking.

It was all in a language I couldn't read, but the illustrations were clear enough, and I knew why my mom must have been reading it. I couldn't grow a vine out of my hands, throw lightning, or stop someone's heart with a touch like the people in the colorful sketches, but whoever they were, my mom thought I was like them. And the pictures told me what happened to people like me. Drowned, burned at the stake, excommunicated. It was enough to make me want to do anything I could to prove that I was not one of those monsters.

Can it possibly be true that everything I bottled up for so long is just . . . *normal?*

Michael continues, "Being a Sire means you can manipulate Ha'i—life force—like when you made the plant grow and how you heal rapidly."

Ha'i. He says it like the Hebrew word chai, the sound coming from the back of his throat in a way I sometimes struggled to pronounce. *Ha'i.* The warmth that flows through me and tingles from my palms is *life force.* I've always thought of that feeling as more of a reaction, like a blush or a shiver.

"So, how can you touch those without them hurting you?" I ask Michael, looking at the gloves.

"Because I'm not a Sire. These"—he holds up the gloves—"are made with antimatter, which counteracts Ha'i and incapacitates Sires."

"You're not a Sire?" I ask. "But your cut healed so quickly."

"Ah. Right." He gestures toward a tube of ointment. "Where I come from, medicine is more advanced."

"I see." I look at his forehead, where the injury still shows, but hardly. "Well, if you guys have such great medicine, how come you haven't shared it with everyone else?"

I don't really have a sense for how much more advanced these exiles actually are compared to the rest of us, but I know that medical knowledge is one of the things the Families most hope to gain from them. Exactly what kind of healing are these people capable of? I can't help but think of how ill Grandfather has been recently. . . .

"We've tried," Michael answers vaguely, his lips downturned. "A lot of our medical advancements are dependent on Sire abilities. If you understood your skills, you could have healed me without any need for the patch paste."

Is that true? For a moment I wonder if perhaps he's recruited the wrong person after all. As far as I know, my abilities are more likely to hurt someone than help them. Could I truly be using them to heal others?

And if there are more people out there with my abilities—all apparently capable of advanced healing—then what the hell are these supposedly idealistic people doing gatekeeping that kind of knowledge?

I get up from the bed and wander over to the window.

"I'm sorry, you must be very overwhelmed," Michael says.

"Yes, but I'm ready for you to explain it all." I don't turn, but I can see his reflection through the glass. He puts down the gloves and turns to give me his full attention. I meet the reflection of his eyes.

"My people are called the Makers, and I'm from the Genesis Institute, which you would not have heard of."

I exhale. My breath fogs up the window, and I trail my finger through the condensation.

He continues. "Though we keep our existence secret, we occasionally recruit Sires like yourself to join us."

It's difficult to swallow past the tightness in my throat. "Look, Michael, or whatever your real name is—"

"My name is Michael. I haven't lied to you about anything."

That makes one of us.

"Well, you failed to mention that you're from some secret society looking to recruit me," I say bitterly.

"I didn't realize it was relevant." He stands. "I had no idea you were a Sire. That was completely coincidental. We got a tip that there was a Sire in the area, but I thought it was the pianist—"

"Then why did you ask me out?" I ask, twirling to face him. This suddenly matters very much. Was it all an act? Did he know I was a *Sire* all along?

"Because I thought you were . . . cool!" His puppy-dog eyes are annoyingly sexy.

"But you would have disappeared, and we would never have seen each other again." I don't know why I'm so upset. But if I'm going to try to play the part to find out more about these people, I need to know who I'm dealing with. I need to know if he's the kind of guy who would use seduction to manipulate me or if our meeting truly was a freak coincidence.

"That's . . . I wasn't overthinking it. . . . I didn't realize how young—I mean, sometimes that's normal, to go out and never see each other again."

I blush at the implication of his words. "It wasn't like that."

He shakes his head. "Maybe not. But what about you? You're going back to school in a few days. You knew it wouldn't work out either."

I mean, he has a point.

"Moving on." He brushes the conversation away. "We're in agreement. It was a mistake."

Even though I am firmly in the "it was a mistake" camp, it still stings to hear him say it.

"Fine," I snap, and I feel so childish.

"Look, Ada, what's important is that you need to learn about your Sire genetics."

"Yeah, well, if being a Sire is as normal as you say, then why isn't it common knowledge?"

More than ten years of my own insecurities would really like to know the answer to this.

"Because in the provincial world, the manipulation of life force using Sire abilities was made illegal more than six hundred years ago. And many Sires have been recruited to join the Makers, limiting the gene pool. So abilities like yours have become rare in your world, or so latent that they never surface in any obvious way."

Your world.

What is *his* world?

Growing up among the Families—but not as an initiate of the order—meant I heard a lot about the exiles *before* they were exiled. Everything else was classified, and I'd been given only the barest sketch of the secret stuff in the rush to prepare me for this trip. I don't even know whether what the Families think they know is accurate.

But I can be the one to find that out. That is, if I don't completely bungle this.

Okay, irritatingly attractive recruiter, time for me to squeeze some information out of you.

"Fine," I say. "Tell me about these Makers."

I gingerly settle myself back on the edge of the bed feeling skittish, like a bird on a windowsill, unsure of what is glass and what is sky.

Michael swivels the desk chair to face me and sits. He takes a deep breath, then says, "Imagine a society devoted to advancing the world scientifically, artistically, and socially. Where everyone is committed to bringing more beauty to the world and eradicating the horrors of inequality and illness and ecological damage."

I hear the passion in his voice, and I envy it.

"You're describing a utopia."

"Not quite, but as close to it as history has ever seen."

A bubble of excitement expands in my belly.

"And you're saying this society exists?"

"I'm saying it exists and that I want to take you there." His eyes sparkle with excitement, and his smile is so wide I almost forget I'm not supposed to trust him.

"But if what they're doing is so great, why does no one know about it? Why aren't these ideas helping the rest of the world?"

"Because we're hunted," Michael says matter-of-factly. "We're in hiding. And we have been since the original Makers were forced to flee during one of the Roman Inquisitions. Before then, they were scholars of an academy in Italy renowned for its advancements in art, science, and philosophy. It attracted scholars from around the globe who wished to be modern 'muses,' like the mythical goddesses said to have inspired the arts and sciences."

This is the confirmation I've been waiting for. These Makers are *definitely* the exiles.

"What happened to the school?" I ask, and I'm genuinely curious to see if his account will match the blurry version I've been told.

"The Makers' science, and their philosophy in general—the Church hated it. Some of the academy's research was definitely . . . ethically questionable.

Amazing, but highly experimental. They believed that humankind being 'made in the image of God' meant it was their job to 'continue the creation of the world,' to perfect upon it. And this philosophy was considered deeply heretical.

"And when the school refused to conform to the Church's narrow restrictions of what could be taught and studied, Inquisitors came"—his voice grows quieter—"and burned the academy to the ground." He looks away, and the column of his throat tightens as he swallows. This is ancient history, yet he acts as if the pain is still raw, as if it hurts him personally.

Michael collects himself and stretches out his long legs; his feet jostle into mine, and he quickly snaps them back. Sitting up straight, he continues. "Luckily, much of the academy's research was rescued and hidden before it could be destroyed. The Makers, like many other groups of the time, were forced to denounce their ways or be expelled or even executed. Some did, and some went into hiding and continued their scholarship. A group of those in hiding eventually arranged for passage to the New World, where they went on to found the Genesis Institute."

My rapt interest in the story is no act. It's wild to hear the things I've only ever been told about in theory confirmed by someone outside of the Families. I try to wrap my head around how much could have been lost with the destruction of such a school.

A flop of dark hair obscures Michael's face, and my fingers itch to push it away. We're sitting close enough that if we both leaned forward, I could. Instead, I lean back, lacing my fingers together in my lap. I school my features to look skeptical and say, "If what you're saying is true, shouldn't everyone have heard of this Inquisition?"

"Have you heard of Galileo's trial for his belief that the Earth revolves around the sun? And the Spanish Inquisition that followed the expulsion, when the Jews and Muslims were exiled from Spain?"

"Yes, but not anything about the loss of major scientific advancements."

"That's because the Church simply denied that any of it ever existed. They buried all the evidence of the Makers' heretical experiments and blasphemous ideas, and they forbade anyone to speak of them. Except for an elite group of Inquisitors who were tasked with hunting down those that fled." His eyes bore into mine, telegraphing sincerity and urgency. "And the loss of all that knowledge, it set advancements back *centuries*. But the Makers kept it all and have continued their mission of advancement in secret."

"I don't understand," I interject. "If these advancements were so great, how did everyone just go along with the Church and pretend they never existed?"

My feet are jostled by Michael's again as he makes another attempt to stretch his legs. He pulls them back and stands instead, pacing the length of the small room. "Sorry," he says, running his hands through his hair. "This version of history is very standard for me, and explaining it to someone with a totally different paradigm is always confusing. But don't underestimate the Church's power." He looks at me. "Even in your own lifetime, you've observed enough to see how world narratives are formed. How easy it is to reshape history through propaganda and misinformation."

He's starting to sound like my grandfather.

"It's scary how quickly truth can be rewritten," he continues. "Within one generation after the Exodus, the truth of the original Makers and their discoveries was mostly forgotten, and by the next generation, completely so. Remnants of their legacy remain, but only under the guise of myths and legends."

There's a part of me that was never sure whether I really believed all the Families' stories, that wondered if it has all just been exaggerated and lost in translation over the years. But hearing how Michael's story fits with what I've been taught—it starts to sink in that this could all actually be *real*. I feel almost weightless, my muscles tight and trembling with a mix of excitement and confusion.

Michael's pacing takes him to the kitchenette. "It's been a long night," he says. "Let me get you something to eat." As he putters around, I observe him with new eyes, looking for signs that he's from a society hidden by some big historical conspiracy. He looks normal. But there are subtle hints. There's no branding on anything he's wearing. His shoes look well worn, well made, and just a little too old-fashioned. He wears no watch. And I don't think he has a cell phone, or if he does, he hasn't pulled it out all night. I mean, that alone is weird.

He sits next to me on the bed and places a tray with a cup of tea and some cookies between us.

I've been too distracted to realize how hungry I am. I take my time eating the cookies and washing them down with tea. Michael's not very good at sitting still. He runs his hands through his hair, chews his nails, drums his fingers on his knees.

"You know that you sound crazy, right?" I ask him, the way I assume a random teenage girl who has not grown up among the Families would. "Hidden society, centuries-long conspiracy, and all that?"

He stills his fidgeting and turns to face me. "I understand that it's hard to second-guess everything you've ever learned. And there's so much more than what I have told you. If you come with me to Genesis, I can *show* it all to you."

It's the exact invitation I've been hoping for. And it sounds incredible. But being kidnapped has really clobbered my enthusiasm.

Michael's eyes brighten, and his dimple makes an appearance. "You know, Michelangelo was a Maker."

This gets my attention. "What?"

"Yes, and a Sire; he was at the academy before the Inquisition. He, and others who didn't want to abandon their lives, chose to stay behind and denounce all Maker activity considered to be heretical. Whenever I look at his prisoner statues, I see the struggle of the life he chose. Like he's the one trapped in an unfinished state, confined by the new rules of the world, most of his fellow Makers gone."

He is annoyingly adorable when he gets passionate about art stuff. And this is not anything I've heard before. The Families revere the well-known masters for sure, but not in the same way as the ones who were exiled.

"And what other historical celebrities would you like to claim?" I ask.

"Many. Da Vinci, Ada Lovelace—both Makers."

"No way." Do the Families know this?

"It's true. Da Vinci was another who stayed behind. Ada was a Sire recruited later in life; she didn't die young as your history says. One of her direct descendants is my guildmaster."

This is far beyond anything I thought I knew. My mind is racing, trying to rearrange what it thinks is true.

"Look, if I haven't convinced you yet, at least understand this." He waits for me to look up at him, and the expression in his eyes has grown urgent. The warmth of his body is far too close to mine on the bed. "Someone has been abducting Sires around the globe, but the Makers can keep you safe."

Why would anyone be capturing Sires? I wonder if it's related to what I saw in that book and why my parents were so insistent I suppress my abilities.

"Your kidnapping means the Inquisitors know who you are, which means you're still a target."

"Wait, Inquisitors? Who are you talking about?"

"The initial group of Inquisitors who were tasked to hunt us down—they never stopped. Our ancestors hoped that they would forget about us, but that hasn't happened. They've passed on their hatred to their children, and we've been hiding from them ever since."

Well, that, at least, he's totally wrong about. I've heard stories from the Families about those Inquisitors, and they definitely don't exist anymore. But *someone* tried to kidnap me. Who would want to harm Sires?

"Ada, don't you get that you're in danger? We need to get you to the Genesis Institute as soon as possible."

As soon as possible. No way I'm waltzing out of the country with this stranger. "I can't go with you right *now*," I say.

He massages his forehead as if it will somehow give him the words to convince me. "Please," he says, "you were abducted because you are a Sire. I can help you."

Sire. It's still strange to have a name for whatever I am. I try to call up the tingling warmth between my fingers, but nothing happens. I want to know how to control it. And I want to show the Families that I'm worthy of being one of them. But I shouldn't make any impulsive decisions on my own. Me being kidnapped was not part of the plan. I've found the recruiter, got the invite, and now I need to get the hell out of Italy. I just hope that refusing to go with Michael won't lose me my chance.

"I believe you, but I need to go home to my family before I make any final decisions."

"That's fair," Michael says, resigned. "I'll send you a formal application to Genesis, and I hope you'll choose to come."

I'm relieved that his offer is open, but selling the lie of my indifference is safer than the truth. "I'll think about it," I say.

"Until then"—his tone sharpens—"you can't tell anyone about any of this."

"Right, hiding for hundreds of years, hunted by dangerous people and all that."

"We've stayed hidden for a long time, but things have changed in recent decades. Your world has airplanes and satellites and the internet—hiding an entire society has become more difficult. Telling anyone is a risk. Can I trust you with this knowledge?"

"Yes." I avert my eyes and aggressively inspect the scars on my hands.

"Good. Because I really don't want to have to muddle you."

I look up sharply. "Muddle me?" Dread churns in my belly.

"Um, can we pretend I didn't mention that?"

"Michael," I insist. "What does it mean?"

"It means to make you forget."

The dread rises into my throat, and I stand, taking a few steps away from him.

"I hate muddling people, but sometimes it's necessary. Don't worry. I'm not going to do it to you."

"You can steal memories?"

"No, no, it's only a blend of tea—"

"You were going to *drug me*?" I look down at my empty cup in horror.

"No!" He stands but doesn't move toward me. He holds up his hands placatingly. "Ada, calm down. I'm not going to muddle you. I'm going to make sure that you get home safely, and then I'm going to hope that you'll come to Genesis when you're ready."

I take a deep breath. He says he hasn't done anything to me, and I'm going to believe him, because I don't really have another choice. "Okay."

By now the sun has fully risen; morning lights up the room, and I realize how thoroughly exhausted I am. I need to sleep and then think about everything with a clear head and copious amounts of caffeine.

Michael pulls a leather billfold from the pocket of his cloak, opens it, and takes out a white folded paper. It's an origami bird. "I'm still worried about leaving you knowing Inquisitors are looking for you. Take this pigeon," he says. "Use it if you need me."

Even if I know it's not these Inquisitors who are looking for me, it seems that someone else is, so I do need to be careful. I take the bird from him, and I'm surprised to find that it isn't made of paper but of something that feels like lightweight clay.

Michael reaches over and strokes the bird's beak. The flat wings unfold and begin to flutter. The bird elevates off the top of my palm and hovers there, wings flapping, its faceless head twitching from left to right.

I'm transfixed by its delicate beauty.

"It's like magic," I say in wonder.

"Or advanced science." Michael winks. "This is a homing pigeon golem. It will find me wherever I am, anywhere in the world. You can write a message inside, or just send it off if you're in danger. All you need to do is flick its tail, and it will know to find me."

"This is . . . impossible."

"Your understanding of what is possible and impossible is about to change," Michael says with a smile. The sentiment tangles in my chest, making it hard to breathe, whether from amazement or fear, I'm not quite sure.

"This golem utilizes magnetoreception—the same force that allows real pigeons to navigate using Earth's magnetic field—and it is entirely scientifically possible." He reaches over and strokes the bird's beak again. It folds flat and floats back down into my hand. Michael's hand comes down on top of it and presses it into my palm. His fingers are warm and strong, and I try my best to ignore the growing tension coiling inside me as his eyes find mine earnestly. "Promise me that you'll deploy the pigeon if you need me and that you'll keep it with you at all times while you're still at risk."

"Okay," I say, quite sure that I am indeed at risk—but of what, I do not know.

"And he was a native English speaker with an American accent?" Counselor Avellino asks me for the third time.

"Yes," I confirm, trying to sound polite instead of pissy. I've been interrogated by the Families about every single interaction I had with Michael and then asked to repeat it all again. And despite my promises to Michael, I've told them everything. Well, besides the fact that I went on a date with my mark before I realized who he was.

"And he said only *some* of the exiles traveled to the Americas?"

Counselor Avellino is the Families' lawyer and, let me tell you, he knows how to cross-examine a witness.

It's been hours of this. My head is pounding, and I just want to go home.

One might think that after the crippling trauma of being abducted and the exhaustion of an international flight, I would be allowed to go home to recover. But if one is now a spy for a historic order, they apparently cannot expect such treatment. Instead, as soon as my plane touched down at JFK, I was whisked to the seat of the Families' Inner Chamber—which is hidden in the basement archives of the Cloisters in Fort Tryon Park—to be debriefed.

The flight back had not been easy. I was constantly looking over my shoulder for some unknown threat. When I attempted to use the lavatory on the plane, I almost had a panic attack from the small space and had to ban myself from drinking so I wouldn't have to go again. And it's not like anyone here has offered me a drink since, so my mouth feels as dry as the ancient illuminated manuscripts displayed in the Cloisters museum upstairs.

Despite being in a building renowned for its epic architecture, the actual room where the Inner Chamber convenes is just a boring boardroom with a long table seating a lot of Very Important People. Not all of the Inner Chamber is present, but those that are include members as illustrious as a US senator—who if the Families get their way may be our next president—the French minister of culture, a big deal film director, an even bigger deal Italian fashion designer, and my mom. They are each a representative from one of the families that have been stewards to the memory of the exiles—or the "Makers," according to Michael—for hundreds of generations. The order is built around this stewardship, with the intent of recovering the exiles' lost innovations and sharing them with mainstream society. And now that I finally have a seat at the table, I don't want to screw it up.

"I'd like to take another look at the golem bird," the senator says.

Kor bumps my knee with his, and when I glance at him, he gives me an encouraging smile. *Just a little longer*, he mouths silently.

Despite the subtlety of Kor's actions, they've still drawn the table's attention, and now everyone's watching us uneasily. I'm used to this when I'm in public with Kor.

With his dramatic cheekbones, pale skin, and almost-black hair, Korach Chevalier is the kind of person who always attracts a lot of admiration but seems completely unapproachable. Whenever someone who thinks they know him sees him acting close and comfortable with me—an average person in every way—it shakes their image of his cool, enigmatic nature.

It's hard for me to see Kor through the eyes of the masses. To them he's a mysterious paragon of artistic genius. To me he's just Kor, one of my closest friends, who is two years older than me and technically a distant cousin. (Very distant. Through marriage.)

Kor clears his throat, and the activity around the table resumes.

"We're sorry for the repetition," Dr. Ambrose says to me. He's a kind physician with salt-and-pepper hair and gold-rimmed glasses. When my mother had grudgingly allowed the Inner Chamber to assess my abilities, he'd been patient and transparent through the whole process. "We know you have been through an ordeal, but we must make sure we have all the proper facts for the sake of our research and for your safety. If we decide to send you to study at this institute, we need the whole picture."

The Inner Chamber is split on whether I should be sent to infiltrate Genesis. Most of them are in favor of it, but there are a few who don't trust me to pull it off.

"Not to mention that your story doesn't add up," the loudest in the Ada-can't-be-trusted contingent interjects.

Alfie Avellino: son of Counselor Avellino and the most annoying person in my acquaintance.

"You still haven't answered why you didn't follow the protocol when you first encountered the exile." He glares at me accusingly as he pats down a strand of his perfectly parted hair—a shade of brown just light enough that he'll try to tell you it's blond.

Alfie liked me fine when we first met a few years ago. In fact, he worked hard to ingratiate himself with me to get closer to Kor, but the moment he realized I wasn't going to be initiated into the Families, I slid below his notice like runoff into the sewer.

"She couldn't follow the protocol because she was *kidnapped*." Kor comes to my defense. It's clear that Alfie has more to say on the matter, but he won't talk back to Kor. He will, however, straighten his ugly paisley tie and scowl down his nose at me, trying his best to make me feel like I don't deserve to be here.

He doesn't have to work very hard. I'm already pretty sure I don't belong.

Nothing can make me feel quite as hazy with inferiority as being surrounded by these people who have shaped their lives around the values of the exiles by actively improving the world through innovation and art. The abilities that earned me my initiation might mean I need fewer Band-Aids than the average person, and sure, I'm good with plants, but no one's looking for a ficus at the Met. Everyone else at this table gained their seats by pushing themselves to be masters of a modern Renaissance.

Okay, maybe not Alfie. I'm pretty sure he just earned his seat through generations of nepotism and his family's deep pockets. But even he went through years of training after being initiated. Whereas I was never even good enough to be considered until the Families needed to use my abilities as bait. Whatever, at least I have abilities. It's not like Alfie's bringing anything new to the table, besides his seemingly endless collection of hideous ties.

If he deserves to be here, so do you, I remind myself as I try to muster up the confidence of a mediocre trust fund white boy.

"Not only did Ada succeed beyond our wildest expectations in Italy," Kor says, "she did so despite having incorrect information about the mark." Whenever Kor speaks, everyone listens with rapt attention. The French minister of culture is making doe eyes at him and twirling her hair around her finger. Even my mother—whose eyes always seem to shift away from me when I speak up—is listening intently to Kor.

Kor has transformed the Families in recent years.

The order's influence had been steadily growing over the centuries as they reintroduced some of the exiles' lost innovations—derived from the order's extensive archives and from centuries of hunting down relics—back into society. They've funded a lot of research based on their knowledge, which has contributed to everything from health care to agriculture to clean energy. But most of that was based on ancient knowledge. Now, because of Kor, the Families have a path to the exiles' actual living descendants and whatever far-more-advanced innovations they may have since developed. And it's all because Kor made contact with Prometheus, the anonymous informant from among the exiles who provided the information about how and where they would be recruiting. Between Kor's success with Prometheus and the influence that's come with his recent fame and public advocacy, the entire Inner Chamber is basically as obsessed with Kor as the teens who run his online fan clubs.

"Ada has the perfect cover, a direct invitation, and has already proven herself to us," Kor continues. "Having her infiltrate the institute is the best course of action." He sounds so sure of this plan. So sure of me. I, on the other hand, am the farthest thing from sure.

"She has no training," Alfie argues. And he's not wrong.

"What of our training would have better prepared her for this?" Kor challenges. "The tutoring in Aramaic and Latin? The art restoration and document preservation techniques?"

"She's an immature and undisciplined teenager, and she could put us all in danger if she blows her cover."

I do so love being discussed as if I'm not in the room. If Izzy were here, she'd tell me to assert my femininity and not let myself be talked over.

Speaking of which, where is Izzy? I've been expecting her to show up. Her older brother, Roman, is already here, sitting quietly at the other end of the table.

Izzy King is my other best friend. She's half Korean, an avid gamer, and one of the cleverest people I know. Growing up, she was the only girl around my age from the New York branch of the Families, so we were always together. I was really hoping to see her before she goes back to Massachusetts at the end of winter break.

"Ada won't have trouble with her cover," Kor assures the room. "She'll need to blend into a school where they already expect her to be an outsider. If anything, her being an average teenager will make her cover stronger." *Average teenager.* Ouch, Kor. "Regardless of everything else, she was abducted because of her abilities. For that reason alone, we should send her to Genesis, where they can keep her safe."

"I agree," Dr. Ambrose says.

"So do I," my mother says, speaking for the first time this whole meeting. She has otherwise been perfectly content to let all the other people in the room plan my life out for me. And how does her makeup and blond bun look so fresh? It seems impossible that she's been stuck in this room for as many hours as my sweaty, frizzy, haggard self. Everyone here has probably forgotten we're even related.

Sometimes I wonder if that's what she wants, for them to forget. Maybe I'm an embarrassment for only getting initiated into the order on a technicality, for not having any of the accolades her friends get to brag about their talented kids having.

As I mope, the argument that I should go to Genesis as a matter of safety seems to be winning over most of the table.

"We will have to consult the Grand Master," Councilor Avellino says, with the snobbery of knowing he's one of the only people in the room with the security clearance to speak directly with the head of the Families.

As I let the Chamber continue their decision making about my future without bothering to ask my opinion on the matter, I lean over to Kor and whisper, "Where's Izzy?"

"She's not coming," he whispers back. "I'll explain later." His eyes hold a sadness that makes my rib cage tighten with alarm.

Right before I left for Italy, Izzy had texted me that she didn't think I should go, though she didn't tell me why. When she didn't respond to any of my messages while I was gone, I figured it was just because of the time difference, or that she was being pissy that I was missing our annual winter break snowboarding trip. Now I worry her silence was due to something more significant.

I hide my phone in my lap, prepared to message Izzy on every single one of her social media accounts until she finally responds. Except, for some reason, none of her profiles will load. I must have a bad internet connection. But . . . no, everything else seems to be working fine.

What's going on? I reload and then reload again.

Nothing. All her profiles are gone.

She's either deleted her accounts or blocked me.

Why would she do that? My breath feels trapped, my mind ping-ponging between worry and hurt.

I pull up the last text message Izzy sent me.

Please don't go to Italy. I saw something I wasn't supposed to, and now I have a really bad feeling about your trip.

When she hadn't responded to any of my follow-up questions, I'd put her warning out of my mind and chalked it up to a drunk text. It certainly wouldn't have been the first. But now I'm not so sure.

Kor sees the look on my face and takes my hand under the table with a comforting squeeze.

"We're starting to talk in circles," Kor says to the rest of the Chamber. "Let's continue this discussion tomorrow. Ada needs to go home; she's been through a lot."

Alfie objects. "She's been exposed to incredibly sensitive information. We can't just let her go home!"

"Of course we can," Kor says with finality. And because Kor is Kor, everyone listens and the meeting is adjourned, giving me free rein to leave.

As soon as we're out of the Chamber, I try to ask Kor about Izzy.

"Not yet." He shushes me and pulls me after him. He uses a bright orange keycard to exit the Families' private archives—I'd asked for my own keycard but was denied—and leads me up the stairs into the museum.

It's closed to the public at this late hour, and in the low light, the echoing stillness of the ancient chapels and galleries is haunting enough to give me chills.

The Cloisters—a building designed by combining different architectural elements taken from medieval abbeys, monasteries, and convents—houses a huge collection of medieval art and architecture. But only part of the collection is open to the public. Up in the tower and down below in the archives are many more pieces, including the Families' private collection of relics tied to the existence of the exiles.

My mom texts me saying she needs to get some things from her office and will be ready to go in fifteen minutes, so I let Kor lead me through the silent, spooky halls of the Cloisters until we reach his favorite gallery, the Unicorn Tapestry Room. Seven beautifully detailed tapestries with life-size figures depict a story that has puzzled art historians for years. The tapestries are infamously mysterious; no one even knows who commissioned or made them.

I have so many questions for Kor, but my exhaustion is catching up with me. I lie down on the floor in the center of the room, arms and legs outstretched. With a loud groan, I close my eyes.

And then there's a warm body lying next to mine, and Kor is pulling me against his chest. I blink against his soft cashmere sweater, inhaling the smell of his expensive sandalwood cologne and a hint of charcoal that tells me he's been sketching.

I suppress the familiar tug that comes whenever Kor is sweet with me.

Of course I'm a little bit in love with him—it's impossible not to be. But he'll never feel that way about me. It took me a few too many years to realize that. Luckily, our friendship managed to survive my painfully one-sided crush, and I came out on the other end of it relatively unscathed. Competing with an ever-increasing number of fans and groupies is excellent for crush-squashage.

Lying in his arms with our bodies pressed together is not.

Kor takes one of my hands and grazes his fingertips over the crescent scar. "I'm sorry about what happened in Italy," he says. "It's my fault you were there in the first place."

I get that he's feeling guilty that I was kidnapped, but I can't help but bristle at the implication that he should have known I couldn't take care of myself.

But maybe that's the truth. Maybe Alfie is right about everything. I wasn't ready for Italy, and I'm not ready for Genesis. I don't have the training, and there's no way I can pull this off.

"Out of curiosity," I ask Kor. "If the Inner Chamber decides I should go to Genesis, would I be able to . . . choose to not go?"

"You're in danger. That's reason enough for you to go. The school can protect you from whoever abducted you."

That may be true, but it doesn't answer my question.

"Do the Families have any idea about who took me?" I roll myself away from Kor's body. Now's not the time to let him play the harp with my feelings. Izzy says he does it on purpose because he needs me to be in love with him. Kor needs everyone to be in love with him. To be obsessed with him. He was born to be adored.

"We've been investigating it nonstop since yesterday," he says.

The museum floor is cold and hard beneath me. Kor and I are no longer touching, but our faces are close enough that, even in the dim light, I can see the small scar that bisects his upper lip. The one *Rolling Stone* described as "the wound the world wants to kiss better." (I have not stopped teasing him about this and don't plan to anytime soon.) I turn away and stare up at the dark museum ceiling. "Michael said there have been other Sire abductions besides me."

"Yes, we've confirmed that to be true. Right now, our most likely suspect is Nora Montaigne."

"The CEO of Ozymandias Tech?" I sit up.

Kor nods.

The French billionaire is always in the news for designing clean-energy private jets that are making waves in the lifestyles of the rich and famous. Not to mention, she's the CEO of the company that just bought Izzy's app. But it's wild to think that Nora Montaigne could somehow be involved in any of this. Despite the ethical ambiguity of her being a billionaire, her public image is generally quite positive—environmentally friendly, philanthropic.

"How could she be connected?"

Kor stays on his back, talking up to the ceiling. "Ozymandias Tech has been performing genetic experimentation that would benefit from knowledge of abilities like yours," he explains. "And the Families have long suspected Montaigne is aware of the exiles. The Families lost a slew of auctions for items assumed to be exile relics to shell companies that were all traced back to her."

"Izzy works with her company now. Can she help find out more?" And maybe now Kor can tell me why she's not here.

This makes him sit up, but he doesn't meet my eyes as he says, "Izzy's not going to help us with anything."

I feel cold all over. "What do you mean?"

He lays his hand on my thigh. "She's left the Families, Ada."

The throbbing in my head returns with a vengeance. "I . . . Is that even a thing you can do?"

He shrugs.

"But why?"

"She just said she wanted out, and she hasn't spoken to me since. It's part of why the Inner Chamber is hesitant to trust you after such a recent betrayal. Especially since you and Izzy are close."

Why would Izzy do something like this? And why wouldn't she explain herself to me and Kor?

I pull out my phone and look at her last message again.

Please don't go to Italy. I saw something I wasn't supposed to, and now I have a really bad feeling about your trip.

The thing she wasn't supposed to see, could that have been at Oz Tech? Did she realize they're abducting Sires and that's why she didn't want me to go to Italy? It makes sense. Are the people she's working with dangerous?

"I hope she's okay," I say.

"Roman has been in touch with her and said that she's doing fine."

I'm so confused. I need Izzy. Quite frankly, I don't have a lot of close friends. I mean, when you're from a family that's part of a weird secret society, it can be hard to connect to people outside of it.

"Don't worry," Kor says. "She made a ton of money selling her app, and she just wants to focus on other things now. She's been pulling away ever since she went off to college. This isn't that big of a surprise."

But that doesn't explain why she would ghost me. Or why she would keep working with a company that she thinks is harming people.

"Hey." Kor gently kicks my foot with his. "We should be celebrating." Once I pocket my phone, he takes both of my hands in his and stands, pulling me to my feet. "You're going to learn how to use your abilities."

My abilities.

It's so weird to think of them as something positive that can be trained and used for good. Aside from the easy healing and my talent with plants, I've rarely ever felt different from other people. Because of my parents' fear, I'd gotten used to suppressing anything peculiar about myself over the years. And it mostly worked. It's easy enough to turn yourself into someone else when your true self scares the people you love.

But in recent months, it had all become harder to ignore. The stress of college applications was making my hands hot and tingly all the time, and keeping it in check was taking way too much emotional energy. I knew from experience that talking to Mom about it was not an option. I finally confided in Kor and Izzy, thinking maybe they could find the book that I had seen so many years before in the archives to help me learn more.

I haven't gotten over the whiplash of what followed.

Kor had been elated, and he immediately convinced me that I had to tell the Families and be initiated.

When I'd asked Mom why she hadn't told me sooner that the Families needed someone like me, she brushed it off, saying that she hadn't realized it was the same condition they'd been researching. But as soon as the idea of trying to get me into the institute had been suggested, she'd agreed, as if she couldn't wait to have the problem of "What is Ada going to do with her life?" off her plate.

Kor is giddy now like he was that same day I first told him about my abilities. "Do you have any idea what you're capable of?" he asks me, squeezing my hands tightly.

No. I have no idea.

"If our research is correct, abilities like yours could change the face of modern medicine. And Prometheus has implied there might be a way to share these abilities with non-Sires. You can help us find the way. You're going to help *change the world.*"

I've always known Kor would change the world. Now he seems to think that I can too.

"You'll learn directly from the descendants of the most talented masters. This is the opportunity of a lifetime. Of hundreds of lifetimes!"

It's true. And it feels too big to believe, especially when it's so obvious that Kor is the one who should have this opportunity, not me. He would fit right in at Genesis. It feels like some cosmic mistake of fate, the abilities given to the wrong one of us. He has the talent and the drive to use them correctly, unlike me.

"I can tell that you don't understand yet." His hazel eyes shine with excitement. "But I'll show you the archives. Once you see the scrolls, the paintings—the innovations we believe these Makers have . . . " He spreads his arms wide, looking from wall to wall at the tapestries. "Like these unicorns!"

"What about them?"

"They were real."

"Oh, come on. No, they weren't," I scoff.

But there's no trace of humor on his face. "The information passed down through the Families suggests they were real. That they were experiments."

"What does that even mean?"

"Whether inspired by the myths of previous generations, or for a utilitarian purpose—perhaps military—the unicorns are an example of the kind of science practiced by the exiles that was deemed heretical and led to their expulsion. They successfully bred these magnificent creatures, and now the world thinks they never existed."

I stare at the tapestries, beautiful but creepy in the low lights of the dark museum. They illustrate a hunt for a unicorn and the unicorn's resulting death. But the last tapestry shows the unicorn alive and domesticated in captivity. I think about everything Michael told me, but this still feels like too much to be possible.

There are endless benefits to being part of the order. All the members use their connections to rise to powerful positions and to influence global change. I've often assumed that's the real reason most members remained involved, not that they truly believe all the fantastical stories of these mysterious people and their wondrous, mythical lives. But it's clear that Kor truly believes it all.

"Look how the tapestries tell the story of the exiles," Kor says. He steps up close behind me, and with his hands on my shoulders, he spins me slowly around to take in all seven illustrated scenes in succession. "Like the unicorn, the exiles were hunted." He points to the tapestry depicting the hunt. "And they were eradicated." He pivots to the illustration of the hunters with the dead unicorn. "But they weren't really." We look together at the most famous of the tapestries, the one of the unicorn wearing a collar surrounded by a fence. "They're still alive somewhere. But they're not truly free."

I see it. I want it to be true.

"We're going to be the ones that set them free, Ada. We'll reunite our two societies and usher in the next Renaissance."

It sounds pretty great, in theory.

"But what if they don't want to be reunited? They seem intent on staying hidden."

"If that's what they want, it won't matter once we have you in there. They don't have the right to keep their knowledge from us, and you will be able to share what you find with us, whether they know about it or not." His breath, warm on my neck, sends chills down my spine as I let his words sink in.

The Inner Chamber talked a lot about me learning from the exiles, finding out what they've been up to and what kinds of things they know. But Kor is clearly saying more than that. He's saying he wants me to steal from them.

"What you're implying, that's not what the Inner Chamber said would be my job."

Kor turns me to face him, and his eyes, glittering with flecks of blue, yellow, and gray, are fierce with passion. "They don't all know," he explains. "You going to Genesis, it will be the most important thing the Families have ever accomplished. You will be receiving instructions that come directly from the Grand Master himself, and some aspects may be classified to only the highest echelon of the Inner Chamber."

"Are you talking about the Oculus?" The Oculus is the most restricted inner circle of the order. It's based somewhere in Europe, and I hadn't even been sure the Oculus still existed, as I'd never known anyone ranked high enough to confirm it. Despite knowing how important he'd risen in the Families, it hadn't occurred to me that Kor could have possibly gained *that* much seniority.

"Yes," he confirms. "While the rest of the Families have been focusing on stewardship of the memory of the exiles and on bringing their ideas into modern society, the Oculus has always been seeking the exiles' physical location in order to work toward reunification."

"How do you know all this? How did you get involved?"

He pulls a thin chain from under his shirt, absently toying with the pendant. It's a silver cross entwined with a gold vine. The emblem of the Families. It belonged to Aragon, Kor's father, before he died. "My father was a member of the Oculus."

That makes sense. I know Aragon was very high-ranking in the Families, and Kor has always strived to follow in his footsteps. Though I can't ignore the pang I feel knowing that Kor has kept this from me for so long. I suppose I can't blame him, as I only recently told him about my abilities. We all have our secrets.

Kor gets back down to business. "To the rest of the Families, your mission will be reconnaissance only. In actuality, we hope to be able to rely on you for more practical matters."

Of course, I haven't been consulted about any of this. Do I even want to go to Genesis if I'm supposed to lie and steal from them?

Kor, as always, can read my mind. He squeezes my shoulders. "Ada, there is so much humankind is capable of, unknown potential buried in our genetics, untapped and untrained. Instead, we're living half-lives." There's a flash of anger in his eyes now. "I don't understand why the exiles have been so selfish until now. I really don't. Just the Sire abilities and medical science alone—we're slaves to viruses and disease, but not them. There's so much suffering that could be mitigated."

I'd asked Michael why the Makers hadn't shared their medical knowledge, and his answer had been vague. If they do have the information that the Families claim, then I know Kor is right.

Kor sniffs, then sniffs again. He releases my shoulders and swipes his knuckles under his nose. They come away streaked with blood. He groans in annoyance as he pulls tissues from his pocket and tips his head back to stem the flow.

"You're still getting those?" He'd told me his nosebleeds had stopped.

"They cabe back a few weeks ago," he explains, his voice coming out distorted as he keeps his nose pinched shut. "Dr. Ambrose said it's norbal frob all the stress, with planning the charity bedefit at the sabe time as studying for biterms. That's why we postponed the album release tour."

Because Kor is the type of guy who works himself until he's sick, and then when something has to give, he deprioritizes his entire career to give all of his focus to his charity work and his commitment to the Families.

Meanwhile, I'm here whining about not being sure I'm ready to give the bare minimum.

As Kor wipes away the last of the blood, the determined gleam is still in his eyes. "Ada, the Families have spent centuries trying to live by the values of the masters, but that's not enough anymore. Now that we know what's out there, it's our obligation to use that knowledge to help the rest of the world, even if the descendants of the masters themselves refuse to do so. And *you* are the key. This is your chance to crawl out of your comfort zone."

My comfort zone, which is safely tucked into his shadow.

Kor has always asked for my help and advice. Feedback on his art and his songs, support behind the scenes during his tours and before interviews. Sometimes, when I feel crappy about my mediocrity, I take comfort in that. That I'm making a mark by being part of Kor's journey.

And now he's telling me I can have my own.

I want to be worthy of our order's mission, to be able to prove all the doubters in the Chamber wrong.

The problem is that the biggest doubter is me.

5

I sleep through the entire next morning and part of the afternoon. It feels so good to wake up in my own bed. Ever since elementary school, when my parents split, Mom and I have lived with my grandfather in his old Bronx mansion. Any luxury it may have once had faded away long ago, but I love it here.

I'm so grateful to be back home that I can almost forget I might be about to leave it all behind, or that unicorns might exist, or that I'm possibly being pursued by a billionaire kidnapper.

I groggily make my way through the wallpapered hallways in search of caffeine, but I halt when I pass my mother's room and hear her voice raised. She never loses her cool, unless she's talking to my dad. But if he's anywhere near a working phone line, he would have called me.

After my parents split, my dad had some kind of early midlife crisis and decided to backpack around the world. He spends a lot of time working on permaculture farms in the middle of nowhere with no phone service. Or at least that's what I think he does. I'm pretty sure he's currently in Central America. The last time I heard from him was in the fall, right before the Jewish New Year. The call had been about ten seconds long; I can remember the whole thing.

"Hi, Daddy."

"Hey, Sprout. Just calling to wish you a shana tova."

"Thanks. You too."

Awkward pause.

"I might be off the grid for longer than usual starting next week."

"Okay."

"But I'll come see you as soon as I can."

"That would be nice."

"Bye, Sprout, I love you."

"Love you too, Dad, and I miss—"

Click.

We had so much to say to each other when I was young, but these days talking to him feels like talking to a stranger. When we talk at all. His prediction that he'd be gone longer than usual has proven more than accurate.

Mom's voice rises again. "Can't they at least first try the standard treatment, even if it's unlikely to change the prognosis?"

That doesn't sound good. I tiptoe closer to listen at the door.

I've seen the creases between Mom's eyes deepening over the past few months (as much as the Botox will allow), and I've heard her whispered conversations with Dr. Ambrose. If I had a dollar for every time I've walked in on her talking with Grandfather and they both become silent the moment they see me . . . I'm not an idiot; I know Grandfather is sick, and I know it must be something serious. He's lost a ton of weight over the past few months, and he barely eats. But I've never heard scary words like "treatment" and "prognosis" bandied about until now. I wish they would just tell me what's going on instead of keeping me in the dark about everything, as usual.

Mom's voice rises as she exclaims, "No, you cannot test Ada's blood. Leave her out of this."

What? Does Grandfather need a blood transfusion or a donor for something? Why wouldn't she let them test my blood? I would gladly give my blood to help him. I try to hear more, but Mom has calmed down, and I can only make out broken mutterings, something about stem cell transplants and then the two-syllable word I was dreading. *Cancer.*

I blink away tears, my fists clenched so tight that my nails dig painfully into my palms. I knew Grandfather hadn't been well, but I'd been assuring myself it was just regular old-person stuff. Not something serious.

Mom's footsteps grow louder, and I scurry away before I'm caught eavesdropping. I immediately head to the sunroom, where I know Grandfather will be. He likes when I join him there; he says his plants are fond of me and that they grow better when I'm around.

The sunroom is bright with afternoon sunlight streaming in through the glass walls. The air is fresh and tangy, and I breathe in the smell of all the memories made in this room. I developed my interest in plants from gardening with Grandfather here. Repotting aloe vera plants, trying to coax blooms from the orchids, trimming the rosebush that had been my grandmother's favorite.

Grandfather sits reading a newspaper in his favorite chair, tendrils of vines creeping up the upholstery. A few months ago, if I'd come in at this time of day, I would have found him wrist deep in soil instead of looking so weary. He definitely looks sick. Worse than before I left for my trip.

"Good morning, mi reinita," he says when he sees me approaching.

"Hi, Grandfather." I kiss his cheek, then sit next to him on a cushioned stool and grasp his leathery hand. His bones are so light. His eyes twinkle, and his crepey skin wrinkles as he smiles. He's thinner, gaunter, less vibrant. He seems to be . . . wilting.

"Something is troubling you."

"Just your health, Grandfather."

"My health? Don't fuss over me, or I'll feel my age."

What am I supposed to say to that? Ask him if he's dying?

"Your mother tells me that you may be leaving for university sooner than we expected. Are you excited?"

It's hard for me to care about Genesis or anything to do with the Families after what I've just learned. "I'm not so sure," I say.

"Why not?"

"I don't know if I'm cut out for the program."

"Nonsense. My granddaughter?" He boops my nose. "In this family, we know how to fight our way to the top and become exactly who we are meant to be."

Despite what I'm used to from everyone else, Grandfather has always had unwavering confidence in me.

I smile weakly, not wanting to disappoint him with my own, less-flattering assessment of myself.

"Your mother was also unsure of herself when she was your age," Grandfather says.

"Really?" Unsure is the last way I'd describe my laser-focused mother.

"Oh yes, she agonized for months before deciding to go to business school."

"How did she decide?"

He chuckles. "I believe she chose whatever was the most different from anything me or your grandmother did." I can't tell if he's joking.

We are connected to the order through my grandmother's side of the family, and it was extremely important to my grandmother that her daughter be an active member of the Inner Chamber. But I'd always had the impression that's what Mom wanted too.

When I'm being generous, I can feel bad for Mom having to live up to even higher standards than I do. I never knew my grandmother well, as she died very soon after I was born, but she was a senior policy adviser for the

United Nations, and she had also played for the New York Philharmonic when she was in her teens. And Grandfather has an MD-PhD and was a world-renowned epidemiologist until he retired. Apparently, he traveled a lot for his job, so he wasn't part of all the Families-related activities that dominated my mother's life, and the two of them were never close the way he is with me.

It's nice to know that Mom hasn't always had it all figured out. Maybe her rebellious phase was how she ended up marrying a directionless musician like my father.

"Come, read with me," Grandfather says.

Reading with Grandfather is a daily ritual. My dad used to play music for me every night until I fell asleep, and when he left, I couldn't sleep for a week. Grandfather started reading to me instead. Every single night, until I started reading to him. I miss my dad a lot, but it's never hurt too much because Grandfather has always been there in his place. But now I might lose him, too.

If Grandfather sees my eyes filling with tears, he doesn't acknowledge it. He just passes me his newspaper.

Grandfather subscribes to at least ten different newspapers local and foreign, and he reads every single one. He says it's important to be aware of what's happening around the world. That generally means knowing about how bad things are and how helpless I am to change any of it, so I'd much rather ignore it all.

As predicted, the headlines are grim. An increase in deaths of homeless people over the winter months, refugees dying from a pandemic, a famous scientist gone missing and presumed dead.

As I read, Grandfather's eyelids droop, and soon he's asleep. At least he looks comfortable. I use my sleeve to wipe my cheeks as tear stains gather on the newsprint.

I hate feeling helpless.

Sal, Grandfather's housekeeper who is basically part of the family, comes in holding a package. I discard the newspaper and get up to give her a hug.

"Welcome back," she whispers so as not to wake Grandfather.

"Hi, Sal." I hug her, breathing in her familiar scent of lavender and jasmine.

"This just arrived for you in the mail." She presses the parcel into my hands. It's wrapped in thick brown paper, and in loopy script it says, *Application to the Genesis Institute*.

As I take it, my heartbeat quickens.

Maybe I don't have to be helpless anymore.

Michael told me I have healing abilities. The Makers have advanced medicine. Could their knowledge help Grandfather?

When Kor had said we could use Maker knowledge to help our world, that had been inspiring but theoretical.

This is personal.

Once Sal is out of the room and I see that Grandfather is still sleeping soundly, I tear open the package with trembling hands.

Inside is a cube. It's about the same size as the music box my father gave me, which I've kept on my nightstand since I was a child. The music box turns out to be an apt comparison, because when I turn the cube in my hands, it plays a range of musical tones. Each wall of the cube is made of a different material. One side is clear like glass, one is wood, one is an ambery resin, one is clay-ish—similar to what Michael's pigeon is made of—one is some kind of metal, and the last side is silk.

Each wall plays a different music note when pressed. I shake the box but don't hear anything inside. I hold it up to the light and try to look through the glass-like wall but see nothing. I think it's a puzzle.

Of course, a straightforward application would be too much to ask of this mystery school. Straightforward, like the city college applications burning a hole in my desk drawer upstairs.

I lift the cube, shake it, and press each side, creating a tune from the different sounds. Maybe there's a musical code that needs to be played to unlock it? Nothing I try works. I don't even know if opening the box is the goal.

I've had enough of everyone being cryptic. I'm overcome with the urge to just throw the thing out the window and see what happens when it crashes on the pavement, but I restrain myself.

I use a pen and try to wedge the tip between the walls of the cube, but it doesn't fit. I look around the room for something else I can try. My grandmother's old Singer sewing machine is in the corner, nothing more than decoration these days. I go to it and rifle through the drawers. There are spools of thread, thimbles, and countless loose buttons. There, in the back corner, I find what I'm looking for: a pincushion impaled with multiple pins and needles.

I sit in the window seat with a sewing needle and try to rip it through the silk side of the cube—which emits a loud, discordant note until I release it—but the fabric is surprisingly strong. I poke the needle into a crack where the walls of the box meet, and I'm able to insert the point in about a centimeter, but then it refuses to budge. I push against the needle, trying to pry the sides of the box apart, but the needle springs loose and stabs my thumb.

Ouch.

That was dumb. A single dot of blood wells up from the pinprick and drips onto the wood side of the box. I immediately try to wipe it away, but the wood wall pops open.

Did my blood just open the box?

I'm not sure it matters considering that, apparently, the box is empty. I look inside, examining the reverse sides of the six different walls. There's nothing there. I try playing the music notes, but now that the box is open, they don't work. Frustration bubbles up within me. If there's another step to this puzzle, I will scream.

My brewing tantrum is interrupted as my phone buzzes, and my temper recedes, replaced by trepidation when I see that it's an email from the Genesis Institute admissions office. I tap the message open to a letter-head with a logo of an androgynous figure, clearly based on the *Vitruvian Man*—da Vinci's drawing of one human body superimposed on top of another, four arms, four legs, in supposedly perfect proportions. The email reads:

> *Dear Ada Castle,*
>   *We are pleased to notify you of your acceptance to the Genesis Institute. Tuition and room and board will be included as part of a full scholarship for the duration of your studies. We eagerly await your response.*
>   *Sincerely,*
>   *Master Michelangelo Loew, Community Liaison*

I tap to their website. "The Genesis Institute: for exceptionally gifted pupils" is splashed across the page with the same logo. The site looks completely mundane, like a regular private school. But I know better.

For an instant I consider deleting the email and hiding the box at the bottom of the trash. No one needs to know I received an acceptance. I could go upstairs right now and fill out those college applications. A worthless liberal arts degree and a lifetime of student debt could still be mine.

And I wouldn't have to think about stealing anything from anyone.

The memory of how I felt when I saw Michelangelo's prisoner statues rises in me. I look at the newspaper on the coffee table, headlines full of calamity. I watch the steady rise and fall of Grandfather's chest, knowing his health is declining by the day.

Or I could decide to stop being helpless.

A tingling warmth prickles the scars on my palms, and this time I don't let myself suppress it.

Three days later I'm wandering around one of the Families' contemporary art galleries as I wait for my ride to Genesis. I spent a grueling morning in the offices upstairs receiving rushed instructions from Family members who all treated me like a kid who shouldn't be trusted with any information. As if they could do any of this without me.

I'd also been up half the night with Kor, who had given me a completely separate set of instructions from the Oculus.

I'm still shaken that the Oculus even knows that someone like me exists. I thought they worked with people more like . . . I don't know, the Pope and the CIA. But, apparently, they also work with Kor, and by extension, yours truly.

In addition to learning about the Makers, they want me to find a way for them to gain access to the school. They also believe that there is some form of ritual or device that can give non-Sires the ability to create and use Ha'i. I am to confirm whether it exists and get all the information necessary to steal it.

Because yours truly is also now a thief, I guess.

I stop in front of a painting of an angel in flight. Confident brushstrokes capture the movement of her outstretched wings and the impossibility of her vivid, ethereal beauty. I know the painting well; it's one of Kor's older pieces. The art world recognized Kor's talent years ago, but now with his music fame, the value of his work has skyrocketed.

I remember when Kor finished this painting. He'd gazed at it wistfully, then wondered aloud if his perfect girl was one too perfect for this world. It was back when I was still hoping he'd realize that I was his perfect girl. Even years later, with that desire far behind me, I can't forget the heartache I felt in that moment, knowing I'd never be good enough for him.

I'm definitely no angel.

The familiar click of high heels and the subtle scent of bergamot and orange blossom make me turn with pleasant surprise.

"You thought I wouldn't come to see you off?" my mother asks.

"We said goodbye last night."

Mom had ordered a ridiculous mismatch of foods from my three favorite takeout spots, and we'd had a family dinner with Grandfather and Sal and Kor. It had been really nice, though it didn't feel right without Izzy there.

"Give me a little bit of credit." She pulls me into a hug. "I miss you already."

I already miss her too. Miss the relationship we used to have compared to how busy and distant she's become. She's always been a workaholic, but these past few months have been next level.

"You know that all I want is what's best for you, right?"

"Sure, Mom," I say into her champagne-colored silk-blend blazer, which I know will still somehow be stain free by the end of the day.

She kisses the top of my head. "Ada, I mean it. I would never have allowed them to send you to this school just to be their errand girl. I'm only letting you go because I think it will be good for you to learn from these people."

I roll my eyes. *Letting* me go. Maybe she could trust me to make my own decisions instead of trying to micromanage everything. I know she's trying to be nice, but all I hear in her words is relief that I might finally develop some actual talent, mixed with her lack of belief that I could possibly accomplish anything meaningful for the Families. Kor said this is the most important thing the Families have ever done, and yet my mom just sees me as an *errand girl.*

She would think that since I've never lived up to her standards of excellence. She is the ultimate perfectionist; from her looks, to her nutritional intake, to the phrasing of her text messages—everything must be perfect, perfect, perfect. Anything less than exceptional is failure.

To be fair, she's never directly said that to me, but it's clearly the standard she holds herself to, so I just assume she already sees me as a sunk cost.

Even so, I hug her tighter.

Our hug is cut short when her phone buzzes informing her of some meeting of great importance. With one last kiss, she rushes off.

I turn to watch the street from the gallery's glass doors, wiping away some pre-homesickness mist from my eyes. The sidewalks teem with bundled-up pedestrians clutching paper cups as they rush to meet the day. I should be one of them. School resumed at the beginning of this week, and it's weird to realize I may never go back to the familiar grind of math tests to bomb and books I only pretend to read. I wonder if I'll regret missing my graduation.

I've been expecting a vehicle, so Michael takes me by surprise when he's suddenly on the other side of the glass, on foot, his floppy hair alive with wind. I push open the door.

"Hi," he says with a dimpled smile.

If he wonders why I asked him to meet me at a random gallery instead of my home, he doesn't mention it. All our interactions are being observed through security cameras so that the rest of the Inner Chamber can over-analyze everything about Michael.

"Ready to go?" he asks awkwardly.

"Not in the slightest," I respond as I step out into the brisk morning, winding my scarf around my face to protect myself from the biting wind.

My luggage was picked up yesterday by a courier—Kor suspects they wanted to search through my stuff—so all I have with me is my backpack. My phone is hidden at the bottom, stashed in a pouch of tampons. I wasn't explicitly told not to bring it, though it was made clear there won't be cell service, but it still feels like contraband. The satellite phone stashed beside it is definitely contraband. One of the Families' tech experts had flown in from Belgium just to give it to me and show me how to use it.

I thought meeting a tech expert would mean I'd get all kinds of cool spy gadgets, but nope. Just a satellite phone that I have been told to never ever use. Apparently they're worried that it is insecure and that the signal can be intercepted, but they want me to have an emergency way to contact them if need be. When I'd asked about spy cameras and recording devices, the tech guy had said the camera on my cell phone would be perfectly sufficient. When I asked about night-vision glasses, he asked why I would have any need to see in the dark instead of flicking the light switch. What a lack of imagination.

"I'm so glad this has all worked out and that your family approved," Michael says as we head west, weaving our way around a mountain of garbage bags.

"Approve of a full scholarship to an elite private school? It was an easy sell." I don't meet his eyes as the first of many lies rolls off my tongue. "The website and phone calls were very convincing."

"Yes, we have a provincial office that takes care of cover stories." Michael pauses at the corner, dutifully waiting for the walk signal despite there being no oncoming traffic. I attempt to suppress my New Yorker instinct to rush.

"Are there many? Recruits who need a cover?"

"Not many in recent years. Faking deaths is our most common method." Well, that's morbid. The signal turns white, and we continue walking. "It's not encouraged for recruits to keep ties with the provincial world, so death is usually the simplest solution."

"But I'll be allowed to come back and visit?" My heart tugs with the need for this assurance.

"Since you are young and in danger, an exception is being made for you."

I'm not sure where I expected him to take me, probably an airport, but I certainly wasn't expecting the subway. And yet here we are, on the crowded 6 train platform headed downtown. It's much warmer down here than outside, and my winter clothes are stifling me. I feel like I've been microwaved—parts of me too hot and parts of me still thawing from the cold. I won't miss the temperature idiosyncrasies of the subway platforms while I'm gone.

"What a dreadfully inefficient system," Michael says as he looks around, but his voice is infused with affection.

I don't like anyone, no matter how adorable their windblown hair may be, dissing my city. "This *inefficient system* transports millions of people a day," I respond dryly.

His smile widens, but when he realizes I'm not smiling back, his look turns thoughtful. "You make a good point. It is both amazing and inefficient."

The train arrives, and it's packed, but we manage to snag two adjacent seats.

There's a series of ads on the subway car's walls announcing KORACH CHEVALIER'S NEW SINGLE "RIGHTEOUS" OUT NOW in bright red letters, Kor's face gazing with romantic mournfulness at the commuters. You'd think I'd be used to this by now, but I'm not.

As we pull away from the platform, the sway of the car and the press of bodies jostles me against Michael. With each knock of our thighs and bump of our shoulders, I become more and more fond of this *inefficient* mode of transportation. I may have many reservations about the dude, but he didn't just stop being attractive.

"How are your hands?" Michael asks me at one point.

"Fine. Scarred. I've never had a scar before."

"Your Ha'i is creative energy. Antimatter is the opposite." He whispers this even though the other passengers couldn't care less. "It's the only existing substance that counteracts Ha'i and can cause injuries that Sire abilities can't heal. Our labs are analyzing the gloves. The Inquisitors have certainly advanced their technology over the years."

This is useful information. I had described the gloves to the Families during my debriefing, but no one seemed to have heard of antimatter. It definitely seems like the kind of thing Ozymandias Tech would have access to, though. The more I think about Izzy's message, the more it makes sense that Oz Tech is behind the abductions.

We ride the train all the way downtown, and the car slowly empties. Once there's no need for us to be pressed close together, Michael shifts slightly so we're no longer touching. Suddenly the ride is a lot more boring.

"So, where are we going?" I eventually ask. There's an entire historic order waiting for the answer to this question.

"We need to catch a train," Michael says, "but the entrance to the train station is a bit . . . tricky to access."

Where could we be taking the 6 line to catch a train? We've already passed the Grand Central stop.

"When the New York subway system's first line was built, the Makers designed their own train to be accessible from the City Hall station," Michael explains. "Unfortunately, in the forties, the station didn't meet the needs of the new subway cars, so it was abandoned." He shakes his head ruefully, wearing that dimpled smile. "So inefficient, so wasteful." He says it like he's proud of a young child for trying but failing. I roll my eyes and hold back from sniping at him again. He continues, "Luckily, we still have ways to access the station; this approach is the easiest."

He sticks his hand inside the front of his coat and pulls out a bag of cheese puffs. "I'm hungry. Are you hungry?" He withdraws a bright orange puff from the bag, pops it into his mouth, then tips back his head with a way-too-sensual moan. "Enjoy them while you can." He holds out the bag for me to take. "There's no highly processed deliciousness at Genesis," he says wistfully.

A few minutes later, the bag is empty and I'm trying to lick bright orange powder off my hands. My attempts are mostly unsuccessful. I look at Michael and find him licking his own fingers just as awkwardly. Our eyes meet with a shared moment of panicked embarrassment.

"Ladies and gentlemen," the polite voice of the train announcement drones, "this is the last downtown stop on this train. The next stop on this train will be Brooklyn Bridge / City Hall on the uptown platform." From my many years riding the subway, I recognize this announcement as standard, but this time it doesn't stop there. "Ladies and gentlemen," the voice continues, "not only is it unsafe, it is a violation to ride or walk between cars except in an emergency or when directed by a police officer or a train crew."

I stand to head to the exit with everyone else, but Michael shakes his head.

"But this is the last stop," I say.

"Yes, but we're the next stop," he replies as the remaining stragglers make their way out.

"Stand clear of the closing doors, please," drones the announcement. I feel awkward and a little nervous. Won't a conductor come kick us out? After a moment the train pulls away from the platform and drives through the dark tunnel.

But it doesn't stay dark for long. Light trickles in from a skylight as we turn into another station. A beautiful station, with intricate tiling.

"Come on," Michael calls. He's already at the sliding doors—which have most definitely *not* opened considering the train is still *moving*—fiddling with his multi-tool. "We only have a moment. And be prepared to jump over the gap." The doors pop open a crack, and Michael separates them further by pulling them apart with his hands.

"I'm going to hold this open for you," Michael says, his long arms high enough for me to duck under. "But you need to jump quickly. Okay?"

I nod, not knowing quite what I'm agreeing to considering the train is very much still rambling down the track. The opening is just wide enough to fit his lean frame. He looks back at me, with my hips and other curves, and then he pulls the door a little wider.

No time to blush.

As the car reaches a bend, it pauses, almost imperceptibly.

"Now!" Michael urges. I grip the straps of my backpack and leap over the gap between the track and platform, my heart thumping so hard I worry for my other organs. I hear Michael land right next to me, and I stumble into him. He steadies me as my knees tremble from the shot of adrenaline.

The train car is gone, screeching its way along the tracks. I take a deep breath, clutching Michael for an extra moment. Then I let go and look around to find that we are in what feels like a totally different time.

I've never been in a subway station so empty, so quiet. And it's so perfectly preserved, under New York City all this time, and not even a secret.

"Never got much use," Michael says. "Now it's always empty except for the occasional private tour. But doesn't it have so much character?"

It does.

"We have to catch our next train, so we'll take the fast route. Or, as I like to think of it, the fun route!" He hops down onto the rails, and I hold in a shocked screech. Touching the tracks is almost as bad of subway etiquette as making eye contact with a stranger.

"Avoid this one." Michael points at the third rail—duh, dude, I'm no subway amateur—then reaches up to help me climb down to meet him, though I need to fight all my ingrained instincts to even consider such a reckless action. My only associations with people jumping onto subway tracks are very unfortunate—loss of life and, worse, rush-hour delays.

As soon as we pass under the archway of the dark tunnel, he lifts what looks like a manhole cover. I look down the hole and see a . . . pole? "Don't overthink it. I'll catch you at the bottom," he says, and sits, dangles his legs into the hole, then wraps them around the pole. "Wait about thirty seconds before you follow." He pushes his way into the hole and gets sucked into the dark, his clothing squealing against the metal. As soon as his head is through, the cover slams shut with a clang that echoes through the dark tunnel.

My heart races at the thought of following him down. But the terror of standing alone on a subway track with no knowledge of when the next train will come to run me over is enough to have me on my butt, shimmying into position as I hold the cover open and wrap my legs around the pole. Thank God I wore pants today.

Oh man. Oh Lord. Oh cheese puffs that I might barf up.

Here I go.

Air rushes around me as I shriek, my fingers burning from gripping the pole instead of loosening them as I should, but I just grip tighter. My eyes are squeezed shut, and my heartbeat is erratic. And then warm arms are catching me, holding me. I'm on solid ground. It's over. It actually was fun.

I still might barf up cheese puffs.

★ ★ ★ ★ ★

A couple of corridors and a few calming breaths later, we arrive at another empty train platform.

"Welcome to the Atlas," Michael says, gesturing toward the stretch of track in front of us, "a highly efficient maglev train system that connects all of Maker society." Opaque glass walls block off the track in either direction, so I'm not sure how it leads anywhere.

"Maglev? Like magnetic levitation?" I read an article to Grandfather a few months ago about investors throwing money at Ozymandias Tech for a magnetic levitation project.

"Yes. The provincials are catching up with this technology. It allows for smooth travel at astonishing speeds."

The climate in here is comfortable, and Michael removes his coat. He has a smart-looking cravat tied around his neck, tucked into a formal jacket that reaches his knees. Well, hello there. There's no denying that this whole vintage professorial vibe works for him. Works for me.

"Ah, here we go," he says, and I turn to see a train entering the station through a round entrance that has opened in the wall. "Airlocks," Michael explains. "By reducing the air in the tunnels, there's less drag on the train, allowing for greater speed."

The train looks like a giant bronze bullet. It stops in front of us with silent grace, and numerous doors slide open. We enter, and the inside is even more magnificent. The walls are polished cherrywood, and there are couches and chairs all upholstered in jeweled-toned velvets. Crystal chandeliers hang from the ceiling.

Michael settles onto an ocean-blue divan, and I sigh into a deep red winged chair as I continue to take in my surroundings. With the changing light through the window, I realize we've been moving for a few moments already.

"If we're going as fast as you say, how come I don't feel it at all?" I ask in amazement.

Michael grins so wide that my own cheeks ache. "Welcome to the possibilities of a world where everyone devotes their lives to creativity and innovation," he says.

Do they really? I'm curious to see how ideal this Maker lifestyle actually is, beyond the advantages they have purely as a result of hoarding their resources.

Michael continues. "The Atlas may not transport anywhere near millions a day, but it can get you from New York City to the Globe Theatre in less time than it takes to perform *Hamlet*."

Okay. That's pretty mind blowing. I wonder when it will hit me that this is all real.

My attention catches on two people sitting together a few seats away from us. One is a woman with an intricately braided hairstyle and a beaded bodice with puffed sleeves, but instead of a sweeping skirt as might be expected, the bodice is tucked into jeans that she's paired with tall riding boots. The man next to her has on a leather jacket over a high-necked blouse and voluminous short pants with tights, and combat boots. I bite my lip to keep from gasping. They look uh-maze-ing. The clash of styles is, somehow, incredibly chic. A blend of classic and modern that rivals anything I've seen during New York Fashion Week. I'm dying to take a picture of the woman's hairstyle so I can try it on myself.

"Are my clothes not going to fit in?" I ask Michael, looking again at his long jacket, then back to the beautifully dressed couple, and then at my own jeans and hoodie ensemble that is my go-to most of the time.

"Don't worry. Maker fashion is varied enough that whatever you have will be fine." He looks at his clothes with mild distaste. "This is faculty dress code. Anyone not on duty wears what they want."

Right. He's *faculty*.

And a distraction from my reason for being here.

"Can I explore a bit?" I ask, getting up from the chair. I should investigate more of the train. Espionage and all that.

"Sure. I'll show you around." He starts to unfold his long limbs.

"No, it's fine," I say quickly. "You've been shuffling me around all day. I can wander on my own." Then, to be safe, I add, "Plus, I need to use the bathroom."

Ugh. Why did I say that? Now he must think I always need the bathroom. He's gonna think I have stomach issues and start associating me with diarrhea.

"I have a small bladder," I clarify, then immediately regret it.

Shut up, Ada.

He clears his throat, settling back down. "There's a lavatory through there." He indicates the adjoining car, and I grab my bag and scurry through the door, my face aflame.

I take my time exploring the train. Each car has its own distinct personality. There's a café car with a beautiful wood bar and candlelit tables, and even a library car with shelves of books and comfy reading nooks. I take advantage of the emptiness of the library and fish out my cell phone. I want to see how far out I can still get service. As I wake the screen, the last bar is just blinking out. No service, no internet, no GPS.

I'm officially on my own.

I type up some quick notes with details of the train station and the train itself so I don't forget, then stow my phone back in its hiding place and go to poke around more.

Near the end of the train, I enter a car not so different from where I left Michael, but the decor is darker and more severe, almost military in style. It's empty but for two boys. One looks younger, with shaggy hair and splotchy skin. He's wearing sweatpants—which makes me feel a lot better about my own clothes—and he's fast asleep with his legs propped up on a teardrop-shaped instrument case. The other boy is seated at a desk writing with a fountain pen on parchment, and—

This. This is what I had expected people from Utopia to look like. He's the type of exquisite specimen that I have rarely lain eyes upon in real life. His hair is a brassy shade of blond pulled into a short ponytail. The slope of his nose and the angle of his jaw are perfectly proportioned and might just as well be chiseled from stone in a museum. Izzy can call me thirsty all she wants for having a new crush every semester, but with Michael off the table, I deserve some eye candy. Not that this candy will ever be on the menu—I know out-of-my-league when I see it. I shouldn't ogle him, but I think it's fair to say that there's a certain tier of attractiveness that is so unattainable it excuses company manners.

The boy looks up at me, his ice-blue eyes aloof and assessing. An amber earring glints in his right lobe. He's probably one or two years older than me—not that I have any trust in my age-radar anymore.

He stands and reaches out his hand to me. "Raphael Vanguard," he says like I should recognize the name.

"Ada Castle," I say, but when I extend my hand, instead of shaking it, he grasps it, and he bends to brush a kiss over my knuckles. Though his lips barely touch me, heat burns my skin, and the base of my fingers warm with that familiar prickle that I now have a name for—Ha'i.

His eyes widen then flick to my right hand, which he's just released, then to my right ear.

Is it possible to want to be an item of clothing? Right now I would like to be Raphael Van-whatever's leather jacket. It looks awfully cozy resting on those sculpted shoulders.

"Castle," he says. "I've never heard that name before. Are you from the Misty Isles?" Even his voice is perfect. It's deep and smooth with an almost imperceptible lilt of a foreign accent that makes me think of fancy pastries and silk pajamas.

"I'm from New York," I respond.

The flirtatious glint in his eyes blinks out, and his expression turns sour. He wipes his hand on his perfectly tailored pants.

My cheeks burn, and my gut twists, though I have no idea why I should be embarrassed. He returns to his seat, ignoring me, and his beauty now feels cold and dangerous.

"Well, uh, nice to meet you," I mumble, feeling the urge to flee.

He doesn't respond, and I turn and head back in the direction I came, working hard to keep a normal pace instead of running like I want to.

I make sure to stop in the lavatory. I don't actually need to go, but I might eventually. I'd rather wet myself than tell Michael I need a bathroom again, so I force the deed.

By the time I make it back to Michael, the train is smoothly pulling into another station. Michael is fast asleep with his head tipped back and his legs spread wide.

I gently touch my hand to his shoulder, and he startles awake. He blinks, looks around, then exclaims, "Ah, we're home!"

Maybe he's home, but I'm far, far from mine.

7

We follow the other passengers into a glass elevator and ride up through a shaft of stalactites and stalagmites and all manner of shimmering rocks. When we reach the surface and exit the station, we're in a small village near the water. I can't see the ocean, but the salt in the air and the cry of gulls tell me it's close. The wind is crisp, but it's nowhere near as cold as New York, and at the speed we were traveling, we could be anywhere in the world.

"Where are we?" I ask Michael.

"Arcadia."

"And where is that?" If he could provide specific GPS coordinates, that would be helpful.

"In the Atlantic Oce—"

Michael is cut off as the disconcertingly beautiful boy from the train pushes past us. He pauses in his stride and sneers at me before addressing Michael. "Pulling weeds again, Master Loew?" His smooth voice is laced with an ugly tone.

Michael tenses and says, "Journey Vanguard, you will treat all members of this institution with respect."

"But of course, my apologies." The boy's words drip with sarcasm as he saunters away.

He approaches a tangle of beautiful people, who all immediately fall into orbit around him. I assume one of the girls must be his girlfriend when he kisses her on the mouth, but then another girl takes firm possession of his biceps and rises on her tiptoes for a kiss of her own. I force myself to look away.

"I should warn you," Michael says stiffly as we continue walking. "There are some among our society who don't approve of accepting those raised in the provincial world. If anyone gives you any trouble, come see me immediately."

Ah. So even Utopia has bigots. Why am I not surprised?

"That's strange," Michael mutters, narrowing his eyes at two guards who are stonily observing everyone coming out of the station. They look like medieval superheroes, wearing black capes over knee-length leather jackets with silver buttons down the front and a silver dragon embroidered on the left side of the chest.

"They're not usually here?" Having guards at the train station of a secret island seems normal to me, but the long swords strapped to their backs are certainly unsettling.

"No. The Avant Guard is a military group trained to protect Maker territories from provincial threats. They're ordinarily based in Avant, where those Makers who didn't want to travel to the New World hid and established our other academy."

I feel like I need to be writing all this down. Do the Families even know about Avant?

Despite the guards, the village itself could not be more inviting. A strip of quaint shops of varied sizes, shapes, and colors—as if a child with scissors cut out buildings from different time periods and pasted them together haphazardly—line a central square with a large fountain. The area is bustling with pedestrians, many of whom are dressed in the same blend of old and new as the couple on the train.

Other passengers from our train join a line of people waiting to get onto gliders that look like a cross between a bicycle and a paper airplane made of old parchment. My stomach drops as I watch one careen down a mini runway, alight into the air, and fly away. It looks flimsy, like it could easily be taken down by an aggressive seagull. We'd better not be getting onto one of those.

"Not quite New York City or Florence," Michael says, looking out at the village, "but it's home to the best biscuits and tea in the world." He motions toward a tea shop that's built out of a repurposed train car. There's a gleam in his eyes, and I can tell he's happy to be home.

As we pass through the central plaza, there's a gap in the line of shops, and an iron fence looks out over a view of a distant waterfall. I rush over to the fence and catch my breath when I realize that there's nothing on the other side of the rail but a sheer drop hundreds of feet down to where water violently crashes against rocks in the cove below. From here, I can see that the whole village has been built on the edge of a cliff, which curves to form the secluded cove. The waterfall blocks the point at which the cliff sides almost meet in a narrow ravine, the only passage from the cove to the ocean.

Wind whips my hair into my face, and I close my eyes and breathe in the smell of breeze and brine. "I'd love to go down to the water," I say to Michael, who has followed me and is watching my awe with a smile.

"That would be challenging," he responds. "The founders of Genesis purposely chose this island for the protection provided by its steep cliffs. It's not easy to get down to the beach."

Right. This island is for hiding. From people like me.

"Let's get to the institute," Michael says. "Would you prefer to walk or take an ornithopter?" He gestures back toward the gliders.

"There's no way I'm getting into one of those oversize paper airplanes. Please, let's walk."

Michael coughs to suppress a laugh. "That's the first time I've heard da Vinci's original design described quite like that." He leads me down a path into the cover of trees, where I'm surrounded by the fresh smell of many shades of green.

A slobbering hound races toward us from the opposite direction, followed by a man who grins broadly when he sees Michael. The man wears a blue gemstone earring just like Michael's, though he looks a bit older. His T-shirt and corduroy slacks are ordinary enough, or they would be if they weren't accompanied by a red velvet cape and knee-high laced boots. I'm going to need to practice not snickering when looking at full-on adults wearing *capes*. But also, I want those boots.

The two men grasp each other's arms below the elbow in greeting, and Michael scratches the dog behind the ears.

"Ada, meet Master Ravi Bose. He'll be your Apprentice Testaments instructor."

I nod politely as if I know what the hell a testament is and as if throwing around words like "master" and "apprentice" is perfectly normal.

"Do you know why the Guard are watching the station?" Michael asks his friend.

The man looks sidelong at me before answering. "Don't know anything for sure," he says. "But it sounds like there have been more abductions of provincial Sires as well as concerns about an informant in Avant, so extra precautions are being taken to prevent infiltration."

The dog sniffs around at my feet.

My chest constricts. Their military is looking for spies? The timing of my coming here couldn't be worse.

The man continues to eye me as he says, "I'm surprised they're allowing any newcomers in."

"Only special cases," Michael responds.

I feel a tremor of guilt, but it sounds like the Makers have someone a lot more dangerous than me to be concerned about. Like whoever kidnapped me. I push the memory aside before the familiar dread can settle.

"Well then," the man says to me. "Welcome, Special Case. I, for one, am glad to see new blood on this island. Hopefully, everything will be resolved soon, and the Avant Guard and their aggressive posturing can return to their gloomy tower." He claps Michael on the back and then whistles to his dog. "Let's go, Munch!" And they head off toward the village.

As Michael and I continue down the road, the foliage thickens, and the air grows heavy with mist.

"The provincials think this is just a privately owned island, and we use the mist to obscure the institute. The moisture likes to collect in the forest," Michael explains. He pats his hair, which has floofed up spectacularly. I'm sure the moisture has styled my own hair into something a lot worse.

Eventually, the tree cover breaks, and the institute comes into view, grand and imposing. The front half of the building has a majestic paneled glass roof with a large dome at its center and towers that rise around it. The tallest spire is obscured by a milky fog that filters the sunlight, making the scene feel painted in watercolors.

We cross the courtyard and enter the building through towering oak doors. Sunlight streams through the glass ceiling of the entrance hall, illuminating walls covered in colorful frescoes. A large tree grows straight up through the floor, its roots creeping across the room, embedding themselves between the marble tiles.

I stop in my tracks and stare at a colossal mural that is a perfect re-creation of one of my favorite paintings.

"*The School of Athens*," I murmur, walking closer to investigate. I've always been captivated by Raphael's fresco that depicts the greatest mathematicians, scientists, and philosophers from classical antiquity under one roof, sharing their ideas and learning from one another.

"That wasn't its original name," Michael says, and I look up at him questioningly. "Famously known as *Scuola di Atene*, it's actually called *Causarum Cognitio, Knowledge of Causes*, but before the Inquisition it was known as *l'accademia Dell Muse, the Academy of Muses*."

I suck in a breath. "Are you saying that this is meant to be the institute that was destroyed during the Inquisition?"

He nods. "The academy is said to have been started by Alexander the Great, but it grew to prominence during the Renaissance when the greatest creative minds from around the world traveled there to form the Makers— or *le muse*, as they were called at the time—including Raphael, who immortalized the academy in his greatest masterpiece."

"But Plato, Aristotle, Socrates . . . Pythagoras? Everyone depicted in the painting, they're all from ancient Greece, not the Renaissance."

"You're right, of course. But look again. Look at Plato's face." I look at the central figure of the painting. "Who else does it look like?"

It's suddenly impossible not to see. "Leonardo da Vinci," I say.

Michael nods. "And Heraclitus?" He needs to point the figure out to me this time since I don't know who he's referring to. But when I scrutinize the face he indicates, I see the clear likeness.

"Michelangelo."

Michael nods again. "And here"—he points to a figure all the way on the right side—"is Raphael himself." It's definitely him, practically identical to the self-portrait I saw on display in the Uffizi Gallery just the other week.

I observe the fresco with new eyes, now seeing Raphael's depiction of himself and his contemporaries learning from one another in a great academy, the memory of which has been stolen from the world. But the heart of that center of learning still exists, here in this very building.

Where I'm going to have the chance to learn. I swallow thickly.

"Let's go see the headmaster," Michael says.

We walk through corridors hung with magnificent paintings and sumptuous draperies, past twisting staircases and strange laboratories.

The headmaster is waiting for us in an office that smells like mint leaves and aged paper. He's an imposing man wearing a cravat and knee-length jacket like Michael's. Perched over his left eye is a monocle of smoky glass. His other eye is trained on me, watching sharply.

He has three hoops in his ear: sapphire, emerald, and pearl. The same earrings I was supposed to be looking for in Florence. I bet this is who Prometheus had intended for me to find.

Michael walks up to him and gives him a quick half hug.

"Welcome back, my boy." The man's face is infused with affection as he returns the hug.

"Ada." Michael turns to me. "This is Headmaster Bloche."

"Welcome to Genesis," the headmaster says, his voice deep and stern. He gestures for me to sit. I sink into an embroidered couch and actively look around the office so as not to rudely stare at his monocle.

"How was Chorus?" Michael asks in a low voice that tells me the conversation is not meant for me, though he must know I can hear.

"She was . . . Chorus," Bloche says with a sigh.

"What did she say?"

"That teaching the girl is the will of the Conductor."

Michael glances at me, then back to the headmaster. "Will that satisfy the rest of the Council?"

"It will have to."

I wonder if I'm "the girl." And who are Chorus and the Conductor? But my attention strays when I notice a large oil painting above the headmaster's desk. It's of a boat caught in a storm, and it looks an awful lot like an original Rembrandt. The perfection in the contrast of the shadow and light matches his signature style. It's breathtaking. But Rembrandt only ever painted one seascape, which was famously and tragically stolen. A bubble of unease floats in the back of my throat.

The headmaster takes a seat and nods approvingly when he sees me admiring the seascape. I do my best to tamp down the questions I have about it. Instead, I swallow and smile at the headmaster.

"Ms. Castle, you have been invited to join this illustrious institution to commit yourself to our mission of advancing society through all manner of art, philosophy, and science."

"Advance all of society?" I ask. "Or just your hidden society?"

He purses his lips, then says, "I see why you like this one, Master Loew." After a moment of contemplation, he says. "Ms. Castle, coming here means leaving your past behind. Most recruits cut all ties with anyone in the provincial world. The Council was willing to allow you here due to the danger posed against Sires such as yourself"—he fixes his gaze on me, the glass of the monocle having gone completely black—"but, eventually, you will have to choose between their world and ours. Do you understand?"

I notice that he hasn't really answered my question. Michael is standing near a grandfather clock—that has pictures of planets and constellations but no numbers—his expression pinched.

The response on the tip of my tongue is that this has all been very fast and I can't commit to anything yet. But I'm not here to be honest. I'm here to make these people trust me. So instead, I say, "Absolutely, sir. I'm excited to learn."

"Thank you, Ms. Castle. You will be given until the next anniversary of the Exodus. At that time, you will have to decide whether you would like to make your home here and forgo your old life, or whether you want to leave here, never to return."

I nod and swallow, having no sense of how much time that actually gives me. And what will they do if—*when*—I tell them I want to leave? Would they really just let me go after learning all their secrets? I'm not so sure.

The headmaster continues, "Our community runs on a guild system. You will need to put together a gallerie to gain acceptance to a guild at Quorum."

"A gallerie is a portfolio of your skills and interests," Michael explains. "Quorum is when apprentices present their galleries to the guildmasters for application to become journeymen. Your guild will provide you with all the necessary education, guidance, and resources for your artistic and scientific pursuits, and in turn, you will share your research and innovations with your guild."

This all sounds complicated. I thought I'd done what I had to do to get into this school, but now I'll also need to apply and be accepted to a guild? I feel the stirrings of the college admission trauma I thought I'd left behind.

Michael continues. "The five Genesis guilds are the Sophists, the Artisans, the Alchemists, the Ciphers, and Bioscience. Over the next few months, we'll help you get acquainted with each so that you will be able to choose between your options at Quorum."

I try my best to hide my abject horror at the intimidating nature of the list.

Bloche says, "As an apprentice, most of your needs will be provided for you, but you should have some currency for incidentals." He reaches into a drawer and pulls out a pouch, which he hands to me. "That should be enough to tide you over until you collect a guild stipend."

I peek inside the pouch and see gold coins, each a little smaller and thicker than a dime. Their shape and texture are imperfect, inconsistent, though they all have the same imprint, an intricate design of a circuit-like maze.

"Sense." Michael names them for me.

"Cents, like pennies?"

"No, sense." He taps his temple. "Like *sens*ibility, and non*sense*."

"Hold on to those. They will be useful to you for more than currency," Headmaster Bloche says.

"Can I exchange dollars for sense?" I ask, nervous now. I hadn't considered that finances would be different.

"No, but you don't need to," Michael assures me. "You'll receive an apprentice stipend from the institute, and all necessities are provided for free—sense is only needed to purchase luxuries."

Necessities are *free*? When the most powerful country in the world can't even provide affordable health care? Maybe this is Utopia after all.

But I can't afford to think like that. Any whiff of utopian ideals only lasts as far as the boundaries of this island, and I need to prepare myself to be able to steal from these people.

The headmaster rises, so I assume I should too. He says to Michael, "I have to travel again, so I'll ask you to cover some of my meetings that cannot be postponed, and someone on the island must have a council key for emergencies."

Michael looks extremely uneasy. "Maybe one of the guildmasters—"

The headmaster cuts him off. "I know that you worry you are too young and that the guildmasters will question your authority, but none of the guildmasters have worked as my direct apprentice. I know I can trust you, and that is more important than your colleagues' professional jealousy. You have proven yourself time and again, and those who haven't seen it yet will soon." He takes a large, ornate key from his pocket and hands it to Michael. "Now, if you would please direct Apprentice Castle to her apartment."

"Yes, Master Bloche." Michael sighs.

Before we exit, I take one last look at the painting that might be a priceless, stolen Rembrandt. I want to ask Michael about it, but I don't know how to without sounding accusatory. I need to appear excited to be here, not suspicious. So I paste on a smile and follow him out.

On the way to my room, Michael provides a mini tour of the institute. The entrance hall is called the Equinox, and it branches into a sunburst of five peripheral wings. One wing is the library, the heart of the school. The Autumn and Spring wings have classrooms, offices, and communal facilities, and the Summer and Winter wings are mostly for residence. My room is in the Winter wing.

I know we've entered the Winter wing when the rich warm hues of the wallpaper and window hangings change to cool blues, deep evergreens, and snowy whites. There are ornaments and light fixtures of crystal and glass, reminiscent of ice, and even the scenes in the paintings on the wall have shifted in season and tone.

We turn into a hallway with walls that somehow manage to be the exact color of twilight after fresh snowfall, and we stop at an arched door. There's a brass knocker in the shape of tree branches and a small hole where the knob should be.

"Your fingerprint is linked with the lock," Michael says, indicating the small hole and wiggling his pointer finger. I had submitted a full set of fingerprints during my application process. I stick my pointer into the groove, and the door swings open to a common area.

The room has the feel of a winter cabin with walls of aged wood full of grooves and knots and a floor of plush rugs in deep reds and soft ochers. Numerous glass spheres hang from the exposed beams of the ceiling, illuminating the space with the glow of Edison coils. A large window looks out onto the mists, and a fire crackles in a woodburning stove. My tower of bags is already here, stacked neatly outside one of the two closed doors, and a third door opens to a small bathroom.

"Hello?" Michael calls out, but no one responds.

I stand at the entrance, unsure what happens next. He seems to be unsure as well, and he awkwardly fingers the sapphire hoop in his ear. All the Makers I've met so far have had gemstones in their ears.

"What's with the earrings?" I ask.

He looks confused for a moment, then follows the motions of his hand, and understanding dawns. "Ah, guildstones. You'll get one when you join a guild at Quorum. The gems communicate guild and rank. So, a sapphire hoop indicates I'm a master of the Sophist guild—"

One of the doors opens, and a teenage girl with a spectacular cloud of blond and purple hair rushes out.

"You're here! Hi! Come in!" she greets us.

"This is Georgia Vega, your roommate," Michael says.

"Call me Georgie." Her smile is wide and infectious, with teeth that are bright white and slightly crooked. She's wearing a plaid shirt, a black tutu with black tights, and purple combat boots. "Hi, Master Loew," she adds, eyeing Michael like it's weird that he's lingering in her—our—apartment, which I guess it is.

"I'll leave you two to become acquainted," Michael says. He gives me an encouraging smile and heads out.

"Yay! Welcome! Make yourself comfortable!" Georgie flops onto a couch and pulls her hair away from her face, messily tying it with a leather band. In addition to a purple guildstone, little men hang from her earlobes that look like they had previous lives as paper clips. I sit on the second couch opposite her and suddenly realize how tired my body is from the long day. Georgie says, "There are so few people from the provincial world here. It's so nice to meet someone else who is."

"Wait, you're also from the . . . regular world?"

"Yup. Came here three years ago when my mom was recruited. She wouldn't come without me and my dad. It was a big deal. They don't normally take anyone who isn't special in some way."

"What makes your mom special?" I wonder if she's a Sire like me.

"She's an art historian, and the Sophist guild supposedly wanted some of her esoteric research. But I think it's more likely that the Makers were concerned about her publishing information that could make people start asking the wrong questions." She tucks her feet up underneath her. "So, how many times have you been called a weed so far?" she asks. She's clearly joking, but there's something dark in her tone. I remember Raphael's comment that had enraged Michael.

Pulling weeds again, Master Loew?

"Once," I respond.

"Was it Rafe?"

"Uh . . ."

"So beautiful it hurts? More arrogant than Zeus? Thinks he's God's gift to all vaginas?"

I laugh. "Yeah, that sounds like him."

"Figures."

"What does 'weed' mean?" I ask her.

She scrunches up her nose. "Someone who wasn't raised as part of Maker society. Like something growing where it doesn't belong." She begins to stroke a fluffy blue pillow that does not at all match the rest of the decor. "There are some people who think that when the Makers left the provincial world behind, everyone in it ceased to matter. And there's a lot of animosity and fear surrounding provincial people."

"But everyone else I've met so far has been really nice," I say.

"Yeah, the majority of the folks here are pretty great." She nods toward the door. "But most don't understand the provincial world the way he does."

"You mean Michael?" I ask.

She eyes me skeptically. "Master Loew," she clarifies.

Right, he's a teacher. That's gonna take some getting used to. But maybe now I have a new friend to help me navigate this world so I won't have to attach myself to Michael like a barnacle.

Georgie's fluffy blue pillow lifts its head, opens its tiny mouth, and yawns. Then, two emerald-green eyes blink open, and the not-a-pillow stares at me suspiciously.

"Good morning, sleeping beauty." Georgie proceeds to scratch it behind the ears. It closes its eyes and emits a buzzing sound, not unlike a chain saw.

"What is that?" I ask. I mean, it's clearly a cat. But . . . blue.

"This is Bastet," Georgie says, kissing the cat's nose. "I found her scrounging for food in the compost garden. She must be a Bio experiment, but it's not legal to experiment on living beings. It was probably one of the Avant transfers—like Rafe. They still do cruel Blood Science stuff in Avant. Everything has been so much worse since they came here."

I'm still fixated on the peculiar feline. "How can they turn a cat blue?"

Georgie looks at me, brows arched. "They didn't *turn* her blue. They probably bred her this way with Sire-based genetic alteration. But a blue cat is the least of what they can do here. If this surprises you . . . sheesh. Just wait until you meet the Valkyries. You're going to freak out." Georgie reaches into her pocket and pulls out a multi-tool just like Michael's, except it's pink and bejeweled. She flicks open a tool and aims a little pink laser dot at the wall. Bastet leaps off the couch trying to catch the light as Georgie keeps the laser bouncing around the room.

I consider asking her if unicorns are real but then chicken out because it feels too ridiculous to say out loud.

"I was given a lot more information than you before I came here," Georgie says. "But don't worry. I'll help you out."

I couldn't have asked for a better roommate. And being around someone from home allows me to breathe in a way that I haven't felt comfortable doing all day.

I'm here, in this place where I can learn to use my abilities, at the same institute great minds like Ada Lovelace attended. I know I have a job to do for the Families, but, for a moment, I let myself imagine that I'm here just to learn from these people.

I can't wait to start.

The next day is a kaleidoscope of newness. My morning starts at the infirmary, where a slender redhead with a slightly hunched back named Kaylie Botticelli gives me a host of inoculations. Kaylie's a master of the Bioscience guild (amber hoop guildstone, I'm learning), and she's kind and extremely patient with all my questions. She also gives me a diamond earring, which is apparently something all Sires wear. I've never owned anything so valuable in my life, and I keep checking to make sure I haven't lost it yet.

The first class that I attend is Testaments, taught by Master Bose, who I met in the forest yesterday. The Testaments are the written records of the Makers, including the History Testaments (recorded Maker history), the Council Testaments (Maker laws), and the Testaments of the Prophets (recorded prophecies because, oh yeah, apparently prophecy exists, and being a Prophet is also a "perfectly normal genetic condition"). The class is currently studying the prophecies of a woman named Psalm, as well as those of her daughter, Chorus, the last known Prophet, who I have not failed to notice has the same name as whoever Michael and the headmaster were discussing yesterday.

I recognize that all the Testaments are full of information that will be useful for the Families, but it seems irrelevant for helping Grandfather, so I'm eager to move on to my next class, which could make all the difference.

Ha'i class is specifically for apprentice Sires to master control of their Ha'i—crucial information for the Families and for me. The sooner I learn how to use my Ha'i, the sooner I can learn how to use it to heal.

The class is in a candlelit room with a grass floor and a man in the corner playing a combination of lyre and singing bowls. The instructor, Master Liu, is a graceful older woman with her hair in a long silver braid who guides everyone through various meditations using movements reminiscent of tai chi.

My head spins with the knowledge that everyone in the room must have abilities like mine. I have never met another person that I knew to share my condition, and my heart seems to pound with the excitement of no longer being alone. I close my eyes and breathe deeply, listening to the echoes of the singing bowls and feeling the grass beneath my feet. But the wonder of it all doesn't quite subdue my frustration at how impractical these slow movements feel when I just want to learn how to use my abilities quickly.

Master Liu has me practice a hand configuration called "shiin," which is ideal for conducting Ha'i. Shiin is made by squeezing the middle, ring, and pinkie fingers together, with the pointer and thumb stretched wide, so that the hand forms the shape of a lopsided W. When I make shiin, I feel Ha'i course through me and warm the skin connecting my thumb and pointer fingers in the same spot as my crescent scar. But while I can feel its warmth, I can't seem to manipulate the Ha'i the way the other apprentices can.

I watch the young apprentices around me ignite candle flames, create glowing balls of light, and sprout plants from the earthy floor. It's amazing, and I'm not convinced I'll ever be able to do any of it. I'm still not sure Michael didn't make a mistake about me being a Sire and that my quirks are not a symptom of something else entirely. My feelings of incompetence spike as I repeatedly make a silly hand gesture with no visible result.

"Do not rush learning the language of your Ha'i," Master Liu reassures me. "Focus on finding the well within yourself."

But I have to rush. My time here is limited, and my grandfather is sick. I close my eyes, pretending to focus on this stupid well within, but really I'm just holding back tears of frustration.

After Ha'i class, one of my classmates approaches me. She's maybe thirteen or fourteen and definitely going through her awkward phase, with white-blond hair in a crooked braid and large hazel eyes that seem too big for her slim, pale face.

"Hi. I'm Hypatia, and I'm new here too," she says. "Is it true that you're from New York?"

When I nod, she looks positively gleeful. "I've never met someone from the provincial world before! I have *so* many questions." As she talks fast, her words slur with a slight lisp, which I find adorable. "Are there really whole islands made of garbage?"

"Uh, I think I've heard about something like that forming by accident in the ocean."

But by the time I have the words out, Hypatia has already moved on. "The other apprentices have lots of questions too, but they're too intimidated to ask."

I am quite sure that I'm more intimidated by them. I ask, "They don't think it's weird that I'm so much older than everyone else?"

"I doubt that. At Genesis they're much more used to recruits than at Avant. That's where I'm from."

"That's a relief. I feel pretty incompetent."

"Well, I'd be happy to help you. I'm highly competent," Hypatia says as she lifts her hand, and without even making shiin, lets loose a string of sparks.

My eyes widen with appreciation. "It's beautiful." I reach out and try to catch the fading light. "What is it exactly?"

"Ha'i?" She shrugs. "Life force. Creative energy."

"Yeah, sure, but what does that actually mean? Everyone has 'life force,' so what's different about a Sire?" Maybe if I can understand this more tangibly, I'll be able to conduct on demand.

Hypatia looks thoughtful. She runs her tongue over her teeth, then says, "Well, Ha'i is everywhere, and most people just move it around. But Sires create new Ha'i inside their bodies and then conduct it outward." She swishes her hand as if she's conducting an orchestra, making more of the lovely lights. "Any person can cultivate potential energy, but a Sire can make it from nothing."

"Is there a way for someone who is not a Sire to create Ha'i?" I ask, thinking of the device, or whatever it is, that Kor wants me to find.

Hypatia shakes her head. But she's only an apprentice; maybe she just doesn't know about it yet.

I try copying her hand motion, but no lights appear.

"Let me show you how," she says.

We sit together in the empty classroom. She's a good teacher, and soon I can make the sparks about one in three times that I try, so I'm feeling a lot better about myself. But my old instinct to want to suppress any sign of my abilities keeps clouding my head.

"You've got a pigeon," Hypatia says, and I turn to see a fluttering golem hovering over my shoulder. I pluck it out of the air, unfold it, and read the handwritten message inside.

> *Please come see me in my office at your convenience.*
> *Pigeon will lead the way.* —M. Loew

I do my best to ignore the jump in my pulse. To Hypatia, I say, "I have to go."

"Okay. I expect you to practice, and we'll have another lesson tomorrow after Ha'i class," she instructs.

"Yes, ma'am," I say, my lips curving upward. And after a helpless look down at my hands, I add, "But first, can you help me refold this pigeon?"

* ★ ★ ★ *

I follow the pigeon through the Spring wing to a doorway at the end of a bright hallway that smells like honeysuckles. I pause to pull my hair out of its messy bun, finger combing the long waves and biting my lips to give them some color.

None of this is because I care how I look for Michael, of course. I'm just aware that I'm coming from a class that involved a lot of physical activity, and I want to look put together when meeting with a faculty member.

Michael's office door is open, and he's sitting chewing his nails while studying a large book that takes up half of his desk. The office is small with a lot of serious-looking bookshelves. Against the wall, there's a sofa in an alarming shade of chartreuse, and next to it is a table with an assortment of oddities including an old record player, a silver menorah, and a shofar.

Is Michael Jewish? Instinct has me checking the doorframe, and there is indeed a mezuzah nailed there, much like the ones my father hung on all the doorposts of our old apartment.

"Oh, Ada, hi," Michael says, looking up from his book. "Thanks for coming." He smiles warmly and gestures for me to take the seat across from him.

I sit and resist the urge to adjust my clothes or hair.

"Are you settling in okay?" he asks. I can't help but notice how detached and professional he appears behind his desk.

Yet I can't forget the warm press of his thigh, the way his breath caught when our fingers intertwined, the certainty of knowing I was going to learn the texture of his lips.

Well, this is awkward.

I clear my throat. "Um, yeah, pretty well. Georgie's really nice, and my room is great." I promised myself that I'll try to keep it clean. I have been promising myself I'd clean my room for the past decade. Maybe a blank slate will finally help.

His face breaks into a grin, dimples and all. "I knew you'd like it here. I'm hoping that when the time comes, you'll choose to stay."

How am I supposed to respond to that? I certainly can't tell the truth about my intentions. Instead, I change the subject.

"Are there many Jewish Makers?" I ask, glancing back at the menorah and shofar.

He shakes his head. "Jews are only about zero-point-two percent of the world's population, and that proportion is about the same among the Makers."

"My father's Jewish," I say. I phrase it that way because I don't know what I consider myself, but I want Michael to know that we share this part of our identity. That despite the very different worlds we come from, we may have learned some of the same prayers and the same traditions.

And it does mean something to him; I see it in the sharpening of his expression, the brightening in his eyes. It reignites a spark of the tension between us. Or maybe that's just in my head.

I look away and say, "I kind of always associated the Renaissance with Christianity. White European Christianity." And the diversity I've seen at Genesis so far doesn't fit that image. The students and staff have been an array of ethnicities as varied as what I'm used to in New York City.

"That's a logical association since the Church dictated known history. But it wasn't just Greek and Roman culture that shaped the Renaissance. Much of the mathematics and science came from Islamic countries. The Academy of Muses had students from all over the world and was known for accepting those not permitted to learn elsewhere. In fact, though Jewish communities were confined to ghettos and limited in what professions they were allowed, the Academy's influence led Italy to become one of the first European countries to allow Jews to attend medical schools. Many Jewish physicians, printers, and patrons of the arts impacted the Renaissance."

"Oh, wow. Okay. So, is there some kind of Maker religion?"

"No. Makers continue the creation of the world, and that means something different to each person. Though it was the Church who exiled the Makers, there are still many Christian Makers. And there are at least twenty other religions practiced in our communities, as well as many atheists. But while religion has been a leading cause of war and division in provincial history, the Makers believe it is something that should bring people together, not divide them. Many Makers will use the umbrella term 'the Conductor,' the one who orchestrates all things, to refer to a shared general concept of a creator."

Ah, that explains that.

"So, now that you've had a chance to settle in, we should discuss your gallerie for Quorum," Michael says, back to business. "I've been assigned as your apprenticeship mentor. Most apprentices become journeymen by around thirteen or fourteen, so I think it would be best for us to aim to have you ready to apply to a guild at the Spring Quorum. Otherwise, you'll have to wait until next fall. The Spring Quorum is less than three months away."

Michael launches into an in-depth overview of each of the five guilds while I take some basic notes. When he's finished, I have the following list:

Sophists (sapphire): social sciences and humanities
Artisans (amethyst): fine art and performance art
Alchemists (emerald): chemistry and earth sciences
Ciphers (pearl): mathematics and physics
Bioscience (amber): biological sciences and healing

A familiar anxious pressure balloons in my chest. I am proficient in approximately zero of these subjects. "So how exactly do I prepare for Quorum?"

"As your mentor, it's my job to help you organize a collection of work that will demonstrate your skills, passions, and talents."

This literally feels like college applications all over again. And three months is *nothing*.

"In terms of your skills, I know you play guitar—"

"Not well," I remind him.

There's a pause as we both navigate the memory of the last time I told him this information, and all the flirting that followed. At least, that's what I'm doing. Maybe he's totally over it already.

"It's a good start," Michael says. "Most Makers play at least one instrument." No kidding. I've counted at least four instrument cases in this room alone. Most in vaguely guitarish shapes and one smaller square case that I assume is some kind of horn. "We should make sure you're proficient in one song that you can perform. Do you write music?"

"I've dabbled." Well, I helped Kor with some of his earlier songs, which kinda counts.

"Perfect. A well-practiced song of your own composition will be a nice touch. We'll prioritize that." He scribbles something in a notebook—the fancy kind with yellowish paper and a leather cover that ties with a cord. "We also know you're good with plants. I'll make sure you're scheduled in the greenhouse and will inform your instructors to guide that strength." More scribbling. "What are your other talents?"

This line of questioning grates on every one of my insecurities. How do I let him down easy about the fact that I'm generally untalented? I'm pretty sure that my snowboarding prowess is not what he has in mind. I settle on, "I like to write stories."

He smiles as he takes this down in his notes. "Storytelling is a strength of my own guild, the Sophists. Definitely a good option for you. What about other art? Do you paint?"

I do like to paint. Well, I like to *start* paintings. I'm marginally better at drawing. Though the last time Kor tried to help me with my drawing, he said my work won't improve until I learn to "observe properly" and am willing to have the patience to "develop the layers of the piece."

"I draw, but I'm not that good," I say to Michael.

He looks up at me, brows furrowed. "Why do you keep doing that?"

"What?"

"Downplaying your abilities."

"I'm not downplaying anything. I'm fantastically mediocre." I paste on an overdramatic smile. "Perpetual jack-of-all-trades, master of none, nice to meet you." This is the last thing I want to admit to Michael, but better to get it out of the way rather than see his disappointment when he figures it out for himself.

He huffs. "You're the farthest thing from mediocre. Do you even know the rest of that saying?"

"There's more?"

"'A jack-of-all-trades is a master of none, but oftentimes *better* than a master of one,'" he quotes. "And do you know who it was referring to?" His tone is scolding. "A young upstart actor who was mocked for trying his hand at writing, better known as William Shakespeare." His voice softens, and that earnest gaze meets mine. "Dabbling is encouraged here at Genesis."

I swallow. It sounds good in theory. But he hasn't seen how amateur my work is, never mind compared to those who have been developing their talents for years.

"If you say so," I concede. He, and everyone else, will see for themselves soon enough.

He breaks our eye contact and shakes his head as he looks back at his notebook. "You're going to have to practice being less hard on yourself if you want to encourage your own growth. I'll make sure to add additional art studios to your schedule so you can prepare some pieces for your gallerie. As we get closer to Quorum, we can meet again to reassess."

He then offers me the use of his phone to call home. While Arcadia is mostly isolated and sadly far from any cell towers, Michael's office is equipped with a phone line that he needs for his job as Genesis's official liaison to provincial society. Before I agreed to come, I was told I could use it to stay in touch with my family.

One of the first directives I have from the Families is to find an alternative mode of communication with Kor, who is to act as my handler. I can't rely on this phone or any mail I send to be secure, but if I can't find a better way to pass information to Kor, I'll wait to give it to him in person when I travel home for the holidays, or in the worst-case scenario, use the satellite phone.

Michael leaves me alone in his office so I can have privacy for my call. I feel sick at the thought of violating his personal space, but I push through it, knowing what I need to do.

I start by actually using the phone to call my mom to let her know that I arrived safely. She doesn't answer, but I leave a message.

Then I hang up and assess the room. Where should I start?

Kor's top three directives to identify are:

   1) A secure mode of communication

   2) The location of the institute and how to access it

   3) A method of giving non-Sires Sire abilities

And I've added my own last one.

   4) A cure for Grandfather

The bookshelves seem like a good place to begin, but there are way too many books to look through. I pull out my phone—that I'd excavated from its hiding place for this purpose—and use it to take photos of the shelves. I can use the pictures later to see if there's anything worth a closer look.

I hasten over to Michael's desk. The large book he was reading is written in Hebrew. I snap a picture, because why not? I rifle through his drawers, but everything seems standard and boring besides a stash of emergency chocolate. Nice.

I take pictures of all kinds of documents, but my anxiety is starting to spike, knowing that Michael could return at any moment. There are a lot of letters stamped with wax seals of a book that has the scales of justice growing up from between the pages—the emblem of the Sophists, Michael's guild. Thankfully, all of the seals are already broken, so I'm able to easily photograph their contents without too much fuss. I record a video flipping through his notebook in case there's something useful in there. I'll check later. Gotta keep moving.

My heart is pounding so loudly in my ears that I'm worried I won't hear if someone's coming. There's a slim drawer underneath the center of the desk that I almost miss. When I open it, it's empty except for the large key that Headmaster Bloche had given to Michael yesterday. It's as long as the length of my hand, fingertip to wrist, and heavy. There's an engraving of the *Vitruvian Man* Genesis emblem, and the teeth of the key look incredibly intricate. I snap a photo, put it back, and close the drawer.

I move on from the desk to a tall cabinet full of files about what looks to be other recruits, or potential recruits. *Snap, snap, snap.* The next shelf is all provincial vinyl records. Very cool but not useful.

I yelp as I hear a door slam somewhere in the hallway. It's probably not Michael, but I've officially reached my limit on how much apprehension I can hold inside my body. I'll look more the next time I'm here to borrow the phone.

I take a few deep breaths before I casually walk out of Michael's office, as if I have every right to be here, because I do.

I'm dizzy with adrenaline as I attempt to navigate the labyrinth of corridors back to my room in the Winter wing, but I find myself totally lost in an unfamiliar hallway. There's fragrant wisteria hanging from the ceiling, and an impressionist-style mural of a garden extends across the wall. I turn to retrace my steps and then recognize the stiff leather and shiny silver of the Avant Guard as two soldiers round the corner.

Gah. Why now?

I try to saunter past them while looking as innocent as possible, but it doesn't work.

"Oi, what's your name?" one guard says. He has a sharp nose and gray hair that doesn't match his youthful appearance.

"Ada." I smile, not stopping or even slowing.

"That's the one," the other guard, stocky and blond, growls.

"Are you sure?" They pause, but I keep walking, and they don't prevent me from passing through the next more familiar hall and into the bright open air of the Equinox.

The one? What's that supposed to mean?

As inconspicuously as I can, I pull my phone from my hoodie pocket and tuck it past the waistline of my leggings and into the front of my underpants.

When the thud of boot steps grows louder behind me, my instinct is to bolt, but I force myself to keep a normal pace. I relax my shoulders and hold in my ragged breaths.

"Halt," one of the guards calls, and I comply, heart racing. I pull my hoodie down over my thighs and suck in my stomach so the outline of my phone doesn't show. The phone is locked, but they could easily force me to unlock it. And there's no innocent excuse for the photos and videos I just took.

But these guards have no reason to suspect me of anything, right? Maybe they just have a simple question.

"Ada Castle." The guard's voice echoes around the Equinox. "In the name of the Blood Crown and the Maker Council, we order you to submit to a search of all belongings on your person."

My stomach plummets. Or that.

I try to swallow, but my throat is too tight. Why is this happening? The hard case of my phone presses uncomfortably against my groin. I attempt to squish my facial expression into quizzical innocence as I comply with the guards and, with trembling hands, empty my hoodie pockets.

All I have are my notes from my meeting with Michael, my pouch of sense, and a quarter and a stick of gum that have been living in the recesses of my pocket since whenever the last time this sweatshirt was washed.

The blond guard scrutinizes the provincial items extra carefully.

The gray-haired one pats me down. Arms, back, stomach. His eyes are as gray as his hair. And cruel.

My heart thunders as he impersonally pats down my legs, my thighs. For the first time ever, I'm thankful for those five extra pounds that now mold a cushy hideaway around my phone, keeping it in place.

A passing journeyman stops in her tracks and calls over, "Does the Council know you're searching a recruit?"

"Move along, lass," Gray-Hair says. But she doesn't move along, and a cluster of other observers has started to form.

"This isn't the way we do things here," someone else insists.

Gray-Hair ceases his frisking, and Blondie tosses my things back to me, confiscating the quarter and the gum.

"We're done," he growls. "For now."

After they stomp away, a few people linger to make sure that I'm okay, which is kind, but I just want to get out of here. I brush them off and rush toward the Winter wing, cursing myself for thinking I could ever do this job in the first place.

When I reach my room, I throw myself onto the couch and pull my phone from my pants. My hands shake uncontrollably as I stare down at the screen. No service, of course. No portal to the instant distractions where I could hide from the humiliation and fear of that entire interaction. Only a bunch of photos that are awfully incriminating.

I feel entirely out of my depth. It's literally my first day here, and I've already attracted the suspicion of the guards. I don't even know what I did to warrant their distrust.

Now I definitely can't risk snooping again. Will they decide to search my room?

I lean back against the couch and close my eyes against the sting of imminent tears.

How am I supposed to do this?

Alfie was right. No one should have trusted me with this job.

I need some guidance on how I should handle all of this. Maybe I should go back to Michael's office and call Kor.

Ha. No way. I'm never leaving this room again.

"You doin' okay?" Georgie asks me when she comes in a few minutes later and finds me unsuccessfully attempting to cuddle her cat.

"Yeah," I say, tamping down my panicked feelings and reaching for a safe excuse for why I've been crying. "I just really miss my family. It's hitting me how isolated we are."

She gives me a sly smile. "It just so happens that I can help you with that."

"You can?"

She motions for me to follow her into her room, and I do, but I stop in my tracks once we enter. Despite the incredible technology of this place, I haven't seen any computers. No screens in general.

But Georgie's room has enough screens for the entire island.

The room is lit with the blue glow of many monitors and blinking lights. It reminds me of Izzy's room, which adds one more pang to my generally miserable mood.

Georgie settles into a cushioned swivel chair and sweeps blond and purple tendrils out of her face as she begins clicking around on one of the screens. "It took some convincing, but Headmaster Bloche caved and let me have my setup here. My plan is to eventually get the Cipher guild on board with computer science."

"Ciphers? They're mathematicians and engineers, right?" She nods. "But aren't you an Artisan?" Georgie wears an amethyst guildstone.

"Yes, but only because the Ciphers wouldn't accept me. The Artisans are a good fit, but I was pretty bummed when the Ciphers turned me down."

"I don't get it; it seems like you're perfect Cipher material." I motion to all the computer stuff that surrounds us.

"It's different here. They don't understand computers. They didn't let me submit any of my code for my gallerie, and I didn't have any experience with their styles of engineering. The Makers' technology evolved completely differently than the provincials', and a lot of it is dependent on Sire abilities and Ha'i manipulation."

Georgie pronounces "Ha'i" like "hai" instead of from the back of her throat, which I know from experience can be tough to get used to if you didn't grow up with it.

She continues. "They use artificial nervous systems for high-level computing and genetic sequencing. But virtual reality, machine learning, the internet—they don't have anything like that here. And they have this weird misconception that anything the provincials do must be inefficient or immoral in some way. But I intend to show them how computer science could advance this world even further." Her eyes are bright with intensity. "In the meantime, I also really love clothing design."

Ah. That explains the bolts of fabric in the corner and the mannequin in a scandalous state of half dress.

"So . . . do you have an internet connection?" I ask, cautiously optimistic.

"Yup. It's satellite, and pinged through a bunch of other locations, so it can be slow, but it's the good ol' internet."

Hallelujah! I cannot believe my luck. "Can I use it sometime?"

"Why do you think I brought you in here? You said you wanted to talk to your family. There's no network for me to connect your phone, but I can set up a video call for you on my computer." She clicks open the necessary window. "Just don't tell anyone. The Makers don't want me spreading 'provincial trash' around. And they're scared the internet could lead people here. They're not wrong, but I'm good enough to hide the signals to prevent that from happening."

"So anything I say will stay private?"

Georgie laughs at this. "Even if there were someone on this island who understood how the internet works, they wouldn't be able to get past my encryption. There are government agencies that can't do that." She grabs a sketchbook and bright pink headphones. "And you don't have to worry about me." She slides the headphones on. "I have a new album drop to listen to and a dress to design. Take your time!" She waltzes out of her room and closes the door.

When Kor answers my call and his smiling, surprised face fills Georgie's screen, the anxiety whooshes out of me like an unpinched balloon.

"This is a secure connection," I say.

"Are you sure?"

"Yep." I feel the muscles of my face soften as the need for any artifice melts away.

"Wow, that was quick. I guess you're pretty good at this." He winks.

It's nice to let him believe that for a moment.

"It's not actually going that well," I say.

"Why? What happened?" His brows scrunch with worry, but whether his concern is for me or for a possible wrinkle in his plan is anyone's guess.

"The whole island is on high alert because of the Sire abductions. There are extra guards, and since I'm an outsider, people already distrust me."

"Have you gotten into any trouble?"

"Well, not exactly, but—"

"Good. Why don't you start by telling me what you've learned."

We're on borrowed time, so I try not to be too annoyed that he's getting straight to business. I tell him about the Atlas and as much as I can about Arcadia. When I bring up the other school in Avant, he informs me that the Families know about Avant because it's where Prometheus is from.

"We targeted Genesis for infiltration instead since Avant has a stronger military presence."

"And do you know anything about the Misty Isles?" I ask. I've already heard these mysterious islands referenced more than once.

Kor's never heard of them, and he tells me that finding out the extent of the Maker world should be a top priority.

I describe my apprentice classes. He's very interested in my Ha'i class and has me show him how to make shiin. He reminds me how important it is that I master my Sire abilities and encourages me to do whatever it takes to improve more quickly.

I go on to tell him how I need to prepare to get admitted to a guild, and

I use my notes from my meeting with Michael to give Kor a rundown of all the guilds.

"Apparently I'm going to have to write and perform a song," I say. "I might need your help with that."

Kor brushes this off. "Just don't get distracted fiddling around. Which of the guilds do you think is most likely to know about the use of Sire abilities by non-Sires?" I have no idea where to start in looking for this supposed innovation that allows non-Sires to generate Ha'i.

"Maybe Bioscience?" I suggest. "Since they focus the most on healing compared to the others? I met a Bioscience master that I can try to ask about it." I think of the kind redhead, Kaylie, who vaccinated me. She'd explained that they've eradicated a lot of illnesses here, including the common cold, the flu, and STDs. It had brought my attention to Bioscience as a guild that might be able to help Grandfather.

"Okay, then focus on impressing the Bioscience guild." Kor's eyes gleam as he types notes.

Yeah, it makes sense for me to aim for Bioscience. I'd been momentarily excited about the art and botany that Michael had discussed with me, but Kor's right. That's not why I'm here.

"I took some photos and video today that I'll share when I can," I say. I'll have to figure out if it's safe to upload to Georgie's computer without her noticing anything fishy about my files. "And I'm pretty sure I learned where the written documentation of all of the Maker innovations are kept, though I don't have access to it yet."

This had been an exciting revelation in my Testaments class. I explain to Kor how we'd learned about the Guild Testaments—the most venerated of all the Testaments. They transcribe each guild's innovations and discoveries, but each Guild Testament can only be viewed by members of that guild, and they're kept in a highly guarded part of the library.

"So you'll be able to access these documents once you're in a guild?"

"I'll technically only be able to see my own guild's Testaments, but once I have access to that part of the library, I can see what else I can find."

"Very good. So getting into a guild should definitely be your main focus. Try to make it the Bio one. It sounds like these Testaments may be a shortcut to a lot of what we need all at once. I'll pass all of this on, and I'll find out if the Inner Chamber or the Oculus have further instructions for you." He gives me one of his soulful looks. "Ada, this is an amazing start. You're doing so well."

I end the call with renewed vigor. We'd never circled back to my concerns. I'd never even told Kor about what happened with the guards. But I've always craved Kor's praise like a flower to the sun, and his clear approval of what I've accomplished so far has me positively photosynthesizing.

Kor will tell the Families I'm succeeding at my mission, and I know what I need to focus on. Finding out more about the locations and extent of the Maker world, learning how to utilize my Sire abilities, and getting into a guild so that I can access the Guild Testaments are all things that can be done without any high-risk activities. Even if I have to bury my phone back in tamponland and never snoop through another office, I can still be of use.

I can do this.

10

Genesis certainly has the most utopian school cafeteria I've ever seen. Everyone eats slowly and with intention, and the food is fresh and has more color and flavor than the same things back home. I mean, there's still a cliquey popular table (three guesses as to who's sitting there), but that's made up for by the generally good vibe of the room, not to mention the impromptu string quartet currently playing Brahms.

Hypatia joined me and Georgie at our table. She looks exhausted; she's paler than she was during Ha'i class this morning, and she hardly touches her food. I'm also not feeling my best. Despite my call with Kor yesterday, I'm still on edge about the Guard. But not being alone and eating a good lunch is certainly helping.

As I indulge in freshly baked herb bread spread with garlic maple butter and a savory nut pâté, Georgie and Hypatia find common ground discussing a topic that has them both very excited—hoverjousting.

Hypatia says to Georgie, "I hope you don't have any delusions that the Artisans will rank in the tournament. Your guild's team is abysmal."

Georgie sighs. "Yeah, they really are."

As their conversation progresses, I gather that a hoverjoust is exactly what it sounds like, a joust—like the ones on horseback at the Renaissance faire—but on hoverboards. The players rush toward each other with lances raised and try to hit their opponent's shield or, even better, knock them off their hover. It sounds awesome, and Hypatia insists that she and Georgie will teach me how to play after classes today.

Their discussion turns to arguing over whether the Ciphers or Bios will win first place in the tournament this year.

Georgie excitedly says, "The title will go to the Ciphers for sure. Having Hera as captain has transformed their team, and she's undefeated."

Hypatia is just as excited, the conversation pulling her out of her lethargy. "Maybe before Rafe joined the Bios, but he's also undefeated, and Hera has the tendency to—"

Georgie interrupts. "Don't say anything negative about Hera Earhart in my presence." She looks wistfully over at a table where two Black girls are sitting. I assume one of them must be Hera. "She is possibly my future wife, and she'll eat that arrogant pretty boy alive."

Hypatia giggles. "That's an accurate description of my cousin."

My head snaps up at that. "He's your cousin?"

"Speak of the literal devil," Georgie says.

I turn to see a beautiful scowl. Raphael "Rafe" Vanguard has risen from his seat at the cliquey popular table and is glaring directly at us.

"Hypatia," he barks. "Come sit here."

Hypatia rolls her eyes and blows him a kiss but doesn't get up. Rafe's eyes burn with anger—but not at her, at me.

"Why are they so—" I motion with my hand, indicating the general aloofness of Rafe and his friends.

"'Cause they think they're better than everyone," Georgie says.

Hypatia doesn't seem to be bothered by this assessment of her cousin. She says, "A bunch of us, mostly Sires, transferred here temporarily from the other Maker school, the academy in Avant. There's rumors of a breach at Avant, and with the Sire abductions, the Council thought we'd be safer here."

I wonder if the Families have made progress in confirming whether Ozymandias Tech is behind these abductions. I need to remember to ask Kor about it the next time we talk.

"Most of you guys are fine," Georgie concedes. "But the ones in Guard training are scary." She turns to me to explain. "There's a military track for Avant Guard training at the Avant academy. You can recognize them because they wear bone rings"—she lifts her hand and waggles her fingers—"and treat everyone else like crap. Especially *him*." She glares at Rafe. "I have a grapefruit-size bruise on my butt from falling after he crashed into me the other day. And he didn't even apologize." She turns to Hypatia. "Sorry, I get that he's your cousin, but he's an ass. Like, why does he care that you're sitting with us? Just because we're recruits?"

"He can be really overprotective of me," Hypatia says, running her tongue across her teeth. "My whole family is because I get sick a lot." She rolls her eyes. "But Rafe can definitely sometimes be an ass."

"I hate having so much of the Avant Guard around Arcadia," Georgie says. "It feels like there's more every day."

"They're very worried about an infiltration and want extra security for all the Sires."

Kor had said they'd chosen Genesis specifically for its lack of military. Oh well.

I try to sound casual as I ask, "What would they do if they actually found an intruder?"

I bite down on a gushberry, and sweet juice gushes over my tongue. I harvested this batch myself from the gushberry groves during my agriculture class this morning. We learned all about the history of the red berry that the Makers engineered decades ago, a superplant full of natural energy-boosting nutrients.

Hypatia thinks about it for a moment. "The Makers are generally pacifists, but not the Avant Guard. They're trained to protect our secrets no matter the cost."

No matter the cost. Great. No big deal. It's not like I came within an inch of my life yesterday or anything. I try to swallow the chewed-up gushberry around the painful lump in my throat.

Hypatia covers her mouth with her hand as she chews her own gushberry, but her large hazel eyes bug out as she looks over at Rafe's table. A wiry boy hunched into a hooded jacket takes a seat next to Rafe. I recognize him as the boy who had been sleeping in the train car with Rafe when I first met him on the Atlas.

"That's Simon Sanzio," Hypatia squeaks, her lisp more prominent than usual. "He's also from Avant. Isn't he beguiling?"

I absolutely do not find Simon from Avant beguiling. Besides the fact that he's at least two years younger than me, he has a pronounced slouch in his back, and his face is covered in acne.

"You'd have thought a utopian society could have cured pimples by now," I say.

"Ada!" Georgie shoves me, and I know it's rightly deserved.

"We *have* cured them," Hypatia huffs, "but Simon forgets to use his tincture. His mind is very busy with songwriting." Ooh. I wonder if I can get ahold of said tincture for PMS breakouts. "He's in a band, and he plays the hurdy-gurdy." Hypatia clearly has it bad for this Simon dude, and she babbles on. "He's guilded as an Artisan, but he'll need to present at Quorum to switch from the Avant chapter to the Genesis one. I need to figure out how to get him to ask me to Carnevale."

"You can't go to Carnevale until you're fifteen," Georgie says. The upcoming festival is months away, but I've already heard many apprentices grumbling about how they can't go.

"Yes, I'm still working on solving that issue." Hypatia purses her lips and appraises Georgie and me, clearly assessing how we can be utilized for whatever plot she's concocting.

But I intend to keep my hands clean of any rule-breaking that could draw attention.

"So if Simon's a transfer, does that mean he's also a Sire?" I ask.

"No," Hypatia says. "He came because he's a Valkyrie. Rafe picked him up from Avant and escorted him here the same day you arrived."

"What's a Valkyrie?"

Hypatia stares at me like I just asked what the moon is.

But before I can get an explanation, a familiar voice above me says, "Apprentice Castle, do you have a moment?"

Michael is so tall that I have to crane my neck to see his concerned face. The spike in my pulse might be fear that he's about to bust me for snooping in his office, or it might be embarrassment over the gushberry juice that's dribbling down my chin. I scramble for a napkin.

"Uh, sure. I was about to head to the Sire lab." I'm both nervous and excited for a class with journeymen who are closer to my age. Well, not a class exactly. Genesis is less of a school and more of a community. Only the apprentices who haven't yet joined guilds are considered students. Guild members have "laboratories," "conservatories," and "studios," which are collaborative environments that include both teens and adults.

"I can walk you there," Michael offers. His friendly smile confirms this is unlikely to be a confrontation about my office escapades, so I relax. And his offer is a relief. I'm not quite sure where the Sire lab is, and I'm still wary of walking around the school alone after my incident with the guards.

Speaking of which. "I heard about yesterday," Michael says as we make our way out of the cafeteria. "I am so sorry about how the Guard treated you."

As we enter the Equinox, my lungs constrict at the memory of what happened in this room. "It's okay. Everyone else was really supportive."

Michael stops walking and puts his hand on my shoulder. It's no big deal, the hand. I'm chill about it. But Michael looks really upset.

"Headmaster Bloche has assured me that the captain of the Avant Guard has been given firm instructions about what will be tolerated while they're stationed in Arcadia."

"Thanks." He's still holding my shoulder. Okay, maybe I'm not chill about it.

"I mean it, Ada. I will make sure you are always safe and treated with respect." His eyes are fierce, and for a heartbeat I believe he could keep me safe from anything.

"Hi!" a cheerful voice interrupts.

Michael removes his hand from my shoulder and steps back. He turns to smile at Kaylie, who's making her way toward us with her own beaming smile. "I didn't see you downstairs," she says to Michael. "I was coming to find you." I hadn't realized the two of them were friends.

"How are you acclimating?" she asks me. "I was just thinking I should send a pigeon to check if you had any side effects from your inoculations."

"No. Everything's great."

"Wonderful. Let me know if anything changes." Kaylie reaches over to Michael and straightens his cravat. "You forgot about lunch at the orchard, didn't you?"

"Oof." He palms his forehead. "I'm so sorry."

"Don't worry. We still have plenty of time." She smiles affectionately, as if she's used to this happening.

Are they going on, like, a date? Not that I care. It would make sense. Kaylie's probably only one or two years older than Michael, and she's sweet and pretty and smart.

"Thanks for putting up with me," Michael says to her with a wink. "Can you find your way to the lab?" he asks me. When I nod, Kaylie loops her arm in his and they head toward the entrance.

This is fine. They would totally make a cute couple, and I am perfectly capable of navigating my way to the Sire lab on my own.

Blech.

*   ★   ★   ★   ·

I am apparently not actually capable of navigating to the Sire lab on my own. First I go up too many staircases and end up in a cavernous astronomy observatory. When I backtrack, I find a lab, but it's the wrong one. A group of journeys are mixing a viscous slime in a foul-smelling cauldron, and they helpfully point me in the right direction.

When I finally find the right lab, a woman in a hijab welcomes me and introduces herself as Master Hayyan. "This is where you can safely experiment and learn to stretch the potential of your Sire abilities," she says.

There are about twenty-five other people in the room, mostly working in pairs, ranging from about my age to my parents' ages. My eyes are immediately drawn to the only familiar face, Rafe. I hadn't realized he was also a Sire, but I guess it makes sense since he's a transfer. His blond hair is in a bun, and his sleeves are pushed up above his elbows, revealing sun-bronzed muscled forearms. He's working with a striking girl with deep umber skin who is just as tall as he is. Her hair, a mix of brown and blond locs, is plaited into a thick braid that falls to her waist, and a necklace in the shape of a snake rests around her throat. She has a green guildstone in her ear—an Alchemist. But neither of them has a Sire diamond. My eyes flick to their fingers, where they both wear matching pairs of rings, one each of diamond and bone. Hypatia had shown me her Sire ring and explained that in Avant they wear their guildstones and birthstones on their fingers instead of their ears, and I remember that bone rings indicate members of the Avant Guard.

Master Hayyan gives me a tour around the room, showing me where the supplies are and telling me about some of the projects the other Sires are working on. There are three older journeys upgrading a massive eight-foot golem that is used for deep-sea welding when making alterations and repairs on the Atlas tunnel. Another pair is experimenting with organ growth as part of a hormonal therapy for gender transition that doesn't require invasive surgery.

I have a hard time imagining that my abilities could make *me* capable of these kinds of things, so I'm equal parts awestruck and intimidated.

Everything I've been taught so far has reinforced the idea that much of the science lost to provincial society is tied in with their loss of knowledge of Sire abilities. If provincial Sires were taught how to use their Ha'i, that alone could transform our science and health care. I wonder how many Sires are out there, their abilities completely dormant, or plaguing them the way mine plagued me. And Master Hayyan is sure to know about a way that Sires can share their abilities, if one does actually exist. The training I can get in this lab could be the most important knowledge I gain for the Families.

"The best experimentation happens through collaboration," Master Hayyan says. "So let's find you a partner." I dutifully follow her as she threads her way through the pairs of working students, but dread descends as I see which table she's approaching. Oh no. This can't end well.

She stops in front of Rafe, who is inspecting what might be a human liver but could also be a spleen because I don't actually know the difference. The tall girl is looking into a complex contraption of lenses and brass that I think is a very fancy microscope.

"Apprentice Castle, until you choose your guild and your focus of study, Journeys Vanguard and Keftiu will make good partners, as they are also new to the institute."

"Actually, Master Hayyan," Rafe says, not even acknowledging my presence, "Mbali and I will continue to work alone." He opens his multi-tool—which

I have learned is officially called a Heliotorch, but everyone just calls them "spoons"—and lights a flame beneath the wobbling organ in front of him.

"Journey Vanguard," the professor responds firmly, "that was an instruction, not a request."

Rafe continues his work, unfazed. "I'm sure you can find someone else to assist the recruit." The saccharine way he says "recruit" makes it clear he wishes to say something else entirely.

"In that case," the professor counters harshly, "I'm sure the Bioscience hoverjoust team won't be needing your assistance either."

Rafe snaps his spoon—which is ostentatiously gold—shut and looks up. His face remains neutral. "That's ridiculous. I'm not an apprentice to be scolded."

"The choice is yours, Journey Vanguard."

He stares her down but doesn't object again.

Master Hayyan turns to me and says, "Why don't you start by making homing pigeons. They're simple golems, and an excellent form of practice."

As Master Hayyan walks away, the tall girl smiles at me. "My name is Mbali." She has a strong, melodious accent. "Sorry about him." She rolls her eyes at Rafe.

There is clear camaraderie and affection between them that makes me wonder if they're more than friends. She's not the same girl who was clinging to him in the cafeteria earlier, but something tells me that a lot of girls cling to Rafe.

"Fie on this!" Rafe sneers. "Just because Avant's Sire curriculum is more advanced than Genesis's shouldn't mean we have to waste our time catching her up." He ends his rant by walking away.

"Don't worry," Mbali says. "I'll help you." She gives a brief explanation of the experimentation she's doing with viper venom.

Rafe returns and drops a box of putty in front of me. "Here. Make some pigeons."

I sink my hands into the putty and pull out a handful. It's soft and pliable and immediately molds to the shape of my palm.

"What is this stuff?" I ask.

Rafe groans. "They sent her to the Sire lab without knowing the basics of the high materials?" He massages his temples. "I can't believe this. I'm not a gravdamn nursemaid."

More like a whiny baby. "Don't talk about me like I'm not standing right here," I say.

"Pardon me?" he asks in surprise.

"You're not better than me, and the fact that I know nothing about the way things work here has already been established, so no need to keep harping on it," I snap.

His eyebrows rise appraisingly, and Mbali stifles a smile.

Rafe draws himself taller and looks down his perfectly shaped nose at me, but before he lets fly whatever insult he has planned, Mbali gently pushes him aside.

"Down, boy," she says, then patiently and graciously reviews all the guilds' high materials with me as I take notes.

<u>High Materials</u>

Loam (Artisans): An easy-to-manipulate clay that is highly porous and sensitive to conductive Ha'i. Good for prototyping and simple golems.

Glace (Alchemists): Like glass but lighter and shatterproof. Nonporous. Easily melted down to reuse without creating any waste.

Sap (Bioscience): Biological healing compound. Main ingredient in patch paste.

Spidersilk (Ciphers): Synthetic fabric. Thin and lightweight *but virtually impenetrable. Used for ornithopter wings,*

military and athletic uniforms, etc.

Sense (Sophists): Coin-shaped . . . something about a neural

network?? Used as money and basic brains for golems.

The concept of sense, the Sophists' high material, trips me up.

"I thought sense was money?" I ask Mbali.

"The coins can be exchanged as currency, but they are also used as neural network power sources."

"So you're saying they're . . . batteries?"

"That's not a bad comparison, but no. It is more like a basic nervous system. For example, these pigeons need to be crafted and animated, but they also need sense to give them the ability to fly on command."

They sound kind of like computer chips. I'll have to ask Georgie later.

The high materials feel like basic innovations that the rest of the world could easily benefit from as well. They all seem practical and sustainable, and I don't see any reason beyond selfishness that such things should be withheld from others. I have to learn as much as I can about all the materials and get samples for the Families. Especially sap, the Bioscience healing compound, which sounds like it could be useful for Grandfather.

Mbali shows me how to roll out the loam into thin sheets and where to place the sense. The intricate folding pattern to form the pigeon is tricky, but I practice.

As we all work, Rafe ignores me, but he is simply too present for me to ignore. He's like a looming rain cloud of discontent and hotness. You know that idea that people become less attractive if they have a bad personality?

All lies.

Once I complete something somewhat recognizable as a pigeon, Mbali says, "A golem can't work until it's animated by a Sire. Rafe is particularly good at animation, so he can demonstrate."

Apparently, the chance to show off is enough to get Rafe to stop pretending I don't exist. He splays his hand in shiin over the bird.

And then the bird, which I made with my own two hands, flutters into the air. I've seen pigeon golems before, yet my heart is in my throat at the thought that I helped create this miraculous thing. That I could potentially learn to use the very same abilities I spent so long being afraid of to *bring something to life.*

"An excellent first golem," Mbali says.

"But the construction is too sloppy for actual use," Rafe interjects. And before I can stop him, he makes shiin again and deanimates the pigeon, which falls lifeless in his hand. Rafe pulls out the sense and pushes the loam back into the container. All of my painstaking, precise work melds in with the rest of the shapeless lump, my sense of accomplishment squished along with it.

The rest of the journeys have begun packing up and trickling out of the lab. Mbali nods goodbye to me and gently presses Rafe's arm before she also heads out.

Rafe reaches for the vat of loam to put it away, but I say, "I can clean up after myself."

"I'll do it," he says. "I'd rather you stay away from the supplies. Wouldn't want you stealing anything."

My outrage is only slightly dimmed by the fact that I had fully intended to scope out the materials for that very purpose.

But I won't let the insult stand, so I reach out to force him to relinquish the box. When my fingers brush against his, I feel the same tingle as when we touched on the train—it's almost like my Ha'i is reacting to his—and he must feel it too because he jerks away so violently that he elbows a rack of beakers, causing a symphony of glace to fall clattering and rolling all over the floor.

"If the two of you could please clean that up before you leave," Master Hayyan says politely before making her own way out of the room.

Rafe clenches his jaw so tightly he may grind his teeth into sand.

Apparently, glace really doesn't shatter, so the cleanup is relatively simple, but being alone with Rafe gives me the strong urge to flee.

When we're finished, Rafe says, "Run along." His blue eyes flash and his forearms flex, muscles tight like a predator about to pounce. "Just know that I'll be watching your every move. And so will the Guard."

What does the Guard have to do with anything?

"Wait, are you the one who told them to search me?"

He doesn't answer, but I know it was him. What a jerk.

"What do you have against me?"

"I don't trust you. I know you're scheming, and I intend to safeguard my people instead of falling for your act." His voice is deep and dark like a shot of espresso, and it elicits the same blend of indulgence and anxiety.

He can't possibly know anything. He just doesn't trust me because he's a bigot.

"And stay away from Hypatia," he growls.

"She's my friend."

"Make new friends." He moves closer, crowding my space. I instinctively step back, hitting the desk behind me. His eyes are hooded, and I suddenly feel like an entirely different kind of prey.

"What if I don't?" I breathe.

"Little Weed, why are you trying to provoke me? You need better survival instincts." His silky words waft in the air between us, and his arms cage me against the desk, causing my pulse to quicken.

"I'm not scared of you," I say, my voice sounding braver than I feel.

He takes one more step, removing the last of the distance between us. He's so close I can smell him. Of course he smells amazing, like leather and spice and seduction. His eyes bore into mine, unapologetic and calculating. He leans toward me, and I stop breathing as he whispers in my ear, "You should be."

I feel his breath on my skin with a heat that chills me. A muscle in his neck tightens as he swallows. The gust of his exhale blows a tendril of hair out from behind my ear, and he reaches toward my face as if to tuck it back, but then drops his hand and clenches it into a fist. I see confusion spark in his eyes before he turns and surges out of the room.

He's out the door before I finally gasp air back into my lungs, my heart pounding so hard it might bruise my chest out of fear . . . and something else entirely as well.

11

Later when Hypatia comes to drag me to the hover park, I almost don't go. As cool as hoverjousting sounds, I'm not here to have fun, and I was planning to flip through the anatomy book I'd been given in one of my classes this morning to see if there are any leads for what my next steps in looking for a cure for Grandfather should be. But then I remember Rafe telling me to stay away from Hypatia, and screw him, I'm gonna go learn to hoverjoust with my friend.

I follow Hypatia through the mists of the forest to where Georgie is waiting for us at the entrance to a clearing. Georgie's holding something that looks a lot like a snowboard, and I rush over to examine it, my excitement rising. I love snowboarding. It's something I'm actually good at, and—oh, this is *so* much cooler than any snowboard. I feel my chest expand with appreciation as I take the hoverboard from her. Of all the things that I have seen since I came to this place—flying origami pigeons and the rearview of hot guys in breeches included—nothing holds a candle to this.

When we enter the clearing, there's a large flat section with separate lanes, which Hypatia tells me is called a magna-mat. The rest of the area looks like an elaborate skate park built in and around the forest foliage with slopes and bridges and all kinds of obstacles.

I admire the hoverboard in my hands, eager to get my feet on it.

Georgie says, "It's a great model. My mom got it for me as consolation for my difficulty in adjusting to moving here. It made me feel better for about a minute until I realized I couldn't ride the thing without—careful! You're gonna—"

But I'm already on the hoverboard and shooting up one of the ramps. There's a subtle tension of magnetism that reverberates all around me with a soft but audible hum.

"Whenever I get on that thing, I end up spraining a part of my body and usually someone else's body too. How are you so good at that?" Georgie calls.

"I'm used to snowboarding," I reply as I subtly tilt the board to give it the lift it needs to whoosh through a tunnel, and then I easily shift pressure from one hip to the other to swerve through a hedge maze, Georgie, Hypatia, and everyone else now out of sight.

The board is incredibly intuitive. I play around, seeing what it can do and testing its limits. It can't go more than a few feet off the magnetic surface, but it's *so* smooth.

For the first time in a while, my head is clear. I'm not thinking about my obligations to the Families, or how disappointed Michael will be when I can't get into a guild, or the fear and humiliation of being stopped and searched by soldiers because a handsome jerk wants to bully me. I'm simply enjoying *being*. I exit the maze and glide over a bridge. My hair comes loose from its tie and whips in my face, obscuring my vision and getting caught in my mouth. My lungs burn from the sting of the crisp air. As I do an alley-oop off the halfpipe, I hear cheers.

"By the Conductor! Look at her go!"

"She must have done this before—no novice is that good on a hover."

When I finally slow to a stop in front of Georgie and Hypatia, quite a crowd has gathered. Drawing attention to myself certainly hadn't been my intention, and it's the last thing I need. But I don't have time to worry about it with Georgie and Hypatia fussing over me.

"That was amazing!" Georgie gushes. "You need to teach me some of those tricks. Well, first you need to teach me how to balance and move in a straight line."

We all laugh.

"You'll for sure be recruited to your guild's team after Quorum!" Hypatia's hazel eyes glitter with excitement. "And then I'll live vicariously through you."

Hypatia will also be presenting at the upcoming Quorum as she's recently come of age to join a guild, but she'd said her family won't let her hoverjoust because of her health. I'm curious about her mystery illness, especially since sickness seems to be uncommon among the Makers with all their advanced medicine, but I assume that if she wants me to know about it, she'll tell me eventually.

"Let's see how you do with a lance," Georgie says. "I can't wait to see how you joust. You need to wear a helmet on the magna-mat though."

The helmet she tosses me is shaped like it belongs on a knight, but it's no shining armor. The cap is made of spidersilk padding, and the visor is fully transparent glace.

Hypatia grunts with effort as she hands me a lance. It's longer than I am tall, and it's heavy and awkward to hold. They set up a target for me in the center of one of the lanes on the magna-mat so I can practice with the lance before attempting an actual match against another person.

I might be good on a hoverboard, but I can barely hold the lance. I drop it on my first and second try. By my third, I make it across the mat still holding the lance, but it doesn't get anywhere near the target.

After a few more fruitless attempts, I pull off my helmet, ready to give my lance arm a break. Hypatia seems captivated with something over my shoulder, so I turn to look.

Ah. At the edge of the clearing, a sweaty Simon Sanzio is doing shoulder rolls while holding dumbbells. Kaylie is coaching him, helping him isolate a specific muscle in his back.

I suddenly have some questions about why Hypatia insisted we come here at this specific time of day. Gotta respect that girl's hustle.

"Seems like a strange place for a workout," I say. "Why don't they just go to the gymnasium?" I ask.

"They need the open sky," Hypatia explains as she weaves a flower into her pale blond braid. "Simon needs to work on his wing strength."

I do a double take, wondering if I heard her right.

Turns out I did hear her right.

As I watch, Simon spreads his wings. Yes. *Wings.*

They're not feathery angel wings or gossamer fairy wings. They're large and strong enough to hold up a human body. They ripple with muscle and bone, and they're covered in skin.

Valkyrie. Got it.

As Simon flaps his wings and elevates off the ground, I'm not sure I fully believe my eyes.

Kor would *die* to see this. He's always been obsessed with mythical creatures, and when I learned Maker history and Kor's belief that some of those creatures might be real, I finally understood why.

"You can do it, Simon!" Kaylie cheers. "You're getting stronger!"

But Simon's clearly not very good at the flying thing. Red-faced from exertion, he starts to rise higher, higher, until he catches a current, and with a joyous "Whoop!" he's off, gliding into the treetops.

He waves at Hypatia.

She waves back with a pleased blush, covering her mouth to hide her too-wide smile.

"Not so high, Simon!" Kaylie yells.

And just then his wings falter, and he comes crashing down into a nearby tree.

A very high tree.

One of his wings is twisted at an odd angle, and his face contorts in a grimace.

"Don't worry. I'm coming to get you!" Kaylie calls up to him. Then to Hypatia she yells, "I can stabilize him, but go get Grey. I'll need help getting him down."

Hypatia runs off, her face pinched with concern. More onlookers gather, all calling up encouragement to Simon.

Kaylie strips off her jacket, and I realize she's much slimmer than I'd thought before. Beneath her jacket, she's wearing a backless camisole, and I watch in amazement as she unfurls her own wings.

She shakes them, and they flounce into shape.

Kaylie has *wings*.

I can't help but stare. Even from a few yards away, I can see that the skin looks tougher than the rest of Kaylie's skin, and it's slightly iridescent. The wings are beautiful in their own, bizarre way. Even more beautiful is watching Kaylie as she gracefully leaps up, flaps her wings, and soars into the treetops, her copper hair streaming behind her like dancing flames.

We all watch as Kaylie lands on a branch above Simon.

I immediately think of the angels in Botticelli's *The Birth of Venus*. I've wondered whether Kaylie was Botticelli's descendant based on her last name. And she even resembles Venus with her pale complexion and flowing red hair.

"They're straight out of a painting," I say to Georgie with wonder.

"Literally," she responds. "Half the paintings you've seen of angels were probably originally of Valkyries, then called angels only after all the living Valkyries were driven into hiding. Some paintings, like Botticelli's, were even altered to make the wings look more angelic after the fact. We learned all about it in Foundations seminar."

There's an Avant transfer—one of Rafe's posse—standing near us, and he keeps turning to glare at Georgie, because apparently a recruit even breathing the same air as him is an indignity. I give him the finger. Not sure if they know what that means around here, but he seems to get the message and stalks away.

"Don't even bother," Georgie grumbles. "Better to just ignore them."

"If you say so," I respond begrudgingly. "So Botticelli was a Maker, I'm assuming?"

"No, he wasn't. And he was vocal in denouncing them. He even burned some of his own work depicting heretical Maker innovations during the Bonfire of the Vanities."

I have a vague recollection of learning about the Bonfire of the Vanities, which took place in Florence, and I make a mental note to find out how it fits in with the Inquisition responsible for the Makers' exile.

"But he had Valkyrie family members who often acted as his muses before they all went into hiding during the Exodus."

"Wait," I say as her words sink in. "Maker innovations. So you're saying the Makers . . . ?"

"Made the Valkyries. Yup. They're an example of the kind of science the Makers were exiled for—attempting to improve upon the original creation of the world."

Kor had said unicorns were Maker experiments too, and now that I have evidence there are literally winged humans, it feels safe to ask, "Are unicorns real?"

Georgie laughs. "You should see the look on your face. They are real. But they're extinct. I think the last unicorn died, like, eighty years ago."

Why do I feel sad for the loss of something I didn't even know existed until now?

"But the wind horses are still around. You have to ask Master Botticelli to introduce you to Peggy."

"So if the Makers can do all"—I motion to the winged people above us—"*that*, can they, like, cure cancer too?"

"I assume at least some kinds."

"Doesn't it bother you that they haven't . . . shared that with the regular world?"

She's thoughtful for a minute before she says, "Years before I knew the Makers existed, my grandmother had a very treatable form of cancer. The cost of her treatment was so high that she burned through her entire life's savings in a year.

"She didn't tell my parents, but we found out after she died that when her money ran out, she'd started reducing and rationing her medications, and she'd even entirely stopped using the ones needed to manage her severe side effects. There were pharmacies full of the medicine that could have reduced her suffering and saved her life, but she couldn't afford it, and so she died in her fifties of something perfectly treatable."

"I'm so sorry." I know what it's like to have a sick grandparent. The whole story is so tragic, and it's definitely not the first time I've heard of a situation like it. Why is our world so cruel?

Georgie continues. "So I guess my point is that my experience with provincial health care was that a lot of cures existed that were only accessible for some. And at least here they treat anyone who needs it."

I have about a thousand more questions, but I'm distracted by the sound of Simon yelping.

I look up and see him slipping from his perch. He grabs at a branch and catches himself. He hangs, his feet kicking, trying to find purchase beneath him, but there's nothing there.

Kaylie helps him keep his grip, but the branch itself is half-dead and close to splintering. She lowers herself to support his weight, but as soon as she tries, her wings falter.

"He doesn't look that heavy," I say.

"Oh, she could probably lift him on the ground," Georgie explains, "but Valkyries' wings are only strong enough to carry their own body weight, and they have to stay light even for that."

The branch Simon hangs from is high. If he falls, he'll definitely break some bones, probably worse.

I have an idea.

I dash over to the tree. I've never done anything like this before, but I'm good with plants. If I understand my abilities correctly, I should be able to push Ha'i into the tree to help it strengthen enough to hold Simon's weight until more help arrives.

The bark is harsh under my palm as I form my fingers into shiin. I close my eyes and try to find the well of Ha'i within me like Master Liu taught me. I imagine channeling the line of energy into the tree. Kaylie yells her encouragement; she thinks I can do it.

But nothing happens.

Maybe the leaves on the lower branches look greener? That's not enough to heal a dying branch.

Simon is sobbing now.

"Just a little longer," Kaylie says to him. "Your brother is on his way."

"Hold on, Simon!" a deep voice booms as a shirtless man comes careening through the sky from the direction of the village. He has a trim build of lean muscles that ripple as he flaps a pair of wings much larger than Kaylie's. This must be Grey, Simon's brother. It takes me a moment to recognize him in the distance, but it's the gray-haired guard who searched me the other day.

I hear a sound like the crack of a whip as the branch snaps.

And Simon is falling.

Directly on top of me.

"Simon!" Grey yells, flying toward us. But there's no way he'll get here in time. There's not even enough time for me to instruct my body to move out of the way.

Simon crashes onto me, and the breath is knocked from my lungs as we collapse in a tangle of wings and limbs. My vision blurs as my head smashes into the ground, and Simon's face collides with mine, my teeth splitting his cheek open like an overripe peach. The metallic taste of blood fills my mouth.

I try to spit out the blood, but there's so much of it. Some mine and some Simon's. I feel like I'm choking on it.

I hear voices, but they sound far away, as if I'm underwater.

"Don't touch them!" Kaylie calls as she swoops down to us.

"Simon, are you okay?" Grey bellows.

Then his voice again, close to my face, fuzzy through the pounding in my head. "Thank you for breaking his fall. You may have saved his life."

12

A long hoverboard ride. A crack of thunder. Simon flying over Rafe, who is lying in a field of red flowers. An unknown beautiful girl pouring wine for Kor.

The dream is a little different every time, but those parts are always the same. I've had difficulty sleeping every night since the flying incident. My injuries healed quickly due to my Sire abilities, but the weird dreams are a pain in my butt.

I'm so tired that I'd fall asleep in this chair if the information we were learning wasn't so fascinating.

"The fact that da Vinci had a boyfriend is not secret Maker knowledge," Michael says. "It's well documented in provincial history if you know where to look."

We're in a Foundations of Maker Culture seminar, discussing famous Makers from before the Exodus (including Luca Pacioli, the father of accounting as we know it, and supposedly Leonardo da Vinci's live-in partner—though they separated when Pacioli joined the Makers in Avant and da Vinci stayed in Italy).

Michael—Master Loew—leads the Foundations seminar, as he's the

resident expert on the relationships between Maker society and the provincial world. The seminar meets in an alcove of the library. It's a small
group made up entirely of recruits, including Georgie and both of her
parents.

There's also a Sophist named Gloria who must be close to thirty years
old and was recruited, like, ten years ago. She clearly knows everything we
learn already, and I'm pretty sure she only comes to these classes to moon
over Michael. Which . . . fair. I have, unfortunately, discovered that Michael
being all teachery does not make it easier to ignore his dimples. But he's
clearly not discouraging her. Honestly, his enthusiasm whenever the two of
them debate is probably encouraging her. Whatever.

The fact that da Vinci didn't want to join the Makers leads to a discussion
about some of the many others that the Makers have been unsuccessful in
recruiting over the years. One of whom was Rembrandt, who resisted multiple attempts at recruitment despite the personal and financial difficulties
that he had in the provincial world.

I think of the painting hanging in Bloche's office. The knowledge that
Rembrandt specifically wanted to keep himself and his art in the provincial
world makes the thought that the Makers may have stolen that painting
even more despicable.

Since I'm grouchy from lack of sleep, I'm not careful to school my expression, so when the seminar is over, Michael approaches me. "Something's
bothering you," he says.

Yeah, something's bothering me. But I'm not about to expose my crit-
ical views about Maker lifestyle. Except my mind and my mouth seem
to be at odds with each other because the question spills out before I can
stop it.

"The painting in Headmaster Bloche's office, is it Rembrandt's *The Sea of
Galilee?*"

Michael grins. "You have a good eye. Yes. It's a magnificent piece, isn't it?"

I feel a flush of confusion and anger. "That painting was stolen over thirty years ago."

He must hear the accusation in my tone. "The Makers had nothing to do with the theft. Bloche rescued the painting from the thieves."

"Then why didn't he return it?" I honestly hope he has a good explanation. I want to respect him. I want to respect the Makers.

"Return it to the people whose carelessness allowed thieves to slash it from its frame? Here it was faithfully restored and is in a place where it can be better protected and properly appreciated."

"Properly appreciated?" I rub at my scars, feeling my frustration build. "How many people, on this tiny hidden island, get to appreciate it when it hangs in one man's office? You think provincial people can't properly appreciate art? Do you know how much the loss of that painting was mourned? Is still mourned? The museum still has the empty frame on display." I bite my lip, realizing too late that I'm showing my hand. But when our eyes meet, it feels impossible to try to pretend, so I don't stop. "You're the one who told me about how much history has been stolen from the provincial world by the Inquisition. And you think *more* should be taken?"

Michael's expressive brows are drawn tight. "Tell me about the empty frame," he says.

"At the Isabella Stewart Gardner Museum in Boston," I explain. "Where the Rembrandt was stolen along with a bunch of other works. The empty frames are left on the walls, waiting for the works to be returned to them." Grandfather had brought me to the museum a few years ago. I'd found the empty frames to be truly haunting. And the feeling of loss they evoked in me lingers in my memory in a way so many other exhibitions I've seen over the years don't. "There's a ten-million-dollar reward for their recovery."

Michael listens earnestly, nibbling at his thumbnail.

"Thank you for sharing that," he says. "I hadn't considered the implications of the loss to provincial society."

No kidding. Not considering provincial society seems to be a running theme here. But Michael's seminar has made it even more clear that what the Makers think about provincial society is wrong. The people of the twenty-first century are nothing like the intolerant religious zealots who exiled and hunted them hundreds of years ago. Well, at least most of them aren't. But there's certainly no longer a reason for the Makers not to share their knowledge.

After Michael says goodbye and heads out, my eyes are drawn to the section of the library with everything I need: the Guild Testaments.

The Guild Testament scrolls, where each guild compiles their greatest discoveries, are kept on their own floor suspended in the center of the library, accessible only by two winding staircases: one leading up from the floor below and one leading down from the floor above. Both staircases are patrolled by members of the Avant Guard. On the floating landing, there is a temperature-controlled glace room—the Ark—where the scrolls are kept, staffed by only a few trusted stewards.

The most secure area on the island? It's gotta be where the good stuff is. And I need the good stuff. None of my efforts so far have turned up anything useful about whether it's possible to share Sire abilities, and my hope that there's an easy cure for Grandfather is waning.

My time in the infirmary after my accident had given me the chance to chat with Kaylie about Maker medicine. She was very enthusiastic about my interest in Bioscience, and she gave me some suggestions of ways to get the guild's attention at Quorum. But my conversation with her pretty much confirmed that if a cure for Grandfather's cancer does exist, it's unlikely to be something that an individual Sire could achieve on their own. If I want to find the details of how my abilities could be used in conjunction with Maker surgical and pharmaceutical practices that might be able to be re-created by the Families' doctors, then I need to see the Bioscience Guild Testament.

I won't have access to the Ark until I'm in a guild, but I've started preparing for then by befriending one of the Ark stewards, a pregnant Sophist master named Xander. Georgie and Hypatia had thought my choice to sit at her lunch table the other day had been completely coincidental. They were wrong.

But even if I can't get into the Ark yet, Kor also wants me to prioritize getting more information about the Makers' other territories, and that's something I can do right now, right here in the library.

The Genesis library is enchanting. Despite its size, it manages to be cozy with endless nooks and sitting areas. And the books! Gorgeous hand-bound books as far as the eye can see.

I ask one of the stewards, a plush white woman with her hair swept up in a beaded hairnet, where I can find information about the Makers' other communities.

"Hmm, I have an idea. You wait right here." She pats my arm and bustles off.

There's beautiful copper detailing throughout the library that I had thought was decoration, but when a few minutes later a glace tube comes whizzing into a cubby next to me, I realize that it's a system of pneumatic pipes. I remove two scrolls and a slip of paper from the tube and send it back through the chute. A cursory glance shows that both scrolls are maps, and the paper is the shelf location of a book.

Once I find the book, I sit down in one of the private study nooks—out of sight of the guards patrolling the Ark—to examine everything more closely. One map is of the world, but it's very different from any map I've ever seen. There are numerous additional landmasses, and the familiar continents are on a completely different scale. Africa is notably much larger and

Antarctica much smaller than I would have expected. The second map illustrates the entire Atlas route, and the book is an illustrated geographic reference text, clearly intended for young apprentices, titled *Exodus & Exile: The Geography of Maker Past and Present*. All of these will be extremely helpful.

There are five areas on the world map that are labeled as "Delegations to the Maker Council."

In Foundations, Michael explained that the Council is the group of delegates from each of the Maker communities who meet to make decisions regarding important issues that affect Maker society as a whole. I know that Arcadia democratically elects the Genesis headmaster, who acts as their delegate.

Avant is indicated to be in the Alps, and *Exodus & Exile* provides some additional information like the fact that it's ruled by a monarchy. A fact that seems to conflict with their supposed utopian ideals, but okay.

Arcadia is in the Atlantic Ocean, southwest of Bermuda. (I note that it is suspiciously right around the area known as the Bermuda triangle.)

Midway between Avant and Arcadia is a cluster of small islands labeled the Misty Isles. I've heard a bit more about the Misty Isles, the domain of the Matriarchy of the Isles, from Mbali. Her mother is the leader of the Keftiu Matriarchy. The reference book explains that at the time of the Exodus, the Matriarchy provided refuge for fleeing Makers, many of whom chose to integrate into their society. Once the Atlas was built, and long-distance travel became easier, representatives of each guild were sent to establish themselves under the auspices of the Matriarchy, and more Makers began to take up residence there. It's not unusual for Islanders like Mbali to choose to study in the Maker schools.

There are two other denoted locations on the map: a tiny island in the Mediterranean Sea labeled "Eden," and an area near the Middle East labeled "Naiot."

I flip through the reference book for more details. Eden supposedly marks the location of the actual Garden of Eden from the Bible. Though from the little information I can find, no one lives there, and it is more of an environmental preserve and perhaps also a retreat for those who need certain kinds of rehabilitation. Naiot is also currently unpopulated, but the book says that's only been the case for close to two decades, ever since the tragic event known as the Fall of Naiot.

Master Bose, my Testaments teacher—the one with the dog—read to us about the Fall of Naiot from the *Book of Chorus* in my Testaments class just the other day.

Naiot had once been a hidden village of prophets who had an alliance with the Makers. After world governments repeatedly used their prophecies for destructive ends, they stopped sharing them, which led to their expulsion. They hid themselves where they could train new prophets to control their prophecy and use it responsibly. But all of that ended with the Fall of Naiot.

I hadn't fully understood the testament that described the Fall. I should probably read the prophecy again.

I close the reference book and maps and bring them with me to the section of the library where the Testaments of the Prophets are shelved.

Having grown up with Catholicism and Judaism, I'm pretty familiar with hearing about old prophecies. But according to *Exodus & Exiles*, this Chorus chick is still alive. That makes the Makers' recorded prophecies a hell of a lot more recent than David and Samuel.

While the Guild Testaments are classified, the regular Testament section is easily accessible. Each of the Testaments of the Prophets has the name of a different Prophet embossed in gold on its spine. It's the very last, extremely slim volume labeled *Chorus* that I pull down. I settle into a nearby love seat and begin to read.

Chorus

Book 1: Testament 1

Seventy souls lived in the village beyond the river. On a day when the rapids of the river were fierce, a girl—only recently granted her Sight—was sent to collect wildflowers.

When the sky began to dim, the girl returned and found the village silent. No other souls roamed the streets, and each door that she opened led to another vacant home. She was not concerned, for strangeness was not strange to the village.

But when she reached the temple and found it abandoned, fear took her hand in a slow dance. There was no one seated in meditation under the palm trees, no one playing the harps to aid in concentration, no one lounging in the purifying baths.

No one guarding the stones and scrolls of prophecy.

The fear became a knife, sharp and urgent, but the girl kept it at bay in clenched fists as she walked into the vestibule.

At the altar, the gemstones had been set and the scrolls unrolled. Everything was arranged for the prophets to puzzle out the meaning within the prophecy. But there were no prophets, only echoes.

The girl disrobed and immersed in the purifying baths to prepare her body before ascending to the altar. There was no one to play the harp or the bowl, but she conjured the memory of the music.

A prophecy is a finicky thing, often misinterpreted, but the meaning of this one was as clear as if it were written on her skin.

Strangers were coming. Men who would steal blood to steal the future.

The girl knew how the prophets would react to such a message, and she knew what she must do. With heart and mind numb, the girl gathered the gemstones and the scrolls and the wildflowers she had picked. She walked to a cave outside the village where she knew everyone else must be.

The cave was fragrant with the scent of foxglove flowers and as silent and lifeless as the village. Hers was the only heart that beat, and hers were the only lungs that drew breath, but they were all there—her family, and almost everyone she had ever known—lying still as if in peaceful slumber, their blood forever safe from those who would misuse it.

She fell to her knees and dug her hands into the ground, pulling out fistfuls of earth. Stones and rubble ripped through her skin and twisted her fingers, but she kept digging.

Outside the cave, a prince—only a man for a few years, but already powerful—dropped out of a shadow in the sky. He could not be in the presence of bodies whose spirits were departed, but he had not cut his hair or imbibed drink, so he lent the girl his strength. He braced his hands on the entrance of the cave and sang. He stood there all through the night while she used his strength to dig until the sun came and hid the stars. But the sun could not chase away the darkness on that day.

On each lump of newly turned earth, the girl placed a stone. Sixty-seven stones. Sixty-seven graves. She scattered the wildflowers outside the cave, and their seeds took root and grew to cover the entrance.

The girl returned to the village and soaked in a purifying bath until it ran black with dirt.

Her grief caused the temple walls to shake as she Saw that there was hope. A child of her blood that she would teach to hone

the Sight, who would also cultivate Life and Sing strength, and
who would reunite all those who had been lost.

Then the prince picked up the girl and held her against his
heart, where he swore he would keep her for the rest of their days,
and the shadow in the sky flew them both to paradise.

Later that day, the waters of the river ran still, and strangers
crossed its banks. They found the village empty. The streets were
silent, and the temple was barren. All the roads and houses were
deserted.

They pondered over the enigma of the black pool in the temple,
and they bathed in it, thinking it might grant them blessing.
They scouted the area between the river and the spine of the
mountains but did not find the cave.

And so they left.

The strangers and their offspring often return on days when
the river runs still. They try to decipher the mystery of the village,
and they continue to bathe in the black water, hoping for a
miracle.

But all the miracles of the village are gone.

A shiver runs through me as I finish reading. I flip through the rest of
the pages, but they're all blank, waiting for new prophecies not yet recorded.
When we'd discussed this Testament in class, the young apprentices had a
lot to say.

"It didn't actually happen like that. You're not meant to understand it literally."

"How could you say that? Everything written in the Testaments is true!"

"No way it really happened. Have you seen Chorus? She's so scrawny. She
couldn't dig even a single grave on her own."

"But Prince Alex amplified her strength."

"They are the most romantic couple ever."

It has not escaped my notice that Prince Alexander and Chorus are a common topic of gossip and the closest thing to celebrities that the Makers have. But at the time I thought they were mythical or historical. Not currently living actual people. Understanding this lends new meaning to the rest of the apprentices' discussion.

"I heard that he proposes once a year, and she always says no."

"Why do you think she won't marry him?"

"I heard he once proposed with a bouquet of handpicked flowers, one from every country in the world."

"Chorus would never align herself with the Blood Crown."

"But Prince Alex is nothing like the king."

"They need to marry so they can conceive the Child of Three to bring us out of exile."

"The Child of Three isn't real, and no one wants to go back anyway."

"Everything written in the Testaments is real!"

I wonder the same things as the apprentices. This particular story doesn't sound like it could have really happened—princes falling from the sky and singing strength—but then again, there's so much I would never have thought possible before coming here.

The Child of Three is another common topic in my Testaments class. Apparently, at the time of the Exodus, when the Makers were first exiled, one of the Prophets of Naiot prophesied that the Child of Three (TBD on why they're called that) would one day come and reunite them with the rest of the world.

The consensus seems to be that the prophecy Chorus recorded having in the Testament of the Fall of Naiot confirms she will be the mother of this three-pronged messiah. The jury seems split both about whether anyone actually believes this will happen and whether they even want it to. But I've taken the existence of the prophecy as a sign that the Makers are at least open to the idea of one day collaborating with the provincial world. Though I sure hope we don't have to wait for this Chorus lady to finally agree to marry the prince and then wait for an infant to grow up before we can make any headway.

The thing I'm most curious about the Fall of Naiot is who the hell the strangers are. The Makers are sure they are the Inquisitors, but I know it must be someone else, and what could they possibly have had planned that was bad enough that the prophets thought dying was better?

I resolve to learn as much as I can about Chorus and the prophets. And I'll need to ask Kor if the Families have any record of Naiot or any events that coincide with the tragedy described.

I take the reference book, maps, the *Testament of Chorus*, and a few other random books to make sure that my selection doesn't look too suspicious, and I find a steward to help me check everything out. Then I head back to my room to photograph everything for the Families.

13

Kaylie leads me to the stables carrying a basket of apples and carrots. We're going to meet Peggy, the wind horse, and Georgie and Hypatia have promised me it will be the highlight of my week.

When I told Michael I was interested in the Bioscience guild, he recommended that I reach out to Kaylie for some additional mentorship since she's a master of the guild.

She's been really helpful. She gave me some suggestions for projects for my gallerie, and today she wants to give me some background on the origin of the guild, which is the newest guild in Maker society.

The stable is large and well kept. Horses stick out their heads curiously as we pass each stall. They stamp their feet and shake out their manes. We approach the last stall, the air pungent with the spicy scent of animal and earth. On the wall outside the door hangs an ornate saddle made of purpledbrown leather. It has no stirrups, and there is a glass compass set into the bronze horn grip.

I hear melodic humming coming from the stall.

"Peggy has an admirer," Kaylie jokes. "He comes here often. He's probably already groomed her, but she needs to be taken out to stretch."

The "he" turns out to be Rafe, who is rubbing Peggy's neck and feeding her an apple. I almost don't recognize him because the soft look on his face transforms him into a completely different person.

Yet even this soft version of him can't keep my attention once I lay my eyes on Peggy.

She is stunning.

She has a silvery blond coat and a lustrous champagne mane, and at her sides lie large, iridescent wings.

I have to remind myself to breathe.

"We're taking her out to fly," Kaylie says to Rafe, who upon seeing us has reverted back to the familiar version I know, all hard edges and contempt.

"I was just leaving," he responds. Ever since our Sire lab confrontation, Rafe has mostly just been ignoring me, though I continue to work with Mbali at his table.

He whispers something in Peggy's ear—of course he's more civil to an animal than to me—and then, with a tight smile at Kaylie, he pushes past us and exits, not even acknowledging me.

I reach over and tentatively stroke Peggy's neck. "How is she even possible?"

"The wind horses are one of many incredible creatures born of Maker experimentation at the original academy before the Exodus."

My lungs feel tight as my world is turned over for another time. Almost a daily occurrence here.

"I just can't believe I lived my life for so long without knowing about . . ."

Kaylie nods in understanding. But there's no way she can possibly understand. To me, she and Peggy are impossible miracles. "How can the rest of the world just . . . not know?" I want to feel angry, but my awe for Peggy doesn't leave much room for negative feelings.

"At the time of the Exodus, the wind horses and other creatures that were the result of Maker innovations were brought into hiding to prevent their destruction, and their existence was denied by the Church until it was forgotten that they were ever anything other than legends."

This is a pattern of what I've been learning at Genesis, that so many stories I'd assumed were myths are actually just the vestiges of the memory of Maker science that was once part of our world.

"Come along, girl," Kaylie says to Peggy, and I follow them out of the stable. Peggy doesn't need a bridle or reins; she listens to Kaylie's soft instructions.

"She's one of the last of her kind. Most have been sent to Eden, and there are three at the Academy of Avant. The Blood Science guild is trying to breed them, but wind horses tend to have very difficult pregnancies and often die in childbirth." She pauses and then adds, "It's much the same for Valkyries."

"And they can't . . . make new ones the way they made the first ones?"

"The knowledge of how to create species like the wind horses is passed down through the Blood Science testament, but it's a practice that ended long ago. These kinds of forced evolutionary practices were risky and occasionally harmed animals and humans alike."

"How so?"

"Well, procedures often required live organ donations. There were many failed experiments that ended in deaths, and there were many side effects that weren't anticipated." She looks away as she says this, and I think about what she just said about Valkyrie births.

She continues. "As the Makers evolved as a society, we had to confront these controversies. Genesis dismantled their Blood Science guild entirely, replacing it with Bioscience. At Avant, they still practice Blood Science, and they definitely involve themselves in some morally questionable behaviors, but even they have limits. When the Council was established and they enacted laws to restrict experimentation on living beings, it was understood that it could mean an end for some of these magnificent creatures. Steps were taken to preserve them, but we had more success with some than with others. Many have already been lost."

"Like the unicorns?"

"Yes." Her voice is wistful as she pets Peggy. "Nowadays, the evolutional experimentation that continues is purely aimed at enhancing and improving the world within a more confined set of limitations while maintaining a strict code of conduct that does not harm any living beings."

I watch in a daze as Kaylie encourages Peggy to gallop for a bit . . . and then to fly. The wind horse flaps her wings—not dissimilar to Valkyrie wings—and rises into the air, huffing her snout and shaking her mane in glee.

How beautiful she looks in flight. Her coat is like liquid gold turning to a platinum sheen as it catches the sunlight. Kaylie extends her own wings and joins Peggy in the air. They frolic together, two impossibly beautiful beings, and my heart aches at the possibilities of creation.

Humans came up with the science to make humans and horses *fly*. Because human limitations—my limitations— are nothing like what I have been previously led to believe. Who knows what I will one day be capable of if I learn from these people?

But first I need to join a guild.

14

The weeks pass quickly, and I find myself in a comfortable groove at the institute. Getting into a guild so I have access to the Guild Testaments is my top priority, so I keep my head down and focus on my classes and on gathering as much intel for the Families as I can. (Fine, also some occasional hoverjousting.)

Even at only the apprentice level, my classes are odysseys away from anything I ever had at home. I haven't had to look at a single monomial, polynomial, or trinomial in months. And while the other apprentices might be a lot younger than me, I've had to work extremely hard to catch up to them. And I'm not even fully caught up yet.

My anatomy class is the one I'm struggling with the most, by far. I'd done perfectly fine in biology back home, but these classes are totally different. We have to do things like re-create detailed models of body parts with loam and theorize about bizarre and theoretical surgeries.

My art classes, on the other hand, are pure joy. The other week I painted an entire picture using dyes I made myself with plants I grew myself.

However, my mission is always front and center of my priorities. I've become adept at sneaking cell phone pictures from various texts in the library and pocketing materials from the infirmary and classroom supplies.

I regularly have calls with Kor, who comes armed with a bunch of specific questions and tasks from the Inner Chamber. Sometimes I speak with other Inner Chamber members as well. The other day I had a very long and very boring call with some United Nations dude about clean energy.

Fun fact, a lot of renewable energy initiatives in the provincial world are actually already based in Maker tech and have been introduced into society over the years by the Families.

Less fun fact, Mr. UN was trying to get more specific details about how much of the island's electricity is renewable. The answer is 100 percent. It is now my very unfun homework to find out the methods by which they achieve this percentage. But I do actually want to help combat climate change, so I'm not mad about it.

I'm still worried about getting caught, but ever since appeasing Grey by involuntarily acting as Simon's trampoline, the Guard hasn't been giving me any more attention than they would a regular student.

My bigger problem lately is that I've been feeling guilty. I've been spending more time with Kaylie in order to learn about how Maker medicine works, and Xander, the Ark steward, to gain a better understanding of the security surrounding the Guild Testaments, and I kind of hate that I'm lying to everyone who is being so nice to me. It's not like they're the ones responsible for keeping their knowledge from the rest of the world.

But I know I'm doing the right thing. I may be enjoying everything I'm learning, and I may have a growing respect for a lot of the Maker ideals, but that doesn't change the reality of their inherent selfishness. I'm here for the benefit of the whole world, not just for me.

Except for this week. Right now I'm way too busy and distracted to do anything other than work on polishing my gallerie for Quorum.

Which is in two days.

Not only will being a journey give me access to the Ark and the Guild Testaments, but I'll also get access to the guild labs and stockrooms. Everything about my job here relies on me getting accepted into a guild.

The guild system is not nearly as confining as I'd expected. Unlike provincial university—where you basically have to choose your career path as a child, and if you choose wrong, too bad—the guilds expose you to all different disciplines aligned with your skills.

A journey can choose to become a master of their guild if they contribute an original study or invention to their guild's testament, and once they master . . . Well, I don't know much about masters yet, but the ones at Genesis seem to have mostly educational or administrative roles. Masters can also join other guilds. Over the course of Maker history, there have even been six people who mastered every guild and were given the title Master-of-All. This tidbit was told to me by Hypatia, who had proudly added, "And two of them have been from my family."

While I'm excited at the prospect of becoming a journeyman for a guild, every time I think about presenting my premature gallerie in front of the guildmasters, I feel like my skin doesn't fit right.

"Has anyone ever not been accepted to a guild?" I ask Georgie.

"I think it's happened before," she answers. "But if I managed to get accepted, you for sure will."

We're in the kitchen performing our cleaning rotation. Master Bose and Mbali are on duty with us. Instead of it being considered menial labor, everyone at the institute—from apprentices to guildmasters—takes turns completing the practical tasks necessary to keep the institute running smoothly.

"Don't let the fear of rejection cause you anxiety," Master Bose says as he works his way through a barrel of serving dishes, scraping any remaining waste into the compost. "Genesis works with everyone to find their place." He stacks the plates in a stone oven that uses energy generated by the methane from the compost to clean dishes using ultraviolet light and steam. "When an apprentice receives no guild invitations, the guildmasters give them assignments to work on, and they then reapply at the next season's Quorum."

That's nice and all, but I can't let that happen. Headmaster Bloche said he will send me away if I don't renounce my provincial life before the next anniversary of the Exodus, which now that I have a basic understanding of the Maker calendar, I think is only a little more than half a year away. I need to join a guild *now*.

"But you really don't need to worry," Georgie interjects. "You're a Sire! Guilds are always dying to recruit Sires. Plus, the hoverjoust teams all want you." She lowers her voice conspiratorially. "Officially, guildmasters don't take that into consideration, but everyone knows they all want to give their teams an advantage. You'll for sure get more than one invitation."

Mbali adds softly, "Do prepare to be rejected by the Avant guilds, but don't let it wound you. They're extremely selective."

And they'd never accept a provincial recruit is the part she doesn't say out loud.

She's referring to the Blood Science and Mysticism guilds, both of which are illegal at Genesis but still practiced at Avant.

Master Bose nods in agreement. "Not that you'd want to go to Avant anyway . . . bunch of stuck-up monarchists." He looks over at Mbali. "Present company excepted, of course, Journey Keftiu. I have great respect for the Matriarchy of the Isles."

Tracing her finger along her snake necklace, Mbali winks and says to me, "If you're truly unhappy with your placement options, you can always join the Pirates."

"Who are the Pirates?" I ask dubiously.

"They're a group of Makers who have rejected both Genesis and Avant.

They live at sea and believe that no one should be limited by a guild or council."

"Never heard of 'em," Georgie says. "But they sound like my kinda people. I've been called a pirate once or twice."

Once we're finished our cleaning duties, Mbali and I head together to the Sire lab. As I work on my woeful attempt at creating a golem that can move its limbs and support itself well enough to walk (but does not yet have any useful purpose), I'm still obsessing over Quorum.

I dubiously look over at Rafe. Since Hypatia, Simon, and Mbali have all decided to like me, he's mostly stopped being overtly hateful, though I can tell it costs him something. But I actually learn a lot from observing him while he barks orders at me and gives me withering glances. As long as I don't talk much or, heaven forbid, bump into him, he's generally tolerable.

And Rafe is in my top choice of guild, the one most likely to have information about Sire ability sharing and the one best suited for me to help Grandfather. I need advice from wherever I can get it, so I decide to chance it.

"Why did you choose the Bioscience guild?" I ask him.

He looks up at me and blinks.

For a moment I lose my train of thought as an image vividly overlays my vision.

Rafe lying in a field of red flowers.

I thought I'd finally managed to be free of that dream weeks ago, but the picture in my mind is as clear and detailed as a photograph.

I blink away the memory and refocus on the real Rafe, who is staring at me as if he can't believe that I've attempted small talk. "It's just that I'm trying to figure out what guild is best for me, assuming I get any invitations," I say.

"You're a Sire. You'll get invitations," he says dismissively, focusing back on whatever is under his microscope. I assume he means to ignore my question entirely, but after a moment he says, "At Avant, I was part of the Blood

Science guild. I had to relinquish that when I came here." He momentarily rubs his bare middle finger, where I assume he used to wear his old guild-stone. "I chose to reguild into Bioscience as it's the most similar."

"Do you like it?"

"Yes. Bioscience is a natural choice for a Sire, given our innate healing abilities." He keeps talking, eyes concentrating on the incisions he's making. "Once I master, I'll probably go on to the Artisan guild to pursue music." This surprises me, but not as much as his volunteering the information in the first place. "I'd also consider Alchemy or Mysticism. I have little inter-est in the Ciphers, and we both know I have no business messing with the ethics of Sophistry. So Bioscience made the most sense as a starting point."

He's never spoken so many sentences in a row to me. He's actually telling me about himself. The experience of him acknowledging me as human is a nice change.

"Well, what about me? Do you think Bioscience would be a good choice?"

He scrunches his brow for a moment, and I'm sure he's about to say no, but then he shrugs and says, "As I said, it's a good choice for most Sires."

Back in the common room of my apartment later in the evening, I recall the conversation and wonder why Rafe doesn't think Bioscience is a good fit for me. He probably just assumes I'm not good enough for his guild. But it's not one of the guilds Michael's been nudging me toward either. However, Kor thinks it's best, and I agree. For Grandfather if nothing else.

I've been using every spare moment I have searching for a way to help Grandfather, but I haven't found anything specific about cures for cancer. I searched the library, tried asking questions to the snooty Bio journeys, and even snuck into the Bio lab after following Kaylie to find out where it is. The only consistent response I get is, "There's information about it in the

Bioscience Guild Testaments." Joining the Bio guild is my best bet at ever seeing those.

So Bioscience is my first choice . . . right? But if I don't get in, I need a backup option.

I wish Georgie were here so I could pick her brain more. As if I haven't been doing that for days. I'm glad for her sake that she's been busy in her Couture Studio sewing pieces to barter at the Quorum faire. She must be sick of my constant spiraling.

All this worrying is fruitless when I could be doing something practical like actively enhancing my gallerie. I *should* be practicing my song.

With help from Michael and from my apprentice classes, my gallerie has come a long way. Madam Adelina, my pitch instructor, has really helped me improve my singing voice. In Apprentice Art Studio, I've made some decent drawings and discovered that, in addition to my plant dyes, I really enjoy both egg tempera and pastels. I've prepared an original recipe in culinary science and, with Kaylie's help, completed a life-size anatomically accurate sketch of a human circulatory system. Through it all, I've gathered a fair number of pieces worth showing. However, my song is still a mess.

But there's no way I can be productive with my brain this preoccupied.

Izzy has talked me through many overthinking tornadoes. If she were here, she would tell me to approach things logically and make a list.

I grab a paper and pen and write down each guild starting with Bioscience.

Bioscience
PROS:
– Medical stuff
– Sire sharing thing??
– Good fit for Sires
– Great hoverjoust team

The negatives for the Bioscience guild write themselves:

> CONS:
> — Snobby/competitive journeys
> — RAFE

I move on to the Artisans next.

> <u>Artisans</u>
> PROS:
> — Georgie
> — Music + art = yay!
> CONS:
> — Bad hoverjoust team

What about the Sophists? They have an amazing guildmaster. I met with her once because she wanted to make sure I was integrating at the institute "spiritually, philosophically, and psychologically." She is, as Michael had told me, the direct descendant of Ada Lovelace. She's also as sweet as a gushberry and a total genius.

> <u>Sophists</u>
> PROS:
> — Michael's guild
> — Nice guildmaster
> — Art history = yes, please
> CONS:
> — Most other kinds of history = boring
> — Psychology, sociology, theology = also boring
> — Michael might be my TEACHER . . .

Mbali is the only Alchemist I've met. I know that their high material is glace, and I've passed the Alchemy lab a few times and it's always smoky and smelly. They're involved in things like chemistry, botany, and agriculture. It takes me a moment to make my list since I haven't given the guild much thought before.

Alchemists
PROS:
– I'm good with plants
– Do they actually do alchemy–like make gold?
CONS:
– I got a C in chemistry last year
– Stinky lab

The Ciphers are my last choice, and I know little about their guild other than that Georgie often talks about their hoverjousting captain, Hera, and that Michael's sister has done some prominent research for them. I'm pretty sure I don't have the head for whatever they do. Even their guild emblem looks like some kind of complicated equation with a golden ratio spiral and the geometric and military compass invented by Galileo. I jot my notes quickly.

Ciphers
PROS:
– Great hoverjoust team
– Engineering and physics are theoretically cool . . .
CONS:
– MATH IS EVIL. STAY FAR AWAY

As an afterthought, I add the two Avant guilds to my list even though I've been told they're only part of the Genesis Quorum as a formality since both practices have been banned here.

Mysticism is the smallest guild, very selective, and shrouded in secrecy. I don't know why it was banned at Genesis, but Hypatia had once mentioned that mysticism is considered dangerous and that some people who studied their testament went mad or even died. Technically, Genesis allows apprentices to be guilded as Mystics and travel to Avant to learn from the masters there, but it's rare.

Mysticism
Not an option, drives people to madness

Blood Science involves experimentation that's controversial and risky. Genesis replaced the entire guild with Bioscience, but Avant still practices it.

Blood Science
Not an option, illegal at Genesis, morally problematic

I sit back and look over my list, just as confused as before.

There's a knock at our apartment door, and I know it's Michael.

He's here to help me with my song—the one I'm supposed to be practicing. I'd taken a scribble that had started out as a poem and added a melody, but something's not quite right. My plan had been to ask Kor for help, but every time we spoke, he seemed too busy, and he kept reminding me to focus on my mission instead of being distracted by projects. So earlier today, I'd asked Michael for help instead.

Except now that he's on the other side of my door, I question that decision. Is this going to be awkward? He hasn't been anything but professional with me lately, so what am I worried about?

I fold my guild list and put it in my pocket. Then I get up to open the door for Michael.

He's not awkward at all as he lets himself into our common room, his long legs taking him straight to the guitar on the couch. It's actually his guitar. Most apprentices make their own instruments, but I haven't had the time to learn that process yet, so Michael lent me one of his older ones that he'd made when he was an apprentice.

"Just wait a sec while I get my music," I say, heading into my room.

I rifle through the numerous piles on my desk until I find my sheet music and then turn to leave, but my stomach sinks when I see Michael waiting for me in the doorway.

I hadn't meant for Michael to follow me to my room. In fact, that is the very last thing I wanted, for the very reason that is reflected on his face right now.

Abject horror.

Okay, it might be more like mild shock, but I know what must lurk beneath his polite mask.

I have failed my oath to keep my bedroom neat, and it's in its usual state of colorful chaos. Explosions of clothing, accessories, and art supplies are all over the floor and bed and pouring out of the drawers.

"How do you find anything?" Michael asks.

I burn with shame while at the same time trying to shove a bright pink bra under the bed with my toe. *Please let him not have seen it. And please let there not be any dirty underpants lying around.* I'm too scared to look.

"Well, you know me, extraordinarily talented," I say, cheeks aflame.

He smiles tightly, and I feel like such a . . . child. I try to use sheer force of will to erase the blush from my face as I shoo him out of the room.

I sit down and grab the guitar, ready to move on from my embarrassment. Michael sits on the opposite couch, and I start to play him what I have so far. I'm stilted and nervous and all too aware that it's not very good.

"It's really good," he says when I finish.

"No, it's not."

"Yes, it really is. It needs some work, but the bones are solid."

He suggests minor changes to the lyrics and melody, but his biggest input comes in ways to improve my playing.

"No, not like that." He comes to sit next to me to adjust my finger placement. As his confident fingers rearrange mine on the frets, my breathing becomes uneven.

He's good at this, and his changes coax something deeper from the song. Make it something I can imagine letting others actually hear.

When I play through the finished version for the first time without any mistakes, I feel a thrill in my blood.

"Honor a Maker!" Michael says, and the thrill spreads warmly through me. That exclamation is what Makers say to offer congratulations for significant creative accomplishments. No one's ever had reason to say it to me before.

Michael takes the guitar and begins absently plucking at the strings. All his frenetic energy vanishes as he plays with sure, steady hands. He starts to tell me about the first song he ever wrote, which he claims was "total chaff"—and it probably was considering it was called "Angel in the Sunrise"—but soon our conversation falls away as we both get pulled into the music.

Michael holds his guitar like an extension of his body. There's a natural twang to the instrument, but he pulls a softness from it in a way I have yet to master. The notes string together into a yearning voice. His fingers break into a flurry of rushed movements, eliciting a thrumming sequence that amazes me in its complexity, made even more impressive by the fact that Michael's not looking at the strings. He's looking at me.

Our eyes meet, and I catch my breath. The muscles in his neck relax and tighten with the movements of his arms, his lips softly parted, his eyes smiling. I feel the music like it's touching me in all the places that Michael's not touching me, and he just keeps . . . looking at me. Like something important is being communicated without words. Like all the things he's not saying are loud enough to drown out the song.

And then it's over.

Michael puts down the guitar and clears his throat. "I've missed this instrument," he says, looking at the guitar as if we didn't just share an intense, soul-bonding moment.

He searches my face and asks, "Ada, are you happy you chose to come here?"

"Yes," I say without hesitation. "Very happy." And I know it's true. I've already changed so much—learned so much—and I wouldn't give up this experience for anything.

In this moment, I'm not thinking about my mission. In this moment, I would rather learn from Genesis than spy on them. And in this moment, I'm pretending as much to myself as to everyone else that that's all I'm here to do.

I swallow. "But I'm still conflicted about which guild is right for me."

Michael smiles. "Trust your gut. Don't think about what anyone else would want. Listen to what the guildmasters have to say and focus on what resonates with you here." He holds his hand against his heart. "And after Quorum, once you've joined a guild"—his eyes soften—"you'll officially be a Maker."

He reaches up to my ear, and I feel the ghost of a touch above my Sire diamond at the spot where my guildstone will go. My heart stutters, and I hold my breath.

The lock of the apartment door clicks, and Michael's hand snaps back.

"Hi!" Georgie chirps.

"Well, I should probably be going." Michael rises from beside me. "Your gallerie is going to be wonderful, and by this time two days from now, you'll be a journeyman."

15

Within the hour, Quorum will begin and my future as a Maker will be decided. I feel stiff in the formal clothes I borrowed from Georgie (which she had to alter to fit me). I'm wearing a navy balloon-sleeved blouse tucked into high-waisted black velvet trousers. And with my new high laced boots and half my hair braided into a crown atop my head, I almost look like I belong here. That is, until I realize that I'm standing in the wrong place.

Hundreds of Makers are crowded into the Equinox for the Quorum opening ceremony. I had automatically walked over to a group I recognized from my Sire lab, but this is the spot for journey Sires. No one seems to care that I don't belong here, except for Rafe, who hisses at me and points to a cluster of children—the apprentices—all the way on the other side of the room. But I'm too embarrassed to cross the vast space with everyone watching, so I stay. Surprisingly, Rafe doesn't push the issue, and I can't help but notice that there's a lightness to his expression I've never seen before. It almost looks like he's . . . happy.

The herald announces the arrival of the delegation from Avant. A parade of important-looking people streams into the room. I've been told that more dignitaries than usual will be present at this Quorum since several notable apprentices are presenting their galleries, including Hypatia and Simon, who are apparently both from high-ranking Avant families.

Suddenly, the low hum of whispers and activity quiets, and I look to the doors. An imposing man with long, wild hair enters. The aura surrounding him sucks the attention from every corner of the room. He looks straight out of a movie set, wearing a long fur coat and leather pants tucked into knee-high leather boots. His chest is bare, an impressive tattoo of a dragon spans across the left side of his chest and up his neck, and some kind of claw hangs from a cord around his neck. How many dead animals is this guy wearing?

As if he knows what I'm thinking, Rafe whispers in my ear, "Would you believe his girlfriend is a vegetarian?" I stifle a laugh, the comment so anachronistic with the pageantry of the moment. And did Rafe just make a joke? To *me*? He *must* be in a good mood.

The man looks so weird and so captivating that I can't stop staring. His long rippling hair is midnight dark, though his beard is shot with gray. Atop his head rests a simple metal circlet.

"Prince Alexander, heir to the Blood Crown of Avant," the herald introduces him. All of the Avant Makers—Rafe included—kiss the knuckles of their right hands. Everyone else acknowledges the prince's presence with a deep nod of their heads.

Prince Alexander sweeps through the entrance hall. As he gets closer, I notice that each of the fingers on his right hand bears a different colored gemstone band, with two on his thumb. Six guilds. Is he a Master-of-All?

For some reason, he seems to be coming straight toward me. No, I realize, toward Rafe.

The prince stops in front of us, a wide smile softening his harsh features. Rafe is smiling too. Really smiling—with teeth and cheeks and twinkling eyes. I didn't think he was capable of such an expression, and now I can't make myself look away.

When the prince speaks, his voice is gravel. "Raphael, it's been too long, brother."

Brother?

The prince grabs Rafe's hand, squeezing it as he leans over and kisses him on the cheek. His long hair shields them from view, but I am close enough to hear Rafe whisper, "I miss you. I miss home."

"You are where you should be" is the quiet, gritty response.

"How are Ben and Mab?"

"Everyone is well and missing you."

"And Gwen?"

"She misses you the most."

And then Prince Alexander sweeps away.

I look up at Rafe, who is back to his stone-cold self.

"Are you kidding me?" I whisper to him. "You're a *prince?*"

He looks at me with disdainful amusement. "Obviously."

★ ★ ★ ★ ★

Once all the delegations have arrived, the crowd makes their way through the archway that leads to the auditorium in the Autumn wing. The other apprentices who will be presenting their galleries are with their families, and I find myself on my own, awkwardly scanning the room for a familiar face.

"So, you're the provincial Sire," a melodic voice says from behind me. I spin around and see a petite woman in all black. She's striking, with olive skin and dark brown hair in a sleek topknot. A pearl hoop hangs from her right earlobe, indicating that she's a Cipher master.

"Aria Loew," she introduces herself.

So this is Michael's older sister. How is she so short when he's so tall?

"Ada Castle," I respond with a smile that she does not return. She is assessing me, looking more through me than at me.

"I know who you are." She lifts her arm and slowly strokes her fingers through the air around me like harp strings. An onyx ring adorns her pointer finger. In my apprentice classes, we'd learned about some of Aria Loew's research—smart, sciencey stuff I never really understood about strings that connect the universe. I knew she was doing further research in Avant, but I hadn't realized she joined the Mystic guild as her ring would suggest. I had been under the impression that the Mystics barely accept anyone. In fact, I think Hypatia had told me they'd only accepted one Genesis student into the Mystics in the past two decades. She must have been referring to Aria Loew.

Aria inspects the air that flows through her hands and says, "Though you've been here such a short time, so many ties bind you to our people." One dark eyebrow arches high in surprise as she adds, "Including to my brother." With a quizzical look, her thumb and pointer come together and pull at something invisible. As if feeling the tug, Michael, who is a few yards away, conversing with a bearded and bespectacled old man, turns to glance in our direction. When he sees us, he says some last words to the man and heads over. Aria releases the invisible something and scrutinizes me more closely. She is now exploring the air with both hands, tugging and pulling at an invisible tapestry woven around me.

It's pretty creepy, and it feels like she's doing some kind of divination, like maybe she can somehow know things I really need her *not* to know. I shift my feet uncomfortably.

Aria brings her fingers close to her face and inspects the emptiness between the pads of her fingers. "You have secrets," she says in a singsong voice, "but don't worry. I won't tell. Your intentions do not oppose my own." I release a tense breath, not at all comforted by her words. "A piece of advice,"

she says, meeting my eyes too sharply. "You should be asking more questions about why you needed to be rescued."

What the hell?

She drops her hands as Michael approaches, gazing at her with a beaming smile and arms outstretched.

"Ari!" He envelops her in a hug that she tolerates more than returns,
though her expression is pleased, with the quirk of a smile that reveals she
has the family dimple. "I see you've met Ada."

"Yes. She's fine. I don't mind her," Ari replies, and Michael's grin tells me
that this is her version of a compliment. "I need to visit the library," she says.
And then walks off, leaving me with an exasperated but still smiling Michael.

"Well, that's my sister."

"She seems lovely," I respond, and from the way he grins, I feel like I've
passed some kind of test.

Ugh, that dimple! I remember the feeling of being the one to make it
flash. I also remember the feeling of him playing guitar while looking into
my eyes the other night.

I want to say something, anything, to reignite that intimacy. But he's
already looking away, nodding at two professorial-looking women, and I
remind myself that I'm not supposed to be playing these games.

"I'll see you when Quorum begins," he says, walking toward the women.
Then he turns, gives me an encouraging smile, and adds, "Stop worrying. I
can tell you're worrying. Just answer their questions honestly. You're going
to be great."

The auditorium has amphitheater seating with a stage in the center. At the
front of the stage, there's a long table where the guildmasters sit taking notes.
I watch from a section to the right of the stage along with the rest of the
apprentices who will be presenting their galleries. Hypatia is sitting next to

me, vibrating with nerves and rhythmically running her tongue back and forth along her teeth. She'd missed lunch with us yesterday because she was receiving treatment for her mystery illness, and today she's positively shining with vitality. She keeps waving excitedly at her parents, who are sitting with Prince Alex. Because, of course, if Rafe is a prince, that makes Hypatia royal too. Can't say I saw that one coming.

The Quorum begins with reassignments from Avant, like Simon. He bumbles through his gallerie, but, honestly, compared to anything I'm used to from teen boys back home, it's quite an impressive display. I especially like one of his inventions—a lightweight portable boat that can be carried like a backpack and assembled quickly when necessary. It's cool, but when he's questioned about it, it's revealed that the motor is too heavy, and the boat has a tendency to leak. He also performs a song on his hurdy-gurdy—a guitar-like instrument with a hand crank and a wheel that is much less ridiculous than it sounds—and when it comes to music, he is, as Hypatia has told us, quite talented. He's reassigned from the Avant Artisan guild to the Genesis one, and he replaces his amethyst ring with a stud in his ear. Hypatia applauds enthusiastically for him.

The reassignments are followed by the masters who are seeking entrance to new guilds. Today's group is small and has no one that I know. The last group will be journeys qualifying as masters, but first the big deal that everyone is most excited for is the apprentice placements.

Headmaster Bloche calls up each apprentice one by one to present their gallerie and to be interrogated by the guildmasters. Pockets of the crowd cheer each time an apprentice accepts a position in one of the guilds.

I take deep, calming breaths the way my pitch instructor, Madam Adelina, taught me, but my nerves are tenacious, and it's hard to pay attention to the other galleries.

"Next apprentice is Hypatia Vanguard, fourteen years of age," the herald announces. "Her mentor is Donatello Bloche, headmaster of the Genesis Institute and master of the Sophist, Alchemist, and Cipher guilds." Wow, I didn't realize that the headmaster himself mentored Hypatia. I guess that's how it works when you're a member of the royal family.

I squeeze Hypatia's hand as she rises. Her clammy fingers squeeze mine in return, then slide out of my grasp as she walks confidently to the center of the stage.

Hypatia begins to present without even the slightest quaver in her voice. I want to see the gallerie she's put so much of her heart into, and I give her my full focus.

Her presentation is flawless, and I'm bursting with pride on her behalf, but at the same time, there's a stone in my stomach. She's only fourteen, and her gallerie is much more impressive than mine. She performs a beautiful song on the harmonica and displays a gorgeous clockwork owl she made. She animates the owl, demonstrating the strength of her Sire abilities, and it flies around the stage. She also presents a variety of fragrances she's developed.

The guildmasters ask her pointed questions, all of which she answers with confidence. She's invited into two of the Genesis guilds—the Ciphers and the Alchemists—as well as, to my surprise but apparently not to anyone else's, Avant's Blood Science guild.

"I would be honored to accept the position of journeyman to the Alchemist guild." Hypatia's voice rings out loudly.

The Alchemists erupt into cheers and cries of "Honor a Maker." I cheer along with them. I'm so happy for her. This world is new to me, but Hypatia has been preparing for this day for years. I clap enthusiastically, and Hypatia smiles at me before she heads off the stage. Her parents, along with Rafe and Prince Alex, flock to embrace her, their faces glowing with pride.

After Hypatia, there is a slew of other apprentices, a few of whom multiple guilds compete over. One apprentice conducts a symphony of tinkling glasses—without even touching them—by manipulating the sound waves utilizing only her voice. The Cipher guildmaster argues hard for her, but the girl chooses to join the Artisans. Another apprentice—who created a hair dye that changes color in different temperatures—accepts an invitation from Bioscience. Besides Hypatia's, the Avant guilds do not make any additional invitations.

Around me, the seats grow sparse.

And then the herald is saying the words "Next apprentice is Sire Ada Castle from New York. Seventeen years of age. Her mentor is Michelangelo Loew, Sophist master and provincial liaison."

I walk up to the stage. The guildmasters all seem to be looking down their noses at me, thinking, *Who is this impostor? She doesn't belong here. Where are we supposed to put her?*

A young apprentice has pushed over my table with my prepared materials.

"You may present your gallerie," Bloche prompts.

I swallow, then begin to present my work, starting with my best drawings, including the circulatory system piece. I read a short story and then demonstrate my ability to revive a dying philodendron plant. I was really nervous about this part, as my Sire abilities tend to be inconsistent, but after a nervous false start, I manage the task quickly. I then exhibit my design for window curtains made entirely out of woven living plants. I'd thought this was too silly to include, but Hypatia had told me it's the kind of thing the guildmasters like. I hope she's right.

It's time for my song.

I grit my teeth. I can do this. I've been practicing nonstop for two days.

I lift the guitar and start with easy strums the way Michael showed me, nothing too intricate or easy to flub until I become more comfortable.

The whole room is focused on me. How the hell does Kor do this in front of entire stadiums?

I start to sing, my voice only a little shaky.

> *These hands of mine*
> *Could sculpt a human out of stone*
> *Could draw the views of worlds unknown*
> *Could paint something with soul*
> *But instead*
> *These hands of mine are stained only with mistakes*

> *These hands of mine*
> *Could pull your heartstrings with a song*
> *Could learn the keys to play along*
> *Could write a symphony*
> *But instead*
> *These hands of mine stumble over clumsy notes*

I remember what Madam Adelina said, to find the truth of the emotions of the song instead of focusing on the technique. "Your world ruined your singing," she'd yelled at me. "They made you think that things need to be perfect. But beauty is in the flaws of truth. Stop covering up the truth!"

I try to sing my truth.

> *These hands of mine*
> *Could reach out so I'm not alone*
> *Could plant the seeds to grow a home*
> *Could hold your face between them*
> *But instead*
> *These hands of mine stay clutched behind my back*

I try my best to block out the crowd, to sing for no one but myself.

Will I do more on this earth than waste away my hours?
Can I do more for the earth than one day become her flowers?

As the last notes die out, I take a moment to compose myself. Following Madam Adelina's advice had brought on more emotion than I had intended, but I think it went okay. Maybe not great but at least a perfectly acceptable level of good.

I take a deep breath. "That concludes my gallerie," I say.

Although I'm mostly pleased, I can't help but notice how anemic my presentation was in comparison to the others.

Headmaster Bloche and some of the other guildmasters ask me questions about my strengths (plants) and weaknesses (math), specific interests (healing), and methods used in the work I presented. I answer everything as best I can.

"One last question," Bloche says. "How did you open your guild box?"

"Excuse me?"

"The box that was part of your application. The method used to open it can be a useful indicator for affinity and guild fit."

Oh. Was there more than one way to open it? And how come no one else was asked this question? Maybe only recruits get a puzzle box. Well, I'm not going to admit I tried to break it.

"I pricked my finger," I say.

Every single guildmaster's head shoots up at this.

"You used blood?" Bloche asks, with the faintest note of accusation. The gaze behind his smoky monocle bores into me.

"It was . . . an accident?" I respond.

The Blood Science guildmaster looks down in derision, but the others continue to stare at me quizzically.

Bloche clears his throat.

And then the Cipher guildmaster rises.

It's starting.

She says, "While we recognize that you have a strategic mind that would be beneficial to the Cipher guild, you have made it clear that mathematics is not a strength, and it does not appear that your interests align with our guild at this time. We do not extend an invitation to our guild."

I hadn't wanted to join the Ciphers, but that doesn't prevent the sting of rejection.

The Artisan guildmaster is already rising. He says, "Though it seems you have a propensity for art, considering that you are a Sire, we are surprised that you had not cultivated a more developed talent in any of the fine arts before arriving here, which may be a sign that it is not your true calling."

My muscles feel as tight as an overtuned string instrument. They're not going to accept me. The easiest guild to get into is going to turn me down.

"However," he continues, "you have made great strides in only a few months, and you clearly have an eye for aestheticism. Considering your potential, we invite you to join as a journeyman to the Artisan guild."

I breathe, panic subsiding.

"We especially enjoyed your song and both the technique and metaphorical expression of your painting entitled *Tree in Autumn*. If you choose to join our guild, we will foster your skills in both visual art and music. We would be honored to have you as a member of our guild." He takes his seat.

They like my work. I can't believe it. I don't yet know if any other guilds will accept me, but I already know I'd feel comfortable with the Artisans.

The Bioscience guildmaster stands next. This is it. My first choice.

The guildmaster says crisply, "Though you are a Sire, which is a quality that often makes for a good healer, no particular information has been presented to indicate that you are a good fit for the Bioscience guild. At this time, we do not extend an invitation to our guild."

My chest constricts. I needed to see the Bioscience Guild Testaments. Kor will be disappointed. But I find that I'm less disappointed than I expected to be. At least I have the Artisans. I shouldn't mind numerous rejections. They're to be expected. I'm a stranger to this place and am lucky to have received even one invitation. But Grandfather . . . I can't think about that right now. I'll find another way. I *will*.

The Alchemist Guildmaster stands. "You lack a steady hand." I guess she saw my trembling despite my efforts to hide it. "And proficiency with numbers, both qualities often necessary in our guild."

Oh no. How do the apprentices handle all these rejections? I want to dissolve into my own shadow.

"However, the fact that you have managed control over plant life before having any Sire training is a strong indicator that you have botanical gifts. We invite you to join as a journeyman to the Alchemist guild. We can foster your affinity for plants and introduce you to apothecary medicine, as you are interested in healing. It would be our honor if you were to join our guild."

Wait, what? The thrill of another acceptance has my heart pounding. And I didn't realize the Alchemists work with medicines, though now that I think about it, it totally makes sense.

The Sophist guildmaster—Professor Lovelace—rises. My stomach has calmed. I can handle more rejection now. I have two good options.

"Though you are unfamiliar with our history, your song and story both demonstrate an intuitive understanding of universal human experience. We are honored to invite you to be a journeyman to the Sophist guild. Our

guild would foster your songwriting and storytelling and could guide you
on various paths that you seem well suited for, including education, guidance, or psychological and emotional healing. We believe that you would be
a great fit for our guild, and we hope you agree."

Three invitations! That's the most offers any apprentice has had so far today.
And Michael's guild no less. My blood sings with triumph. I *can* fit in here.

A small voice in the back of my head reminds me that my purpose in
fitting in here has nothing to do with developing the skills the guildmasters
are speaking of, but I shush it.

It's now time for the Avant guildmasters. I square my shoulders ready for
their rejections.

The Blood Science guildmaster, Rafe's old master, doesn't even deign to
stand to acknowledge me. He speaks tightly, hardly opening his lips, yet his
voice booms across the room as he says, "The Blood Science guild does not
extend an invitation to Ada Castle of New York."

I expected as much. It's fine.

At least this is almost over.

The Mystic guildmaster—an extremely old man with a long white beard
and a large skullcap—rises on shaky legs. He grips his ivory cane with both
hands, and in a heavily accented voice that crackles like dead leaves crunch-
ing underfoot, he says, "The Mystic guild invites Sire Ada Castle to join us
as a journeyman."

There are numerous audible gasps around the room. His words were
somewhat muffled by his waist-long beard, but I'm pretty sure I heard him
correctly.

The Blood Science guildmaster's face is pinched. The Genesis guildmasters all have wide eyes. Even Bloche looks ruffled.

The Mystic continues. "You can complete your foundational studies here
at the Genesis Institute and come to the Academy at Avant to train in the

mystical arts after next winter's thaw, when the threat to our young Sires will have passed. We hope you will consider our offer, cousin."

Cousin?

He leans heavily on his cane and creakily lowers himself back into his seat.

I look around the room, at a loss, unsure of what just happened. The entire room is ghost quiet. All I can hear is my own heartbeat.

An Avant guild has invited me—a recruit—to join the most exclusive of all the guilds. And now I have more invitations than any other apprentice today.

It's time for me to make a choice.

16

I stand on the Quorum stage feeling the pressure of countless gazes watching, waiting for my decision. Other apprentices have had most of their lives to prepare for this choice, but all I have is now. I've been rejected by my first choice, but I now have several other offers, including a tantalizing new option that has just presented itself.

Should I consider the Mystic's offer? Hypatia said it's dangerous to study mysticism. Yet I can't deny that I feel a pull to it. Aria Loew had fascinated me, not to mention that I desperately want to find out why this mysterious guild that is so selective would ever want *me*. The idea of it makes me feel . . . elite, maybe even powerful. I'd be lying if I said I wasn't feeling some temptation to throw my plans to the wind and see what learning from the Mystics could mean.

But no. The Families need me at Genesis, right? And everything I've heard about Avant makes it clear it won't be hospitable for a recruit. I wish I could consult with Kor to be sure.

Everyone is still silently waiting for my answer, and I feel like I should just make an impulsive choice—the way I do whenever a waiter comes to take my order. Ugh. If I can't even choose an entrée, how am I supposed to make this decision that absolutely should not be rushed? I close my eyes, trying to think clearly.

I think about how Aria Loew seemed to *know* things. The idea that the Mystic guild probably has members who could divine my secrets reinforces my decision that it's not safe.

I have to choose between the Artisans, the Sophists, and the Alchemists. Michael had said to trust my gut. So I try. And when I do, strangely, the difficulty of the choice melts away. One guild feels like the obvious best fit, both for my talents and my priorities. I open my eyes.

"I would be honored to join the Alchemist guild," I say, my voice steadier than I feel.

And then I am deafened by the sound of cheers. The Alchemists in the audience are on their feet, applauding and roaring their approval.

I squint into the crowd, surprised to see all the beaming faces. Surprised by their whoops of welcome. They want me. I didn't expect that. I'm an outsider, a stranger who's been taking children's classes. I see Hypatia and Mbali standing among the Alchemists, applauding along with them, and I know I have a place by their side.

★   ★   ★   ★   ★

Michael approaches me when Quorum is over. "Your song was superb! I love how you altered the key in the bridge." That had been a mistake, but I guess it worked out.

"Thanks," I say, fingering the new emerald guildstone in my ear, my emotions still a blur from the whole experience.

Everyone is heading to the faire in the village, and we follow the crowd. Since so many people come from the different Maker communities for each Quorum, it's become tradition for craftsmen, traders, and performers to travel with their wares to the faire.

"I wait for months to get my favorite fudge," Michael chatters as we walk along the crowded forest path. "This one old lady from the Misty Isles makes it from a secret recipe. But she's getting on in years. I hope her recipe doesn't die with her."

"If you're charming enough, maybe she'll leave you the recipe in her will," I suggest.

"Don't think I haven't considered it. Most people I bother to charm have something I hope to inherit."

I look at him with one eyebrow raised.

"Your fuzzy polka-dot socks," he says in answer to my unspoken question. "The ones you were wearing when we traveled from New York."

"Your feet are almost double the size of mine. My socks will not fit you."

"But they *will* fit my hands, which is all that matters since I intend to wear them as mittens. I have always wanted fuzzy polka-dot mittens."

"Noted," I say with a laugh.

When we arrive at the village, it's unrecognizable. The normally sleepy stretch of road is bustling with people. Hundreds of stalls are propped up, their brightly colored canopies creating a patchwork tunnel of noisy and pungent activity.

I thought once we got to the faire, we'd part ways, but Michael stays by my side. "Today I will be your guide and introduce you to your first Quorum faire, and together we will celebrate your accomplishment!" I'm pretty sure he just wants to keep an eye on me since the faire is teeming with nonlocal Makers who may be uncomfortable with recruits. But I'm certainly not going to protest his company.

There are performers everywhere—mimes, musicians, magicians—along with unique crafts and aromatic foods. Clothing, sheet music, pigments, puppets. The air is wafting with every kind of smell: freshly baked bread, sizzling meats, spicy perfumes, earthy clays, wood, and wax.

And the *noise*. It's harmonious in its deafening discord. Instruments, singing, laughter, bells.

I gravitate toward a stall of beautiful Venetian masks—all intricate and delicate, made completely of glace—but Michael bounds in the opposite direction.

"Eureka!" he exclaims, heading toward a small stall piled with chocolate confections. His old lady and her fudge. I watch as he exchanges a flute—which he whittled out of a reed—for a brick of fudge wrapped in waxy linen. From the way the rickety old woman smiles up at him and pats his cheek, I wouldn't be surprised if she does indeed leave him her precious recipe.

We continue to navigate the rainbow of stalls, stopping often to watch performances or chat with friends. There's a strong Avant Guard presence. I steer clear of them as much as possible, though with Michael by my side, I'm not too worried.

We see Hypatia, who introduces me to a bunch of Alchemists she's already befriended. I should probably be making new friends in our guild too, but, well, there's always tomorrow. Or any other time when I haven't been offered Michael's undivided attention.

I make sure to visit Georgie, who is helping Elsa—the island's premier tailor—in exchange for her allowing Georgie to sell some of her own designs. Georgie is having a lot of success. She's sold more than half her wares, and she has a satisfied glow about her. I run my hands over a pile of fingerless silk gloves.

"These are beautiful," I tell her. Then, struck by a thought, I ask, "Did you have to open a guild box when you were recruited?"

"Yeah. That was a real head-scratcher."

"How did you do it?"

"I wrote a program that input every combination of the music notes until one tune finally opened it. It took three days."

Georgie amazes me. She's so talented with her clothing design, her art, and her coding. She's a Renaissance woman if I ever saw one. I wonder if I'll be able to accomplish anywhere near as much as her if I spend more time at the institute.

An elegant woman comes to look at some of Georgie's wares, but another woman rushes over and whispers something in her ear. The customer looks at Georgie with a mix of fear and distaste, drops the scarf she's holding, and says, "Never mind. I won't barter with an outsider."

Bright spots of pink flush Georgie's cheeks.

I'm incensed, and I start to follow the retreating woman, but Georgie holds me back. "Confrontation isn't good for business."

"Has that happened a lot?"

"Thankfully not too much, and only from nonlocals."

I take the discarded scarf and fold it. "Do you ever wish you could go back?" I ask. "To your old life?"

"No." She answers without any hesitation.

"Even after dealing with . . . ?" I wave my hand in the direction of the rude customer.

"Even with all that, being here is worth it. The opportunities for what I can accomplish here—despite the discomfort and prejudice—are a hundred times better than anything in the provincial world."

"The provincial world," not "home." Georgie has accepted that this place is her new home. And in a few months Headmaster Bloche will want me to do the same. But that's never been a real option for me.

Michael is browsing the wares of a bookseller, and I head in his direction, but the pleasant notes of a wind chime draw my attention to a tiny stall hidden behind the others. My curiosity is piqued, and when I draw closer, I see a sign that says HELIOTORCHES. I should get myself one of those customizable multi-tools—spoons—that everyone uses. I've been wanting one for a while. A handy tool always available for any and all spontaneous creative endeavors.

An old man with a shiny bald head tends the stall, muttering to himself grumpily.

"Hello?" I ask cautiously, wondering if he even wants customers.

"What?" he barks.

"I'd like to get a Heliotorch," I say.

The man sighs, then pulls out a large drawer and lays it on the table. A variety of tools are on display. "What mods are ya lookin' for?" His knobby-knuckled hands shift through the various items. He wears an onyx ring, a large one, indicating he's a master of the Mystic guild.

"Uh, what do you recommend?"

"Everyone needs a blade, a pencil, an' a torch." He plucks out the relevant mods—a sharp blade the length of my middle finger, a stick of graphite, and what looks like a sewing needle, but I know from seeing Georgie's that the tip lights up to be a very powerful flashlight.

He looks at the diamond in my ear. "You're a Sire, so you'll be wantin' a sparker." He adds an unfamiliar mod to the tray. In the drawer, I see what looks like a nail file and glance at my overgrown nails. "I'll take that," I say, "and that please," I add, pointing to miniature scissors.

I'm long overdue for a haircut. I've been meaning to ask Georgie to give me a proper cut, but I can at least trim off some of my dead ends in the meantime. I twirl a lock around my finger. It's almost at my elbows these days. I ruefully think of how annoyed my father would be. He always liked my hair to look tidy, and he used to trim it for me every week on Friday afternoon.

The man observes my hair and sucks his teeth, his watery eyes sharp. "Now, for the spoon itself," he says, with what sounds to me like a little less grump than before. "I have somethin' I think you'll like." He kneels to search through the recesses of an old chest, then rises holding a nondescript box. "Instead of a new Heliotorch, maybe consider this one, which needs a new owner." He opens the box, and my eyes widen.

The size of a small harmonica, the spoon is inlaid with a mosaic of dark green stone around a harp made of mother-of-pearl.

I want it.

"I don't have much sense, and that looks expensive."

"The cost is a lock o' your hair, three inches long and one inch wide."

My skin prickles. "Um, that's super creepy."

"That's the price if you want it."

I don't want to give this crotchety man my hair to do who-knows-what with, but the spoon is so lovely.

"Who did it belong to?" I ask.

"An old friend. He told me to hold on to it till he comes back, but I have a feelin' he won't be comin' back anytime soon."

I should just buy a new, simple spoon for a normal price, but my hand itches to hold *this* one, as if I'm meant to have it. "Okay, I'll take it," I find myself saying before I've even finished deciding.

The man assembles and attaches all my chosen mods to the spoon and then uses the new scissors to discreetly clip off his payment from an under-layer of my hair.

With my hand in my pocket clutching my new spoon, I join Michael, who's still distracted at the book stall. Among the piles, I find a beautiful deck of hand-painted cards with dragons, wind horses, and unicorns instead of royal face cards. It makes me think of Izzy. She's always been excellent at card tricks. I miss her so much. I'll have to ask Kor if he's learned anything new about what she's up to and see if he can convince Roman to put her in touch with me.

When Michael sees the cards, he says he wants to teach me a Maker game called Beg and Plea, and he purchases the deck.

"A Quorum gift," he says.

We find a table near the fountain, and a girl in a gauzy dress brings us glasses of fresh spiced juice. I listen to the instructions for the game with half an ear, and we casually play as we chat, but I keep losing because I'm too distracted by how very perfect the day is.

Michael presses me a bit on why I didn't choose the Sophists. What I don't say is that I'm relieved to be in a guild where—besides Foundations class—I can easily avoid having him as a teacher. Not that it should make a difference anymore. We've found a rhythm in which Michael is my mentor who I am fond of, in more of an elderly brother kind of way, all awkwardness behind us.

His eyes gleam as he wins another round of the game, and my heart speeds up when his hand brushes mine as he grabs the rest of my cards.

A brotherly kind of way? Blah. Who am I kidding?

Something neither of us has yet mentioned was my invitation to the Mystic guild. There's a niggling doubt at the base of my neck tormenting me over whether I should have taken their offer more seriously.

Michael deals me a new set of cards, but instead of starting another round, I say to him, "I didn't realize your sister was a Mystic."

He smiles. "Yes, it shocked a lot of people when she left the Genesis Ciphers. But physics and mysticism have more in common than you might think. Especially when it comes to theories surrounding the Universal Tapestry—similar to what is known as string theory in the provincial world. Have you heard of it? As I recall, you're a fan of theoretical physics." He winks.

I shake my head, unsure whether I'm comfortable with the fact that he's brought up a reminder of our first date. That is, our *only* date. This is not a date.

Michael continues. "The Mystics haven't extended an invitation to a Genesis apprentice in my lifetime, and Ari was one of very few Master applicants in that time."

"I don't understand. Then why did they invite me?"

"I guess I'm not the only one to realize you're special."

I feel a blush spread up my neck in a sensation that starts as pleasure and morphs quickly into irritation. We're supposed to have boundaries. That kind of teasing is not boundaries.

"Seriously," I say. "Should I have considered their offer?"

"Oh, absolutely not. Avant is no place for you, and mysticism is hazardous."

"But your sister—"

"Ari has always . . . painted using colors no one else can see. I understand why she needs to do what she's doing, but it doesn't stop me from worrying about her." He nibbles on his thumbnail, and I instinctively reach over and push his hand away from his mouth.

Why did I do that? It's not my place to police his habits. I drop my hand as I realize I'm still touching his.

As twilight paints the sky an inky lavender, the faire takes on new life. More of the stalls begin to serve food and drinks, and the mood shifts to one of feasting and dancing.

"Ada! Honor a Maker!" Kaylie passes our table, and she pulls me up into a hug. We invite her to sit with us, and Michael gets more drinks and a platter of scroll pastries (dough rolled up with chocolate, cinnamon, and jam into flaky spirals of deliciousness).

A young Valkyrie runs over to Kaylie. I thought I was used to seeing humans with wings, but this little girl—with her rosy cheeks, blond locks, and wings spread wide—looks exactly like a cherub from a painting. Kaylie dances with her and some of the other children, and Michael makes them all giggle by playing a silly song on a borrowed lute.

Soon a band—Simon's band, the rest of the members in town for Quorum—starts to play, and Kaylie pulls Michael into a dance. They twirl in happy circles.

I spot Rafe among the dancing bodies. He's with a gorgeous girl in a teal sari—though dancing might not be the right word for their slow-moving, sensual embrace. Rafe looks up, and our eyes meet for an instant before I quickly turn away, only to catch Michael's eye. He smiles at me before turning his attention back to Kaylie, who he theatrically dips toward the ground, both of their faces shining.

I get up from the table and walk over to where the fence looks out at the view of the cove. I gaze down to where the water roils in its own ferocious dance, years of crashing waves carving a beautiful sculpture from the cliffs.

Michael follows me over a few minutes later and pulls out his packet of fudge. "It's time," he says dramatically. He carefully unfolds the linen and hands me a small square.

I take a bite; it's pure bliss. "They definitely don't make fudge like this where I come from," I say.

Michael licks chocolate off his thumb in a way that really shouldn't be so appealing. "They've got some pretty good food over there too."

Michael is the only Maker I've met who has anything positive to say about provincial society. "What made you want to work as the provincial liaison?" I ask.

"I'm only a third-generation Maker," Michael says. "My mother's mother—my bubbe—came to the Makers as a teenager on a Kindertransport that was diverted to Avant during the Holocaust. Many of those children were sent back after the war, never really knowing the truth of who their caretakers had been. But my bubbe had met my grandfather and stayed to marry him."

The wounds of the Holocaust seem to haunt every Jewish person that I know, but I didn't expect those wounds to extend to the utopian bubble of the Makers. I guess it's a mild relief to know that the Makers did offer some help to those persecuted during the Holocaust. That they occasionally extend the barest of interventions.

My father doesn't have much family still alive, and he's never seemed able to talk about them, but I know that his mother's mother was a Holocaust survivor. I feel the echo of shared generational trauma with Michael. I never thought I could share any kind of history with a Maker.

Michael continues. "My mother always tried to hide her heritage, not wanting to call attention to having provincial ancestry, and she often spoke of the atrocities of the world that had allowed so much hate and destruction. But Bubbe—she wanted me to know that even though she'd left it behind, there had been beautiful aspects of her old life. She told me that while she had seen the worst of the world during the war, that was not all there was to provincial life. I was a thirsty audience for all her memories of the place that she had loved that no one else here seemed to care about or want to remember."

The sounds of laughter and chatter float by on the breeze.

"Does your sister have the same affection for the provincial world?" I ask.

Michael laughs. "Not at all. She was always more enamored with my grandfather's side of the family. My great-great-great-plus-a-few-more-greats-grandfather was a religious Kabbalist recruited by the Mystics."

"Oh. Was it more common for the Avant guilds to recruit from the provincial world in those days?" I ask.

He laughs again, but this time the sound is hollow. "Yes. Our society is made up entirely of recruits. We are a people defined by exile. Outcasts who wanted a better life than one under the Imperialists we fled from. But try pointing that out to those who resist new recruits now, and you'll find them spouting the same rhetoric our society was founded to combat." He sighs and looks down at my face, and that's where his gaze stays.

We sink into a quiet kind of communication that involves only our eyes and my fast-beating heart. The sun has all but disappeared, and it's one of those magical hours where the edges of reality begin to fade, and the moment itself has the fuzzy edges of a memory. We tiredly gaze at each other, the silence heavy and meaningful.

"Did you enjoy today?" He breaks the silence, and I can't tell if he's looking at my eyes or at my mouth, because I have stopped looking at his eyes to look at his mouth. There is tension in his lips, in his jaw, in his throat.

"Yes," I say.

"I'm glad." The words are almost a whisper, and they feel so intimate. More intimate than touch.

Michael blinks, then looks away. "It's late," he says. "I should get back." I nod, and he bends at the waist in a small bow. "I'll see you tomorrow, Journey Castle." The detachment in his voice almost blows the moment out of my grasp, and I immediately start to doubt whether it was even real.

"See you." I smile at him, and he walks away.

I turn my face to the breeze, close my eyes, and listen to the soothing sound of the waves violently pulling their sculpture from the stones below. I breathe in the air of this place that, if a million things were different, I might begin to call home.

17

As Hypatia and Georgie had predicted, I'm quickly invited to try out for the Alchemist hoverjoust team. I was hesitant at first, since I need to stay focused and not attract unnecessary attention, but Hypatia pointed out that it would be a great way for me to quickly integrate into our guild. It didn't take much to sway me since I wanted to do it anyway.

The hoverjoust arena is carved out of the bedrock on the westernmost side of the island. Its design is inspired by the Ancient Theatre of Epidaurus, and the amphitheater-style stone seating forms three-quarters of a bowl shape that is open to the ocean. In the center of the bowl is a dirt pit bisected by a fence, where the jousts take place.

I approach the pit with trepidation, but the team is warm and welcoming as they introduce themselves with lots of arm clasps and high fives. High fives aren't a thing here, but they seem to think it's a provincial greeting, and they do it enthusiastically, wanting me to feel welcome.

"I've been hoping you'd guild as an Alchemist ever since I saw your moves at the hover park!" says a tan boy with dyed green hair and very large biceps who I think is called Sebastian.

"Were you on a hoverjoust team in the provincial world?" asks a girl named Carlota.

I laugh. "There's nothing as cool as hoverjousting in the provincial world."

Miriam, the Alchemist team captain, claps her hands for order. "Let's see if you're a fit for the team! You already know how to use that, right?" She gestures toward Georgie's hoverboard, which is clutched under my arm.

I nod. I've been practicing more at the hover park and have even started to manage hitting the targets with my lance.

Miriam rummages through a basket full of protective gear and tosses me a padded vest, some kneepads, a shield, and a helmet. Most of it is made of spidersilk in shades of Alchemist emerald green and resembles medieval armor.

I pull on the gear and mount my hover. While the floor is packed dirt, there's a magnetic surface beneath it that engages the maglev of the hoverboard with a now familiar hum.

I feel good going into my first practice match against Carlota—that is until she's careening toward me with a massive lance aimed at the shield on my left arm, which suddenly feels far too small. I squeeze my eyes shut and do everything in my power not to follow my instinct to veer away. Carlota's lance crashes hard against my shield, my whole body jangling with the impact as I zoom past her to the other end of the pit. At least I stay on my hover and don't drop the lance. Carlota beats me 3–0.

Miriam has us do various balance and aim drills and rotates us through more practice matches, all of which I soundly lose.

The entire experience is . . . painful. The team is made up of competitive, well-trained athletes who have been playing this game for most of their lives. By the time we pause for a break, I've fallen numerous times, I'm sore in places I didn't even know existed, and I'm pretty confident that I'm not getting onto the team anytime soon.

But Miriam is surprisingly pleased with my performance. "For a total novice? We didn't expect anything different. In fact, we expected much worse. Welcome to the team!"

"I mean, you'll have to work on keeping your eyes open and on your lance control," Carlota pipes in.

"Who cares about lance control when she can stay balanced while moving that gravdamn fast?" Sebastian responds with a wink.

A gong indicates that the team's time using the pit is over, and everyone gathers their things as players from another team stream in for their practice. I glide toward the exit, but I overestimate my ability to jump a barrier and crash into it, landing on my hip, my face scuffing the dirt. I groan and roll onto my back.

A harsh laugh echoes above me, and I glance up to see Rafe. He looks scrumptious in his tightly fitted padded armor—all in Bio shades of amber—with his helmet in his hand and his blond hair flowing like some kind of punk rock Lancelot.

"You're the prospect the Alchemists have been excited about?" He does not look impressed. "I guess the Ciphers will be our only rivals for the title this year." He hops on his hover and glides off, making no effort to reduce the amount of dirt he sprays into my face.

"Hey!" Carlota shouts, gliding after him, but Sebastian and another boy, whose name I already forgot, hold her back.

"What did he say to you?" Carlota huffs. "I've already reported him to the Jousting Lodge once, and I will happily do it again if he's being a prejudiced son-of-a-sphinx. . . . "

"Ignore him," Sebastian says. "He's purposely trying to get a rise out of us."

"No, don't ignore him," Miriam objects. "Raphael Vanguard was the captain of the Blood Sci team in Avant before he transferred here. We have to take him seriously. He's our biggest competition—him and Hera. He knows how to use shame and intimidation against us. So don't ignore that kind of thing." There's fire in her eyes. "Let it make you angry, and use your anger to fuel your game."

We all clasp arms, and I see my determination reflected back at me on my new teammates' faces. When tournament season begins, we're gonna take that arrogant prince down.

⋆ ★ ★ ★ ⋆

I've been calling home every Sunday, so after practice I knock on Georgie's door, hoping to use her internet.

"Come in!"

When I enter, I find her excitedly typing and glancing back and forth between her monitors.

"I was going to ask if I could call my family, but you seem busy."

"Nah, I'm just working on one of my pet projects. Actually"—she waves me over—"you'll like this." Her fingers clack a percussive symphony on her keyboard. "I've been tracking different forums for conspiracy theories about our existence."

"You mean the existence of the Makers?"

"Mm-hm. They think we're so well hidden, and for the most part we are, but stuff gets out every now and then."

This gets my attention, for obvious reasons.

"Here, check this out." She's pulled up a web page. It's a conspiracy forum dedicated to "the Hidden."

"Some of their info is scarily accurate; there's no way it's only speculation. The main moderator goes by the handle Cicero. He seems to know the most."

I lean over Georgie's shoulder and skim through the posts, certain phrases sticking out. ". . . *poison that makes people forget . . . born with wings . . .*" I take control of the mouse and continue scrolling, goose bumps breaking out on my arms. ". . . *hidden location for hundreds of years . . . faked death . . .*"

Georgie's right; this is definitely more than just speculation. At the same time, plenty of posts are way off base. I see more than one entry about vampires and even one about the philosopher's stone, both of which I'm pretty sure are fiction.

I slow my scrolling when I reach an entire section on illness. According to these rumors, "the Hidden" can cure almost anything, including cancer. More than one person claims to have received miraculous medication from a mysterious benefactor.

"Have you warned anyone about this?" I ask Georgie.

"Nah. I haven't found anything concerning enough, but I thought you'd find it amusing. You're all set up to call your family whenever you're ready."

Once Georgie leaves the room, my first impulse is to check social media, but I decide not to. The last time I scrolled through my feeds, it left me feeling depressed about the superficiality of what used to matter to me. I can't decide whether my forced distance from those parts of my old life is a relief or a loss.

When Kor answers my call, it's clear that I woke him up. He tells me he's been under the weather and that I should give my updates to Alfie Avellino instead. Bluish veins show through his pale skin, there are dark circles under his eyes, and his hair, which he's normally so vain about, is badly in need of a cut.

"I'm fine." He waves his hand dismissively when I ask him if he's okay. "It's just a cold I caught while volunteering at the clinic."

I think guiltily of my own coldless, flueless winter due to my Maker inoculations. Why should he be sick when the cures exist here?

We say goodbye and I call Alfie, and it takes him less than a minute to start pissing me off. He bosses me around about things he wants me to do, even though he knows nothing about what goes on here, and he refuses to answer any of my questions.

Our raised voices must attract the attention of Dr. Ambrose, who appears on-screen and gestures away a seething Alfie—who flips me off with both hands before he leaves—to take over the call himself.

Dr. Ambrose listens patiently, peering through his gold-rimmed glasses as I give him my updates about what's changed now that I've joined a guild.

The institute begins a new term after each Quorum, and now, as a journey, my classes are entirely different from when I was an apprentice. It's nice to be around people closer to my own age, as the journeys are all mostly in their teens and twenties.

I still attend Sire lab and Foundations, but I now must also be a contributing member of my guild. I have Alchemy lab, where we work on projects to add to the guild's testament, and Phytology, where I've been studying plant life in a three-story greenhouse. The other day I learned to use my Ha'i to sprout a full-grown sunflower from a seed in a matter of minutes. I've also been studying nondestructive and nonwasteful agriculture methods (I go into depth with these for Dr. Ambrose since they should be perfectly easy to implement back home), and I've joined a rotation creating our guild's high material, glace. So far I just clean and melt down old products, but I hope to soon be able to understand its production enough to be able to pass on practical instructions to the Families.

I don't only take Alchemy-related classes. I also have multiple art studios and conservatories. In one class we've been learning about the physics of sound so we can physically manipulate things with music—it feels like actual magic.

When I talk about art classes with Kor, he often remind me to remain focused on gathering the information more important to the Oculus. But Dr. Ambrose doesn't do that. He seems equally interested in all my studies, and he takes detailed notes about my new classes so that he can consult with the Inner Chamber about whether there's anything specific they want me to glean for them.

When we're finished, I call Mom. She tells me she misses me and asks about my general well-being, but, as usual, she's too busy to do more than see my face and make sure I'm safe before she has to go and passes me on to Grandfather.

When his gaunt face appears on my screen, I almost burst into tears. He looks so ill. He's thinner than before—if that's even possible—and his skin is sallow.

"Grandfather!" I yelp. "I miss you so much."

"I miss you too, mi reinita. I miss you too. But maybe we'll see each other soon. Can you come home for Easter?" He starts coughing—a shuddering, phlegmy cough—and my heart hurts. He's getting worse. If anything happens to Grandfather that I could have prevented, I'll never forgive myself.

"Come, Tomás." Sal appears on-screen. "Sit back. I'll bring you some hot water with lemon."

Once I say my goodbyes, I go back into the common room and promptly start sobbing as I flip through pictures on my phone.

"You okay?" Georgie asks, pulling off her headphones.

"Yeah, just missing my family again."

She comes and sits next to me, and I show her my phone, scrolling through photos and pointing.

"This is my mom." She looks carefree and happy in this photo, sitting on a rock at the Ravine in Central Park, not a stitch of makeup on, her blond hair loose and blowing in the wind. It's an old photo. I haven't seen her that relaxed in years. There are a few more similar shots, reminding me of a time when my mother knew how to have fun. When did she change? And when did I start to forget this version of her?

I keep scrolling and almost show Georgie a picture of Izzy, but calling her my best friend doesn't feel true anymore, so I flip past all our selfies, trying not to start crying again.

"This is my cousin, Kor." I bring up a selfie of us making stupid faces on the set of his *Rolling Stone* photo shoot.

Georgie stares, bug-eyed, with her mouth open in a perfect round O. When she finally regains her speech, she asks, "Your cousin is Kor Chevalier?"

"Very distant cousin," I say defensively. "More of a friend."

"I might die." She puts the back of her hand to her forehead in a swoon. "Like, if there's a single guy on this planet who could turn me bi, it would be him."

Sigh. I didn't realize how nice it's been to be away from 24/7 Kor-mania.

"While I love Kor, I might puke if I am subjected to too much of your adoration," I say to Georgie, who is dramatically fanning herself.

She grabs an empty sewing box. "Here, puke bucket. I'm not about to stop."

"How do you even know about him?" Kor only shot to notoriety in the past two years, after Georgie had already moved to Arcadia.

She puts her hand on her heart. "Ada, I was a fan of Korach Chevalier before he was famous. I've been listening to his music for years." She closes her eyes and takes a deep breath. "Okay, I'm over my fangirl paralysis. Show me pictures of the rest of your family."

I open the most recent pictures I have of my dad. He's waving at the camera from a beach in Costa Rica, where, last I heard, he was spending his days playing guitar for tourists and surfing. His wavy brown hair is grown out almost as long as mine, so different from the neat cut he always had when I was young. I've been missing him more than usual lately. He'd love to know about my new interest in sustainable agriculture and that I've been getting better at guitar. We might finally have something to talk about.

I swipe to a photo of Grandfather. I only took it a few months before I left, but he was already so much thinner the day I said goodbye, and even worse today. I feel my tears returning. I hope he's okay.

The Makers could help him. I must get ahold of their cures or find a way to make Sire abilities more accessible. For Grandfather, for the Families, and for the rest of *my* world. Now that I'm an Alchemist, I have access to their Testament scrolls. I've gotten too distracted by guilds and guys and hoverboards.

It's high time I visit the Ark.

18

I asked Hypatia to come with me for my first visit to the Alchemist Guild Testament, and she scheduled us a time slot in the Ark for today.

As I approach the winding staircase that leads up to the Ark, I'm surprised to see that next to the ever-present stone-faced Guard stands Simon, wearing a matching black uniform. His shiny silver buttons are smudged.

"What are you doing here?" I ask him.

"My family doesn't want me to fall behind in my Guard training while I'm away from Avant, so I'm doing some basic training here. Congratulations on joining the Alchemists, by the way."

I have to blink away a vivid image of him flying over a field of flowers—Why am I still getting flashbacks from that annoying dream?—before I respond with, "Thanks. I really liked your hurdy-gurdy performance and your boat."

He lights up. "Thank you! Are you here to see your guild's testament?"

"Yeah, I'm just waiting for Hypatia."

"I'm here!" Hypatia sings, coming up behind me. The other Guard grunts, wanting us to move things along.

They search us—Simon's cheeks pinkening as he pats Hypatia's pockets—

and take everything we have, including both our spoons. Once cleared, we make our way up the twisty staircase.

At the top of the landing, there's a large circular desk. The pregnant steward I've been befriending, Xander, is on duty.

"Ada! Hypatia!" she greets us. "Congratulations to you both for becoming journeys."

At the sight of Xander's warm smile, an icy shard of guilt spears through me. Hypatia, Simon, Xander—they all trust me, and I'm planning to use that trust to steal from them.

But I know it's the right thing to do.

Xander escorts us into the sealed glass room of the Ark and carefully retrieves the Alchemist Testament. She removes the emerald-green velvet cover embroidered with the Alchemist emblem of a mortar and pestle in front of the Tree of Life, and she shows us how to unroll the scrolls and use the index system to find what we need. We wear protective gloves so as not to damage the parchment with the oils on our hands and use a pointer to direct our eyes over the cramped calligraphy. Touching the Testaments feels . . . important. It's just a scroll written by humans, yet it feels holy. I know some Makers would say it *is* holy. That human innovation is divine, the continuation of the work of the Conductor. It's easy to believe that sentiment when surrounded by the evolution of human advancement so carefully collected and treasured here inside the Ark.

Thinking of it as sacred certainly doesn't help me alleviate my guilt over appropriating it.

"What do you want to look at first?" Hypatia asks once Xander has left the room.

"Medicines," I say resolutely.

While I see absolutely nothing about giving Sire abilities to non-Sires, no conversation with Kor or online forums could have prepared for what we do find. The breadth of information in the index alone is overwhelming. I've only looked at one section in the actual scrolls, and already my mind is reeling. The recipes, trials, experiments, and results. The magnitude of how much the Makers have solved, how much they can prevent, how much they can cure.

Unrolled beneath my gloved hands are cures for genetic diseases, infections, cancers; references to Bioscience surgical procedures utilizing Sire healing. I don't know how I'm going to manage to get my phone in here, but I'm going to have to find a way. This information must be shared.

The words before me blur together as I think of packed children's wards, overflowing intensive care units, of global pandemics that have killed so many. The Makers could stop it all. I guess I've kind of known all along. But now I know *for sure*. And that makes it so much worse.

My anger grows until my hands tremble so hard that Hypatia takes the pointer from me before I accidentally gouge the sensitive parchment.

"Are you okay?" she asks.

"I'm fine," I snap. "Actually, no." I close my eyes and take a deep breath. "I'm not feeling too well. I think I should go."

"Of course," she says. "We'll come back another time. I'll get Xander to help me put everything away. You go lie down. You look pale."

I stand frozen for a minute. Then stalk out of the glass room.

I need to talk to someone about this.

We're slaves to viruses and disease.

Kor warned me that the Makers were hoarding more than I could fathom, but even being here for months, I didn't understand how right he was. I've been wasting valuable time. I remove my gloves and leave them on the desk, ignoring a startled Xander. I hurry down the stairs past Simon, who chases after me and returns my things, but I don't even thank him as I storm directly to the Spring wing.

I bang on Michael's office door, my eyes burning from unshed tears. Not everyone here knows about the rest of the world, but he does. Plus, he's a master and close to Headmaster Bloche; he has the influence to make change.

Michael opens the door. "Ada? What are you doing here?"

Kaylie is there too. "Are you okay?" she asks, rising from the ridiculously colored sofa. "Come sit. You don't look well."

I make direct eye contact with Michael and, without masking the accusation in my tone, I say, "I looked at the Alchemy testament."

"And?" Kaylie's expression is open and concerned, but Michael looks down. He knows why I'm upset.

"How can you let so many people suffer when you have the means to help them?"

"Help who, Ada?" Kaylie puts a calming hand on my shoulder.

I turn to her, softening my tone. "The world," I say. "Everyone else. There's so much wrong with the provincial world that could be solved with Maker knowledge. But you just stay in your bubble, helping only yourselves."

Kaylie looks at me with pity. "It's not so simple—" she says.

"That's not how it works—" Michael starts at the same time.

I throw up my hands in exasperation, glaring at Michael. "We're talking about an entire world of suffering!"

I brace myself for indifference or more excuses, but instead he says, "You're right. I wish it could be different." He turns away, slamming his hands onto his desk. "You think it doesn't pain me, too? My grandmother only escaped genocide because it was a time that the Makers deemed it acceptable to interfere. But these days we're not doing enough. I worry about it constantly." He pushes off from the desk, drags both hands through his hair, and starts to pace.

Kaylie seems taken aback by his outburst, and Michael tries to explain to her. "You don't understand; you haven't seen it. Their world . . . There are so many things we could make better—" He gives up and turns to me with a hopeless look. "But you don't understand either. You think if we just ship off boxes of medicine, everything would be solved? The Sophists have debated this for years. I've petitioned the Council myself. But the risks aren't worth the little we can do."

Kaylie adds, "Our advancements involve extremely sensitive knowledge that is bound to be misused. Every innovation that lands in provincial hands is eventually used for violence and war. They can't be trusted—"

I know that Kaylie has grown up brainwashed by these ideas, but it's still hard for me to keep the outrage out of my voice as I say, "You don't know them. How do you know you're more trustworthy than them?"

"It doesn't matter, Ada," Michael says, resigned. "Their world has plenty of solutions already, and it's not enough to truly fix things."

It's *my* world, not *their* world. I want to shout it, remind him that this is personal for me. But I hold it in. I just joined a guild, made an unspoken commitment that I'm on my way to accepting this society as my own. I can't let anyone, even Michael, doubt my allegiance. I need my cover to remain flawless because, ultimately, if I can't convince the Makers to share their knowledge willingly, I'll have to steal it. And I'll need to be trusted to pull that off.

Michael continues. "Anytime we've tried, they find ways to hoard the knowledge, create scarcity, drive up prices, and make a profit."

"As opposed to hoarding it for one tiny, insular society?" I challenge.

Michael's brown eyes flash defensively as he steps closer, his tall frame towering over me. "You know hardly anything about us, Ada. We have expanded beyond our insular society many times in history. We shared everything with the Matriarchy of the Isles and the Prophets of Naiot. We share with those who place the needs of humankind above their own wants. With those who actually make an effort to tap into their creative potential and contribute to the advancement of the world."

The absolute nerve of him. "Newsflash, Sophist master." I jab my finger at his chest and am met with the solid resistance of stubborn man. "Most people can't use all their creative potential because they're too busy devoting their energy to daily *survival*. It's easy for you to celebrate yourself for advancing society when all your basic needs are met for *free*. When you don't have to devote the majority of your time to whatever soulless job will pay the rent."

"It's a broken system. I don't disagree."

"A broken system you have the power to help! And it should be your top priority. Never mind individual suffering. Think of the planet. I *saw* those scrolls, Michael. That information could be used to battle pollution, global pandemics, climate change." I think of all the information that Grandfather forced me to read up on, the suffering of our planet that I didn't want to face when I was powerless to prevent it.

But I'm not powerless anymore.

"If the provincial world starts crumbling to the ground, you think your hidden communities will remain safe? If you ignore their problems, they'll become your problems."

"You think we don't know that?" Michael responds, his voice rising. "You think more knowledgeable minds than yours haven't been debating these very issues for decades? You think we haven't tried sharing information about sustainability, medication, vaccinations? It doesn't make anything better. Giving the provincial world quick fixes won't change anything until they deal with inequality and corruption."

"You have solutions for that, too!" I shout at him.

"Not ones they are willing to implement!" he shouts back.

Kaylie puts up her hands and tries to interject. "Why don't we relax—" But we both ignore her. I'd practically forgotten she was here, my entire world shrinking down to just Michael and me, standing too close together. Yet there is a chasm between us that may be too wide to ever bridge.

Michael tries a little more calmly. "If you would let me explain—"

"There's no explanation for selfishness." I turn away from him. Before I had doubts that maybe the Makers didn't actually know how bad it was. But they've known all along, and they're still not willing to help.

Kaylie says to Michael, "Maybe she should meet Hilde."

"I guess, maybe," he says, exasperated.

She looks to me. "Hilde is a friend of ours who . . . feels similarly to you. She's devoted her life to helping those suffering in the provincial world. Last I heard, she was at a refugee camp with an outbreak of—" She turns to Michael and asks, "Malaria?"

"Cholera, I think," he says with a sigh.

"Why aren't more Makers doing what she's doing?" I ask, my curiosity piqued.

"Well, her methods aren't very practical—" Kaylie starts.

"She's foolish and reckless," Michael interjects.

"That's not how I would put it," Kaylie says.

"She was perfectly fine, then one day went completely out of tune." He shakes his head. "But I do think it could be good for you to meet her, to help you understand." He looks pained. "I'll make the necessary arrangements."

"I'll gather some supplies to send with you," Kaylie says, heading toward the door.

When the door closes behind her, Michael says, "I'm sorry. I shouldn't have raised my voice." When I say nothing, he steps closer. "Ada, I don't want to fight with you."

I don't want to fight with him either, with this man who has always felt like an ally, who had faith in me even when I didn't have faith in myself. But I've built him up in my head as something he's not. He may be handsome and generous and kind, but he's no paradigm of idealism. He's just as hypocritical as everyone else here. And he's definitely not on my side.

I meet his eyes. "This is not a fight, Michael. This is me getting a reality check. You've spent so much time trying to prove to me how special, how superior the Makers are for their dedication to making a difference. But that idealism is nothing if it ignores the majority of the world."

"Ada, my entire job as liaison is to make inroads to eventual change in our relationship with the provincial world. I'm not ignoring anyone. Improving this situation is what I've dedicated my life to."

"Keep telling yourself that if it makes you feel better," I respond. Michael flinches. I shouldn't let my true feelings show like this. I need him to trust me. But as usual, Michael draws the raw truth from me, even as I lie my ass off to everyone else. "You may have a little more respect for *my people* than other Makers. You may be more willing to bring in strays to join you in keeping your secrets. But that's not real change."

"It's not up to me, Ada." He sounds tired, resigned. "I'm limited by the permission of the Council—"

"No. Don't shift the blame. I don't care about the Council. They're just waiting for some prophesied baby to be born instead of making anything happen themselves." I walk over to his shelf of provincial records and run my hands along the sleeves. Elvis, the Beatles, Nirvana. In Florence, Michael had confessed to being scared of letting people down by questioning what he'd been taught is right. The memory pricks at me now, surprisingly painful.

"You're not like them," I say. Unsure if it's a statement or a plea. "Corrupted by Maker propaganda, fearing an overblown enemy. You know that most provincial people aren't a threat." He's followed me, and when I turn, he's so close that I have to look up to meet his gaze. "You say you've tried? What have you actually done?" His jaw is clenched, hands balled into fists by his sides. "Or do you just bite your nails and then keep playing the role of the headmaster's perfect poster boy until the next time you're inconveniently reminded that you should feel guilty?" He swallows, his eyes blazing.

Maybe it's not fair of me to say these things to him. After all, I'm just as experienced at ignoring the pain of the world to assuage my own guilt. But I'm ready to wake up.

We stare at each other in silence. We're standing too close. He parts his lips as if there's something he wants to say. I feel the huff of his frustrated breath, but he swallows his words down. I watch his Adam's apple travel the column of his throat, and even now a part of me wants to touch it. My eyes flick to his lips, and the way his teeth sink into his bottom lip makes me think he wants to touch me, too. But when I slip past him and stalk to the door, he doesn't stop me.

I'll meet this Hilde, but I don't think she'll change my mind. The Families had the right idea in sending me here, in wanting a share of the Makers' knowledge. And I'm over my apprehension about deceiving them. They don't deserve my guilt.

19

A couple of days later, I'm in the library car of the Atlas, exploring the stacks. Michael sits stiffly, his right knee bobbing up and down faster than a heartbeat.

This is the first time we've been alone together since our fight, and I'm awkward and unsure how I'm supposed to feel. I stay focused on combing through the bookshelves instead of having to face him, but the sound of his constant fidgeting is making me nervous.

"Why are you so anxious?" I ask him.

"What? Oh. It's been a while since I've seen Hilde." He sighs. "Seeing her can be . . . emotionally draining."

"How so?"

"She's very intense and has a way of making you question your decisions. Also, well, we used to . . ."

"Oh."

"It was a long time ago."

The awkwardest of pauses.

"Do you still have feelings for her?"

"Yes, but it's not . . . like that." His gaze is far away. "You'll see what I mean. You'll love her too."

Who said anything about *love*?

Soon, the Atlas arrives in Morocco, where we catch an airplane that takes us somewhere very sandy. Michael has arranged for a jeep, and he drives us through stretches of desert and in and out of poverty-stricken towns. The areas we pass look completely foreign, and for the first time I think about the fact that most of the provincial world is just as much a mystery to me as the world of the Makers.

After a lot more desert, the jeep stops when a small camp comes into view. As I climb out, hot, dry air engulfs me, and I'm instantly thirsty and itchy.

A girl in dirty cargo pants trudges over from the camp.

"Let me guess," she says to Michael. "You're here to present me as a cautionary tale?"

She looks incredibly familiar, though I'm sure I've never met her before. I try to puzzle out where I could have seen her. She has a unique kind of loveliness, a blending of varied ancestries that I've noticed in many Makers. Sun-bleached loose brown curls frame a russet face with a liberal sprinkling of freckles.

"Hills." Michael walks to her and wraps her in an embrace. She doesn't reciprocate, but she doesn't draw away, either.

Once he releases her, he holds her at arm's length and examines her. "Are you well?"

"Of course not."

Michael sighs and drops his arms. He waves me over. "Hilde, this is Ada. She's a recent Sire recruit."

Hilde nods curtly to me, then moves on without missing a beat. "Listen, Michael, I need you to speak to Ari and tell her to stop her games."

"What?" Michael asks, clearly perplexed.

In a swift motion that has Michael sucking in his breath and me freezing in place, Hilde lifts her shirt.

There's a tattoo on her abdomen, words scrawled in a spindly script. The skin around each letter is pink and sensitive. The words are flipped in mirror image, so it takes me a moment to decipher what it says.

Hildegard, go home!

"I'd recognize Ari's handwriting anywhere. We exchanged pigeons during class all our years as apprentices," Hilde says. "This hurts to perdition, mind you."

But Michael isn't looking at the tattoo. A sour feeling churns in my gut as his gaze roams over her exposed figure. However, it's only concern that fills his eyes.

"You're not eating enough," he says tenderly. "What happened to the nutrition loaves I sent you?"

"Oh, don't be ridiculous," she snaps. "I'm fine. There are others who need that nutrition more than I do." She points petulantly at her tattoo. "Hello, Michael? Your sister is writing on my body from oceans away, and it grav-damn hurts."

"I didn't know she could do that," he admits.

"Some weird Mystic thing, I'm sure. It probably involves a Ha'i stone or Kabbalah or something."

"I'll talk to her," he sighs, "though she's not wrong. You should come home."

Hilde pulls down her shirt and rolls her eyes. "I have dying children to see to. Are you here to help, or just to nag me?" She trudges back to the camp, and we follow after her, each holding a bag of the supplies Kaylie sent.

Nothing could have prepared me for the horrors of the refugee camp. Hilde explains that it's relatively new, so I'm surprised by the sheer size. The number of displaced people living in such appalling conditions. They had to leave their village because of a war only a few months before, and the disease swiftly followed due to a lack of clean water. The nearest medical professionals are aid workers at a larger camp about a two-day walk away.

Hilde sends Michael off to help with the healthy children and gives a young teenage girl, Asha, instructions in a language I don't understand about what to do with all the supplies we brought. Then she leads me to another part of the camp.

"Did they tell you I went crazy?" she asks me over her shoulder. My silence is her answer. "People like to call women crazy when they don't understand us. We feel things too strongly, we're hormonal, we overreact. Well, if getting a glimpse of the truth of the world makes us crazy—maybe the world is the problem, not us."

Behind one of the tents is a small green garden that stands out against the endless sand.

"How do these plants live in this environment?" I ask.

"They don't. Despite the fact that they're all tough breeds—mostly weeds that will grow anywhere—I still have to revive them daily using my Sire abilities. But they're invaluable for medicine and nutrition."

"I'm good with plants."

"Excellent. Then you can help me grow what I need. It takes some finesse in these harsh conditions, but I'll show you what works for me."

After we tend and harvest the garden, Hilde brings me along to check on her ill patients. Many of them are quite sick, and I have to suppress horror, disgust, and fear.

She also has me help draw her blood.

"I have universal blood. Comes in handy here." Thankfully, she does all the sticking of needles herself, but even just helping with the process has me dizzy and nauseated. "Maybe don't mention this part back at Genesis," she cautions. "They can be weird about blood stuff."

As I watch Hilde arrange a fridge full of her own blood, I can't help but think that she doesn't seem "foolish and reckless" or "crazy" to me. In fact, she might be the sanest person I've ever met.

"We should test your blood. Sires can donate frequently, but if you're universal too, it would be nice to have extra on hand to give myself a break."

As she draws some of my blood, she says, "So, Michael recruited you from the provincial world?"

"Yes."

"He's weirdly obsessed with provincials. We used to tease him that he'd end up recruiting himself a lover."

Heat rushes to my cheeks. "It's not like that," I say.

"It's always like that with Michelangelo Loew." She looks me up and down. "And I've been there before. I know the signs."

The desert might swallow me whole.

The sound of yelling has us rushing out of the tent. Asha is running toward Hilde, her eyes swimming with panicked tears.

Hilde jumps into action. "Follow me!" she instructs.

"What is it?"

"Her baby brother."

We arrive at a tent with a dirt floor and mattresses taking up most of the space. A crying woman holds out a toddler in our direction.

Hilde grasps the boy and swears under her breath as she takes his temperature and listens to his heartbeat.

She extends him out to me and says, "You need to use your Ha'i to shock his heart while I administer fluids."

I refuse to take the boy, terrified. "You do it. I don't—I'm not good at conducting."

"No. I have overactive Ha'i and a tendency to burn people when I get emotional. He's very small, so you're safer."

My heart pounding, I take him in my arms. He seems so frail.

"Here, make shiin on his chest," she encourages. I do so, my hand trembling. I feel the child's erratic heartbeat beneath my fingers. "Just a light pulse."

"I can't do it." I'm too scared, too riled up; I have no control.

"Yes, you can," Hilde instructs calmly. "I saw you make chickweed bloom in a desert; you can help this child. Tell me what you're thinking, how you're trying to access your Ha'i." She speaks so calmly while at the same time inserting an IV into the boy's tiny hand.

"I . . . I'm trying to pull it up from the well within me." Like Master Liu had taught me. I taste salt on my lips and realize that I'm crying.

"Okay. The problem is that a well draws water from a preexisting source, so if your source is dry, you are left with nothing. As a Sire, you *are* the source. You're making something from nothing. Don't think of yourself as pulling the Ha'i. Imagine bringing it into being."

Holding my breath, I close my eyes and imagine my belly as a black void, and then I envision a mini burst of light exploding into golden rays. I pull those rays through my hands and feel the warmth of Ha'i spread into the baby's body.

"There you go," Hilde encourages. "Now one more time."

I conduct, and with the pulse of Ha'i, I feel the boy's heartbeat stop, then start again in a more natural rhythm.

Only then do I breathe.

As soon as the baby is stable, Hilde has me pass him back to his mother, who can't stop crying and kissing me.

And then we move on because there's more to be done and no time for rest.

I help Hilde for hours. Crushing plants into mixtures. Distributing food. Purifying water. Administering medicine.

Digging graves.

I'm working on autopilot, like a golem, overcome by feeling so much that I can't feel anything at all.

"You're holding up well," Hilde says to me at one point. "I'm impressed. I thought you'd run crying after an hour."

"If this is their daily life, what right do I have to run from one day?"

Hilde nods approvingly.

I say, "I just don't understand how the world allows this to happen . . . how they can neglect all these people." There's plenty of wealth in the world, plenty of food, water, medicine going to waste daily.

"This is not just a result of neglect," Hilde explains. "The people responsible for this? For so many other humanitarian crises? They're allied with the leaders of powerful countries and multinational corporations. You're from the United States? They fund the corrupt governments who should be taking care of these people, and they don't demand this treatment stops. It's too easy to let tragedy happen far away when you're not the one suffering and when interference would directly affect the affordability of the resources and products you rely on for daily life."

There's a part of me that wants to close my eyes and stop seeing, that wishes I could go back to not knowing. "Why would anyone at Genesis think that showing me this would make me understand why they don't do more to help?"

"They want you to see that your world can't be helped by easy fixes. The solutions that these people need—access to clean water, minimal food rations, humane living conditions, basic health care? Your world has all those things already, and yet these people still suffer. There are a small few that can be helped by people like you and me and the aid workers, but there will always be more."

"Then why are you here?"

"Because I can't *not* be," she says simply. "But I know that not everyone can be here. Genesis is solving new problems, and that's needed too."

"But you think they should do things differently?"

"Some things." She shrugs. "No society and no individual is perfect."

When I lived in New York, this horrifying reality was so foreign. Why worry about catastrophes so far away when there were homeless people on my own doorstep—sometimes literally. But now that I've been living among the Makers on Arcadia, coming here feels like coming back to my people. They may not speak my language or look anything like me, but this is *my* world crumbling to ruins.

Perhaps coming here has made me realize no solution is simple, but it has not convinced me that the Makers couldn't make things better if they shared their knowledge. Not just of medicine and technology, but of philosophy and structures of government that could lead to widespread change.

Hilde has me sanitize before I leave, but I feel like I'll never wash away the smell of death. The reek of a whole world's apathy.

Before he ushers me back to the jeep, Michael takes Hilde's hands in his. "I know you've received our messages. You know Sires are being hunted. If you still refuse to come home, you need to hide better."

"I'm hidden fine."

"I found you easily."

"Maybe that's because I wanted you to find me."

"Hills, I'm serious. Sires are being kidnapped all over the world. You need to move on from here and disappear. Even from me. Tell me you understand."

She narrows her eyes at him. "What are you planning?"

"I'm not planning anything. I'm just doing what has to be done."

She stares at him for a long moment, their hands still gripping each other. "You think you're so different from me, Michelangelo Loew, but you're wrong."

I agree with her. He would be doing what she's doing if he weren't so set on trusting his precious council. I wonder if that's what broke them up. That question ties my feelings into a complicated knot of disappointment and relief.

On the ride back to Arcadia, I can't stop thinking of the faces of the children, of the bodies.

"Do you understand now?" Michael asks me.

"Yes," I say.

I understand, all right. But I definitely haven't changed my mind. The opposite, in fact. More than ever, I blame the Makers for letting my world destroy itself.

20

A week later, I'm on the Atlas again, this time with Georgie—and pretty much every Arcadia resident over the age of fifteen—on our way to Carnevale. Much of the furniture has been removed to accommodate so many people. Our train car is particularly busy as the bar is one carriage over. My neck aches from craning to see everyone's splendid outfits, which range from elaborately fancy to casual to full-on space age. There are styles plucked from every era and every culture—the wonders of fashion not dictated by commercialism.

It's exactly the kind of distraction I need.

The days since meeting Hilde have been intense and charged with a lot of emotion.

But I've also begun to relate more to my Maker peers. I had previously kind of lumped them all into the category of guilty for hoarding their resources from my world. But my time with Hilde made me realize that most of them are really no different from me. I have always benefited from resources and privileges denied to many and had never truly understood to what extent. I get that most of the apprentices and journeys I interact with daily are not the ones responsible for Maker choices on the whole.

It's the ones who know better who have kept my anger bubbling and fueling a new level of laser focus on my mission. And Carnevale has been the perfect encouragement. While I've been able to show Kor things over video call, knowing how good Georgie is with computers, I've never felt I could safely email anything to the Families without her knowing. So I've been looking forward to getting off the island to the vicinity of cell phone service where I can finally send all my collected materials over.

With my renewed focus and Carnevale fast approaching, I've been on a spree of gathering as much information as I can—detailed notes from all my new journey classes, sketches of the layout of the island and institute, photos of samples from the Alchemist lab. Last week I camped out in the library for an entire night to observe the security protocols for the Ark and the Guard changes and schedule.

But it's been a lot, and I'm worn out and ready for a break.

I can't wait to just have fun and dance and not think about the atrocities of the world, or my responsibilities, or boys who don't like me back.

Michael had explained the history of Carnevale to us in Foundations class. During the Renaissance, Carnevale—once a major holiday in Venice celebrating hedonism—gave the original Makers of Avant the chance to come out of hiding and celebrate with old friends. The practice of wearing masks made it easy to keep their identities hidden. Hundreds of years later, when the celebration was banned by the Church, the Makers continued to celebrate beneath the streets of Venice as an act of rebellion. Nowadays, so many years after the Makers have stopped caring about the goings-on of the provincial world, and with the invention of the Atlas allowing the Genesis Makers to join, Carnevale has become a tradition where all the Maker youth get together to celebrate their freedom of creativity. Masks are still a common accessory, but they are made of glace so as not to obscure the wearer's identity—a sign that in Maker society, no one need hide their creative pursuits.

"I'm loving the new you," Georgie says. She's referring to my outfit, which is not at all my usual style.

Carlota from my hoverjoust team lent me a white Grecian-style dress that deeply plunges down the back and has a high side slit. It clings and reveals more than I'm used to, but it certainly accentuates all the right curves. It even has pockets. Mbali gave me her recipe for an elixir that's transformed my unruly waves into an artful mass of loose curls, which I topped with a delicate gold-leaf circlet (that I crafted myself). I feel pretty, like I actually want to be looked at.

I gesture at Georgie. "You look amazing. I still can't believe you designed and made that from scratch."

Her outfit is resplendent—a tailored ocher coat that sweeps into a long floor-length A-line. The front of the coat is open, revealing a high-necked ruffled white blouse tucked into purple velvet trousers and heeled combat boots. A black homburg hat is perched at an angle on the large bird's nest of her hair, which has been teased and swept up like gold and purple spun sugar. She looks beautiful, outlandish, and totally Georgie.

Whispered giggles and the expectant straightening of postures inform me that someone desirable has entered our car. I turn to see Rafe as he traipses through, a stunning blond on his arm. They're followed by his regular retinue of beautiful people, all wearing the same holier-than-thou expressions. But Rafe stands out from them all. Many pairs of eyes—lashes fluttering— follow his movements, and as he gets closer, my own lashes betray me and join in.

His loose golden hair just barely brushes his broad shoulders. He rarely wears it down. I don't really like long hair on men, but he's pulling it off. He's pulling it off so well, in fact, that my mouth grows dry as he nears our seats. He has a regal air about him in a burgundy cravat and jacket that looks straight out of the Victorian military, a rich navy velvet with double-breasted rows of gold buttons. The whole outfit is pulled together with a pair of tightly fitted jeans.

Rafe's date is a Valkyrie, her backless dress exposing an elegant pair of wings, which glimmer under the train's lighting. I don't notice much else about the dress, as I'm too distracted by how much it doesn't cover—endless tan legs, and curves, and shimmery skin that she's maneuvering to press up against Rafe every which way. She looks vaguely familiar from Rafe's posse at the institute, but she's not one of the girls he's been flirting with recently (not that I'm keeping track). Guess she got a promotion.

As they approach us in a cloud of perfumed air, Rafe looks over and catches me staring at him. I expect no acknowledgment, but he elegantly arches a solitary brow and peruses his eyes languidly up my body. Heat rushes to my face, and as our gazes lock, his icy irises flash with a familiar predatory gleam. Then his expression turns bored again, and his eyes slide back to the adoring crowd ahead. Georgie watches the interaction, ignoring the sneers coming her way from Rafe's lackeys, her brows raised with a question that remains unvoiced even once the whole too-pretty group has sauntered into the next car.

I could write a sonnet on all the ways I loathe how hot Raphael Vanguard is. Whatever. Even if we didn't despise each other, I've learned my lesson about guys who have that kind of magnetism. Having one shining star with his own gravitational force in my life is more than enough.

At the thought of Kor, I clutch my phone in my pocket. I've come prepared for entering the realm of sweet, sweet cell service. When we traveled to Hilde, I'd timed the distance from Arcadia to the New York City station. I've been keeping track, and we should be close. "Be right back," I say to Georgie. All I need is the barest of a connection to send off all my materials.

I duck into a lavatory just as the train passes through the air locks into the City Hall station. I check my phone, and as two service bars appear, a string of messages lights up my screen. Most from school friends who don't know where I've been. I'll look through them later and use Georgie's computer to DM the people who deserved better than me dropping them with no explanation. For now I focus on quickly setting up and sending everything the Families need, and then I head back to Georgie.

As I make my way back down the aisle, I'm jostled by a short person in a bat mask as they hurry past me. Weird that they're already wearing their mask and that it's opaque black instead of glace. I turn in curiosity to get another look and see an awfully familiar crooked blond braid disappearing into the next train car.

That little minx! I thought Hypatia had given up on her stowaway plans. I change direction to catch up to her, but by the time I pass into the bar car, I've lost sight of her in the crowd.

"Excuse me. Excuse me. Pardon." I make my way through the loud throng. Hypatia is still nowhere to be seen. I head toward the exit to the next car but then I jolt forward, blinded by sudden darkness as the power blinks out and the train comes to a screeching halt.

I hear more than a few cries of pain. I'm not hurt because I've collapsed into something solid and warm. A hand steadies me and prevents me from toppling. I instantly know who has caught me by the way my skin flares to life when his hand grazes my exposed back.

Rafe.

It's clear when he realizes it's me by the way his body stiffens. He releases me and steps away, and I'm immediately jostled by the panicked swarm. I teeter and try to reach blindly for the ceiling rail, but I'm too short to reach it, and the crush of bodies pushes me to my knees. I let out an inelegant squeal, praying I don't get trampled.

As the initial panic settles, people start pulling out their spoons to light their torches. Rafe and a few of the other Sires produce flares of Ha'i, illuminating the car with an eerie glow. When Rafe sees me on the floor, he sighs in exasperation and pulls me back up against him. He mutters something that sounds like, "She can't even stand on her own two feet."

I ignore the words and breathe in the relief of not having to worry about dying by poorly placed stiletto. "Thanks," I say to Rafe, and I try to make my own Sire glow, but it keeps winking out.

"Stop wiggling," he says, stilling my hand. "Something's wrong. Nothing should ever cause an outage like this." His eyes narrow, and he glares down at me accusingly. "Have you done something?"

"Seriously? You're still going down that road? I thought we were past distrust and on to simple, tepid loathing."

Before he can answer, the lights flare on, and the chaos calms as the train lumbers back to life. It occurs to me then to tell Rafe that Hypatia snuck aboard so he can look out for her, but he's already releasing me and stalking off without so much as a goodbye.

I see Georgie in the crowd and head toward her, but even though the shoving has stopped, I feel unsteady with the absence of Rafe's strong body supporting mine.

21

We're here. As the crowd presses toward the exit door, I lose sight of Georgie, but when I spill out onto the train platform, I find Michael and Kaylie.

At the sight of Michael's tall form and floppy hair, adrenaline shoots through me. He's wearing a dapper wool suit, the jacket open over a Beatles T-shirt. I've grown used to seeing him in his long professorial jacket and dress shirts, but now he looks more like the guy I met in Italy. More boyish, so if I squint, those inconvenient few years between us can almost melt away. I haven't seen him since our trip to visit Hilde, and suddenly I'm nervous. I'd been holding on to my righteous indignation, but now I can't quite remember why I'm supposed to be mad at him.

"You look beautiful," Kaylie gushes at me. Her hand is lightly grasping Michael's arm, and he gives me a small smile. Did they come together? And, like, as friends together or *together* together?

The wave of people pushes us into a cavernous station with high ceilings and walls covered in frescoes. I don't know exactly where we are, but it's somewhere in Italy, near Venice.

"Remmy!" Kaylie breaks from us and rushes toward a figure in the distance.

When she reaches him, he grasps her in a fierce hug. Once he releases her, she excitedly drags him to us. "I wasn't sure if you'd come!"

He's lean with pale skin and short hair the same copper as Kaylie's.

Kaylie is babbling with excitement. ". . . just a short train ride away from New York City, and yet I have to travel halfway around the world to see you!" As Michael embraces the newcomer with clear affection, Kaylie turns to me. "Ada, this is my brother, Remmy."

Did she just say he lives in New York City? I'm burning with curiosity about how a Maker—from a family of Valkyries, no less—could live in my city. How come Kaylie has never mentioned it? I have so many questions, but he's quickly pulled away by more Makers who are excited to see him.

Between Remmy and Hilde, I've now met two people who left Maker society for the provincial world, both of whom seem to still be welcome among the Makers. And based on that conspiracist Cicero blog, there might be others out there. Maybe they'll be my people one day when I leave. Because that *is* the plan.

"Finally, I found you!" Georgie says, grabbing my arm and pulling me toward my very first Carnevale.

Everything I've been told about Carnevale pales in comparison to the real thing. We're in an enormous underground hall packed with people. There are numerous stages around the room, each with a performance going on—music, dances, acrobatics. It's a spectacular, reverent dedication to art.

Most people have donned their masks, so I take mine out of my pocket. It's a simple sunburst design that covers my eyes and nose. Georgie's is shaped like a cat face.

We get sucked onto the central dance floor and become part of the vibrating crowd. Here we're not aberrant recruits; we're part of something larger.

We stop to watch Mbali, who has joined other members of the Matriarchy of the Isles—all wearing serpent masks—in a hypnotic ceremonial dance.

Next to them is a choir, each member splashing paint of a different color onto a giant tapestry as they sing a complex harmony that starts to take visual shape on the joint painting.

Whooping shouts and cheers direct our attention to the main stage at the front of the hall. Two dancers—both Valkyries—have begun a ballet. A spotlight illuminates their shirtless, lithe figures; one has deep mahogany skin, and the other is tan and covered in tattoos. Both dancers wear bird masks and are clearly favorites of the crowd. The music is harsh with a strong bass line, thumping percussion, and electric violin. The dancers are precise and elegant, all rippling muscles and breathtaking speed. With a dramatic drum roll, their wings unfurl, and the dance rises into the air.

There are more whoops and cheers as another figure leaps onto the stage, tears off his dress shirt, and joins the dance. It's Remmy, Kaylie's brother. He's magnificent, spinning on the stage while the others dance hovering above him.

Remmy leaps into an impressive grand pirouette that has the crowd roaring even louder, and then he slows, his body stretched low to the ground, and I have a clear view of his back. There are wings on Remmy's back, but not like the skin and bone wings of his sister or the dancers above. His are elegant angel-like wings drawn in ink on the canvas of his shoulders and back. The tattoos are beautiful, but they are sprouting from two parallel patches of red, angry scar tissue. And I have no doubt what once grew from that ruined flesh. I wonder in horror what must have happened for him to have lost his wings, but the beauty of his dancing drags my attention away from his back.

Despite the fact that he remains grounded, he's flying, weaving a tale of loss that I feel deep in my gut. I never knew dance could tell such a story; I never knew it could touch me as music does or as brushstrokes do. But here I stand, completely undone.

Music from every corner of the room is crashing into itself, discordant and harmonious at the same time, rising into a glorious crescendo, and just as I'm sure my heart will explode into a million tiny pieces of grief, the two flying dancers lift Remmy off the stage and fly him above the crowd. As all the faces in the room lift toward the ceiling, the three dance together, the two Valkyries swing and toss Remmy between them as he soars in rhythmic, intricate flips and turns, a shooting star across the night sky.

Longing turns to hope, the whole room feeling it together, our bodies moving with the music. My sense of self dissolves into the crowd as the music echoes in my skull all the way to my teeth. It melts into my blood, rewriting the rhythm of my pulse, painting me as part of this communal masterpiece.

I am incandescent

a gust of evening wind

the last note of a song

the gasp between kisses . . .

Moments, or hours, or lifetimes later, I turn and find Michael beside me.

"There you are!" he says. I hardly hear the words over the music, but I can read his lips. "I wanted to see your reaction as someone here for the first time. Isn't it amazing?"

I step closer to be heard over the deafening music. "It's incredible!"

His face shines, all dimples and joy, and I can't help but reach up and push the flop of hair out of his face. I would normally never dare, but the atmosphere of Carnevale makes it feel as if the rules are suspended for a whisper of time.

He laughs as it flops right back. "That's a battle I lost long ago."

Michael spreads his arms, lifts his face toward the ceiling, and spins. I laugh and spin with him, like the music will carry us away, until I careen into his body, dizzy and drunk on the moment. He grabs my hand and twirls me under his arm, then twirls me in reverse until the front of my body is pressed up against his. He releases my hand and loosely grips my waist. I put my arms around his neck hesitantly and look up at his handsome face, a face that makes me feel known, makes me feel home. He may have his faults, but he's trying. And maybe I can help try harder because his people, all *this* surrounding us, is worth it.

As our gazes lock, our laughter dies down. Michael's eyes glitter caramel and chocolate beneath his thick dark lashes. His Adam's apple bobs, and I wonder what it would feel like against my lips. Guitar-calloused fingers skim my cheek, cup my face. I no longer hear the music or feel the shift of dancers around us. The only sound is the echoing thump of my heart in my ears.

Thump, thump.

The press of his tall, lean body against mine pulses warmth through me. I feel sexy and fierce and reckless. I tip my face toward his, and now our mouths are so close that I breathe in his shaky exhale.

Thump, thump.

I dig my fingers into his shoulders, and—ever so lightly that I almost miss it—he presses a kiss to my cheek.

Thump, thump.

So soft, like the wings of a butterfly passing by, and just as fleeting.

The touch is gone as soon as it began.

"You look radiant tonight," he whispers in my ear, words tinged with a tender note of regret. And then he releases me and steps away, instantly disappearing into the undulating crowd. I'd almost doubt it ever happened, but the spot where his lips brushed my skin is branded with the sting of a newly inked tattoo.

The noise comes crashing back, and I'm standing alone on the teeming dance floor, my heart warring between excitement and disappointment, my body keyed up and frustrated.

I mentally clutch at the already fading memory. I don't normally let myself want Michael, but I'll allow it for the next few hours. Until I have to return to the reality of why I can never have him. Why I can never have any of this life.

Georgie breaks away from a nearby clump of dancers. "I saw that little dance with Master Tall, Dark, and Emotionally Promiscuous." She yells to be heard. She swats at my arm. "How long have you been drooling over that particular slice of cake?"

"Drooling?" I respond, "More like starving." I roll my eyes. "Forever, it seems."

Her eyes are sympathetic but glinting with the conspiratory excitement of a good secret.

"That's one dangerous dessert." She eyes me meaningfully.

I groan. "You have no idea." There's no room for denial in a moment like this. I raise my arms out to my sides, languidly spinning around again. "I'm already so goooone. . . ."

She laughs. "Well, I would *not* advise distracting yourself with His Highness Raphael VanJerkface, no matter how hot he is. I saw that eyeball moment on the train." She looks at me knowingly. "And it definitely seemed consensual."

"That's probably even more dangerous." I sigh, dropping my arms.

She laughs again. "You're right about that." She reaches for my hand and forces me to keep twirling. "But who needs guys anyway. Dance with meee!" She swings me around, hyper and elated, and we're soon both lost in the music and the meditative beauty of the infinite.

Time passes in a blur. Eventually fatigue and thirst bring me back to reality.

Not long ago, Georgie danced away with a tall girl in a fox mask doing a ridiculously adorable Lindy Hop.

I head toward the bar in search of water and see Rafe making out with a different blond than the one he came with, no real surprise there. She starts to kiss down his neck and his gaze flicks up, meeting mine. He winks, then turns his face to kiss a boy pressed to his other side. The sensuality radiating from the three of them makes me blush and abandon my quest for a drink in my haste to get away.

I'm pulled back into the dancing milieu. A harp and flute ensemble is playing, and I twirl in time with the music, contributing to the spectacle by trailing small ribbons of sparks from my fingertips like Hypatia taught me.

I stop when two striking boys approach me. One I recognize as a beautiful member of Rafe's entourage who is in my Sire lab and who I have avoided ever since he gave Georgie the stink eye in the hover park. The second boy—who is wearing a lion mask—has harsh features and is extremely tall; the top of my head doesn't even reach his shoulders.

"Nice trick," the tall boy says to me. "You're a pretty thing to be dancing alone." His accent sounds like a combination of British and French.

The beautiful boy from Genesis has an amber guildstone in his ear, but the tall boy wears no earrings. Instead, he wears a ruby ring on his hand, along with a bone ring. Blood Science and Avant Guard.

"We can keep you company," the beautiful one says. I don't like his mocking voice, and I don't like the appetite in his expression. Maybe I would rather be alone.

"Thanks," I say, "but I'm actually waiting for someone."

The taller boy's eyes are sharp and assessing. "Bram," he says to his pretty companion, "why don't you get us some drinks. I'll keep this lovely lady company while she waits." Bram smiles coldly and saunters away.

The tall boy gazes at me intently. "You don't like my friend," he says matter-of-factly.

"Maybe I don't like you, either," I respond.

"Well, I would certainly like to change that." There is bite in his smile, but unlike Bram's, it doesn't bother me, and I let him pull me into a dance. His hand is large and cool, and as he holds me against himself, I marvel at his sheer size. He is lanky and slim, but so incredibly tall that I feel comically tiny. He's very self-assured in the way he handles me, far too familiar for a stranger. One hand roams dangerously low down my exposed back, and heat floods my cheeks. "Well, isn't that a pretty blush." His hand moves lower still. Why have I not pushed him away? But after the disappointment of Michael's earlier caution, a part of me craves this stranger's boldness.

"I've never seen you around before. I thought I knew all the Sires in our small little world." He's telling me he knows I'm a recruit. I momentarily still from our dancing, but his smile and grasp remain inviting.

"Show me your lights again," he says. I lift my fingers and let the shimmering ribbons sparkle between us. He runs his fingers through the lights and catches my fingers in his. "Beautiful."

It occurs to me that, though I can't deny I'm attracted to him, I don't even know this boy's name or anything else about him. But I like the way he holds me—like I'm something special to claim—and the way he looks at me, like he *wants* me. I feel the rush of being wanted deep in my belly.

Bram returns bearing a carafe of water. He hands us goblets and liberally fills them. I'm parched and overheated, and I gratefully sip as the tall boy's brazen fingers skim up my spine. I like his touch a little too much, and I step away, not trusting myself. The long night has started to catch up to me, and I'm feeling drowsy.

"I should really go find my friend," I tell the boys. Tall Guy takes my cup, handing it back to Bram.

"Just one more dance, pretty little light spinner." It's not a question, and his eyes hold wicked promises. He pulls me toward him possessively, and I know I should protest, but I don't. I really am tired, and it feels nice to let him support my weight. I lean into him, my cheek resting against his chest, the top of my head barely reaching the open collar of his suede doublet. He lifts my hand and soft lips trail my inner arm, making a pleasant dizziness spread through me. With the slide of warm tongue against my skin, the music suddenly seems far away. A large hand strokes my hair as I lean more of my weight into his solid body. I close my eyes and drift off.

22

The sound of a slamming door startles me into consciousness. I squint against a wave of dizziness and try to move my arms, but I can't. It seems I'm tied to a chair.

This gets my attention.

Adrenaline courses through me, and I blink until the room comes into focus. A tall boy looms nearby.

Oh. That guy. The memory of our dance washes over me.

That scumbag drugged me! I wiggle, trying to break free so I can give him a piece of my mind. But the spidersilk rope doesn't budge.

How have I gone from having a boring, average life to being abducted and restrained twice in a matter of months? Sheesh.

"Let me go," I try to yell, but it comes out as more of a croak since my mouth is so dry. How long have I been out?

"Well, hello there, little light spinner." The tall boy no longer wears his mask, and his predatory gaze is no longer appealing. Fear raises the hair on my arms. My head is pounding, and the ropes binding me to the chair bite into my wrists as I continue to struggle.

We're in a dank, low-lit room. Bram is standing a few feet away with the gorgeous Valkyrie who was with Rafe on the Atlas.

"Soon the halls should be clear enough to get her out of here unseen," the girl says to the others.

"Where are you taking me?" I ask, a quaver in my voice, but they all ignore me. I begin to thrash hard enough that the chair thuds against the tiles.

"I guess you'd like to go back to sleep." The tall boy strides over, but he's halted by the squeak of a door behind me.

"What's going on here?" The voice is deep with an overt sense of authority, and everyone in the room goes completely still.

I know that voice. I turn as much as my restraints allow.

Rafe.

I'm unsure if I should feel relief or fear. He's a familiar presence, but there is certainly no love lost between us, and I don't trust him.

His gaze meets mine, but his eyes are apathetic, giving nothing away.

"Hi, Rafe." The tall boy speaks casually, though his shoulders are tense, and his gaze has locked with Bram's in silent communication.

"Why do you have my lab partner restrained to a chair?" Rafe asks coolly.

The tall boy twirls a lock of my hair around his pointer finger. "Just having some fun with a weed," he responds. "I didn't know you knew her, cousin." My heart sinks upon hearing they're related. The boy unwinds the hair from his finger, then places his hand on my shoulder and squeezes in a way that makes acid rise in my mouth. He leers and asks, "Do you mind sharing?"

"Get off me!" I struggle against his touch. How did I ever let this slimeball touch me?

The adrenaline boost from moments before is starting to wear off, and I feel woozy.

"You're a fool, Leo," Rafe says in a bland, bored voice. "Do you know what she is? You shouldn't be standing so close."

"This philistine excuse for a Sire?" Leo scoffs. "She's harmless."

"She could kill you with one touch." Rafe raises his hand, palm out. "The right amount of Ha'i zapped to your heart"—he snaps his fingers—"pop." His lips lift into a cruel grin. "And perhaps you would deserve it for acting so rashly. Now, let her go."

Okay good, this is going in the right direction.

"We need her," Leo responds, resisting Rafe's command.

"And what could you possibly need her for?" Rafe asks, menacingly stalking toward Leo.

"There's a bounty . . . on Sires," Leo explains, meeting Rafe's gaze without backing down.

"What?" Rafe growls, and the fierceness of his tone freezes my blood.

"The reward is astronomical," Leo says, seemingly unshaken by Rafe's obvious anger, though Bram and the girl cower as if they might disappear if they're quiet enough.

Rafe speaks sharply, each word slicing through the tense air. "You know who must be collecting. How could you even consider helping them?" His blue eyes have darkened to a terrifying shade of midnight. "What are they offering you? You have no need for their filthy provincial money."

Rafe reaches over and splays his hand in shiin over the left side of Leo's chest. The threat is clear. *Pop.*

Leo's eyes show the first flicker of fear, but he stands his ground, and realization dawns on Rafe's face. "Antimatter," he breathes, and Leo nods affirmatively. Rafe lowers his lethal hand. "So they're offering antimatter as a reward for the abduction of Sires?"

"Rafe, you know I would normally never consider it, but this one's just a weed. It's worth what they can give us."

"*This one* is my lab partner."

"She can't possibly matter to you." Leo scoffs. "Imagine what we could do if we acquire antimatter—"

Rafe cuts him off. "You should be censured by the Guard for abetting Inquisitor scum." He practically spits each word. "You too." He glares over at the other two, and the girl begins to cry.

"Cousin, why are you defending a weed? She's not even that pretty. What's Genesis done to you?" Who knew there existed an even ruder elitist ass than Rafe Vanguard?

"I'm defending a Sire over helping our greatest enemy." Rafe grabs Leo's hand and points to the bone ring, the stone of the Avant Guard. "An enemy you have sworn on your life to guard our world against. What has greed done to you?"

Leo is taller than Rafe, yet Rafe talks down to him as if he towers over him.

Rafe drops Leo's hand with contempt. "Tell me everything you know."

"We don't know anything. I just received this anonymous pigeon." Leo pulls an unfolded pigeon from his pocket and hands it to Rafe. "And when I heard about the Sire weed, I thought it might be worth pursuing."

Rafe reads the note, pockets it, and strides over to me. He uses his spoon to cut the ropes binding me to the chair.

"Thank you," I murmur as I stand. But once I'm on my feet, all the blood rushes to my head, and I stagger with dizziness. Rafe brusquely pushes my hair aside, checking my neck. He also inspects both of my wrists, ignoring the red chafing from the ropes. I don't know what he's looking for, but I can't seem to find the strength to protest the contact. He's quick and clinical, but every graze of his fingers elicits the strange tingle I've come to associate with his touch. He doesn't acknowledge it.

"Don't worry. She's fine," Leo says, resigned.

"She'd better be," Rafe responds. Then he goes still, so motionless that he seems inhuman. The black fury has returned to his eyes. He's looking at a faded light pink line on the inside of my forearm. Was it there before? It looks like a scratch that's almost healed. Rafe traces the line with his own finger.

Tingle.

I'm scared by the rage in his eyes, and of the fact that, besides for his finger on my arm, he is so unsettlingly still. "You lie to me, Leonardo de Montaigne," he finally says, icy words that chill the room. Everyone is clearly afraid now.

"Oh, c'mon, cousin, don't be like that—"

Rafe turns furiously on Leo. "Fie upon you! There's already one traitor in your family, and you risk doing something like this?" Rafe points at me. "She may have been born a philistine, but she is a *Maker*. And she is a Sire. A *Sire*! You have crossed a line that should never be crossed." My skin prickles with cold, and my knees are weakening.

I don't understand what's going on, and I'm so dizzy that it's becoming difficult to follow the conversation. I try to grasp at all the pieces slithering away from me.

They took me to trade for antimatter, and they did something else to me too. Rafe thinks it's Inquisitors they're working with, but that's not possible because the Inquisitors don't exist anymore. And someone in Leo's family is a traitor? What did Rafe say his name was?

"Give it all to me. Now," Rafe commands. I close my eyes to make the room stop spinning. Noticing my sudden weakness, Rafe grabs my arm to support me. "Gravdammit, how much did you take?" As I blink my eyes open, Leo is handing something to Rafe. I would wonder what it is if I could only focus, but my brain feels like it's wrapped too tightly in cellophane.

Rafe surveys the room and then says, "I will keep your dalliance with the Inquisitors a secret, as it could lead to your exile, and you are family. But Alex will be hearing that you bled a Sire." There's a chorus of sharp inhales at the mention of Prince Alexander. The air tastes like fear.

The Valkyrie girl starts to cry again. "Rafe, honey," she whines. "I'm so sorry. I wasn't really part of this. I was just in the wrong place at the wrong time."

"Enough, Yvette." She instantly silences. "All of you, get out of my sight."

The air moves with the rush of bodies swiftly abandoning the room. Leo stops at the exit and turns to stare me down with a curious kind of malice.

Then he leaves, the door slamming behind him, and weariness overtakes me. My eyes flutter shut and my head lolls against Rafe's arm. His biceps are so big. He's so warm. I feel funny. Through the veil of my fuzzy thoughts, I see Rafe send off a pigeon.

Soon Kaylie arrives. At some point I must have sat back down in the chair, though I still find myself leaning against Rafe's arm, clutching his wrist. Kaylie and Rafe converse in quick, urgent voices, but I'm in and out of lucidity and catch only bits and pieces.

"It wasn't Inquisitors; it was journeys from Avant, from Guard families," Rafe is saying.

I guess he plans to keep the promise he made to Leo about not mentioning who they were working for.

He continues. "They bled her. I have it all here. Her Sire healing may mean she doesn't need an infusion, but I thought you should examine her to confirm. The drugs are clearly not out of her system."

"We should tell Bloche immediately," Kaylie says.

"No. Let me tell Prince Alexander. It's a bad time to create tension with the Guard. This is not something the prince will take lightly, I assure you."

Michael comes crashing through the door. His face is flushed, and his eyes are overly bright.

"Oh, thank the Conductor," he exclaims when he sees me, but his eyebrows draw together when he notices my appearance. "Are you okay?" he asks, making his way to my side. "Is she okay?"

I'm okay now, I want to say. I smile up at him. He's so handsome when he's panicked. His hair is so sloppy.

"Where have you been?" Kaylie whispers urgently. "I've been trying to track you down for an age."

"What happened to her?" There's a ringing in my ears, and his voice sounds far away. "There's talk of a captured Sire and a potential provincial breach. I came looking for her as soon as I heard. She's not trained—"

"She's fine," Kaylie says soothingly. "Some boys spiked her drink. I've examined her, and she's okay, but she needs to rest. We need to get her back to the institute." Kaylie's voice is soft, and her hand strokes Michael's arm.

I watch how he's calmed by her words and her touch. He squeezes her hand affectionately.

This doesn't bother me.

I don't care.

Please, stop touching him.

"I'll take her to the Atlas now," Michael says. "There's a train leaving soon."

But Rafe interrupts him. "I'll take her," he says. "If there's a provincial threat, I'm sure you're needed here."

Michael nods hesitantly, a note of distrust in his gaze.

Wait, he's going to let *Rafe* take me back? No. I want Michael to do it.

"Be careful with her," Michael says to Rafe.

A short nod is Rafe's response. He gently pulls me up from the chair. My legs are noodles, and my knees buckle. Before I stumble, Rafe reaches down, smoothly catches me behind my knees, and swoops me up into his arms as if I were as light as my pet cat, Elliot. I miss Elliot. She's fuzzy. She's been dead since I was twelve.

Rafe holds me like a child. My legs dangle over his arms, and my head lolls against his solid chest. I try to protest, but his body heat is warming away my chills, and I feel less dizzy this way. Also, he smells good.

As he walks down the hall, he mutters, "You have no sense of self-preservation. You should not be so trusting." When I don't respond, he asks me dispassionately, "Are you okay?"

"Your eyes are pretty" is my woozy response. The comforting rumble of his chuckle lulls me to sleep.

23

I wake sometime later, my head pounding.

Wait. This isn't my bed.

I don't have this many pillows or a luxurious fur throw. Wow, it's soft. I bury my face in the cozy warmth and inhale the somehow familiar spicy scent.

Where am I anyway? I sit up. Instead of piles of clothing on the floor, there's a large piano. Further confirmation that this is not, in fact, my room.

I didn't hook up with anyone last night, did I?

I'm still wearing my dress.

My dress. Carnevale.

Right. I was drugged. And something else had happened to me that had made Rafe and Kaylie worried. My skin crawls with unease as I take stock of myself. I can't find any evidence of the red mark that Rafe had seen on my arm, and nothing hurts.

Along with the general foreboding, I'm also frustrated that I slept through the Atlas journey home, missing a second chance at cell service.

My phone!

Who knows what damning messages might have come through while

I was unconscious? I was with Rafe. What if he saw? In my panic, I have difficulty fumbling for my pocket, but thankfully, my phone is there, locked and seemingly undisturbed.

I hear a soft knock, and I shove the phone back in my pocket before the door opens. Rafe strides over to me, owning the space in a way that can only mean this is his room. His bed. I swallow with the realization of the source of the heady scent from moments ago.

He hands me a goblet of tea. "I brought this from the infirmary. It will help you feel better, though you should be mostly healed by now."

"Thanks," I croak, my voice dry and raspy.

As I drink, I avoid looking at Rafe. I can't believe I slept in his bed. Where did he sleep? My cheeks grow warm at the thought.

As if he can read my mind, he says, "Don't worry. I left you to sleep alone. This is the first time I've been back since last night." I nod in thanks and try to finish the drink as fast as possible so I can get out of here. We're both being awkwardly quiet. Or at least, I am. Rafe seems lost in his own thoughts.

The drink—some kind of herbal concoction—really does make me feel better. As my head begins to clear, more hazy memories of the previous night come back to me. I'm surprised by Rafe's helpfulness. But he lied to Kaylie, saying the Inquisitors weren't involved when he thought they were. Even if it couldn't have actually been the Inquisitors, I don't understand why Rafe would hide seemingly important information.

Being in Rafe's bed is uncomfortably intimate, so I climb out. Cool air on my exposed skin reminds me of my party attire, which feels far too revealing for these circumstances. I slide on my shoes and cross my arms, hugging myself. Rafe stoically hands me his leather jacket. It's too big, but I burrow into it, seeking a barrier between myself and all this awkwardness.

"Why did you help me?" I ask him. He looks like he might be wondering the same thing, his expression even scowlier than usual.

"Losing you to the Inquisitors would have been wasteful and inconvenient. You're useful to Maker society and should not be in the hands of our enemies."

Useful. What an ass.

And he's not finished being offensive. "You're a gravdamn Sire. They shouldn't have been able to overpower you. You have no sense of your own abilities."

This dude literally can't open his mouth without criticizing me. But I don't rise to his bait. I'm not in the mood for a fight, and there's too much I need to understand.

"What did your date and your cousin do to me anyway?" I ask accusingly.

"Leo is only a distant relation, but he, like so many others, likes to use the title liberally to garner favor by claiming connection to the Crown."

"Well, I need to understand what happened."

He rocks back on his heels and runs his hands through his hair, sighing as if this is the last conversation in the world he wants to be having. "I suppose you have the right to know." He looks up and states it frankly. "They stole some of your blood."

The blood that is still in my body chills. "What for?"

"They practice Blood Science, which occasionally necessitates actual blood. But never another Maker's blood, *never* a Sire's blood."

"Whose blood is normally used, then?" I ask, pretty sure I don't actually want to know the answer.

"Animal or philistine."

I have heard others from Avant use the term philistine to mean provincial. "So they *do* use human blood?" I ask, my anger rising.

"Provincial human," Rafe clarifies, as if it makes a difference.

I grind my teeth at his insinuation that provincial people are equal to animals, but it's nothing new for him.

"Regardless." His tone turns menacing. "I won't let them get away with what they did." He clenches his jaw, and the veins in his neck stand out. "I wasn't forthright with Master Botticelli last night because I'd rather Genesis not see Guard insubordination, but I will tell Alex, and those miscreants will suffer the consequences. Once I've gotten all the information I need out of them."

"What kind of information?"

"I received news after we arrived back last night." He looks away, and his shoulders slump. I notice for the first time that his hair is lank, and his skin lacks its normal luminescence. He's . . . rumpled. It's perhaps the first time I've seen His Royal Highness look anything less than perfect.

"The Inquisitors are running rampant, and no one is doing enough," he says, speaking more to himself than to me.

"What was the news?" I ask with a growing sense of foreboding.

He speaks so softly I can barely hear him. "Hypatia didn't come home last night."

I gasp as dread and panic flood me.

Rafe turns to face the wall, hiding any emotion from me. "She's too young to attend Carnevale. She shouldn't have even been there! But she snuck onto the Atlas."

"I . . . don't understand." Guilt is building along with my fear. I'd *seen* her. I should have said something.

"What's to understand?" He whips around, glaring at me accusingly. "Sires were being hunted down, and I managed to help *you* but not my own family." The regret in his voice is clear. "There are rumors going around of another capture attempt last night that was thwarted. Two rescued Sires and one lost." He stalks toward me with conviction. "I *will* find Hypatia and bring her back. I need to find out everything about the other attempt and whether anyone else was contacted with the offer of an antimatter trade.

Leo would never have touched Hypatia, but he must know something about whoever did. Until I've interrogated them all properly, you cannot say anything to anyone about their connections."

Ah. Suddenly Rafe's helpfulness, not to mention the fact that he kept me isolated in his room all night, begins to make more sense. He needs my cooperation. But if it means helping Hypatia, I'm happy to give it.

"I won't say anything," I promise. "I want to do whatever I can for Hypatia, but aren't there more . . . qualified people looking for her? Won't giving them more information make it easier for them to find her?"

Rafe barks out a bitter laugh. "The gravdamned *qualified* people follow too many rules. They've known about this risk for months, and they chose to ship all the Avant Sires off to this island for protection instead of dealing with the root of the issue. They claim they're trying to find the missing Sires, but they'll never accomplish anything while being so careful not to interfere, not to harm—" His eyes blaze. "I'm not afraid to do harm. I'll do whatever it takes."

"What about Prince Alexander?"

"He says he's taking care of it. That he worked out a plan with Chorus—she gave him some cryptic prophecy like she always does. But Alex wasn't around to watch Hypatia grow up the way I was. I can't imagine he feels the same urgency." His voice breaks. "She and I haven't been on the best of terms lately." He shakes his head ruefully. "Because of her friendship with you and your roommate. But I shouldn't have . . ." He suddenly stalks to the other end of the room, obviously annoyed with himself. "Why am I even telling you this?"

"It's not a bad thing to talk sometimes."

"Talking is useless. I need to *do* something. I've spent the past few hours trying to get off this rock, but they're not letting anyone leave. I need to find out if those fools from last night can lead me to the Inquisitor scum who abducted my cousin."

"How are you so sure it's the Inquisitors who are behind the abductions?" If I let him chase the wrong culprit, he's less likely to find Hypatia.

"Of course it is. They've been hunting us for generations, hoping to steal our knowledge and then finally wipe us out. We have the evidence, and we should have acted on it long ago."

What evidence could they possibly have? Maybe I should tell him about Ozymandias Tech? But I don't have enough proof that it's actually them kidnapping Sires. Is their genetic research and Izzy's text message enough to convince Rafe he's barking up the wrong tree?

"I can't believe it's come to this." Rafe covers his face with his hands. "Hypatia has urgent medical needs. I don't know how she's going to manage."

I blink rapidly, trying to banish the memories of my own kidnapping, which are creeping along the edges of my sanity. I still don't know much about Hypatia's illness, but I do know what it's like to be abducted. I can't imagine her going through what I went through. It's hard to speak past the lump in my throat.

"Rafe, I'm so sorry."

He stiffens, the look on his face making it clear that he again remembers who he's speaking to. "Your roommate and Master Loew were both hounding me about you all morning. As you seem to be feeling better, you should go to them."

Even as he dismisses me, he looks so lost . . . so sad.

"Are you okay?" I ask.

Abruptly he bangs his fist against the wall. "Get out," he says.

I'm not offended by his anger. In fact, I'm drawn in by it. I recognize that he doesn't want me to see him vulnerable. But I don't want him to feel so alone.

Why, oh why, do I care?

I walk over to him and lightly put a hand on his back. I feel his muscles relax as he almost imperceptibly leans into my touch. But only for a moment.

"Just leave," he says, his eyes squeezed shut.

So I do.

* ★ ★ ★ *

I head back to my room to change my clothes. Georgie's not there, but I find her at breakfast, where she accosts me with a fierce hug.

"I've been worried sick!"

"I'm fine, but I'm not the one you need to be worried about."

She holds me at arm's length, assessing. "Is . . . is that Prince Jerk's jacket?"

"Uh, yeah." I'd put it back on after changing with plans to return it to Rafe. Also, it smells good.

"Did you hear about Hypatia?" I ask her.

"Hear what about her? Where is she?"

"She was abducted last night."

Georgie covers her mouth in horror. I summarize the details of Hypatia sneaking out to Carnevale and the bounty on Sires.

"This must be why Master Loew has been so panicked. He's been looking everywhere for you. You should probably go see him."

I've been too distracted with concern for Hypatia to think about Michael. But after last night, I don't feel ready to face him alone. "Will you come with me?" I ask Georgie.

She nods and says, "Finish your breakfast first. Whatever happened to you last night, I can tell you need to eat." Since my breakfast is banana bread with clotted cream and date syrup, I'm happy to comply.

As we head through the Spring wing, I try to remember whether I said anything mortifying to Michael while I was woozy. I have no idea if our dance was what I thought it was. But even if we did have a moment of shared attraction, that doesn't mean he's interested in anything more. Now that Georgie knows how I feel about him, I'm glad to have her with me for moral support.

I knock tentatively at Michael's office door, which immediately swings open.

"Oh, thank the Conductor!" Michael says, and for a moment I think he might hug me. Instead, he steps back, allowing Georgie and me to come in. "How are you feeling?" he asks.

"I'm a little shaken up, but that's it." Entering his office brings a lingering memory of our argument and the reminder that I'm supposed to be mad at him. But the truth is that just being in his presence brings me a sense of relief, and after everything I've been through since last night, I don't have the energy to conjure up my ire. "I'm fine, really."

"Good," Michael says, but when our eyes meet, he quickly looks away.

"Do you have any news about Hypatia?" I ask.

"Ah, yes. I know you two are close. We have a few leads as to where she may be."

"You do?"

He nods. "I assure you, many people are working hard to bring her back."

"Hey, um, Ada?" Georgie says in a strained voice. She's staring at a photo lying on top of a stack of papers on Michael's desk, her eyes wide as saucers. I step over to see what's caught her attention. My stomach sinks.

"Who is that?" I ask Michael, trying to sound as casual as possible.

Michael leans over to see the picture that I'm pointing to. It's blurry but clear enough that I have no questions about at least two of the faces I see circled in red ink. Neither, apparently, does Georgie.

"That's a photograph of the inner circle of the Inquisitors," he says. "The Guard have determined it's legitimate. We haven't had intelligence on the activity of the Inquisitors this specific in decades, and we're confident this information can help lead us to Hypatia."

None of this makes any sense.

"How do you know that they're the ones who have her?"

"We have compelling evidence linking them to all of the recent abductions."

Time seems to slow, the beating of my heart echoing in my skull. I glance at Georgie, and her eyes look like they might pop out of her face.

"We have to go," I say.

"But you just got here—"

I dash out of the room with Georgie on my heels.

"Wasn't that your—" she starts.

"Shh. Not here. Let's get back to our apartment."

The moment we're there, the door closed behind us, Georgie bursts out, "Ada, your cousin and your mom were in that photo."

"Yes."

We're horrified for different reasons. She by who is *in* the picture. Me by who *has* the picture.

"What does this mean?"

"I don't know!"

What I really don't know is why Georgie hasn't already put it together. Why she hasn't accused me of spying. The evidence is clear as glace.

"If you had to guess?" She is looking up at me without an ounce of accusation. For some reason, she trusts me. I press my lips together, the lies I'm about to tell already sour on my tongue.

The Families had coached me on various responses to getting caught. I have a reasonably plausible justification that I could tell her right now, but Georgie is the last person I want to lie to.

So I find myself telling her the truth instead.

"My family is part of a secret society that knows about the Makers. But they're not the Inquisitors."

This is not a lie. The Inquisitors that the Makers fear so much, they really *don't* exist anymore. The order that is now the Families started out as Inquisitors, sure. But that was literally centuries ago.

I explain to Georgie, "The Inquisition did create a task force to hunt for the lost exiles, but they haven't continued to hunt down the Makers. The descendants of the task force were horrified by their ancestors' actions, and they made it their mission to bring back what had been taken away. They became stewards, seeking out and preserving the memory of the Makers while emulating their values. That's the group my family are a part of." While the people in that photo may have a tenuous connection to the long defunct Inquisition, they are something entirely different. And certainly not interested in or capable of abducting anyone.

. . . right?

"But you never told any of this to Master Loew when he tried to recruit you?" Georgie asks.

As much as I want to tell her the whole truth, I know I can't tell her the real reason I came here. So I spin a version where my family worked to get me recruited specifically because they knew I was at risk from whoever was abducting Sires and that I had to hide who they were because I knew the association with the Inquisitors would make me unwelcome.

And she seems to accept it all as if she has no reason to doubt me.

"More recently, with the realization that Maker culture had survived and was still thriving, the Families began to search for them again, but with the goal of reunification, not destruction. The Makers only think that the Inquisitors are still after them because they're stuck in the past," I continue.

"But what about, like, Naiot?" Georgie asks. "Who were the prophets fleeing from if not the Inquisitors?"

That's a good question. One I want to know the answer to as well. But it can't have anything to do with the Families.

"I don't know, but whoever it is, it's probably the same people who have

Hypatia. My family could never have taken her. They're good people, not kidnappers." I meet Georgie's eyes, and I'm practically begging. "You have to believe me."

"I do believe you," she says, and my shoulders and heart both relax. "Can you ask your mother about it?"

"I need to," I reply. There's a lot I need to ask her about. Including any new information they have about Ozymandias Tech. It must be them who are really behind all of this. They got their hooks into Izzy, and now they have Hypatia, and the Makers will never suspect them because they're too busy fixating on the wrong people.

I need to help redirect them.

"What do you know about Nora Montaigne and Ozymandias Tech?" I ask Georgie.

"That's the company that makes clean-energy private jets and does all that controversial genetic testing, right?"

I nod.

"Okay, so it's really funny that you ask that because I saw this post just the other day." She ushers me over to her desk, opens the Hidden forum on one of her screens, and clicks around until she finds what she's looking for.

I read over her shoulder. It's a detailed theory that Nora Montaigne is actually one of the Hidden and that the success she's had with her company is because she's using their secret technology.

I wonder if this could be possible. Could she be Prometheus? No. She can't be helping the Families if Kor thinks she's working against them.

And then it clicks. I gasp and grab on to Georgie's chair for stability. Leo, who captured me at Carnevale—Rafe had called him *Leonardo de Montaigne.* And he had said there was already one traitor in Leo's family.

Nora Montaigne.

They have to be related. Of course Leo and Bram weren't working for the Inquisitors; they must have actually been working for *Oz Tech* all along. And Leo's talk of antimatter and making Rafe believe it was the Inquisitors would avert suspicion from his sister.

Any lingering doubt I have dissipates. Izzy works for Oz Tech and tried to warn me about something she saw. Nora Montaigne used to be a Maker and has been doing genetic testing related to Sires. And Nora's brother tried to kidnap me for being a Sire. Oz Tech *must* be responsible for the other Sire abductions as well.

I have no idea how to explain any of this to Georgie, but she seems happy to let me use her computer to deal with it on my own, and she heads to the common room to play with Bast.

After I recover the pieces of my skull left from having my mind blown, I try to come up with a game plan.

I absolutely must talk to the Families. I need to tell them that the Makers have their photo, share my suspicions about Nora Montaigne, and see if they can help me find Hypatia.

And despite the strength of my Oz Tech theory, I'm still filled with dread from the absolute assurance that both Michael and Rafe had about the Inquisitors being the ones who took Hypatia. I need to understand why they think they have proof of that and confirm that the Families have nothing to do with it.

Kor doesn't answer, which makes sense for this time on a Sunday. So I try my mom.

As soon as I connect, I get straight to the point. "Mom, I need to tell you—the Makers have a picture of some of the members of the Inner Circle, and they think you all are behind the recent abductions."

"Ada, what are you doing? You can't be talking about this openly." She looks panicked, and it makes me even more scared, because Mom never looks anything other than poised.

"No one is listening. You *have* to talk to me."

"The most important thing right now is for you to protect your cover."

"Mom, they think the Families are the ones behind the kidnappings."

The look on her face makes me stop breathing.

"Mom . . . ," I choke out. "Are they actually somehow connected?"

"The Oculus is involved in a lot of activities that the rest of the Inner Chamber knows nothing about."

"What are you saying?" My voice squeaks with panic. "Are you part of the Oculus?" Up until recently, I hadn't even known the Oculus was still active, never mind that my mother might be part of it.

"I'm not a member, but all the New York Chamber members have been brought on to help with a specific operation based in the city. Ada, this is not something we can discuss here and now."

"If you won't talk to me while I'm here, then I'm coming home."

"You need to stay where you are. You'll be safer there, and you can't jeopardize your cover."

"Safer from who? Ozymandias Tech? I can't keep doing this without knowing what I'm part of." I force myself to lower my voice, which has been rising to a screech. "I'm not even that safe here. Do you know that I was kidnapped again last night? And I was rescued, but my friend wasn't so lucky." The emotions I've been holding in are breaking through, and I start to tear up. "She's only fourteen, Mom."

My mom's eyes widen. She looks horrified.

No, she looks *guilty*.

Only moments ago I'd been so sure the Families couldn't possibly have had anything to do with the abductions. But the look on her face has all my hope draining away.

How could this be happening without me having known? How could my mother and Kor be aware and okay with it? And . . . I helped them! I remember seeing Hypatia on the train. I think about everything I might have done to lead to her getting caught, and I feel like I'm about to puke.

"Is she safe?" I ask.

"I don't know anything for sure. But if she was taken by the Families, then I'm sure she is."

"Can I talk to her? How can we arrange to send her back here?"

"Ada, that's not how this works. I don't have that kind of authority. If I did, none of this would be happening."

"Mom, she has serious health issues."

"This project is being run out of a medical facility with some of the smartest doctors and scientists in the world. She's going to be okay."

What project? What facility? None of this has anything to do with anything I thought I knew about the Families.

"You need to explain to me why this is happening."

"I can't, Ada."

"Fine. I'll ask Kor."

"No!" For a moment my mother looks genuinely scared. I can't fathom why. "Listen to me, Ada. I'm not going to tell anyone about this conversation, but Kor would. He's young and gaining influence, and he trusts the Oculus and the Grand Master implicitly."

"Are you telling me that Kor is part of these kidnappings?" It feels impossible that my soulful, idealistic best friend could have anything to do with this.

"Of course he is, Ada. And if he thinks you're a risk to the mission, he'll tell the rest of the Oculus. Counselor Avellino is calling the shots in New York right now, and you know he's not your best advocate." Alfie's father, the Families' lawyer, is definitely not my biggest fan. He'd been insufferable when interrogating me after Italy and had been one of the strongest voices trying to keep me ignorant of anything remotely confidential. "If the Oculus has any concerns about you, they'll bring you home immediately. But you *need* to stay at Genesis."

I want to scream, but I can't risk Georgie or anyone else hearing me.

"You can't expect me to do this without telling me anything. Mom, the Makers have a *photo* of *you*. Which means that you're at risk, and so am I if they figure out we're related. If you can't tell me what's going on, I need to come home."

"Ada, your safety is what's most important. You're safest where you are. Please don't do anything stupid!"

"I'm not stupid!" I'm *not*. I'm ignorant because they haven't been telling me anything, but I won't stand for this anymore. I refuse to be a pawn.

"Ada—"

I end the call and storm out of the room. The only way I'm going to find answers is if I get them myself.

"I'm going to New York," I announce to Georgie.

"What? How?"

"I'll get on the Atlas and go." I need to confront the Inner Chamber or the Oculus or whoever in person and make sure Hypatia is okay.

"You can't. Didn't you hear? There's a lockdown."

"What do you mean?"

"Due to the abductions, all Atlas service has been suspended. No one's allowed to leave Arcadia."

I throw my hands up and growl.

"Maybe you should talk to Master Loew about it," Georgie suggests.

"No way! He can't know about this!" The mere thought of Michael knowing about my betrayal ties my stomach in knots.

"Why not? He's your friend, and he'll know what to do."

"He'll never trust me if he realizes I'm related to the people in that picture." And then I start crying and admit what I really should not. "Georgie, maybe I was wrong and they are the ones who took her. If they did, there has to be a good reason, but I need to help her."

"Maybe it's some kind of mistake?"

"I have to find out. Until then, please, promise me that you won't say anything to anyone."

"Of course, I would never." She walks over to me and wraps me in a hug. I sink into the comfort of her support, forcing myself to take some deep breaths and to think logically.

I need to get home to help Hypatia, and I need to make it clear that I'm not coming back to Genesis until they explain everything to me. I can't keep helping them if my own actions are putting my friends in danger. But first I have to figure out how to get off this gravdamn island. And I know exactly who can help me.

This is a crazy idea. And maybe a mistake.

The door swings open the moment I knock.

"What are you doing here?" Rafe asks coldly.

"I think we may be able to help each other."

"That's unlikely," he says, deadpan. But he opens the door wider and lets me in.

What am I doing? Should I really tell him? He's the last person in this place I can trust, but also, he's not afraid to break the rules. I'm gambling on his drive to help Hypatia being strong enough that it will outweigh the rage he's about to feel toward me.

"I have connections who may be able to help us get to Hypatia."

He moves so quickly I don't even have time to blink before I'm pinned against the wall, his hand pressed over my heart.

"Connections? To the Inquisitors? That does not sound good, Weed."

My heartbeat thunders under his hand. I can feel how strong he is, and I haven't forgotten what he said last night, about how a Sire can end someone's life with Ha'i to the heart. Rafe's a mercurial one all right, saving my life one moment, threatening it the next.

I'm also very aware of his closeness to me and his hand pressing into my breast.

"Get off me, creep. I'm offering to help you." I try to shove his arm away, but he's strong, and it doesn't budge. The realization of my own weakness only makes my heart beat faster.

Maybe he will hurt me.

I try to push him away again, and the vulnerability of feeling so trapped causes my panic to rise. "Let me explain."

He releases his hand, and I manage to swallow my instinct to sob. I glare at him. "What's your problem?" I try to yell it, but it comes out as more of a squeak.

He looms over me. "What connections do you have to the enemy of my people, the abductors of my cousin?" The steel accusation in his eyes sends terror shooting through my limbs. "Don't make the mistake of thinking that my not reporting the scoundrels from last night is a sign of softness. They are useful to me, and they are my kin. You may be a Maker and a Sire, but you're still a weed. The Inquisitors, and anyone connected to them, are the enemy. If you are in league with them, I will hand you over to the Guard without hesitation." His voice lowers menacingly. "Or I'll just take care of you myself."

Though he is no longer touching me, the air is thick with his threat. I'd been fooled by sleeping in his arms and in his bed. Rafe is clearly not my friend, and telling him anything may have been a lethal mistake. Unless I can convince him that I'm not a traitor and that I really can help Hypatia. Though I don't know if that's true. On either count.

I take a deep breath. "If you give me the chance, I'll explain everything."

Well, some version of everything.

"Fine," he replies, straddling a chair. He folds his arms over the chair back and stares at me, unblinking. "Talk."

I sit on the edge of his couch and tell him one of my in-case-of-emergency-break-glass prepared explanations—that I was sent here without any understanding of my family's affiliations and that I'm starting to realize my trip to Italy was orchestrated as a setup all along, and that I'm only realizing now that I've seen the picture in Michael's office that I have been being used as a pawn, but that I have not known about any of it until now.

Even to my own ears, the story feels as flimsy as single-ply toilet paper, but I put my all into selling it, and Rafe must buy at least some of it because he doesn't immediately start threatening to kill me again.

"So, what you're saying," Rafe responds, in an as yet nonhomicidal tone, "is that you can direct me to the people who sent you here so that I can find where they're keeping Hypatia and rescue her?"

"Yes . . . but I need you to take me off the island with you."

"No chance."

"I need to learn how my family is actually connected to all of this."

He sneers. "You expect me to help you after what you've just admitted?"

"Do you have any other leads? I can't ensure that I can get you to Hypatia if I'm not with you."

"You can simply tell me where she is, and I'll do fine on my own."

"I don't know where she is," I admit. "But I can try to find out if I have your help. I care about Hypatia too. We can get her back if we work together."

Rafe stands and begins pacing the room, talking as if to himself. "For hundreds of years, the Guard has protected the Makers from discovery by the Inquisitors. Now, for the first time in centuries, our enemy is taking risks, working with traitors in our society, and doing things that might finally lead us to them."

He stalks toward me, staring, as if my eyes hold the answer to a riddle. "Then you come out of nowhere claiming to be able to bridge the gap." He scratches the stubble on his jaw, still staring. "I need to think about this more. Leave me." He begins pacing again as if I'm already gone. No indication of what he's planning, no assurance that he won't turn me in to the Guard. All I can do is hope that taking this risk was the right move.

I realize only after I'm halfway to my own room that I'm still wearing his jacket.

It's difficult to focus during my classes when I know Rafe could decide to blow my cover—or plot my murder—at any moment. In Alchemical Arts Studio, I completely miss the instructions for how to mix a pigment so black that it swallows the light. In Testaments, I'm too agitated to follow the analysis of the history and family tree of Chorus's mother, Psalm.

When I get to the Sire lab, Rafe is conspicuously absent, which only heightens my anxiety. It doesn't help that Gloria—the recruit who always monopolizes Michael during Foundations—is apparently the other Sire who was captured last night, and she's recounting the tale of her rescue by a heroic masked stranger to a rapt audience.

Mbali must have heard about my own Carnevale adventure, because she hugs me and utters something that sounds like a prayer in a foreign language. Today her long locs are wrapped into a large bun on the top of her head, and she's wearing a jumpsuit in a patterned fabric of royal blue and sunshine yellow. She notices my attire too, eyeing my jacket, which she clearly recognizes. Why, oh why, have I not taken this gravdamn thing off already?

Rafe barges into the room and grabs my arm. "Come with me."

"Hey!" Mbali exclaims sharply. She grasps his wrist and squeezes gently until he loosens his grip on me, though he doesn't let go. "You need rest," she whispers to him. Clearly, I'm not the only one who's noticed he looks like compost.

"I will when I can," he replies.

"Has there been any news about Hypatia?" she asks. He shakes his head gravely, and she leans in to give him a quick embrace, pressing a kiss to his cheek. Rafe closes his eyes and momentarily rests his forehead against hers. I wonder again about the nature of their relationship.

"I have reached out to the Matriarch to see if she can help in any way," Mbali says. Her snake necklace slithers with the vibrations of her voice. I've seen it move many times, but now I realize, for the first time, that it's a real living snake. Goose bumps break out over my skin.

"Thank you," Rafe says with sincerity. Then, to me, less aggressively than before, "Let's go. We need to talk."

He practically drags me out of the lab and through the halls to the Summer wing, his fingers burning hot on my skin, the buzz of our contact never diminishing. I feel the metal of his rings pressing into my wrist—his Sire diamond and the bone ring that reminds me that above all else, he is a Guard, sworn to protect the Makers from people like me. My heart beats fast with trepidation. I have no idea how this conversation will go, and I know it could mean the end of the line for my mission.

When we arrive at his room, he finally releases me and lets the door swing shut behind us. I slept peacefully in this room last night, yet now I feel like I'm trapped in a cage with a wild animal. I shiver as I recall the helpless feeling of him pressing me against the wall, and I stay close to the door.

Rafe starts talking, his words clipped and precise.

"I questioned the other Sire who was rescued, and she had no useful details about her captors or even about her rescuer beyond him wearing a full-face harlequin mask and no guild stones. I just finished with Bram and Yvette, and they're clearly just pawns who know nothing. With this ridiculous lockdown, I can't properly deal with Leo. I need to *do* something, and right now you're my only option." He does not sound happy to admit this. "We're bound to the island until the perceived threat has receded, so we're going to have to sneak off. I'll plan our departure for after May Day, which will give us some time to prepare." He paces the room, his gate matching the intensity of his voice. "The Beltane bonfire after the hoverjoust opening games will be the perfect distraction for me to steal the supplies we need, and we can leave the next morning while everyone is still too hungover from the festivities to take notice." He stops his pacing to glare at me. "You will use the time between now and then to find out where Hypatia is being kept so that we can retrieve her. Are you sure you can do that?"

I nod, though I'm not at all sure. I'm still not even one hundred percent sure the Families have her, but that, at least, I can probably get Mom to look into, if nothing else.

He continues. "You're also going to need training. You need to learn how to defend yourself from those who should be weaker than you. To at least be able to put up a fight, even if it's just from me having a tantrum. You'll train with me daily until you're more useful than a frightened bird."

"*Me* train with *you* for weeks? Sure, us spending time together won't make anyone suspicious," I say, my voice dripping with sarcasm.

He grins coldly. "No one has ever questioned me spending quality time with a pretty girl."

"No way," I retort. "I'm not pretending to be one of your sex bunnies."

He makes a sound that might be a laugh. "Don't be so sensitive. You think people will be suspicious if we spend time together, and I'm providing a perfectly adequate explanation."

"I'm not the fling type."

He rolls his eyes. "Fine. Would pretending it was something more serious make you feel better about your misplaced morals?"

I cough in surprise, and once I gain control of my vocal cords, I say, "You don't really seem like a fan of monogamy." There's a bit too much squeak in my voice.

"I'm not."

"It's a terrible idea," I say. "Everyone knows you hate me; it will just draw unnecessary attention."

"We're surrounded by virile youth. The easiest part of this entire plan would be suffering through pretending to be . . . better acquainted. Anyway, people already saw us arrive back from Carnevale together, and I'm sure they noticed you spent the night." He smirks, but it's really more of a sneer, and I can tell he dislikes this idea as much as I do. "Not to mention, the fact that you've come back to my room twice since then, after spending an entire day wearing my jacket."

I blush and start to remove the offending garment.

"No," Rafe says. "You'd better keep it for now."

I pull it back over my shoulder. "Well, if we do this, is there anyone who would be upset? Maybe Mbali?"

"What does Mbali have to do with anything?"

"Are you guys, like . . . ?"

"Oh, no. Absolutely not." His face scrunches up. "I've been engaged to her sister three times since we were children. That would be extremely awkward."

"You're engaged?" I yelp.

"Not currently, no. But the Blood Crown and the Matriarchy of the Isles have been trying to form an alliance for years, and the coupling of their children has always been their favorite strategy." He states this as if he couldn't care less about such an irrelevant matter.

"But for the sake of our current discussion, I can assure you that, though I'm certain many hearts will be broken, there is no one who will be wronged by my involvement in a fake relationship with you."

"But everyone knows that you hate me for being a weed—"

"Gravdammit, don't call yourself that," he snaps.

"Why not? You call me that all the time."

"Yes, because I'm insulting you, but don't demean yourself."

"So, only you can demean me?"

"The point is that my idea is a good one, and you should agree with it. Not only will it help us get off this island, but you'll be treated better if you're associated with me. Don't you want that?"

"In case you haven't noticed, almost everyone besides you and your cronies treats me just fine. Besides, you don't care how people act toward me. What is it that you're really trying to get out of this?"

I'm right. He has an ulterior motive. But it's Rafe, so he has no problem clearly explaining the way he would like to use me to his advantage.

"Rescuing my cousin is my top priority, but I won't deny that this plan has an additional benefit for me." Now I'm certainly curious. "Some moral crusaders have petitioned to have me removed from the hoverjoust league for bigoted behavior. I'm about to be promoted to captain of the team, and an alliance with you would demonstrate that—"

"Are you kidding me? Wouldn't it just be easier to stop acting like a superior pig?"

He aims his eyeballs at the heavens. "They're not actually coming from a place of morality; they just know that their own team can't defeat me, so they're trying to get me kicked off the league to improve their chances of winning."

"Their motivations don't matter if they're right."

He huffs dismissively. "Another reason it would be useful is that there are a few of my past partners who . . . don't seem to understand that what we shared was a one-time thing. . . ."

This boy is truly unbelievable. He wants to use me to keep his clingy conquests off his back and make him appear less reprehensible than he is.

"It sounds like you'll be getting a lot more out of this than me," I say.

"You want my help to get to the mainland, and this is the best way to make it happen. Are you in or out?"

"Would you even be able to keep it in your pants for that long?" I can't believe I'm actually considering this.

"Honestly"—he thinks for a moment—"I don't know."

"Well, you'd better. I'm not interested in being the pathetic girl that everyone knows is being cheated on behind her back."

"Understood. I'll be respectful of your reputation. But we don't tell anyone about this."

"Nu-uh. I have to tell Georgie." I don't want to lie to my friend any more than I already have. I need her now more than ever.

"Unacceptable. If anyone knows, we won't be able to control who else finds out. I can't get us off this island with gossipmongers breathing down our backs. And I *need* to get off this island."

"I trust Georgie."

"I don't, and for better or worse, we're in this together."

"Okay," I concede. I mean, I totally still plan to tell her. I just won't let Rafe find out. "But you need to act civil toward her. And make your friends be nicer too. I can't be pretending to date someone who acts like my best friend doesn't exist."

"Fine," he agrees through gritted teeth.

"And no more death threats."

"Also fine."

"And I have one more stipulation." This might be pushing my luck, but I know that this plan might mean the end of my time at Genesis, so I have to risk it before I lose my access. "I need you to help me cure my grandfather's cancer."

Rafe's expression hardens. "I'm sorry to hear that your grandfather is ill, but that's not possible."

"Why not? You're in Bioscience and have access to their Testament, and you know how to use your Sire abilities for healing. You must be able to do something."

He stares at me, quietly contemplative for what feels like a full minute before saying, "If we successfully rescue Hypatia, you can bring me to your grandfather. I will examine him and look at his medical information. I can't promise anything can be done, but—and only if we rescue Hypatia, mind you—I will do what I can to help."

I almost start crying in relief.

We iron out a few more details, but the awkwardness is getting overwhelming, and I'm anxious to be alone to think about what I've just committed to.

As I leave, Rafe says, "Get some rest, because after classes tomorrow, you're going to need energy for our training." Then he adds with a wicked grin, "And don't look so miserable as you're leaving my room. . . . I have a reputation to maintain."

I roll my eyes and let the door slam in his face.

25

At the end of my Sculpture Studio, Rafe is waiting by the door to escort me to lunch. I walk stiffly by his side.

This is new. This is weird.

It draws eyes when we arrive at the cafeteria together. Including Michael's. I smile at him, and Rafe must see something in my expression, because he asks, "What is it with you two?"

"Nothing," I respond too quickly.

Understanding dawns on his face, and he grins spitefully. "Naughty." He leans closer to me and says into my ear, "He likes you too. I can tell."

"I don't know what you're talking about," I say with as much flippancy as I can muster, but my heart leaps at his words. Or is it from the feeling of his breath tickling my neck? He's standing very close, and I know how it must look to those around us. An apt display for our charade.

Michael is watching Rafe and me with a stormy look in his eyes. Is he upset? Rafe sees the look too, and he's entertained. He puts his hand on the small of my back and leans in closer, causing a flurry of thrills in my belly.

Rafe whispers, "I'd go for him too if he weren't so infernally self-righteous and dull." The way he winks makes it look to everyone else as if he's said something a lot more . . . intimate.

Michael's jaw clenches, and his hands ball into fists.

I feel a power that I haven't felt before. It's intoxicating enough that I hardly notice the increasing heat of Rafe's hand through my shirt or the way the warmth spreads as he moves that hand to grasp me around the waist and steer me toward his table.

Michael follows us. "Journey Castle," he says stiffly. "I need to speak with you."

I feel Rafe chuckle under his breath. "See you after," he says, gently kissing the air close to my cheek. All a performance for Michael's benefit, I know, but it doesn't stop the heat building in the space between us. My breath is unsteady as I approach Michael, and I'm honestly confused about which of the boys is most responsible.

"Yes?" I ask Michael once Rafe has breezed out of earshot.

"I had some books to give you." He rifles through the contents of his leather briefcase, not meeting my eye, then shoves two books at me, his hand stilling momentarily as our fingers brush. "The rest of the Foundations seminar read them earlier in the year; you'll have to catch up." It's *Utopia* by Thomas More and *The Prince* by Niccolò Machiavelli. They're so different from the books of the same name back home. These leather-bound volumes have stylized script and textured pages, and oh so much character, like a letter written from the author as a gift to the reader.

The hope I feel from noting his earlier expression causes me to be brave, so I ask, "Maybe you can help catch me up?" Not that I'm hoping anything will happen; I'm supposed to be pretending to be in a relationship with Rafe after all. But I miss the mentor sessions with Michael I had as an apprentice.

He doesn't meet my eyes. "Sorry. Bloche's away again, and my schedule is full this week. It's nothing you can't manage on your own." He does look up now, his eyes clear of any kind of care. "If you have any questions, you can ask them during seminar. Enjoy your lunch."

And with that look and those words, suddenly all my doubts come crashing back. What's a jealous glance? Easily misinterpreted, that's what. Words and actions speak louder than imperceptible, probably imagined body language. I need to move on from my fantasies. They're distracting me from what's important, and, though I hate to admit it, they're tearing me apart inside.

Rafe has saved me a seat next to him, but the thought of eating with a bunch of Guard trainees is not appealing. Bram and Yvette are at that table. They're both clearly trying to get back into Rafe's good graces, and he seems willing to put up with their presence, which I don't understand. But he doesn't protest when I bypass his table to sit with Georgie. Simon eagerly takes the empty seat instead. He's been following Rafe around as if he's auditioning for the role of his tail.

Mine and Rafe's behavior has not gone unnoticed, and Georgie has a questioning, mildly offended look in her eyes. But everyone near us is clearly eavesdropping; they're not even being subtle about it. I'll have to wait until later to explain everything to her.

But no time presents itself before I need to meet Rafe for our first training session.

He's reserved us a studio in the Spring wing, an area I've hardly explored. I enter a corridor that has an actual river running through it and soft moss growing on the walls. The river turns into a waterfall as I reach a staircase, which I descend, breathing in the fresh, cool mist. I should really hang out here more often. There are breezy rooms with pools, saunas, exercise equipment, and a lot of scantily clad journeys taking advantage of the amenities.

I find the room where Rafe has instructed me to meet him. He's lying on a mat on the floor, shirtless, glowing with sweat, clearly having just finished a round of crunches, or perhaps shooting an underwear ad, because I'm pretty sure that's the only other place in the universe where men look like this.

"Hey, Little Weed," he greets me, the epithet holding no malice.

There's a tattoo of a dragon on the left side of his chest. I drag my eyes away from his sculpted torso and very consciously focus on staring at his nose so that my eyes don't accidentally wander anywhere else.

"Can you put on a shirt?" I reply in a higher pitch than intended.

Look at his nose, Ada.

He grins, gracefully leaps to his feet, and walks to the corner of the room, where he fills a glass from a small waterfall. Now I'm panicking because his nose is gone, and I don't know where to look.

The room is mostly empty, with many windows and a fresh earth floor covered in rugs. There's a crop of rocks in the corner where the waterfall flows into a small pool, the stones forming multiple storage cubbies. Across the room, there's a crack where a root grows through the wall. I focus on that.

"Are you ready to train?" Rafe asks. I'm still aggressively staring at the root, but I see him in my peripheral vision, carelessly toweling off his sweat, his muscles doing all sorts of ripply things.

"About that shirt," I remind him.

"I'm glad you like what you see," he responds.

"Also, pants," I add. His tight shorts provide a little too much information.

He laughs. "Little Weed, you're gonna have to get used to all this perfection"—he gestures at his exposed figure—"if we're going to be training together."

Right. Training. Once I finish contemplating the deep philosophical truth—that I have only just come to understand—about the etymology of the term "washboard abs."

To my relief, Rafe conjures a shirt from one of the cubbies. Then he stands, hands on hips, and says, "Okay, where should we start?"

I clear my throat. "You tell me."

He slowly circles me, assessing, and I start to seriously regret the faded leggings and frumpy *Teenage Mutant Ninja Turtles* shirt I'm wearing. Couldn't I have at least fixed my hair? I still haven't bothered to trim it, and overgrown waves are frizzing everywhere.

"How can we turn you into some kind of actual threat?"

"Gee, thanks," I respond dryly as I try desperately—and hopelessly—to ignore the heat I feel emitting from his body so close behind me.

"If the Inquisitors have antimatter, you'll need knowledge of basic combat so you're not completely useless if your abilities are neutralized."

Combat sounds very hands-on. One side glance at those tight shorts and I want to be decidedly hands-off.

"Let's start with the Sire stuff. You seem to think that's a particular weakness."

"Yes, one of many."

I roll my eyes.

"Do you have a sparker on your spoon?"

"Yes."

"Take it out. Do you know how to use it to create a flame?"

"Yes." Well, I do in theory, but I'm not particularly good at it. The mod creates a small spark that can be ignited with Ha'i.

Rafe takes out his own spoon, opens to the sparking mod, and effortlessly creates a flame. "Now you."

I follow suit, rather clunkily.

"Again," he says, watching my hands closely. "What's causing you to fumble?" he asks when it takes me three tries.

"I've never been great at calling Ha'i on demand."

"You're thinking too hard. It should be effortless." He's not the first person to tell me this, but no one seems to understand that it's anything but effortless for me. Maybe I'm just a weak Sire.

He has me try a few more times, and once I get a little smoother at it, he says, "You won't always be able to access your spoon, so you need to be prepared to improvise. In this room, what can you manipulate with your Ha'i?"

"Um, you. Me."

He waits for more, but my mind is blank.

"The lights," I say when the thought comes to me. "Maybe the water can be electrified?"

He nods. "What else?"

"I'm all out," I say.

"Think!" he snaps. My spine straightens from the sharpness of his tone.

"I don't know, okay? I thought that's why you're here to help me."

"There's a rug on the ground, a source of static electricity. Out that window and through this wall, there are trees, with branches and roots near enough to break through." His words are clipped and full of judgment. "The rocks in the corner can be heated. If you have sense with you, the mud could be sculpted and animated into a golem. You need to learn to think on your feet. You need to know what you can control!"

"Fine. I'm here to learn. I'll do my best, but stop yelling at me!" Though I am annoyed at myself for not having thought of the tree. Plants are my thing.

"I'm not yelling; I'm speaking passionately."

"Please reduce your passion."

"I am a passionate person."

"So I've heard."

He grins but moves on without missing a beat. "Let's start with static."

He demonstrates, rubbing his socked foot against the rug, then, lifting his leg bent at the knee, he—exhibiting a distracting level of dexterity—passes his hand in shiin below his foot. A flame sparks into existence and then is quickly extinguished as Rafe claps it between his hands.

It's awesome. But I'm not going to give him the satisfaction of saying so. "Can you do that again?" I ask.

Rafe rubs his toe on the rug. I move to watch more closely, and this time the flame he sparks swooshes into a large blaze, igniting a lock of my hair.

Rafe's surprised expression makes it clear this wasn't supposed to happen.

I instinctively slap at the flames, screeching, my face heating as the fire licks its way up my hair.

Rafe quickly flicks opens a mod on his spoon that immediately stifles the flames.

The room is acrid with the scent of burning hair. "What just happened?" I ask.

"I'm not quite sure. That wasn't a normal response. I didn't use that much Ha'i. It's almost as if . . ." He trails off, looking at me curiously, but he doesn't complete the thought.

"As if what?"

He ignores my question. "You should practice this on your own until you get the hang of it."

"I'm not sure I should; it doesn't seem very safe." I take stock of my hair, but there's so much of it that the locks lost to the fire are hardly noticeable.

"You should be fine. That was an unusual circumstance. Just make sure to have your snuffer mod on hand." He brandishes the mod he used to extinguish the flame.

"Uh, I don't have one of those."

"I have an extra I can lend you."

"Thanks."

Rafe has me create static with my own foot and try to set it alight, but he seems distracted, and I'm scared of another fire. While I can make a spark, I can't seem to make a flame. Eventually, with a huff, Rafe says, "I think that's enough for now. Let's call it a night."

I nod, a bit disappointed. We didn't cover much ground.

"Walk back to my room with me," Rafe says. "I can get you that snuffer."

I nod again.

The path through the Summer wing is becoming familiar, and I know we're almost to his room when the tapestries turn the color of freshly cut grass and the walls illuminate with firefly lights. When we reach his door, Rafe asks, "Do you want to come in?"

He could easily just grab the mod and bring it out to me, so obviously the answer to this question is no.

"Sure," I say.

As he rummages through a drawer for the snuffer, I wander around his room. He doesn't have a roommate. I guess that princes are above sharing accommodation. On top of the piano that dominates his sitting area, there's a small sculpture of a dragon made of reflective hematite with amethyst eyes. Next to the dragon is a gilt frame with a picture of the Vanguard royal family—who, since Quorum, I have made sure to learn more about. They're all sitting in a line on a dais, as perfect as a painting in a museum. Rafe's father, King George, sits next to his wife, Princess Lilith—who looks younger than some of her stepsons. Alexander, the heir, sits on the right side of the king, and Rafe and his younger brother, Benjamin, are next to the princess. Though they don't wear crowns, they exude royalty. With the exception of Prince Alexander, they are all blond, and with no exception, they're all beautiful.

Benjamin sits with less grace than the rest of them, slightly reclined like the one picture frame off-kilter in a line of symmetrical ones. There's less severity to his face. Fewer sharp angles and lines. His eyes hold more humor than haughtiness, more question than declaration.

Rafe comes to stand next to me and hands me the mod.

"Thanks." I take it, but he makes no move to shoo me out of the room, so I say, "He looks fun." I gesture to the youngest prince.

Rafe smiles, his whole face softening. "Ben is the most like our mother. He's the sweetest of us—we're not a particularly sweet family." I let out a snort. "But Ben is different. He's . . . kind. And funny. I miss him."

"Why didn't he come with you to Genesis?"

"He's not a Sire, so he wasn't considered to be at risk." His expression hardens. "I wish Hypatia had remained there with him. Her condition is far too unstable for her to have been sent unsupervised so far from home. That's why I had to come too."

"What do you mean? Weren't you sent here for being a Sire?"

"I was close to mastering in Blood Sci, and I'm eighteen. No one would have made me come, but I chose to, to look after Hypatia. And I failed to do the one thing I came here to do." His nostrils flare, but then he inhales and blinks away all evidence of his emotions.

Perfectly controlled, he indicates the piano and asks, "Do you play?"

"Terribly," I respond. Kor's taught me a bit over the years.

"Show me," Rafe commands.

I sit on the bench and begin to pluck out a passable rendition of the "Moonlight Sonata." It's not a song I particularly enjoy, a bit too simple and slow for my taste, but that's what makes it easy enough for me to do it some kind of justice.

Rafe sinks down next to me and brushes my hands away from the keys.

"You'll deafen me if you keep that up. You're tearing the soul out of a beautiful song."

"I suppose now you'll tell me that Beethoven was a Maker or a Sire or something?"

"No, just a genius."

"A *philistine* a genius? Such a thing is possible?"

"It was different in the earlier generations. The more time that passes since the Exodus, the more the provincial world is separated from the truth they denied, and the more they devolve in their ignorance."

Ugh. I've been trying so hard not to hate him. Why must he keep making it impossible?

But then he begins to play the sonata. And he does it properly.

It's beautiful, like no version of the song I've ever heard before. Damn him. Why does he have to be so good at everything? I was wrong to ever consider it simple; when played correctly, it's anything but. The notes wrap around me and pull my pulse into the melody.

I'm envious. I wish I could speak my emotions through music. It sometimes feels like there's something inside me but I don't know the language to let it out, so I'm doomed to never be able to fully express myself.

Rafe leans into the music, the muscles in his back and shoulders rippling. It's like there are two separate masterpieces: Rafe, his whole body engaged, his hands doing a deliberate and intricate dance on the keys; and then the music itself, so beautiful, so haunting, so rich. He transitions into the third movement of the piece, one I hardly know and could certainly never play. His hands move so swiftly that they become a blur in my vision. He bangs them almost violently, and yet the sound released is melodious. When I play piano, I just use my fingertips. Rafe uses his whole hand. The tendons stretch as the sides of his fingers, his knuckles, all get pulled into the dance.

He's forgotten that I'm next to him, probably forgotten that I'm in the room at all. I can tell because I see the difference in his demeanor. The way he's shifted out of himself and into the song. The way he rocks his body into each note. All his usual harshness has melted away. Angles and lines disappear, revealing an unrecognizable face. One I have only seen the barest glimpses of before now. An expression so passionate that it makes me wonder what it would be like to kiss him. To do more than kiss. If he gives this much to his music, imagine what he could—

Um . . . scratch that thought.

He starts to play a different song, though it takes me a moment to notice as one song merges smoothly into the next like a rushing river flowing into a calm ocean. A familiar ocean. And though I don't want to break the spell that's been cast over the room, I'm so surprised that I say, "I know this song."

"You must be mistaking it for something else," Rafe responds, his attention never leaving the keys.

"No. I would never forget this." My voice comes out dreamily because that is how this song makes me feel. It wraps me in a memory that smells of cinnamon cocoa and feels like cold cheeks and toes sticking out of a warm blanket. "My father used to play this for me when I was a child," I say. It's the same tune played by the music box beside my bed.

"That's impossible." The certainty of Rafe's deceleration pulls me out of the warmth of my memory.

"Why?" I ask.

"This song was written by a Levite for meditative use by the Prophets of Naiot in order to help them achieve a prophetic state. There's no way you could have ever heard it." It amazes me how such sweet music can come from his fingers while such contempt drips from his voice.

"Whatever," I respond. "Think what you like. I know what my father played for me." I close my eyes, wanting to slip back into the song. I clasp my hands, rubbing my scars against each other. I won't let Rafe's music be ruined by his attitude.

But my words have angered Rafe, and his fingers bang down against the keys with a clang of sour notes. "I'm telling you, there's no way 'Yosef HaLevi's Nocturne' was your silly lullaby in the philistine world."

I momentarily forget how to breathe. "What did you just say the composer's name is?" I ask.

"Yosef HaLevi," he drawls.

If I hadn't spent the last few months constantly suppressing my reactions, I would never have been able to pull off the nonchalance that I achieve as I say, "You're right. I must be mistaken." But I know I'm not.

What am I even doing here? This plan of ours doesn't necessitate us becoming friends. "I've been in here long enough for all the necessary tongues to wag. I should leave." I shift off the bench and stand.

He doesn't walk me to the door.

26

For the next week, I do my best to avoid Rafe while still pretending to date him. But our fraternization has drawn just about as much attention as I figured it would. Which is to say, quite a lot.

"So, I hear you've been spending time with Vanguard now?" Sebastian pries as all the members of our team soak in a hot spring after a particularly intense early-morning hoverjoust practice. The opening games are fast approaching, and practices have amped up.

"Um, kind of, just seeing where things go." I breathe in the thick geothermal mist. The hot springs are one of the sources of the fog that blankets the island. It should smell like sulfur, but as with so much else, the Makers have improved upon nature, and it smells more like French toast.

"That's all we're gonna get?" Sebastian, always a sponge for gossip, looks terribly disappointed. "This is the same princeling who laughed at you while you were in the dust? Our biggest competition, who notoriously spent every night in a different bed until you came along . . . and that's all we're gonna get?"

Carlota comes to my defense. "Have you set your eyes upon him? Can you really blame her?" She flicks water into Sebastian's green hair.

He laughs. "You're right. I'd do the same. Oh, wouldn't I do the same."

After showering, I use Georgie's computer to call Kor. I haven't been in touch with anyone since the kidnapping revelation. I'm angry at my mom and unsure how to interact with Kor without confronting him, but I need to confirm that they for sure have Hypatia, and if so, where they might be keeping her.

I know that the Families have many facilities around the city—connections with the Met, Columbia University, and the United Nations, but Mom specifically said that Hypatia is at a medical facility. I need more leads.

Except the call is a whopping failure. Kor debriefs me, like usual. But I awkwardly freeze up and neglect to ask any of the questions I need to ask. Instead I stare at him, fixated on wondering how this person that I thought I knew so well could possibly be capable of abducting a helpless preteen girl.

The worst part is that it doesn't seem impossible. Kor has always been so single-minded in pursuing what he wants.

I'm barely paying attention as he tells me about a performance he did for a children's cancer charity. "It was weird doing a show without you," he tells me, and there's so much tenderness in his familiar eyes.

I feel like I need a system reboot so that everything can start to make sense, and instead of probing for information, I make excuses to sign off quickly.

When I call to Georgie that I'm finished, she comes in and quietly gets to work as opposed to pulling me into her normal fizzy chitchat. I'm pretty sure she's withdrawn because of the whole Rafe thing. I should explain it to her now. Explain our need for non-suspicious collaboration and that I'm not actually dating the guy who treats her like dog poop on his shoe.

I start talking. "So, I have an idea about how to get off the island—"

She whips her head to look at me. "Have you found out where Hypatia is?" She looks so eager. So worried.

I sigh as I shake my head, sickened with myself. Hypatia is in danger, and

I'm her best chance of rescue. But I can't even figure out how to have a useful phone call with my own family. Some spy I turned out to be.

"Is there any way I can help?"

I'm about to thank her and decline politely, but then I stop and think twice.

Georgie has dropped enough hints for me to understand that her online activities are not, to say, strictly legal. I don't know if it's impolite to ask your friend to hack someone for you, but I decide to give it a shot.

"Uh, theoretically, would you be able to find a place that I know exists if I don't know where?"

She thinks for less than three seconds, then says, "Know anyone who is likely to go there? Theoretically, of course."

Mom had said that all the New York members of the Chamber are involved in whatever is going on, so that gives me some options. "Yes."

"Oh, then this will be easy peasy. Choose whoever is most likely to open a link from you on their phone without any suspicion." She's already clacking away at her keyboard, flitting between monitors.

Kor and Mom would both be suspicious if I sent them a random message since they know I don't have phone access. But Alfie probably wouldn't think too hard about it.

"Got any insulting memes?" I ask her.

Georgie sits up straight. "Do I have any insulting memes?" She rubs her hands together gleefully. "Let me introduce you to my arsenal."

For just a moment, she reminds me so much of Izzy that I almost feel as if I'm cheating on Izzy with a new best friend.

We spend a little too much time giggling at ridiculously captioned classical paintings and grumpy cats delivering Shakespearean insults. I'm glad to know that despite Georgie having been isolated from most of provincial society for so many years, she's still acquainted with the best parts of the internet.

We settle on a picture of the Last Supper, but everyone at the table is giving the middle finger.

Georgie messages Alfie from her computer with my cloned number.

Saw this and thought of you. With an attached link to the meme.

Moments later he replies with a string of middle finger emojis.

"And . . . we're in," Georgie says triumphantly. "Oh, this doofus has his location services turned on, so we don't even have to wait to see where he goes. I can pull up where he's been for the past week." *Clack, clack, clack.* "Jeez, aren't these people supposed to be, like, super secret? They need way better digital security protocols." She starts to tag locations on a map on her screen. "So, what am I looking for?"

"A place that could house a covert medical facility? I'm not exactly sure."

"Say you haven't tracked someone before without saying you haven't tracked someone before," she jokes dryly. "We'll want to rule out anywhere he has reason to visit on a regular basis and see what's left." As she works, Georgie talks through what she's doing. She pairs his location data with other information from his phone to easily establish what can be ignored: his apartment, gym, school, girlfriend's place, favorite take-out spots.

She has *definitely* done this before. And now I can't help but wonder who else she's ever needed to track.

"Is there a reason he would be visiting this area?" Georgie asks, pointing to the East River on a map.

I peer over her shoulder as she enlarges the window for me. "Not that I know of."

"He's been here three times in the past two weeks." She zooms in on a couple of small islands.

"That's near Riker's Island, New York City's prison," I say. "Maybe he's been visiting an inmate?"

"No." Georgie shakes her head. "This here is Riker's Island, but that's not where he's been going. He's been going here." She points to a much smaller island. "Is there a park there or something?" She clicks around a bit more, then says, "North Brother Island. That's what it's called."

I inhale sharply. North Brother Island is the home of an abandoned hospital and is completely restricted. Or so I thought.

Before I can explain this to Georgie, she's already reading through an extensive web search. "There's a hospital there that has a past life as a place for quarantined disease patients, veteran housing, and a rehab for drug addicts. Now the whole island is a bird sanctuary and off-limits to people." She zooms in on a photo of the old hospital. "Definitely looks like a hidden medical facility to me," she says with a grin.

I nod. "That has to be it."

"So you're saying you think this is where they're keeping Hypatia?"

I nod again.

"Okay, let's make this happen!" She claps her hands together. "How else can I help?" She doesn't even wait for me to answer. "I bet I can make you a map." *Clack, clack, clack.* On one monitor she's researching North Brother Island, and with the other she's continuing to go through Alfie's phone, moving so fast through his apps, files, and internet history that I can barely keep up. "Has this dude not heard of incognito mode? I did not need to know that he's into—"

"I don't want to know!"

"Good call."

I'm not quite sure what Georgie thinks she'll find by scrolling through endless selfies of Alfie flexing in his bathroom mirror, but she clearly knows what she's doing.

"Jackpot!" she exclaims when she finds a series of pictures of what looks like a construction site. "He took pictures of the renovations they've made to the old hospital. I don't blame him—it looks super cool. I can cross-reference these photos with the old blueprints I found in the Historic House Trust archive to make a map. It won't be fully accurate, but it should be better than nothing."

"You are an actual wizard," I say with genuine awe and only a hint of concern for why she would have ever needed this specific set of skills.

An alarm buzzes, and Georgie starts to gather her things. "Well, this was fun, but I have a reservation to use one of the looms, so I gotta go." She blows me a kiss and bounds out of the room while my confession about Rafe stays trapped in my throat.

27

Michael seems distant during Foundations. Or not *distant*, per se, just . . . normal. Like a *teacher*.

I hate it.

But there's something I've been meaning to ask him, and I can't sulk forever. I catch up with him as he's leaving class.

"Hi." He smiles politely at me. I have to take two steps for every one of his to keep up with his long stride.

"I heard a beautiful song last week," I say. No need to mention with whom. "I was told the composer is . . . Yosef HaLevi?"

Michael lights up at the name, and he slows his pace just a little. "One of the greatest composers of our time."

"Of our time? So he's still alive?"

"No one knows. He hasn't been heard from in many years, and it's unknown whether he was in Naiot during the Fall."

"So Yosef also had the Sight?" I ask as I follow Michael into the cafeteria.

"No. He was a Levite—a musician who played to help the prophets achieve a peaceful mind to receive their visions. And since he's a Nazir, he also amplified their Sight."

My head is spinning. "A Nazir?"

"It's a rare genetic ability—even rarer than Sires. When a Nazir makes a vow to adhere to a strict code, they can amplify the strength of those around them."

"What kind of code?"

"They vow to abstain from drinking alcohol, cutting their hair, or being in the presence of dead bodies."

Michael fills his tray from the buffet, but I'm too distracted to get any lunch. I strain to remember the Sunday morning Hebrew school lessons my father insisted I attend. "Like Samson? And then Delilah cut his hair and he lost his power?"

"Yes. Samson is one of the most famous Nazirs given that his story is recorded in the Bible."

"And you're saying Nazirs give up these things for, like, ever?"

"If they choose to take the vow. But it's a difficult commitment, and many Nazirs never do. I believe they still have some natural amplification abilities if they don't break any of the criterion for a cycle of forty days. But if you're so curious about Nazirs, you should ask Journey Vanguard. He was raised alongside the most famous Nazir in recent generations." The precise angle of Michael's brows when he says this makes it clear that he has a lot of questions about my association with said journey.

"Do you want to sit?" Michael gestures to the seat across from him, and I take it.

"You're saying Prince Alexander is a Nazir?" I ask. I take a crunch-bomb from Michael's plate, which he has graciously pushed in my direction. It's a ball of brittle pastry and nuts drizzled in honey that crunches satisfyingly between my teeth, the honey making my bites sticky and slow.

"He is."

"Is he also a Sire?"

"No. To be both is extremely rare. But Sire genetics are strong in the Vanguard family, which is consistent with the theory that Chorus—Prince Alexander's partner—will be the mother of the Child of Three, the prophesied one who will be a Nazir, a Sire, and have the Sight."

"Do you believe that prophecy? That their kid will end the exile?"

He takes a few moments to think before he answers. "I've always been taught that the recorded prophecies are meant to be a guide. So I believe there is a message in the prophecy, instructions—even if we don't yet understand what they are. But I don't think it's any kind of promised future that is fated to happen."

Interesting. "Has there ever been someone else with all three abilities?"

"There are conflicting accounts, but possibly Jesus."

"Ohhh. Yeah, I'm definitely gonna have to ask Rafe more about this." As soon as the words leave my mouth, I regret them.

Michael scowls. "I don't understand what you're doing with him."

I swallow a sigh. "You two aren't so different, you know."

He looks up sharply. "I'm nothing like him."

"You're both highly principled—though your principles might be different— and you're both fiercely loyal to your friends and family. You're both passionate about music and politics, and—"

He cuts me off. "Oh please, I'm not purposely prejudiced and proud of it, and I don't lead people on just to get them into bed."

I steal another crunch-bomb and laugh.

"Why are you laughing at me?"

"Michael, you are completely emotionally promiscuous." Georgie had used that term, and it has stuck with me ever since.

"What is that supposed to mean?" The vein in his temple throbs.

"Oh, come on. You might not be jumping in and out of beds, but you, like, merge hearts with people and then keep them dangling on a string as you move on and do the same thing to someone new." I've had years of experience with Korach Chevalier to prepare me for Michael Loew.

His eyes look betrayed. "Being able to be open emotionally with my friends doesn't make me . . . promiscuous."

"I'm not saying you're purposefully being an ass. I'm just pointing out that you're not so innocent in the way you manipulate people."

"Ada, that's really harsh," he says. And I know he's right. I know I'm being a little cruel and that what I'm saying is only partially true. But there's something inside me that wants to hurt him. That wants him to see that he hurts me every day.

"Sorry, I'm just calling it like I see it. Look at what you do to Kaylie."

Michael sighs in exasperation. "My relationship with Kaylie isn't like that."

I scoff. "You totally use her as a stand-in for a girlfriend, even though she's clearly hoping for more."

"That's not true!" There are twin spots of red on his cheeks. He takes a deep breath, and his throat bobs. He slumps back in his chair and lets out a breath. "Is that really what you think of me?"

"I . . . " I look away, guilt taking over. I shouldn't be taking out my frustration on Michael just because I wish things were different. I try again. "I think you're a great guy. I just don't think you realize how your actions might sometimes be perceived."

"And you think I'm hurting Kaylie?" he asks.

"Um . . . I mean, you don't see her dating anyone else." Grey has been positively mooning over her since the Simon-in-the-tree incident, but she hasn't seemed to have noticed.

He piles his dishes on to his tray. "So, what?" He meets my eyes, almost accusingly. "You think I should date her?"

The crunch-bombs turn to lead in my stomach. But I remember his look when he dismissed me the other day. I know that my wishes are nothing more than wishful, so I say, "I think it's not a bad idea."

I lean back in my chair, the fight drained out of me. "And if it's not what you want, then you should make that clear to her." And to me.

He nods, then tenses as he looks over my shoulder.

I turn and see Rafe stalking over to our table. "There you are." His voice is a low growl, his eyes as cool as sea glass. "Let's go," he says, and grips my wrist, tugging me up from my chair.

"Don't order her around," Michael says, reaching for my other hand.

"It's okay," I say to Michael. But he ignores me and stares at Rafe, seething. Rafe reaches over, and without breaking eye contact with Michael, he pries Michael's fingers off my hand, puts his arm around my waist possessively, and herds me toward the door.

When we're out of the room, I shake his arm off. "What was that about?"

"You asked me to be mindful of your reputation, and yet you have no problem having a—whatever that was, a lover's quarrel?—with another person so publicly."

"It's not like that. He doesn't see me that way."

"And how do you see him?"

"I don't know."

"Don't insult me."

"Don't be so controlling."

"I'm not trying to control you. It was you who said you wanted to pretend fidelity for the sake of your reputation, and yet you don't seem to be considering mine."

I sigh. "I'm sorry. Okay? There is nothing going on between Master Loew and me, but I will be more thoughtful about how things could be perceived going forward."

"Much obliged."

"Anyway, I think I've identified where Hypatia is being kept," I say.

"What?" He stops in his tracks. "That's amazing!" He grabs me by the shoulders as if to hug me. I'm surprised by the action, and from the look on his face, I think he is too. He clears his throat and says, "Let's go to Sire lab early. I have something to show you."

I haven't had a proper lunch, but I did just eat all of Michael's crunch-bombs. "Sure, let's do it."

We pass Georgie in the Equinox, and I watch her face fall as her gaze tracks us. She and I normally eat lunch together, but I'm clearly headed in the wrong direction with one of her least favorite people. Right after she's gone out of her way to help me, no less. She waves stiffly, then hurries off. She has every right to be upset at me. I need to find some time for us to talk. I'll make sure to catch her later tonight, when I can explain everything properly.

"What did you want to show me?" I ask Rafe when we arrive at the Sire lab. No one else is here yet.

"My plan for getting us off the island." He pulls out a bundle from under our desk.

"That's the plan?"

"It will have to do. I had a better plan, but the one Ha'i stone on this island has apparently gone missing."

"What's a Ha'i stone?" I ask. And who could be stealing things? I'm the most likely culprit, and I certainly haven't taken any stones.

"The Blood Science guild's high material. A Ha'i stone channels very concentrated amounts of Ha'i and can be wielded by anyone, even those without Sire abilities. They are extremely rare and difficult to make."

"Ah," I manage to say, but my brain has frozen.

Even those without Sire abilities can wield it to channel concentrated amounts of Ha'i. The Blood Science high material, which explains why no one at Genesis has info about it. This is *it*. What I was supposed to find for the Families. But someone else found it first.

The question is, *who?*

Someone else must be up to something on this island besides me. I didn't steal this Ha'i stone, and while I'm devastated to know that the Families have had a part in any of the abductions, they're not the ones who took me. Twice.

I file away the information about the existence of the Ha'i stone for later. It's not one of my current priorities anymore. Getting off this island to find out what's going on with the Families, rescuing Hypatia, and bringing Rafe to help Grandfather are all that matter to me right now.

"This is the backup plan." Rafe begins to unfurl his bundle. It takes me a moment to refocus and realize what it is.

"Is that Simon's fold-up boat from his gallerie?" I ask, my adrenaline still humming.

"It is. Good lad, that one," Rafe says with surprising affection.

"It didn't work very well, as far as I recall."

"True. But we're going to fix it. We need a boat to reach the mainland."

"Well, what do you need me to do, Your Highness?"

"Don't call me that," he says.

"But I'm here and ready to be bossed around, and you do so love telling me what to do."

He rolls his eyes and puts me to work using spidersilk to fix the aspects of the boat prone to leaking. He does some intricate surgery on the motor. Work that clearly requires very steady hands as well as concentration. Or at least I gather as much from the way Rafe scowls at me whenever I move or breathe a little too forcefully for his liking.

"Must you do everything as inelegantly as an apprentice-made golem?" he demands in frustration.

"Sorry. I'll try to be quieter," I say, concentrating on a silent exhalation.

"I hate when you do that."

"What? Apologize?"

"Act civilly toward me when I'm mean to you."

"Of course I'm going to be civil with my lab partner and fake *lover*."

"You cannot make me like you through sheer politeness."

"Frankly, I don't care if you like me," I say.

"Frankly, I don't believe that, considering you look at me in a way that suggests you care very much what I think."

He's teasing me. Rafe Vanguard is teasing me, and I don't know how to handle it.

"Just because I find you aesthetically pleasing does *not* mean I care what you think," I respond.

"You think I'm handsome?"

"Fishing for compliments is really not necessary when I'm clearly bestowing them freely. And you know what you look like."

"Yes, it's true. I'm much better looking than you."

I don't manage to hold back my wince, and I know he sees it because, just for a moment, he looks as if he might regret his words, but when I plaster a smile on my face, his own expression shifts into frustration.

"Why are you smiling when I've said something rude?" he asks, exasperated.

"It was rude but also true. And I—how can I make this clearer to you—Do. Not. Care. What. You. Think. So you can call me ugly all you want, and it doesn't particularly bother me." I'm proud of how confident my voice sounds.

"I didn't say you were ugly."

"Don't worry. I'm not the one fishing for compliments. No need to retract your sentiment."

He throws his hands up. "You are frightfully irritating."

"Keep the insults coming, Your Highness."

He shakes his head ruefully. "If it pleases you, m'lady."

Other journeys have been meandering into the lab, their heads turning our way, clearly noticing that the bubble of frigid silence that generally surrounds our table has thawed. My neck warms at the attention.

Rafe discreetly tucks the boat away, and he spends the rest of the lab assisting Mbali in her attempt to make fingernails secrete viper venom. I test how different levels of Ha'i affect the thickness versus the length of a vine grown from a seed without sun or water. I keep my head down, ignoring the fact that everyone keeps looking between Rafe and me and whispering.

Nothing to see here.

28

"Tonight we're going to focus on basics," Rafe says when we meet to train later in the evening.

"Why? Haven't I been getting better?" I ask as I kick off my shoes and twist my hair up out of my face.

"You need to learn control," he replies. "You know how to conduct, but you need to be able to do it without thinking."

He's clearly just come from hoverjoust practice, so his clothes are, thankfully, less revealing than usual. But really, could those riding pants be any tighter? My arms ache from my own practice earlier in the day. I should get Rafe to also train me in how to hold a lance.

Not that lance, brain. Stop it.

"You're getting stronger, but you're still wildly inconsistent, and we have to get to the root of what's preventing you from calling on your Ha'i instinctively."

I grumble.

"Beltane is in just over a fortnight. Once I acquire the necessary supplies during the bonfire, I'm off this island whether you're ready to come with me or not. Do you understand?"

"Yeah, yeah. I got it, Your Highness."

"Don't call me that. Make shiin."

I tentatively hold out my hand in the formation.

"Now conduct."

"Conduct what?"

"Just start with a glow."

He holds up his own shiin and effortlessly emits a soft ball of light. Even his hand is beautiful. Fine and muscled, like a sculpture. Like the *David*'s hand.

I can usually manage a glow easily. I go through the steps in my mind like I've done so many times before, but nothing happens.

"Um. I can do this."

"This is what I mean about consistency. Try again."

I do, and again, nothing happens.

Rafe is watching me critically, with a dash of loathing. "Are you even trying?"

"Of course I'm trying!"

"It doesn't look like it. It's like you don't even want to conduct." He steps closer, crowding me. "You are *made* to do this; it should be as natural as breathing. Stop holding back!"

"I'm not holding back! What reason could I possibly have for not wanting to conduct?"

"Desire is nuanced. Being a Sire comes with responsibility, and you wouldn't be the first person in history to be overwhelmed by that. You need to face your fears, figure out what you truly want, and let down the necessary walls to get it."

Who does he think he is? He has no idea about what I really want. I drop my hand. "What if I'm just not meant for this?" It comes out as a whisper. My eyes burn with frustrated tears. Maybe years of repressing my Ha'i has broken it.

I expect that he'll back down, but this is Rafe, not someone who would actually be sensitive to my feelings. His voice and tone stay just as demanding. "You can't give up. Being an unfulfilled Sire is painful. It's why Sires have a higher rate of melancholy and self-harm. You were born to create, and if you don't, your mind will suffer for it. A piece of you will die."

I know what he means because I've felt the blackness at the edges of my worst days. That encroaching endless dark pit of mediocrity. Coming to Genesis has begun to mend that hole.

I can't help but think about the provincial stereotype of the tortured artist, the disproportionate number of creative souls who fall to substance abuse, mental illness, and suicide. How many of them have been untrained and unfulfilled Sires? Would I have veered down that path if I hadn't come to Genesis?

"Try again," Rafe commands.

I take a deep breath and confront all the conflicting instructions jumbled up in my head—Master Liu's well, Hilde's source—the contrasting guidance yelling over each other, completely paralyzing my flow of Ha'i.

"You're the master of your Ha'i. *Demand* that it do your will," Rafe says.

Great, another contradictory method. But I'll try it.

In my mind I adjust my thoughts to match Rafe's demanding tone, and I try to bully the Ha'i up from my core through to my fingers. It's completely ineffective. I feel nothing.

So much nothing that it gives me an idea.

What is the opposite of a demand? A request? That's more my style.

And so I ask.

I close my eyes and envision a glowing source of Ha'i at the base of my belly, and instead of pulling from it by force, I ask politely, *Will you help me?*

And it does.

My hand warms. I ask again, this time for a glow. A controlled ball of lights shines from my fingers. In my mind, I silently thank . . . myself. Then I cast my attention to the wall sconce, make another internal request, and I am elated to see the light flicker.

I try again to make glowing light flicker to life on and off in my hands. It happens seamlessly and instantly.

"You've had a breakthrough," Rafe states.

"I think I have."

Spending years holding back my Ha'i didn't ruin it; it made it shy. I've been hitting a rock that needed talking to.

Giddiness rushes through me. I want to jump up. I want to hug Rafe. But I stay where I am and content myself with only a wide grin.

"Good," Rafe says. "Let's harmonize so I can feel it." He steps closer, makes shiin with his left hand, and lines it up next to mine. A harmony is the practice of two Sires connecting their shiin at the pointer and thumb into a triangle to combine the power of their Ha'i. The energy between mine and Rafe's hands is charged with . . . something.

"I can feel you conducting. Now see if you can control the direction of the energy." His hand—so much larger than my own—emits sparks. They curl around my wrist and form a bracelet—or a shackle. The sparks fizzle out as they hit my skin.

"Now you try."

Sparks. I forget to frame it as a request.

There are no sparks. Instead, the air between my hand and Rafe's buzzes like a magnetic force, pulling our palms together. His hand presses into mine. It burns—a pleasurable burn that rocks through my whole body. I look up at Rafe and see that his eyes are transfixed on the union of our hands, his brows pulled together in confusion. He looks up, and our gazes meet.

I can't breathe.

We both look back at our hands, and Rafe twines his fingers into the empty spaces between mine. One by one. Causing all sorts of fluttering feelings in my fluttery parts. Our clasped hands are humming with an intense and tangible energy, and neither of us seems to be willing to break the connection.

Every particle of my body is now feeling the magnetic pull toward Rafe. Like I want every inch of us to be in contact and like that would not be close enough, like I want us to merge into one being.

I take a breath and force my hand out of his. But when I look up into his eyes again, I see raw want. I dread the knowledge that the same look is probably mirrored back to him in my own eyes.

"You're not really my type," he says in a breathy voice, "but apparently our Ha'i is highly compatible. I've heard of that happening but never experienced it before."

His expression makes the fluttering in my belly turn into a full-on swarm. And not of delicate butterflies. More like moths and bats and other night things with wicked intentions.

He takes a step forward, his eyes hungrily exploring my body. I'm aghast at his arrogance that he actually thinks it would be appropriate to make a move right now, as that's clearly what he has in mind. I open my mouth to tell him off, but my dismissal dies on my lips as he closes the distance between us, and my body only wants him closer.

"Stop." I gasp, backing away from him. I bump into the wall behind me without anywhere else to go. "You're doing some kind of trick with your Ha'i."

He laughs. "Me? Little Weed, you can't blame this all on me." He trails his pointer finger along my arm, and we both watch in amazement as sparks light up where our skin meets. A physical, electric hum seems to buzz under my skin, and every part of me feels warm and tingly. He leans over and murmurs huskily in my ear, "Your Ha'i has definitely come out to play too."

I may not understand it, but I know he's right.

A moment passes when all that can be heard is our ragged breathing, and then we give in at the same time. I reach for him as he presses forward, grasping my hand and restraining it above my head against the wall, then leaning in to kiss up my neck. His fingers curve around my throat, and I gasp as he tightens his grip, the metal of his rings pressing into the soft flesh. His mouth trails up to nip at my ear, and everywhere we touch is on fire. Not the licking flames of a candle, but the destructive blaze of a forest in flames. I feel parts of my body reacting, parts of me that I never even knew existed until this moment, now all deliciously aflame. My free hand makes its way up the back of his shirt, my nails digging into his solid, muscled back. I can feel his heart hammering through his chest pressed up against my breasts, and I involuntarily buck my hips against his with a delirious whimper.

He speaks, almost in a whisper. "I've been with other Sires before; it's not usually like this. My Ha'i *really* likes your Ha'i." And then his hand is on my thigh, hitching my leg up so he can press even closer, making me moan. His open mouth is skimming my cheeks, warming my skin with his gasping breaths as his lips move closer to mine, and I swear I've never wanted anything more in my life than this kiss that I know is coming, but I turn my face away at the last second, and his mouth catches the side of my neck instead. He moans in frustration and bites down. I feel each tooth pressing into my skin, as if he's about to tear into my neck and drink out my soul. It is not a gentle bite. It hurts. Fireworks burst behind my eyelids, which have fluttered closed. I'm dizzy and light, as if all my blood has been replaced with helium. Then his tongue is gently swirling around where he bit me, soothing, causing me to moan again.

"Rafe, stop, we can't," I gasp.

He emits an agonized groan but stops and replies breathlessly, "You're going to kill me."

"No." I gently push him away, and surprisingly, he doesn't resist. I work to catch my breath, then say, "I'm going to walk out of this room . . . and then I'm going to avoid you." I woozily wobble to the door, unsure how I'm managing to stay upright. I turn back and add, "And no more touching during training."

He looks almost drunk as he replies in a breathy voice, "I was wrong." He grins. "You are totally my type."

29

The Equinox is humming with energy. Even though the island is on lockdown, nothing can take away from the excitement of today being May Day and the start of the hoverjoust tournament season. Everyone is wearing their guild colors and emblems and the occasional mismatched token to support their favorite players from other guilds. (The Bioscience team is clearly favored to win; their emblem—a hand of muscle and a hand of bone holding a double helix—seems especially common among the fans.) All the league players are getting a lot of attention, myself included.

I'm waiting for Rafe under the tree in the lobby where a giant Galilean thermoscope is set up to track hoverjoust player rankings. Inside a glace tube float small colored bubbles that represent each player.

Hopefully today I'll get the chance to see my bubble rise, but that could be as high as it will ever go. Rafe and I are planning to leave the island tomorrow. We should be back before either of our teams compete again, but I don't know what will happen in New York, and I can't say for sure that I'll be coming back at all. The thought of that shouldn't hurt as much as it does. I've always known this could never be home. And yet . . .

"Good morning," a silk voice whispers in my ear as I'm hugged from behind.

I immediately get all awkward and stiff-limbed.

"Relax," Rafe scolds. "Everyone is watching."

The whole Rafe-and-Ada-are-a-thing has been relatively subtle until now, but today is going to be the full-on Oscar performance.

Rafe may be a prince and all that, but what he is most celebrated for by the youths of Maker society is his hoverjousting prowess. With today being the opening games for the tournament season, every single eyeball on the island will be trained on Rafe. And therefore on me by his side. I'm really not looking forward to the attention, but everything we've been putting on this charade for comes to a head today.

As we navigate the crowded room, Rafe's arm is warm around my waist. Too warm. But not in a bad way. In a too-good way.

"Why can't we stay with our teams and just, like, blow each other kisses across the room?" I whine. "This feels like overkill."

Not to mention, very dangerous territory. I have been vigilant about keeping things very hands-off between us during training—this did make it difficult yesterday for him to teach me how to induce a harmless faint by overwhelming someone's vagus nerve, since I refused to let him touch my neck, so I'm hoping I won't need that particular trick on our travels—but getting cozy for an audience on the day of a hoverjoust tournament is, apparently, a full-contact sport.

"We don't want anyone to question why both of us won't be at the bonfire tonight or at breakfast tomorrow. I'm sure you can endure just one more day of this," Rafe says, his tone packed with annoyance despite the soft smile he has on his face for everyone else's benefit. "And you promised to help me make a good impression on the hoverjoust lodge."

Sigh. I did.

But the problem with the fact that we haven't touched in a while before now is that I'm not primed for how very potent it is.

Rafe and I have acknowledged that our particular blend of Sire phero-mones has resulted in a certain . . . chemistry. (This is apparently, and dis-turbingly, a thing—that Sires exude My Body Likes to Create Things and I Would Like to Create Something with You vibes, and sometimes those vibes are particularly magnetic with other Sires' vibes.) But we've chosen to ignore it and have settled on something that vaguely resembles friendship.

But Rafe is not content with looking like mere friends today.

"Oh no, you don't," Rafe says, pulling me closer against him as I try to hang back to feel less perceived. To those around us, the action probably looks possessive, but he's just trying to keep me from bolting.

I grit my teeth and continue to smile and nod at all the people we pass who enthusiastically greet Rafe.

I'll be playing my first ever official match today, and these additional nerves are really not helping.

Suddenly, the sun comes out. And by that I mean Rafe turns on his absolute most charming smile, which I have to look away from so I'm not blinded into forgetting just who is grasping me by the waist. I look over to see who it is he's beaming at. It's the table of stern-faced heads of the hover-joust lodge.

I smile at them too. See, lodge people, those complaints about Rafe being mean to recruits couldn't possibly be true. Ugh.

The truth is, it doesn't bother me as much as it should. I don't want to be complicit in helping Rafe get away with being a jerk, but I've come to know him better over the past few weeks—not that it's been easy when he keeps his emotions locked down like a Vatican vault. But something I've realized is that hoverjousting is one of Rafe's only sources of joy on this island. He left his life, his guild, and his whole family to come to Genesis with Hypatia,

and now she's gone too. When his position on the league was threatened, it
wasn't just a game that was on the line for him. If me helping him makes a
difference to his standing in the league, I'm not mad about it.

Keeping away his conquests, on the other hand, still has me rolling my
eyes. But that part is, I have to admit, kind of working.

A handsome boy saunters over and tries to give Rafe his handkerchief as
a good luck token.

"I'm afraid I already have a good luck favor," Rafe says to him. "Isn't that
right, my dove?"

I snort at how ridiculous that sounds but try to play it off as a flirtatious
giggle. "Indeed, *babe*," I reply.

He strokes my cheek as he gently tugs one of the green ribbons from my
braid and ties it around his wrist.

"So, it's true?" the boy with the handkerchief asks sulkily. "You're really
with *her*?"

Nope. He's not really with me, folks.

Rafe holds me by the waist and uses me like a human shield to navigate
past the rest of his admirers until we reach the front doors.

It's time for the games to begin.

"Hypatia would love this," I say wistfully as we follow the parade of
people to the arena at the edge of the island. I'm full of guilt for enjoying
my first hoverjousting match without the very person who introduced me
to it in the first place.

Rafe tenses beside me, and I regret my flippancy. If I'm feeling bad and
missing Hypatia right now, I can only imagine how he feels.

The expression on his face is as steely as ever, but I've been around him
enough to see the signs that he's working to maintain the cool facade.

It's instinct more than anything that has me taking his hand to offer him
some reassurance, some solidarity. I'm the only person who knows the steps

he's taking to help his cousin. He laces his fingers with mine, squeezing gently, and—well, that doesn't feel like just solidarity anymore. Our Ha'i reacts as always, but it feels different this time, solidifying instead of sizzling, making me feel an undeniability that our hands *fit* together.

I glance up, but Rafe isn't looking back at me; he's casually waving at one of his teammates. Apparently, the handholding is no big deal to him, whereas I feel like I've just been downed off my hoverboard.

I have to stop getting lost in the act. Rafe is a master of acting this part without it meaning anything. Though I'm sure it helps that he has touched many, many more, um, hands, than I have.

Separating to sit with each of our teams is a relief.

My own match isn't until midday, so I get to watch the games unfold from up close while enjoying crunch-bombs and spiced juice and the gorgeous ocean view from the open amphitheater built into the cliff.

There is a lot of pageantry. Each league has a herald, and as it's the opening games of tournament season, they go all-out with their performances, introducing each player and their history and strengths.

When it's time for Rafe's match—against a muscly Sophist who looks fully double his size—the cheers increase tenfold. It feels like the whole island has come to watch.

The Bio's herald begins with a flourish. "Honorable Makers, it is my privilege and pleasure to introduce, for his very first tournament on a Genesis league, Prince Raphael Vanguard."

The crowd's cheers are deafening.

". . . captain of the Blood Science league in Avant for two years, and to this day he remains undefeated!"

The green ribbon on his wrist stands out in sharp contrast to the amber of the rest of his armor. I hear the people near me whispering about how he's never worn someone's favor before, speculating about whose it is.

And then he turns to me and winks, and the speculation stops. And so does my heart as I perish from embarrassment.

But luckily the gong begins the match, and no one is looking at me anymore.

Rafe is quite simply . . . magnificent. Like, now I *get* it. He plays the game like it's an art, and he is a master.

He trounces his opponent in the first two rounds, but the second time the Sophist is downed, he has trouble getting back up. It's clear at the start of their third round that the Sophist is injured and is in for a humiliating and painful defeat.

Except he's not.

As the two approach the center, Rafe lifts his lance upward, and the two pass each other without impact.

The third round is a draw.

Rafe could have easily made that strike for a few more points to influence his rank—and I hear a few boos from members of his team who clearly wish he'd done so—but instead he let his opponent end with dignity and without the risk of further injury.

That was so . . . honorable, and the crowd agrees. They're all on their feet celebrating and cheering, "Honor a Maker!"

It makes me proud to play the role of doting girlfriend and flurry over to congratulate him.

Instead of hugging me, he lifts me up and does a little spin. He should not be able to accomplish this so easily as I am not a light person, but I guess there's more to those ridiculous muscles than how good they look because he sure makes me feel light. He also makes me feel like a real girlfriend, the way he's smiling at me with the genuine joy of the game, as if I'm really the one he would want to celebrate this moment with.

It occurs to me that if we were really together, this is when he would kiss me.

Oh no.

I will simply not be able to survive if he does, and I have my own match to play in just a few minutes.

But I needn't have worried. Rafe takes the winner's sash he's been awarded and ties it around my arm. He leans in close, and his hair, most of which has come loose from its bun, acts like a curtain, blocking the view of our faces. So no one else knows that when he leans in closer, all he actually does is whisper, "Your team doesn't have a chance against us, Little Weed."

I don't miss the chorus of *aww*s and sighs from onlookers.

"How do you play so . . . elegantly?" I ask.

He explains as I walk with him toward his team's tent. "The reason that Sires are so prized in the league is because of our ability to bounce back from injury and continue to play. When I tilt, I do so with the complete assurance that I can immediately heal any pain dealt my way. The elegance comes from the erasure of fear. Without fear of impact, I am in control of the tilt."

Forcing reality to his will, as usual. What a prince.

Before he leaves me to go clean up and change, I say, "What you did, offering the draw—I thought it was really cool that you did the right thing."

"I always do the right thing," he scoffs. "You and I just have different ideas about what's right."

★ ★ ★ ★ ★

As the games progress, the Ciphers and Bios lead the rankings as expected. In the Alchemists' first match, Sebastian wins against the Artisans, but then we lose a close match against the Sophists. By the time it's my turn to compete, I don't have to all-out win my match, but I'll need to do well to keep us in the running. If I lose all my rounds or get downed too many times and fork over a bunch of points, then unless every remaining member of my team plays a perfect game—which is rare if your name isn't Rafe Vanguard—we're at risk of being eliminated.

Considering I'm about as good with a lance as I am at choosing my crushes, this is a lot of pressure.

Once I've donned my spidersilk armor, I take deep breaths and shake out my body. My goal is to win at least one round and stay on my hover for at least one more.

"Honorable Makers." I hear Zo, our herald, starting her spiel. "For her debut tournament . . ."

As I pull on my helm, I block out the sounds of Zo's exaggeration of my skills and instead tell myself to imagine that I'm snowboarding on a mountaintop—it's just me and the board and the cold wind on my face.

The gong sounds, and I glide into the pit. My heartbeat is so loud it echoes in my ears, drowning out the roar of the crowd. The shouts, chants, and screams melt into a thrumming bass line that buzzes through me, synchronizing with my pulse. This is the moment. My moment. Everyone is watching me. The Alchemists are counting on me.

I look across the arena to see who my opponent is. I probably should have listened to his herald.

Orange armor. A Bio. I don't recognize the coat of arms on his shield, but even from beneath his helm, I recognize his sneer—Bram.

My own green shield—since I don't have a coat of arms it just has the Alchemist emblem—is sturdy against my left pauldron (shoulder armor), my lance is heavy in the grip of my gauntlet (hand armor), and my knees bend slightly, shins pressing against my greaves (leg armor), which feel just like snowboarding boots, grounding me on my board.

I can handle Bram.

He's known for having strong force behind his strikes, which he accomplishes at the expense of his balance. So, basically, he's better than me, but even though my aim sucks, there's a chance that at some point I can down him. And I'm fueled by spite. There's no one else in this school I'd rather see choking on my dirt than Bram.

I just have to do my best to hit his shield and focus on staying on my board. The gong sounds, and we're off and shooting toward each other. It all happens very fast. One moment we're careening toward each other, and the next Bram's lance is crashing, with precise aim, into my pauldron. He is *strong*. And it *hurts*. And my body really wants to topple off this board.

Everything that was going so fast suddenly seems to slow.

Stay. On. The. Board.

Oww. My shoulder is in serious pain. Like, something-might-be-fractured kind of pain. The armor usually protects from this kind of injury, but I was going really fast, and Bram hit me really hard.

I remember what Rafe just said about how Sires can heal themselves as they play. I can do that too, right? I pulse Ha'i toward the injury, and the throbbing immediately diminishes.

Keep moving forward. Get to the end of the pit.

I drop my lance to help my balance because I'm having a very hard time staying upright. But only moments later my team is crowding around me at the other end of the pit.

I made it, and I didn't fall.

"How did you possibly stay on after a strike like that?" Sebastian asks with a look of pleasantly surprised bewilderment.

"That was quite a hit. Are you okay?" Miriam asks.

"I'm fine. I think." I close my eyes and focus my Ha'i toward the aching area, rolling my shoulder backward and forward. "I'm okay."

Bram is awarded a point for his hit, and I get nada because I didn't even come close to hitting anything. But everyone expected that strike to down me, so the fact that he's walking away with only one point feels like a win all around. And now I know what to expect from him and can strategize my next move accordingly.

I can't guarantee I'll stay aloft with another hit like that last one, and I won't be able to strike if I'm entirely on the defensive. My only option is to get to Bram before he builds enough momentum to have much force behind his strike. Which means going really, really fast. The kind of fast that is highly discouraged during hoverjousts because most players can't keep their balance at such speeds. But staying balanced while going fast on a hoverboard is maybe the one thing on this island that I truly excel at.

It's a good strategy, and it works.

I go fast enough that by the time I approach Bram, he's still far from the center. He hasn't built much momentum, but I have plenty.

Our lances crash against shields. This time Bram's strike is barely a glancing blow. And I hit him too. Hard. Yeah, baby!

We're each awarded a point. I can see how upset Bram is even from all the way across the pit. According to my team, he came really close to going down from my hit.

"You need to watch out this round," Miriam warns me. "Bram feels humiliated that the new girl is showing him up. Someone like him becomes unpredictable when he's angry."

I shouldn't try the same trick twice because now Bram will be ready for it. This time I'm going to adjust my stance to make it harder for him to aim at my shield. A hit anywhere else won't count for points.

I stand sideways, which wreaks havoc on my balance since I can't hold my lance the way I've trained, but if I can pull this off, I'll be able to hit Bram's shield a full body length before he can even attempt to reach mine, and hopefully, by then, my strike will be enough to diminish his aim and striking force.

But as soon as we're heading toward each other, I can tell something is wrong. The angle of Bram's lance is all off; he's aiming too high. He knows he's at a disadvantage if he aims for my shield, so he's not aiming for it at all. The slimeball is aiming at my head.

I don't have time to consider what a strike like his would do to my skull. I just act on instinct.

I've been experimenting with my hoverboard's versatility and practicing some skateboard tricks in the hover park, so I'm about 60 percent sure that what I'm about to try should work. If not, it's gonna hurt.

Right as we approach impact, I throw my lance, trying to vaguely aim it at Bram's shield. Then I lean back into my board and leap up onto the fence that divides us. The bottom of my board squeals against the metal of the rail—which has no maglev tech—and I glide like that, completely out of range of Bram's hit, riding the rail to the end of the pit. Then, feeling pretty good about myself, I showboat a little and do a kickflip on my way down.

The crowd is going absolutely bonkers.

The lodge has to convene to determine whether my moves were legal, but they rule that since I was continuously moving forward, it counts as a fair match. And apparently, when I tossed my lance, it did, just barely, touch Bram's shield, so they're counting it as a hit.

With two hits each, the game is a draw.

From the soup of noise in the stands, I hear my name rise from the crowd. I look over, and my cheeks ache from my smile when I see a large banner that says, Go, Ada, Go! It's so very . . . provincial. Georgie must have made it. Despite being mad at me about Rafe, she's cheering me on. And she's only one of the people holding the sign aloft, along with Mbali, a heavily pregnant Xander, and Kaylie. They're all cheering for me, wearing Alchemist tokens and waving and blowing kisses.

Suddenly the knowledge that I'm leaving tomorrow hits me like a direct lance strike.

These people have become my family here. How can I choose one family over the other?

Will I have to?

Michael's also there, sitting next to Kaylie, with a green token to cheer me on. But he's not looking at me. He's seething in the direction of the Bioscience team. Is he jealous Rafe and I are wearing each other's favors? Or is it Bram he's glaring at for taking reckless aim at my head? It's hard to tell because Rafe and Bram are standing together at the other end of the pit.

Bram isn't getting the hugging and high-fiving support that I am from the Alchemists. In fact, Rafe is yelling at him and practically pushing him toward their team's tent. If screaming at his teammates when they don't win is his style, I can't imagine he was a very good captain for his last team.

I head toward the team tents, but instead of going into mine, I follow the boys into the Bio tent.

When I enter, Rafe is still yelling, but when I hear what he's saying, I hang back out of sight to listen.

"You could have seriously injured her. What were you thinking?"

"It's a dangerous game, Vanguard. That's the whole point."

"Not the kind of dangerous where you purposely try to inflict injury. First the power strike and then a headshot—are you mad? You're lucky the lodge didn't call it a foul."

"Are you being serious right now? We've played on the same team for three years. Something like this has never bothered you before."

"We're not in Avant anymore. You know that at Genesis they have less tolerance for skirting the rules. This kind of play could get our entire team disqualified."

"No, it won't. You're just angry because I bruised your untalented, weed girlfrie—"

Bram doesn't even have the words out before Rafe has him by the throat, pressed up against a post. "Don't you ever speak that way about her again."

He really is very impressive at this possessive boyfriend act. He looks seriously angry. But it's actually scaring me a bit. I don't like violence, especially not on my behalf.

I rush over and put my hand on his arm. "Leave it. He's not worth it."

"Apologize to her." Rafe shakes Bram forcefully.

Bram looks at me, more afraid than remorseful. "I'm so sorry," he says.

Rafe lets him go, and Bram scurries off like a pathetic mouse.

Rafe is still fuming.

"Calm down," I say. "He didn't actually hurt me. See, I'm totally fine." I spread my arms and wiggle my fingers.

"You may be unharmed, but you continue to accept disrespect far too easily."

"You're actually upset about what he said? Why? You say worse to me all the time."

Rafe steps into my space, staring daggers into my eyes. "Let's get something straight, Little Weed. If all of them"—he points toward the exit of the tent in the direction of the crowd but doesn't tear his gaze from mine—"have to think that we're together"—he puts his hands on my shoulders and steps even closer—"then *no one* can insult you but me."

Wow. My heart is beating really fast right now. I bite down on my lower lip, and Rafe grunts in a way that sounds suspiciously like a growl.

"Okay, okay, I'll stop letting all the boys talk mean to me, *my dove*," I try to joke, but it comes out a little breathy.

"Be sure you do, *babe*."

That sounds way better than it should. I might be in trouble.

Once he's taken his hands back and given me breathing room, I say, "When I saw you yelling at Bram, I thought you were lambasting him for not winning."

Rafe leans his head back against a post with a sigh. "It's hard to even care about winning right now. Other things feel so much more important."

Hypatia.

"I get it. I feel the same way."

"Anyway, congratulations to you. You played a good game for a debut."

My brain is blinking out from the experience of receiving a compliment from Rafe. "And you were so sure I wouldn't be any kind of competition."

"You? Are still not competition."

"You're an ass."

"You have a nice ass."

Two compliments in one day. I'm really in trouble now.

30

Everyone is celebrating the opening games at the Beltane bonfire, even the Artisans who came last in the tournament and won't be moving on to the next round. I wish I could join the revelry and party with my team, but Rafe is using the distraction of absolutely everyone Beltane-ing it up to sneak around and "borrow" some equipment we're going to need. So I can't go. People will definitely notice that Rafe is absent, and he wants them to assume it's because we're together.

Instead, I head to my room to pack.

I guess not *everyone* is at the bonfire, because I encounter Michael exiting the library.

"Oh, hi," he says, flustered.

"Hi," I say back, so very eloquently.

It's sad that things have gotten so awkward between us. But I've been keeping my distance ever since our last conversation. The one where I told him he should date Kaylie.

Now that I'm leaving tomorrow, and I don't know when I'll see him again, I suddenly regret that choice. Our last few weeks together, wasted.

"Um, great game," he says. "Your match was really fun to watch."

"Thanks," I reply. There's so much more that I want to say to him, but it's too tangled to come out. None of it matters anyway. Michael and I have no future. If I don't come back, I'll never see him again. And if I do . . . well, if he ever finds out what I've done, he'll hate me.

We both start talking at the same time.

"I should get g—"

"I wanted to tell you—"

Awkward pause.

"You first," I say.

Michael clears his throat. "I just wanted to say that I took what you said seriously. I . . . needed to hear it."

Does that mean he's dating Kaylie now? I might actually cry.

He continues. "You were right, and I'm thankful that you didn't hold back on confronting me about it."

I'm not even sure which confrontation he's talking about at this point. I guess that goes to show how much time I spend scolding the poor guy.

He runs his hand through his floppy hair, making it even more floppy. "Yeah, so, I just wanted you to know how much I value your friendship."

"Oh. Thank you. I mean . . . you too."

That was so . . . sweet. So why does it hurt so much?

"I'll just . . ." He motions forward and then, with a last smile, heads off in the direction of the bonfire.

I head to my apartment, and when I enter, I hear Georgie humming in her room. I guess she's not going to the bonfire either.

With everything going on, Georgie and I have hardly seen each other, and she's seemed more than happy to keep her distance. But she showed up for me at the game today and has been a consistently amazing friend. I owe her better. Now's the perfect time to finally speak to her. To explain that everything with Rafe is fake. Which is absolutely still true.

I'm hesitant as I knock at Georgie's door, but she eagerly shoos me in. She's excited about something enough that she seems to have forgotten we've been awkward with each other for days.

"Congratulations on your match!" She has the harp and rose of the Artisan emblem painted on one cheek and the Alchemist emblem—for me, despite everything—on her other cheek. "It was totally awesome, but there's something I want you to see. Come look!" She claps to herself. "Cicero—"

"The guy who runs the conspiracy forum?"

"Yes!" She's as giddy as the time Hera Earhart complimented her bow tie. "Except he isn't a guy! I don't know why I just assumed, but his—I mean *her*, I checked her pronouns—her identity was so well hidden, it took me ages to track her down. Look, this is Cicero." Georgie gesticulates to her monitor, which has a photo of an Asian girl with thick round glasses and half of her hair shaved off. The haircut is new, but I'd recognize her anywhere. My heart swells with missing her.

"Izzy King," I say. Nothing should surprise me anymore. But there always seems to be at least one more thing.

"You know her?" Georgie jumps up from her chair. "How? What are the chances?"

Well, now that I realize who Cicero is, the chances actually make a lot of sense. All this knowledge about the Makers? It's more surprising that I hadn't already considered Cicero might have connections to the Families.

"She's an old family friend."

"This girl knows computers, already knows we exist, *and* she's cute. Can you, like, introduce us?"

"She's a *family* friend." I emphasize the word "family" for meaning. "And these days she works for Oz Tech with Nora Montaigne."

"Oh." Georgie's eyebrows gradually rise as understanding dawns. "So that's how she knows . . . stuff."

"Her family, and mine, and all the others, would be furious if they knew what she was up to." Even though I haven't spoken to Izzy in months, she's still one of my best friends, and I hope she's not getting into any trouble.

Georgie stares at Izzy's photo with wide eyes. "It's so weird to think that the Inquisitors we hear so much about don't actually exist. Really makes me wonder what else the Makers are wrong about. Ya know?"

I get what she means. Since the mourning day for the Fall of Naiot is approaching—it's the day before my birthday, so I have a chance of actually remembering it—we've been discussing the Inquisitors at length in Foundations. The Makers talk about it as if the "strangers" mentioned in the stories are, without question, the Inquisitors.

"Yeah, I feel like they must have some other enemy out there they don't even know about."

Maybe the Fall of Naiot was Ozymandias Tech too?

Except now I find myself questioning whether Izzy's warning message was about Oz Tech after all. With what I've learned about the Oculus and Hypatia's abduction—could whatever she saw that scared her be related to the *Families*? Could it be connected to why she left them in the first place?

But even if Oz Tech aren't the ones who took Hypatia, they're not innocent. They did try to take me. *Twice.* Leo de Montaigne roofying me to hand me over to his sister is proof of that.

I wonder for the millionth time what Izzy knows that she's not telling me. I wish she had trusted me instead of cutting me off.

Georgie trusts me. She completely took me at my word that the Makers must be wrong about the Inquisitors.

That kind of trust deserves my honesty. I take a breath and then say, "So, about Rafe."

She immediately stiffens, her lips pursing.

"It's not what it looks like," I start, with way too much guilt in my tone.

She looks at me like she can't believe I just said that, and then she laughs. A bitter laugh. "So you weren't wearing each other's favors during that game we were both just at?"

"What I meant to say is—"

"Ada, you don't have to lie to me to spare my feelings. I'm not going to tell anyone about your family either way."

"No! Georgie! Please listen. We're not dating or anything. It's just practical to let people think that. We're working together to get off the island to help Hypatia."

"And you *trust him*?"

"I . . . It's complicated. But I do trust that he wants to find Hypatia. Please don't be mad at me."

Georgie turns away and heads into the common room. I follow her as she makes kissy noises calling for Bast. The cat, who's lounging on the couch, completely ignores her, but Georgie picks her up and nuzzles her face into her blue fur, smearing the painted emblems on her cheeks. Bast puts up with the affection for very little time, then contorts her body out of Georgie's arms and dashes off.

"Georgie, I never meant to hurt you. No one here gets me like you do."

She snorts. "It's nice pretending we 'get each other,' Ada." Her tone is hurtful, but when I see she's clearly holding back tears, my annoyance melts away. "We may both be from the same place, but you're a Sire. Everyone respects that. You have no idea how long it took for me to get to a point where I'm tolerated—barely. At least it's better now than it was." She turns her face away. She's replaced Bast with a couch pillow, and she's clutching it to herself, curled up small on the couch. "Even the people who are nice— they see me as a stranger. I'm not at the bonfire tonight because without Hypatia and with you busy with team things, I don't have *any* other friends.

When you arrived . . . There's a reason your room was available. None of them wanted to live with me—they don't know how to act around me."

"Georgie, I get it. I do."

"No, you don't. You've had one foot out the door since you got here. This is supposed to be my *home*. For the *rest* of my life. And I will *never* fit in. When I do occasionally manage to blend in, I sometimes wish I hadn't, because I hear the way they talk about people from the provincial world. Like they're less-than, like they should be feared." She runs out of steam.

She's right. I haven't been here for nearly as long as her, and just today I was feeling like I truly belong. Finally I say, "I . . . I didn't think . . ." But Georgie's top lip is trembling, and I feel so horrible for hurting her that I'm not quite sure how to go on. What I'm supposed to say is that I'm sorry. And I am. I'm the one in the wrong here.

She's looking at me expectantly, waiting for me to find my words. I would have stormed off and slammed the door in my face by now.

I take a deep breath. I can fix this.

But the sound of knocking interrupts us.

"Hello?" Rafe's voice emanates through the door like a premonition of doom.

"I'm so sorry," I say to Georgie, ignoring the way my heart begins to race at the sound of his voice. "I'll make him go away."

"No, it's fine." Her tone is a mixture of benevolence and sarcasm that I can't even begin to parse.

I open the door. "It's not a good time," I say. I'm not going to let Rafe into Georgie's personal space right now. I can grant her that one courtesy at least.

Rafe's eyes don't miss a thing as he assesses the scene. Georgie isn't looking meekly away from him as she usually does. Instead she's staring him down, obviously pissed off. He leans close as if to kiss my cheek and whispers, "I came to help you pack, and it's a good thing because it looks like you need a chaperone so you don't divulge things that should be kept *secret*, as agreed." He then plasters on a fake smile and pushes past me.

"Well, look at you, little beauty," Rafe says when Bastet pads over to him curiously. He reaches down to scratch her on the head in exactly the way she loves. The blue cat immediately nuzzles against Rafe's hand and allows him to pick her up. Georgie glares at her for being such a traitor. "Looks like someone's been illegally experimenting on you," Rafe coos to Bast, who has nestled comfortably in the crook of his arm. She purrs so loudly I wouldn't be shocked to find out she was also bred with a motor.

Georgie isn't having any more of it. "Give me back my cat." She pulls a mewling Bast away from Rafe. "I'm going to bed." She stalks off to her room and slams the door.

"See, no risk of me telling her anything," I say to Rafe. "No need for you to stick around."

"Maybe your roommate is the one who stole the Ha'i stone," Rafe muses.

"What? Of course not!"

"Why are you so sure? She clearly has a grudge against Makers, and she has a blue cat."

I entertain the thought for a brief—very brief—moment before I shake it away.

"She has a grudge against *you* because *you* are an ass. And she has a blue cat because she *rescued* her." But I'm also curious about the missing Ha'i stone; the mystery of who might have taken it has been distracting me for days. Now I wonder if Bram and Yvette took it for Nora Montaigne.

"Either way, you can't tell her about our plan. We can't afford anything getting in the way of us leaving tomorrow."

"Rafe, I already told her. And you should be glad of it. Georgie's knowledge of provincial computers is the only reason I was able to locate Hypatia."

I watch the progression of emotions play out on his face as he takes in this information.

"You can go now." I try to herd him toward the door.

"I'm not going anywhere until I'm sure you're packed," he says. "I got the equipment we need. We'll leave at first light, and no one should notice anything is missing until midday, but hopefully we'll be long gone by then."

"Fine, if you insist. But you have to stay here." I grab him by the waist and physically force him to sit down on the couch. "You are *not* coming into my room."

For once I'm relieved my room is such a mess. The possible embarrassment of Rafe seeing my mayhem has a much louder voice than the one whispering dark ideas to me about what might happen if he did come in.

"Don't overpack. Your bag needs to stay lightweight," he whisper-yells at my back as I firmly close the door.

Oh, what a mess. Where do I even start? I'd tried to clean up. I really had. But then life got in the way. And there is nothing I loathe more than cleaning my room. Except packing. Packing is worse. Packing involves finding all the things buried in the piles.

"This is ridiculous," Rafe calls to me. "I'm coming in."

He is so gravdamn impatient! "Please don't."

I hear the doorknob turning.

Oh no. Rafe's about to get a glimpse of my crazy. As if he didn't already have enough scorn for me. I mean, I've seen his room, and it would not be an exaggeration to call him fastidious.

But when he opens the door and takes in the view, it's not disdain I see on his face, but amusement.

"You," he says pointedly, "keep packing." And then he does what is positively the most mortifying thing he could possibly do.

He starts to clean up.

Within a relatively short amount of time, he's introduced a brand-new organizational system to the room, and he's methodically putting everything away.

I'm interrupted from my folding—okay, fine, my stuffing of unfolded things into my backpack—by the sound of Rafe clearing his throat. I look up, and he is standing by the bed, eyebrow raised, my bright pink bra dangling from his index finger.

The mortification that burns through me is so hot that it may actually melt my bones. I'm pretty sure my face is currently turning the same color as the traitorous item. I've been looking for that gravdamn thing, forgetting that I'd kicked it under the bed the last time a boy was in this room. Why the hell is Rafe cleaning under my bed? Doesn't he know that's where secrets go to stay buried?

I may never recover from this moment.

"Did you want to borrow it?" I joke, hoping to relieve the tension.

"No, thank you, but I was hoping you might pack it for our trip. It really is a lovely color." He tosses it with perfect accuracy into my bag.

I didn't think it was possible to blush any harder, but apparently I was wrong.

Pretty soon I'm all packed and the room looks amazing. My mind calms from being surrounded by order.

I walk Rafe to the door, and it's awkward because it feels like he should kiss me, but there's no one watching. Instead, I hug him, because he just cleaned my room and I'm honestly grateful. He seems surprised, but he tentatively hugs me back, friendly-like, with only the smallest fizz of tension as my ear barely grazes the skin above his collar.

Tomorrow we're going to sneak off this island and face my family. And tonight I'll sleep in a bed without any crumpled clothes beneath me. What a thought.

31

We start off the next morning before sunrise. I try to take note of the way down to the water for future reference, but I'm quickly out of breath from the difficulty of what is turning out to be a full-on hike. When we reach a break in the overgrowth, I halt. A hint of sun is beginning to purple the sky, just enough for me to see that the trail leads right down the side of the cliff. A narrow, steep descent of boulders make natural steps—each no more than a foot wide—with the cliff on one side and on the other side, only air. As in, a straight drop hundreds of feet down into the ocean below.

"How exactly do you expect me to climb down this?" I ask Rafe.

"With the two feet that the Conductor has benevolently granted you?"

"My hips are wider than this path."

"Your hips, while lovely, are not relevant to your descent."

"Was this plan all just a plot to kill me? Because there is no way I'll make it down that alive." I say this in jest, but I don't fail to recognize that it wouldn't be a bad way to take care of the girl that Rafe now has incontrovertible evidence is connected to the enemy.

He moves closer behind me, and his breath tickles my neck as he whispers into my ear, "If I wanted you dead, I would have found a much more delicious way to kill you."

It's official. I must be broken because a death threat should not make my breath catch.

Rafe tugs me around to face him, looks directly into my eyes, and says, "You can absolutely do this. This is no different from walking down stairs, and you walk down stairs all the time."

"Most staircases won't kill me if I fall."

"When was the last time you fell on a staircase? The only danger is in your head. And if you do slip, I have excellent reflexes." He winks.

I look back toward the trail. I may not frequently fall down the stairs, but most stairs aren't liable to crumble beneath my feet either.

My mouth is dry. "Rafe, I'm really not sure I can do this."

"You really don't have a choice." His momentary support has reached its limit. Now there is an impatient edge to his voice. "Did you think sneaking off a secret island was going to be easy? I watched you flip your hover off a nearly five-foot railing yesterday; you can manage some stairs."

"You go first."

He makes his way down the ledge, and I have no choice but to follow. For the first few dozen steps, as long as I stare at Rafe's back and don't dare look anywhere else, I'm fine. But over time the steps become less even, and we have to scramble instead of walking upright.

"Why are we doing this again?" I ask when my knees and calves start to burn from the angle of our descent. The wind whips my hair into my face and steals the words from my mouth.

"It's the only safe way to get off Arcadia other than the Atlas."

"You call this *safe*?" I concentrate on making my feet follow his feet. If I just do what he does, I'll be fine.

"And it's fun."

"Painful and terrifying is really not my idea of fun," I grumble.

"Oh, come on, it's not that bad. We need to launch the boat at the right time to avoid being seen by the Guard on watch. Stop complaining and keep up."

"You do realize you are stronger, have longer legs, and are in impossibly better shape than me?" As if to prove the point, I slip on a loose stone. Rafe instantly grabs my arm, stabilizing me. "Keeping up is a tall order."

"As usual, you're setting far-too-low standards for yourself."

"Or you're holding me to an impossible standard." I shake off his arm and keep trudging down.

"I'm pushing you to be your best."

"Sorry if me not being a professional mountain climber means that I'm somehow not good enough for you, but news flash, this is me, mediocre and fine with it."

He laughs. "I think I've made it clear that you are more than good enough for me."

"I have never once confused your willingness to jump into bed with me as respect." I wipe the sweat from my eyes with my sleeve.

"You're right. I couldn't possibly respect anyone who is mediocre and fine with it."

"You're obnoxious," I say to his back.

"Or just correct about your capabilities?" He's stopped walking, and when I look up, I see the beach.

I rush down the last few steps and run toward the water, my arms outstretched. All my muscles are burning, and I'm covered in sweat and dirt, but I did it. And it feels pretty gravdamn good.

Okay, and it was even a little fun.

Rafe is beaming at me with his too-pretty smile, but I refuse to give him the satisfaction of having been right, so I turn my face into the salty wind.

Rafe quickly inflates the boat. He sits at the back and has me sit between his legs, my back resting against his chest. Well, this is awkward. I'm super grimy from the hike, and I can't stop fidgeting because of the particular alignment of my butt and his crotch.

Rafe hands me a canteen, and I gulp liberally as he sets the motor and guides the boat. And then we're off, and it's *fast*. We shoot through the water, white foam in our wake. I sigh and lean my sweaty head against Rafe's unfairly dry and non-smelly shirt. The sun glares, so I close my eyes.

I wake with my head lolling against a ridiculously hard chest. To my embarrassment, my cheek is wet with drool. If Rafe noticed the offense, it doesn't seem to bother him. His hands are casually resting on my thighs.

"Good morning," he says. Then he points his chin in the direction of the coast we're approaching. "Just in time."

32

I'm pretty groggy as we land on a beach that a sign informs me is in St. Augustine, Florida. Rafe folds up the boat onto his back and navigates me through a cave entrance to an Atlas station—supposedly the first ever built in the New World when the line was first being constructed.

Though the Arcadia station is locked down, the rest of the train line is still running, and no one who sees us board asks any questions.

"Aren't you worried that you'll be recognized?" I ask.

"I never assumed we wouldn't be discovered," he responds. "Genesis will soon notice the missing magneto gun and put all the pieces together. Our only rush has been to get to New York before they stop us."

The trip to the New York station is short, and we're soon pulling into the familiar platform, the air locks closing behind us.

We exit the City Hall station—the non-fun way, up a simple elevator into an inconspicuous office building where every door needs a separate special code—and then . . . we're back in my city. The Brooklyn Bridge towers over a beautiful spring day. I don't know why this surprises me since it's spring in Arcadia too, but last time I was here, the city was wearing its winter coat of frost and holiday decorations.

There's a familiar concert of honking horns, blaring sirens, and shouting pedestrians. It smells like street food, exhaust, and garbage—but in the best way. It's so *alive*. The Maker population is tiny, nothing in comparison to the bustling life of New York City.

"You look happy," Rafe says somewhat begrudgingly as he darts out of the path of an oncoming man who is texting aggressively without looking where he's going.

"I love it here. Have you spent any time in Manhattan?"

"No. The only time I've spent in the provincial world has been in Europe."

I feel my own grin stretching wide. "Well, then, I'm going to have to show you around." Finally, we're on my turf. I want him to see my world. I want him to see how amazing it can be and that the people have as much depth and creativity as Makers.

"Let's first get to the hotel, clean up, and get rid of these bags." Rafe booked us a hotel room, and though I have no idea how he managed to do so without internet, I'm glad for his foresight as we are a total disaster—sweaty and dirty from the climb, damp and muddy from the boat.

"Great. We can take the subway."

"Let's get a taxi."

"The subway is a classic New York City experience, and today you are a tourist."

"And slow and dirty. From my understanding, a yellow cab is also a classic New York City experience. And I have money that I'm willing to spend." Despite the Maker world not using regular money, Rafe is fabulously wealthy in the provincial world. The Makers—the Vanguards especially—have numerous old business holdings for when money is necessary.

"Mass transit is better for the environment."

He is silent for a beat. "Okay. But in this instance, I am willing to forgo my own personal morals for the sake of convenience. Let's get a cab."

For a boy who's grown up in a world without proper money, he sure does know how to spend it. And for someone who has never been to New York City, he sure knows how to live it large here. The hotel we pull up to is the kind I've never noticed as a local, because I have never had reason to be on such a polished block.

As we walk in, I feel like a complete impostor, especially being so dirty and underdressed. I'm sure that at any moment I'll be informed that this shiny lobby is only available to guests of the hotel, which I must clearly not be. But everyone is extremely polite.

Especially the receptionist. She's immaculately beautiful and flirts unabashedly with Rafe, smiling her perfect toothy smile and flipping her perfect blond ponytail. She even says we can have our room right away although it's hours before check-in. But when she mentions that her shift ends at four thirty and slips Rafe her phone number, I get pissed. What's her problem? Isn't it obvious that we're here together? We're not actually together, but she has no way to know that. *Rude.*

"I thought you hate provincials," I say to Rafe. "But you don't seem to be having any trouble making friends." I hear the grouchiness in my voice.

"I'm just doing my part to fit in," Rafe replies. "But I must say, I find your jealousy . . . hot." He tries to put his arm around my waist, and I slap it away.

Rafe knows how to speak to all the fancy staff and flash all the right smiles and all the right plastic cards. He knows how to be escorted by the bellhop to our tenth-floor room and how to tip him without being the slightest bit awkward.

I'm insanely resentful. This is my world, and he's doing it better than me. But it's hard to stay annoyed when I see our room.

It's opulent and cozy at the same time. Lots of crisp white and rich gold. There are two queen-size marshmallow-soft beds and a view of New York that makes it look like the sanitized movie version of the city instead of the real one I grew up in.

The bathroom has more gold and more white with beautiful marble tiles and a bath big enough to swim in. Once I've dumped all my things, I take a luxurious shower with sweet-smelling soaps and towels made of clouds. It's only when we're both scrubbed clean and wearing fresh clothing that I realize that I'm *alone in a hotel room* with His Highness Raphael Vanguard.

"I'm famished," Rafe says. "Let's go get some food." Well, that solves that problem . . . for now.

Rafe stands out on the streets of New York. Even though he's wearing his regular-people clothes—jeans and a T-shirt and his leather jacket, which I did eventually return to him—with his looks and his build and his man bun, admiring eyes are constantly drawn to him. I see the assumption that he must be someone famous, an actor or a model, because regular people just don't look *that* good. Those eyes all then slide over to me questioningly, then quickly away when they realize I'm no one special. It's an incredibly familiar feeling. The exact way I always feel alongside Kor. It's been months since I've felt this invisible.

Rafe is under the mistaken belief that he has tasted good pizza since he had some in Naples where "pizza was invented." So I have no choice but to set him straight with real New York pizza, which we eat on a bench in Central Park. Then, because we don't plan to move forward with our plan until nightfall, we wander around the Metropolitan Museum of Art.

I've been to the Met countless times, but now it's with new eyes. I see the foundations of Maker life chronicled in the Renaissance art. Rafe gets very worked up about one Raphael painting that he says is absolutely a forgery, as his family has the original hanging in their home in Avant. I steer him to the modern art section so he doesn't make a scene, but there he quickly loses interest.

"Ada, this has been lovely, but I'm fatigued and want to rest up for later. I'm going to go back to the hotel for a nap. Why don't you stay here? You're clearly having a good time, and there's so much more to see." He doesn't give me a chance to respond. He lifts my hands to his lips, brushes a kiss across my knuckles, and says, "I'll see you later." And then he's gone.

I can't help but feel disappointed. I didn't want to go separate ways. I was having a nice time together. I continue to explore on my own, my enthusiasm deflated. Why did he even suggest coming here if he was gonna ditch me?

Then it hits me. Like a truck through a red light. What time did the receptionist say her shift was over? Four thirty? It's four forty-five now. Of course he's horny after weeks of not getting any while pretending to date me. I feel sick to my stomach. And angry. Before I can think about what a bad idea it is, I'm storming back to our hotel.

I crash through the door to our room, ready to let my anger burn hot, but what I see stops me cold in my tracks.

Rafe looks up sharply, shocked by my entrance. He is indeed with the receptionist in an intimate embrace, but not in flagrante delicto, as I had expected. They are both shirtless, but I assume that's for the practicality of cleanliness rather than anything else. Rafe sits on the bed, and she is draped over his lap. I'm pretty sure she's unconscious.

And then there's the blood. Lots of it.

Rafe's mouth is wide open in surprise. His teeth glisten red in stark contrast to the pearly white peeking through. Blood drips down his chin, down his neck. His chest is a sculpted canvas for a messy Jackson Pollock painting of crimson spatter. None of it is his blood. It's all hers. Oozing out in a wine-red river from a gash in her slender wrist. Rafe's spoon is on the bedside table, open to a mod with a sharp, now scarlet-tipped, point.

"I didn't expect you back so soon," he states, as if I've caught him borrowing a book without permission or something equally ordinary. His words sound moist and sticky from the blood coating his teeth. He notices this too and closes his lips. As if in slow motion, I watch the skin around his lips rise and fall into slopes and valleys as he sweeps his tongue around the inside of his mouth. His throat bobs as he swallows. He looks straight at me, as matter-of-fact as ever. "I do apologize. I didn't want you to see this."

33

I'm dumbly, numbly trying to process what I'm seeing.

"What—" I don't even know what to ask. I contemplate just turning around and running as fast as I can.

"Blood doping," Rafe explains simply, as if it should be obvious to me. His pupils are dilated, and his muscles look pumped and defined, bigger than usual.

The feeling of him biting my neck tickles my memory. I remember thinking he wanted to break through the skin and suck out my soul.

"By consuming her blood, I absorb her blood cells into my bloodstream, which gives me extra energy, stamina, and strength." He states it all so factually while the woman lies limp in his lap. "The Vanguard family line has enhanced digestive systems that produce protective enzymes that prevent the blood cells from being broken down. Blood consumption is used at times when we need an extra advantage."

"You drink blood to make you stronger?"

He nods.

"You're telling me you're a vampire?"

"The earliest Vanguard experimentation did make the subjects more reliant on blood than we are now, and some even had fangs. They are likely the source of the vampire mythos."

Consider my mind officially blown.

I look at the girl. "Is she . . . ?" I can't even say it.

"She's fine. I didn't drink that much, and I muddled her." I see the empty cup on the bedside table. "She'll wake up, think she fell asleep watching a movie with me, and be on her way, no worse for wear."

And then I gasp as the pieces click together. I grasp my arm, remembering the light pink scratch from Carnevale. Rafe sees the movement and nods. "Yes, when the Guard traitors stole your blood, they took it for doping. They were likely looking to have some fun at your expense before they handed you over to the Inquisitors. As a Sire, your blood would have a much more profound effect than usual; it could even temporarily grant the drinker your Sire abilities." He shifts the girl off his lap and smears patch paste on her wrist. "However, the Testament of the Guard has long forbidden the consumption of another Maker's blood. Only philistine or animal blood can be used for doping."

"How . . . can you just compare humans to animals like that?"

"Oh, come on, you treat humans like animals all the time."

"That's not true!"

"Don't be so self-righteous," he snaps. He swipes blood off his chin and licks his fingers. "All of humanity has been benefiting from the blood of other humans since the beginning of time. This entire country has been leeching off innocent lives since they decimated the indigenous population and built your economy on the backs of slaves." He uses the ruined bedsheet to wipe the worst of the blood from his neck and torso. There's obvious power pumping through him. I can almost see his dragon tattoo ripple as his heart—which I now realize is a lot colder than I'd begun to hope—beats with power from stolen blood. "You pretend you're more enlightened now, and yet you all still buy your technology and fashion and fuel your cars by putting money in the pockets of regimes that are killing and oppressing their people to continue making a profit. You spent your life ignoring the price for your modern conveniences, yet you're always so willing to crucify anyone who is a little more honest about humanity's parasitic nature."

My mind is reeling at his accusations. He sounds like Grandfather, always trying to explain about big companies who take advantage of immorally cheap labor. But that's not the same as the bleeding girl lying on the bed. "So you think that makes . . . this . . . okay?"

"It means that you and I aren't so different as you like to think. I'm just honest about it. You can go ahead eating meat from animals you would never kill yourself and send children off to die in a war you wouldn't fight yourself. If you're going to profit off someone dying across the globe just because you've never seen their face, then you're a gravdamn hypocrite. I know who I am and what I do. You can keep living in your world of denial. Keep lying to yourself, but don't judge my actions."

"Why didn't you just drink my blood?"

This suggestion enrages him. "Don't ever compare yourself to them." His voice is an angry growl. "You are a Maker. You are a *Sire*. You are made in the image of the Conductor and live a life dedicated to continuing the creation of the world, instead of living a destructive life of wastefulness, on instinct, like an animal." His face is full of disdain. "You may have come to us as a weed, but you have the potential to be so much more. Being my food was the most relevant thing she"—he motions to the poor girl's limp body as if she were a plate of discarded leftovers—"will ever do."

"She's a *person*," I respond quietly. I don't understand how he doesn't see this. Is that how he thinks of Georgie? Like *food*? "They're all people, with the same potential that Makers have. Don't you see this amazing city?"

"More denial. You know how useless your life was before you came to

Genesis." He starts spraying everything down with stain remover—because of course the Makers have one that actually works. It's done wonders for my period underwear. "They're all lazy consumers. Only a handful of philistines have made any useful contributions to the world since the Maker Exodus. And it has all been used to fuel greed or war."

He has no idea how wrong he is. "I'm just like them, and you seem to have stopped detesting me. Can't you realize that if you gave them a chance, you would see their worth as well?"

He steps close to me, looks me straight in the eyes, his doped-up gaze a shiny, unnatural shade of steel, and oh so angry. "You. Are. So. Much. More. Than. *Them*."

He's so close that my clothes are in danger of being stained by the blood. So close that I don't even see the blood anymore. So close that I hear his heart hammering at preternatural speed.

I look away first.

He says, "I'm going to get cleaned up." I hear the bathroom door slam.

I wait for a moment, breathing heavily. Then I follow him in a huff. This conversation isn't over, and I can't be alone in the room with the girl's unconscious body.

I enter the bathroom with my eyes shut. He's already in the shower, water turned on full blast. I squint my eyes open, and when I see the curtain safely drawn, I open them fully. The remains of his clothing lie in a messy pile in the corner of the room. A lonely hair tie is discarded on the vanity near the sink. I close the door behind me so I don't have to see the girl lying there, prone and limp.

"I can't be part of this anymore." I raise my voice loud enough to be heard over the sound of the water.

"We'll get Hypatia and see to your grandfather, and then it will all be over," he responds from the other side of the curtain. "I'll bring you back to the institute, you can go on living in denial, and we can commence ignoring each other once again."

The room fills with steam. Everything I've just seen and heard makes it easier to ignore that we're having this conversation while he's completely naked. There's a crack where the curtain doesn't quite meet the wall, and through it I see pinkish water whirl down the drain.

Blood. Her blood. I turn away from the shower as I gag.

The steam is thicker now, the mirror fogged over. I can only make out strange parts of my face, distorted into a deformed image I don't recognize. It's becoming difficult to breathe the heavy, moist air. I draw in a deep breath, and my lungs fill with the metallic smell of blood mixed with the florals of the hotel soap. My head is swimming, and telltale saliva pools on my tongue. I know what's coming next.

I drop to my knees in front of the toilet just in time. My pizza lunch burns my throat as it comes back up, and I retch into the bowl.

What am I even doing here? Planning to ambush my family with Rafe? Why did I never apologize to Georgie? Why did I tell Michael that he should date Kaylie? I'm severed from everyone who truly cares about me, and the one person I chose to trust turns out to be a monster. I retch again.

A rush of cool air tickles my neck, and the sound of water has silenced. I turn, and Rafe is behind me in a fluffy white robe. He's opened the door to let out the steam, and I take in some long breaths of clean air. But there she is, lying on the bed with a vague expression on her sleeping face. I hastily turn back to the bowl to retch again, and Rafe kneels on the ground behind me, pulling back my hair as I empty the last remaining contents of my stomach into the toilet. I'm shaking and clammy all over; even my hands are damp as they slip around the sides of the porcelain bowl. There can't possibly be anything more to come out. I spit into the bowl a few times, trying to clear the taste from my mouth. I sit up, pushing Rafe away.

"Don't touch me." My voice is strained. I'm exhausted, drained. Why did I trust him? I knew he was dangerous. Why did I let myself get caught up in our charade? I know that part of the pain I'm feeling now is the sting of disappointment. I can admit to myself that while this has always been about getting to Hypatia, it was starting to be about something else, too. Something I should have never entertained. Now it's one more thing I'm losing as I regret this entire decision. I feel complicit in what Rafe has done. I should have known better than to be fooled by his good looks and whatever chemistry there is between us.

I'm trembling with chills, and my teeth are chattering. The shock of the situation enrobes me in a cloak of cold. We're both still sitting on the bathroom floor. Up close I can see the fading of the years in the degrading grout between each marble tile. It's not quite as glamorous a view from down here. Rafe is on his knees behind me. He reaches over and grasps my shoulders, trying to calm my shaking and pass on some of his warmth.

"Please don't touch me," I say again, but he doesn't move. "Get off," I weakly insist. But his hands are still there, grounding me as my body threatens to shake so hard it will shatter into a thousand pieces.

"Ada." He speaks softly in my ear, his voice as deep as ever but unusually tender. "I'm not going anywhere until you calm down." I hold my nose as the soft breath of his words plays along my face. I'm scared that if I inhale, I'll smell her blood on his breath. He wraps his arms around me, swaddling me into stillness, his damp hair hanging into my face. The water has transformed it from golden blond into a dull, pale brown. I try to wriggle out of his grasp, but once again I find him to be as solid as a rock. A rock wrapped in soft terry cloth. I try to push away one last time, but I am well and truly trapped. After what I've witnessed, this should terrify me beyond words. But for whatever reason, it has the opposite effect.

I hate him. That's what I tell myself. If I had the energy, anger would burn through me. I would scream. I would claw at him. I would spit in his face. But instead, I do what he's waiting for me to do. I surrender, collapse into his chest, and let myself cry. It can't be a pretty sight. This is no dainty, damsel-in-distress crying. My breath probably smells like puke, my face is wet from tears and, likely, strings of snot. My body shakes as I weep, and he continues to hold me tight while he strokes my hair and murmurs into my ear. He's repeating something over and over, whispered words I can't comprehend over my sobs.

When I'm finally all cried out, I stand and put some distance between myself and the still mostly naked boy who now feels like a stranger. I search his eyes, for what, I don't know. But all I find is cool practicality.

He gathers his clothes and says, "We should get moving." He exits the bathroom, and I follow him out. "It's almost nightfall, and I want to act while the blood is in peak effect."

Ugh. Does he have to keep reminding me about the blood?

"How long will it last?" I ask, my throat raw.

"It will be in my system for a few days, but the most powerful effects will only last about five hours. You must be warned, though, that if I need to exert a lot of power, I will exhaust myself much more quickly than normal unless I consume more blood."

"No." I shake my head emphatically. "That's not an option."

"Either way, you need to be aware of the risks."

"What do we do with . . . her?" I gesture to the bed.

"She'll wake up and leave. She'll be perfectly fine, I promise."

"What about the part where you, ya know, slit her wrist and drank her blood?"

"She won't remember any of that."

"You still violated her." I gather the clothing I packed for tonight.

"That's not—"

"It is." I grab my bag, then head back into the bathroom to change, slamming the door behind me.

I tug on black jeans and a black turtleneck. When I packed them, I'd imagined feeling like a sexy cat burglar. I'd imagined wearing the ensemble over my hot-pink bra. I'd thought there was a good chance that Rafe might actually find out what bra I was wearing.

That seems like a lifetime ago.

Now I just feel ridiculous. I look at myself in the mirror, all the black making my pale skin stand out in ghostly contrast. I tie my hair in a tight bun on the top of my head.

When I exit the bathroom, Rafe has also changed, and he definitely looks like a sexy cat burglar in his tight black jeans and black leather jacket. His hair, still coppery from the shower, is tied in a bun at the nape of his neck, and his large bag is slung over one shoulder. But his appearance no longer moves me, especially with Miss Good-Enough-to-Eat passed out behind him.

Rafe has cleared away any signs of what happened, and she lies in a bed of perfectly clean white sheets. I can almost convince myself the scene is normal.

I turn away from both of them and head to the door. "Let's do this."

34

"So, to clarify," I ask Rafe as we make our way uptown, "if a person without your genetics drinks blood, it won't affect them?" Tension aches through my jaw all the way to my clenched fingers, but Rafe walks with the same confident coolness as always.

"Not unless they first endured an invasive digestive surgery that they probably wouldn't survive."

It's the time of night right before the city lights itself up to push away the dark. We find a private spot along the East River, and Rafe erects the boat in the shadows.

I feel queasy knowing I'm about to do exactly what my detractors among the Families were worried about. Handing the very information they didn't trust me with right over to someone who could endanger them. There will be no going back after this. But it's not like I have a choice; they have Hypatia.

"Remember the deal," I whisper, hardly audible. This part of the river is restricted, and dealing with police is the last thing we need right now, but I can't move on without the reassurance. "No matter what, you don't hurt my family."

Rafe nods. "As long as Hypatia won't be harmed by my inaction, your mother and the celebrity will be left alone."

"And after, you'll do everything you can for my grandfather."

He nods again.

We don't say anything else. There's nothing to say. We board the boat, and Rafe unfolds an oar to use instead of the motor so we don't make noise. The only light comes from the reflection of the city in the river. The only sounds are my breathing and the ghostly slip of the oar through the water. I don't want to touch Rafe, but there's no room not to. He's warm against my back, his thighs hugging me, anchoring me, as we fade into the blackness of the night.

When we reach the island, we dock behind an overgrown bush. I ignore the hand Rafe offers to help me out of the boat, then trip and sink into water up to my knees. When I'm finally on the shore, my shoes squelch with mud, and my legs are weighed down by the sodden denim. I scurry to catch up to Rafe, who is cutting quickly and silently through the overgrown path.

"How can you see where you're going?" I whisper. My breath is ragged from trying to keep up as I continuously trip on stones and shrubs while shrinking away from twitching shadows.

"I forgot you can't see. I'll slow down. All my senses are heightened."

As if I needed another reminder about the blood.

A giant white bird with a fluffy head jumps into my path and squawks at me. I yelp, and Rafe gives me a death glare for making noise.

We approach a large building, a great deal of which has been reclaimed by nature, green vines devouring brick and stone. Using Georgie's map on my phone, we find a crumbling entrance, the door long gone, and we navigate through hallways that feel as if we're more outdoors than in. The map indicates that we're close to new construction, and sure enough, when we peer around the next corner, there's a steel door barring access to whatever lies ahead. A guard is pacing the hallway, and when he turns in the opposite direction, Rafe silently darts over and makes shiin against the guard's neck until he falls slack in his arms.

"You can't just keep hurting people!" I whisper angrily as Rafe lowers the guard to the ground.

"Don't worry. I only overloaded his vagus nerve."

So *that's* what it looks like when done correctly.

"It's only a mild faint, so he'll wake up soon. Very soon. Let's get moving."

I rifle through the guard's pockets and find an orange keycard exactly like the one refused to me. Because I might have used it for this very purpose. I ignore the stab of guilt and use the card to open the door.

Inside, a staircase leads down to a dimly lit basement level. It's been completely renovated. We pass a room that looks like a medical lab except that it's barred like a prison cell. A middle-aged man in a white lab coat is looking through a microscope, seemingly indifferent to his imprisonment. I worry he'll alert someone to our presence, but as we walk by his cell, he doesn't even look up from his work.

There's an empty lab without any bars, and I go in to look around. There are three large refrigerators, and when I open one, I find that it's filled with . . . blood bags. Why would the Families need a blood bank?

Rafe looks over from where he's keeping watch at the door, and when he sees the blood, he shakes his head. "This is very, very bad," he whispers.

We keep moving and pass more cells. There's one that has a sleeping man with long hair and a long beard. He looks like he's been here a while, and the broken furniture that seems to have been flung around in a rage makes it clear he's not happy about it. But all of the other cells are unoccupied. If the Families are responsible for all the other missing Sires, this is clearly not where they're kept. I start to fear that Hypatia may not be here either.

When we reach the end of the hall, there's another cell that's skeletally furnished with a chest of drawers, a table, and a bed. A tray of food sits hardly eaten on the table. Huddled in the corner is a girl with her head resting on her knees. My limbs feel weak with relief.

Hypatia.

Rafe rushes toward the cell, grabbing the bars. He instantly recoils, yelping in pain. I didn't know Rafe Vanguard could yelp.

"Where in perdition did they get enough antimatter to build something like this?" He looks at the bars with an astounded and helpless kind of rage.

I have the same question. No one in the Families seemed to know anything about antimatter when I told them about the gloves that tortured me when I was abducted. But these bars suggest otherwise.

"Hypatia?" Rafe asks. There's a tremor of fear in his voice that causes me to look toward her with alarm. She's glanced upward at the goings-on but has otherwise not moved or made any attempt to acknowledge either of us. She doesn't look at all like her feisty self. Her pale blond hair hangs loose down her back, and the whites of her eyes are tinged red.

We need to get to her. But there is no discernible opening or lock on the cell, and the bars will neutralize any use of Ha'i.

Rafe unzips his bag and pulls out the most ridiculous gun I've ever seen. It's plastic with a lot of weird tubing and kind of looks like a Super Soaker.

Rafe aims at the cell and pulls the trigger. The gun emits a laser that he uses to cut precisely through the grid of bars to make an opening. The laser only affects the bars, bouncing harmlessly off anything else it touches. With the last cut, the bars fall inward, clattering to the ground with a shrieking clang that makes me jump. Rafe rushes through the gaping hole and embraces Hypatia, who flops weakly against him.

"What's wrong?" His voice is a pained growl.

Hypatia touches her neck.

I see the collar at the same time as Rafe. The same metal as the bars, as the gloves. Antimatter.

"Gravdammit," he curses. "Ada, help me." His eyes are wet.

I run to his side and help support Hypatia as he positions the gun carefully. But he doesn't pull the trigger. He looks at me, his eyes full of fear. I didn't think it was possible for Rafe Vanguard to be afraid.

"A magneto gun shouldn't harm anything besides antimatter," he explains to me, though it sounds more like he's reassuring himself.

"You've got this," I whisper.

There's an unmistakable sound of footsteps approaching from the direction we came. We need to hurry. I consult Georgie's map on my phone for an alternate exit. A door slams. Heavy steps are coming our way. Fast.

"Rafe," I prompt, as calmly and reassuringly as I can.

He pulls the trigger.

The collar falls away, and the flesh beneath is red and swollen. With the antimatter off her body, Hypatia sighs deeply, and I watch as the skin heals itself, leaving only a thin pink ring of scar tissue behind.

"Thank the Conductor," Rafe breathes. "It must not have been on for too long." I remember what Michael had said when he'd rescued me from the gloves, that prolonged exposure to antimatter can make a Sire lose their ability to conduct. "Are you okay?" Rafe asks Hypatia.

"I'm thirsty," she rasps weakly.

"You're safe now. I promise." Rafe chokes on his words as he returns the magneto gun to his bag.

According to Georgie's map, the only other way out without going back down the hall is up. There's a window in the cell, but it's too far to climb, and even if it weren't, we couldn't make it in time.

"I can make that climb," Rafe says. "I'll bring up Hypatia, then come back down for you."

"Are you crazy? There's no way you can do that, never mind holding us and your bag!"

"I can." He flexes his arms, and I see the rippling muscle and the throbbing veins in his neck. I remember the stolen blood running through him. I look away.

"Take Hypatia and go. There's no time for you to come back for me, but I'll be fine. They won't hurt me. I'll meet you at the boat."

"Are you sure you'll be safe? I can outrun them, even holding both of you."

"Go. I need to find out what's really going on here before I leave."

With that, he slings his bag over his shoulder and bends low. Hypatia climbs onto his back, clinging to his neck. As if she weighs no more than a pillow, he springs upward, jumping way higher than an average human can, and catches the ledge of the window with his fingertips. He pulls himself up, and then, supporting his entire body—and Hypatia's—with just one arm, he uses his leather-jacket-clad elbow to smash through the window. Sheesh, I guess he wasn't exaggerating about the effects of blood doping. Within seconds, he's scrambled through the window, and they're gone.

Moments later, four security guards approach, blocking my exit from the cell. They're followed by Alfie. His tie of the day is a mustard and purple striped monstrosity.

Alfie assesses the broken window and missing prisoner. "Find them, and get the girl back," he says to the guards. "I can take care of this one." The guards hurry off the way they came.

I try to push past Alfie. "Take me to Kor or whoever else from the Inner Chamber is here," I demand.

"Not a chance."

"What's your problem?" I shove him, but I don't have much leverage while trying to avoid touching the antimatter bars.

"Why would I help *you*?" Alfie sneers. "You've turned out to be the traitor I expected all along. The only place you're going is into one of these cells and staying there until my father gets here."

Oh, *hell* no. I guess I'll have to find someone reasonable on my own. I turn to check if there's anything in the cell that I can use to my advantage. Nope. When I swivel back around, Alfie's eyes blink upward too quickly, and I'm pretty sure he was checking out my butt. It does look good in these jeans.

"My eyes are up here, perv," I say as I step forward so that we're nose to nose. There's probably some way to effectively use my Ha'i to get past Alfie, but I stick to what I know best and knee him straight in the balls. As he grabs himself with a satisfying shriek, I push past him and run.

He doesn't catch up with me until I'm already up the stairs and out of the building. As I stumble through the dark overgrown landscape, he comes barreling into me, tackling me to the ground. And then he unceremoniously sits on my back to keep me down.

"Get off me! What are you doing?"

"I'm apprehending you, traitor."

He has a rope and seems to be contemplating whether he should use it on my hands or feet.

"I'm not a traitor, idiot. Just call Kor or my mother. I can explain everything."

"If you want a positive result, perhaps you should speak more respectfully."

"Respectfully? You are literally *sitting* on me." And he's heavy. My attempts to push him off are proving utterly futile.

He mutters some more about how everyone only trusts me because of my family while he trained so rigorously blah, blah, blah. As if he doesn't take every chance he gets to remind people that he's the direct descendant of a Borgia.

He decides on using the rope for my feet, which he adeptly ties together at the ankles. Maybe knot tying was one of the many things I missed during those "rigorous trainings."

I make shiin and try to conduct, but nothing happens. I'm used to repressing my Ha'i around the Families. Not to mention that with the pressure of Alfie sitting on me scratching loose the memories of being trapped in a box, I'm a far cry from the calm mindset I generally try to cultivate when summoning Ha'i.

When Alfie finally moves his weight off my body, I try to reach for my spoon, but he's quicker than me and twists my arms behind my back, binding them together using, of all things, his ridiculous tie. Then he takes both my spoon and my phone from my pocket.

Once I'm all trussed up, he steps back, and I shimmy into a sitting position. Rafe would be furious at me for managing to get into this situation without defending myself.

Alfie is pacing back and forth while rapidly messaging on his phone. "Do you understand what you've done?" he asks me.

"Saved a child who was kidnapped and suffering?"

"You've exposed one of our most covert locations. You may have undone years of work. We could be forced to destroy this entire site if word gets out." He shakes his phone at me. "And don't think I didn't find the trojan horse in your immature meme."

"That's right. Your lack of caution is the real reason this covert location is at risk."

"You little . . . " he blusters in a contained internal tantrum, and though it's too dark to really see, I'd like to imagine his stupid face is an angry shade of purple. "You can gloat all you want once I have one of those collars on you."

Horror sears up my spine at the memory of antimatter stinging my palms.

"That's not necessary." I try to remain calm. "Just call the rest of the Inner Chamber. Call Dr. Ambrose if you don't think my mom or Kor will be impartial." There's no way any of them would put me in a collar, except for—

"My father's already on his way."

Panic tightens my throat. Councilor Avellino wouldn't hesitate to lock me up just like Hypatia. But I've already had exposure to antimatter, and if they put a collar on me for too long, I could lose my ability to conduct Ha'i permanently, when I've only just learned to use it properly.

My next words come out as a sob. "Please, let me go."

Alfie turns away from me. "Don't act like this is my fault. You brought the enemy here. I will not be the one to take the blame for any of this when I was the one who tried to warn everyone about you!"

"Please call my mother too," I beg. "I swear no one will blame you."

But Alfie ignores my pleas, and I know that, this time, no one is coming to rescue me.

Inhale.

Exhale.

I'm going to have to save myself.

I take stock of my surroundings the way Rafe taught me. If I could make a flame, I could burn through my restraints, but Alfie has my sparker, and there's no way for me to generate static. Where's a rug when you need one? I fumble my hands behind my back, hoping to feel something, anything that I can use. Weeds and mud and sticks.

Useless.

An idea surfaces. Not anything Rafe taught me, but an old memory from summer camp. We'd studied wilderness survival skills and learned about how to start a fire from the friction of rubbing twigs together. It takes a lot of effort, and I'd never managed it at the time, but I have to try.

I grapple for two sticks, and though I don't have a lot of range of motion, I rub them together as vigorously as I can while pushing my Ha'i out, seeking any spark to ignite.

Please, help me.

Nothing happens, other than my skin getting rubbed raw. I know that the goal is for the friction to make the wood hot enough that it will burn, so I pause my rubbing and make shiin, focusing all my Ha'i on heating the wood. Once I feel it practically scorching my hands, I again rub the pieces together and pump my Ha'i outward. My Ha'i that is a part of me. Not separate from me.

Ada, help yourself.

A flame whooshes into being. I can't see it, but I can feel it, burning the skin off my hands as it makes quick work of Alfie's tie. And the hem of my turtleneck.

At my triumphant cry, Alfie comes rushing toward me, but I throw a fireball in his direction, and he jumps away. "Stay back!" I yell.

My hands are already healing, but not fast enough. I do my best to ignore the pain as I untie the ropes around my ankles. Each movement is agony to my fingers as I disturb the blistered flesh.

When I stand and there's no more fireball in sight, Alfie approaches. But I will not be knocked over or tied up again. When he grabs me, I don't struggle; instead, I lean into his pull, which causes him to stumble from the unexpected lack of resistance. I use the moment to reach for his neck, praying I picked the right spot. I conduct Ha'i toward his vagus nerve, and I must have done it right, because he slumps to the floor in a faint.

I feel like my heart could explode from relief.

I fumble through Alfie's pockets and take my stuff back and immediately use my phone to call Mom.

Ugh! Why does she never answer? I hang up and try Kor, but it goes straight to voicemail.

Rafe and Hypatia can't wait for me forever. I'll have to head back without learning what I came to learn. I use the torch on my spoon to try to find the path back to the water, but without Rafe to lead me, it's too dark and overgrown for me to navigate.

I suddenly notice light coming toward me from a much clearer path than the one I'm on.

"Ada? Is that you?"

In the poor light, it takes me a minute to recognize that it's Kor. He's thinner, which brings out the exquisite bone structure of his face even more than before, and his hair has grown out longer than I've ever seen it. But he looks as calmly commanding as ever, and I feel a sense of relief come over me. He'll know what to do, and he'll be able to explain to me what's going on.

"Hey," he says as if we're not on the grounds of a rotting hospital.

"Hi," I say as if I'm not out of breath from escaping capture.

Then he rushes to me and wraps me in a hug. "It's good to see you."

I hug him back, hard, delaying the moment when I'll have to face the difficult questions that might change everything.

"Ada," he says into my hair, "what are you doing here? With a heretic?"

I break our hug and step back. *Heretic.* That's how the exiles are referred to in the Families' earliest texts—in the *Inquisitor* texts—but no one calls them that anymore.

"I came to—"

There's a squawk from the tree above Kor, and he moves a few feet away, motioning me to follow.

"Herons," he explains. "We need to be careful not to disrupt the birds too much. Our activity on the island has already decreased their breeding, and we don't want the Audubon Society poking around. You were saying?"

"I came to warn you about how much the Makers know about you and to rescue Hypatia."

"Why would she need rescuing?"

I remember the state in which we found her, and renewed anger and confusion surface. "Well, it certainly seemed like she needed it." I'd planned to spin the rescue as a benefit to the Families, explain that keeping her is not worth the risk since she's part of the royal family, but I'm too enraged after witnessing her abused condition.

Kor continues. "We sent you to the heretics' school to get necessary intelligence, not for you to make friends and help them steal from us."

"What are you even saying? You're literally kidnapping people!"

"Almost all the Sires have agreed to cooperate willingly. As soon as we explained the importance of our work and helped them to understand their abilities, they were thrilled to help us."

"You abducted a child from her home and kept her in abusive conditions—"

"She was not mistreated. We tried to make her comfortable and happy, but she barely ate, and we had to keep her in the cell since she tried to escape, which is dangerous for her in this area at night. Last night she attacked a guard—bit his wrist so hard he bled. That's the reason we put on the collar. Even so, she shouldn't have reacted so negatively, and I'm sorry for that." His brows are knit together, genuine concern in his eyes.

"Yes, she's chronically ill and needs to be returned home so you don't unleash the ire of the entire royal family and their guard."

"Unfortunately, we need her, and I can't let her go."

"I don't . . . Who even are you right now?" I sniffle and realize I've started crying again. Crying because I don't understand what I'm seeing on this island or how Kor could be a part of it. "Kor, you have to understand, the Makers, they're not bad—those in charge have made selfish decisions, yes, but they're good people."

"Stop, Ada. I defended you when others said they didn't think you were ready for this job. I believed in you. But they were right; you were easily brainwashed. I'm sure the heretics have many fine qualities, but these are the same people responsible for letting the rest of the world suffer when they had the power to help."

"Their ultimate goal *is* to reunite with the rest of the world. They have a prophecy about it and everything!"

"Yes, the Oculus has found evidence of years and years of recorded prophecies that could help the entire world, yet those too they've kept only for themselves. The Grand Master won't be happy to hear about your sympathetic mentality. I'm pulling you from the mission."

"What? No, you can't—"

He straightens his back and looks down at me. "I can. I'm the right hand to the Grand Master himself."

"But I'm learning so much, like how to control my abilities and advancements we could use—"

"And it's a shame you'll lose that, but it's preferable to me losing you."

"You're not going to lose me."

"I haven't already?" His expression is dark with sadness and disappointment. "You didn't even tell me you were coming to the city. You snuck here and broke out a prisoner! And I shouldn't doubt where your allegiances lie?"

"What was I supposed to do? You told me nothing. Nothing! I came here to warn you. To tell you they have photographs of you. And to find out what I've been helping you do. I thought I was helping you improve the world, not kidnap children!"

"All you had to do was keep your cover, and instead you tell a dangerous royal who you are and bring him directly to us? We're going to have to move everything to another facility now that he's been here."

"Think what you like, but I made the right decision. The fact that I got myself off that island and am here talking to you now is the sign of my success. It was your choice to keep me in the dark, so I was forced to act on my own. And I chose the perfect person to tell. The person most likely to underestimate me so he may actually think I'm innocent in all of this despite my familial connections. A person who has his own agenda and his own secrets, so he'll stay quiet when this is all over. Now stop underestimating me like everyone else and trust me with the information I need to do the job you sent me to do." I'm not sure I'll want to keep doing any kind of job for them once I find out what the Oculus has been up to, but right now ensuring I'm the one in control of making that decision feels paramount.

"You've completed your job already. The information you sent us is enough. With it, combined with what we have from Prometheus and our new lead, there's no reason for you to return."

"But I finally have information about a stone that allows non-Sires to use Ha'i. I'm the only Sire in the family. You need me to—"

He cuts me off. "That's no longer quite true." Kor plucks a leaf from the tree next to him and presses it into his hand, which makes shiin. I feel the hum of Ha'i and—much more easily than I managed with the sticks—the leaf bursts into a momentary flame. Then it's gone, a puff of ash snowing to the ground.

"You're not the only Sire in the family anymore, Ada."

35

or isn't a Sire. He can't be. He doesn't have the symptoms I grew up with. I look at his upper lip, and his scar is still there. Sires don't scar. Could he have gotten ahold of a Ha'i stone? But his hands are empty. "I don't understand."

"Isn't it amazing? Do you know how much good I've done already?" His face is glowing. "I've been helping at the charity clinic. There are so many little things I can heal with my energy alone. I've saved lives, Ada."

He closes his eyes, brow furrowed. "There used to be so much *noise*. All these fans thinking I was someone special, treating me as if singing songs was bringing meaning into their lives. I felt like such an impostor with nothing real to give." He opens his eyes. "But now, now I have *so much* to give."

He takes my hand in his, his gaze growing somber. "I'm sure there are some nice people on that island, but I will do *whatever* it takes to help *our* world."

There's something about the way he says this that makes my body grow cold. "Kor. What have you done?"

But I already know how someone who wasn't born a Sire can gain Sire powers.

"You've been drinking the abducted Sires' blood," I choke out in shock and disgust.

He nods.

"But . . . you're a vegan!" I hardly recognize the person talking to me.

"I've accepted that this power comes with a cost."

"Human blood!" I back away from him in horror. "How are you even able to digest it?"

"Prometheus gave me the information I needed to change myself." Prometheus. Kor's ally from Avant. I know he's given important information to the Families but nothing that would give them direct access to the people. Nothing like what they were hoping to get from me. "It was not an easy surgery."

I gasp as Kor lifts up his shirt. There's a brutal crisscross of scars, a map of torn flesh. "Sire abilities only heal your body as it is now, not any damage from before they kick in." There is bitterness in his voice. Kor had worked hard for the body that had earned him a slew of shirtless magazine covers. His scarred abdomen is a far cry from photo shoot worthy now.

If Prometheus taught Kor how to do this to himself, I can only imagine what other medical knowledge he may have.

"Can Prometheus help cure Grandfather?"

"Tomás?" Kor pulls his shirt back down.

"From his cancer."

"Tomás isn't sick."

I'm so confused. "He *is* sick."

"He's an old man, Ada. He had a routine operation while you were in Italy, and another since then. There was a difficult recovery period, but he's fine now."

"But what about all the stem cell stuff and the blood transfusions?"

Kor's posture stiffens, and he won't meet my eyes. "That was for me."

"You mean . . . for all . . . that?" I motion to his body.

"No. Ada, I'm the one who has cancer."

"What?" Kor is young and vibrant and healthy.

"Leukemia. Stage four." His gaze is calm and resigned.

I raise my hand to my mouth in horror. It feels like time slows as I try to put the pieces together.

"But if I can stay well enough for long enough to succeed with our plan, no one else will have to deal with this wretched illness ever again."

I think of all his visits with Dr. Ambrose, the nosebleeds, the postponed tour. "How come you never told me?"

"I wasn't ready to tell you, and then you had to leave. But it's okay now. The Sire blood keeps me well."

"Why couldn't Prometheus have just given you a cure?"

"The cancer was too far gone. It was too late for any of their cures."

Too late. Kor was *dying*, and he never told me.

"But now that you are a Sire, you're . . . better?" Despite everything I've learned tonight, I want him to be better.

"No. The Sire blood gives me abilities and keeps me well while it's in my system, but once I stop taking it, I deteriorate quickly. The girl seems to have a universal blood type that could have been more effective. But she's been too unwell for me to try it."

Try it. As in, try *drinking* it. My brain is tangled trying to rearrange all my feelings. I'm furious and disgusted by what Kor's been doing, but the part of my heart that has loved him for so long is breaking from knowing how sick he is.

"Why didn't you use my blood? I would have gladly given it. I'll give it to you now."

"I considered it, but your mother wouldn't allow it."

I hear rustling on the path behind me, and I turn my head to find my mother approaching. Despite the late hour, she's as well groomed as always. I want to rush to her, fall into her arms, and have her protect me from all this unwelcome truth. But she doesn't even look at me until she's standing right next to me.

"I won't let them turn you into one of their experiments, freely stealing your platelets whenever they need," she says. A practically professional squeeze of my shoulder is the only affection I get.

She says to Kor, "Just let her go, and let her take the girl."

"You can't give me orders. You're not my superior anymore."

"That may be true, but I am your aunt." She crosses her arms. "Prometheus was unhappy about the girl as well. He's been demanding her release before he helps us further, and rescuing her will make Ada look good to help her cover. It's to our benefit to let them go."

"Ada doesn't need to help her cover," Kor retorts. "She's not going back."

"Ada will decide what's best for herself," my mother says with finality. Words I'd never thought I'd hear her say.

Kor looks as if he is about to protest, but I say, "I want to go back."

He turns to me, eyes wide. "You'll leave me for *them*?"

How can he look so hurt? *I'm* the one who has been betrayed.

"No. I'm going to *help* you. There's something called a Ha'i stone. If I can find it, maybe you won't need anyone's blood."

His expression hardens. "Fine. Go. And take the girl. If she's ill, she should be returned to her family. But think twice before you leave. We don't need you there anymore. We have a new informant at Genesis."

"What?"

What?

Who could it possibly be? Are they the one who stole the Ha'i stone? And if it wasn't Nora Montaigne, how is she involved? Gah. Everything is muddled in my mind.

"Go on." Kor turns away from me.

"Wait. What more have you learned about Ozymandias Tech?"

He freezes, and without turning, he says, "We no longer think they're involved."

That can't be right. They have to be involved somehow. I want to tell Kor what I've learned about Nora Montaigne's family connections, but something else takes precedence in my mind.

"If it wasn't Oz Tech, then who kidnapped me?"

Kor's shoulders fall, and he finally turns back to face me again, his face devastated.

I can barely breathe.

I look to my mother, and she has tears in her eyes. "I swear I had no idea," she says.

I look back to Kor. "But *you* did?"

He nods in affirmation. I feel as if I might crumple onto the ground, but, somehow, I remain standing.

"How could you?" I finally choke out, unable to stop the tears that well up. "Kor, they put me in a crate. I couldn't move. I could hardly breathe." I choke on a sob. "And the gloves, they burned me. It hurt so much—" My voice breaks, and I try to swallow the painful lump in my throat.

"I had no choice."

"They knocked me out." I instinctively reach to the spot at the back of my head.

"They should not have done that," he says with steel in his voice. "They were *never* supposed to hurt you."

"Why didn't you warn me?"

"I wanted to. I should have. I . . . Your response had to be genuine."

I blink up at him. "You've got to be kidding."

"I'm sorry," he says softly. "I couldn't be positive that you having abilities would be enough for the heretics to recruit you. They needed to think you were in danger. And the rest of the Inner Chamber had to be convinced you were at risk so they'd agree to send you away."

He not only didn't tell me about it, but he was the one who planned the whole thing.

I look to my mom for some kind of explanation.

"No one outside of the Oculus knew about the abductions until recently. Most of the other Sires came willingly," my mother explains quietly. "So your abduction seemed like an external threat to the rest of us."

I don't even have words. I've known Kor for so long, and this is so far from anything I can imagine him doing, but so is drinking a young girl's blood. There's not enough room inside me to contain so much shock and confusion.

I saw something I wasn't supposed to.

That's what Izzy's message had said. But whatever she saw, it wasn't at Oz Tech. It was with the *Families*. Whatever it was made her want to leave the order, and she'd tried to protect me from them too.

I hope that wherever she is, she's safe.

"Please understand." Kor's expression is genuinely contrite. "I did this for you, not just for the Families. Everything has worked out better than we could have hoped. I'm sorry you were afraid and hurt. I will never forgive myself for your scars." He grabs the cross at his neck, squeezing it in his fist. "But I'm also glad it worked."

I just shake my head, at a loss for how to respond to so great a betrayal from one of the people I love most in the world.

"You will forgive me," he insists with the conviction of someone who always gets his way. "You'll go back to get more information from the heretics, and together we'll bring radical change to the world. Then you'll realize it was all worth it and forgive me." His tone is confident, but his eyes are pleading.

"You need to leave, Ada," my mother says. "The entire Inner Chamber was alerted about the breach, and they won't all want to let you go." I follow her, turning my back on Kor without saying goodbye.

Mom leads me with a flashlight to the area of shore where Rafe's waiting. When we're almost there, I second-guess myself and stop walking.

"This doesn't feel right. I thought the Families were *good*."

"It's not so simple. And many in the Families are not okay with what has been happening here."

"Then should we even be helping them? Or should we be stopping them?"

My mother is thoughtful for a moment, then says, "I have always believed in the mission of the Families. Kor has a new, radical plan to help make it happen, and the Oculus approves. I'm not the only one who doesn't agree with his methods, but he's just one person who holds temporary influence within a greater organization, and he may yet make the world a better place."

"Maybe I should stay."

"*No.*" Her voice is suddenly sharp. "It's safer for you to go."

My stomach churns at how clinical she is about me leaving again. "You just told Kor that I can choose what's best for me." That had felt like a breakthrough between us, like she was finally starting to treat me like an adult.

She sighs. "Of course you should choose. But you also don't have the full picture to make the best choice. Your safety is my priority, far above the duties of being part of the Families. I can't keep them from using you for your blood if you stay here."

"Mom, you need to protect yourself, too. Part of why I came here was to warn you. The Makers know who you are."

"Don't worry about me. We know what they know. Just keep yourself safe."

"And what about Grandfather? Is he really okay?"

Her expression is strained. "He's fine."

"Even if it's not cancer, is there something else wrong with him? He seemed so sick. Rafe is a . . . healer. He agreed to try to help Grandfather. Maybe we should go to him before we—"

"No. You have to leave. I promise you that he's not sick. He had a series of surgeries, but they were successful, and he's recovering well."

"Why didn't I know about them?"

"He didn't want you to. He thought your concern for him might affect your choice about whether to leave."

Why does it feel like she's not telling me everything?

Mom's pocket has been buzzing nonstop. She hands me the flashlight and takes out her phone. Her eyes flick to the screen and then back to me with a familiar detached determination. She says, "I'll figure out a way to smooth things over with the Oculus." Between sentences, she expertly reapplies her lipstick, no mirror needed. Her armor before heading into battle. "Go now. When you get back to the institute, you can continue to spy, or not if you don't think that's the right choice, but make protecting yourself your main goal."

I return her flashlight, then move to give her a hug, but she's already turning and walking away. So I do too.

When I push through the brush, Rafe is right there. Not down by the boat as I'd expected. We were whispering, but I know that blood doping has given him enhanced hearing. I know he's heard our entire conversation.

Continue to spy.

My mother said those exact words. "It's not . . . how she made it sound." I try to swallow, truly afraid. I know how he feels about traitors to his people, and this time the proof is much more damning.

His eyes are like ice over a frozen lake, cold and harsh and hiding endless depths. He's surrounded by the bodies of the unconscious security guards that he somehow managed to overpower single-handedly.

"Please . . . ," I squeak. "I'm not planning to spy."

"Ada." His commanding voice silences me. "Don't worry. I believe that you did not know what they were doing and do not want to help them anymore."

"Rafe, I swear . . ."

He shushes me with a finger to my lips. "Ada, I trust you." He steps closer. "You're shivering." He shucks off his jacket and wraps it around my shoulders. "Now, we have to get out of here. Let's go." And without another word, he walks to the boat where Hypatia is resting.

It takes me a moment to recover from the surprise, and then I follow him.

36

We quickly cross the river and rush back to the hotel. Hypatia is still very weak, and Rafe carries her most of the way. As soon as we're back in our room—the receptionist must have woken and left, as she is nowhere to be seen—Rafe lays Hypatia on the bed and begins rolling up his sleeve.

"What are you doing?" she protests.

"You need blood now." He extends his hand to her, but she feebly pushes it away with a shocked expression.

"Not from you. Find someone else."

"You need to eat now, and Sire blood will help you heal more quickly."

"Mother said never from a Sire." But her voice is small and frail. Rafe ignores her and presses his inner forearm against her mouth. She hesitates for a moment, then grabs his arm and bites down.

I turn away to give them privacy, but not before I see small fangs puncture Rafe's skin.

I expect to spiral into a total freakout over the fact that my dear friend is apparently even more of a vampire than her cousin, but it seems that I've reached my mental limit on shock for the day. My brain has thrown up her hands and is willing to accept anything right now.

I sit on the other bed, pretending to busy myself with my phone until Rafe comes to sit next to me.

He says softly, "She's sleeping, and she needs to rest. We'll stay the night, and my brother will collect us in the morning. I've already been in touch with him. What you said about your grandfather not being the sick one means we don't have to go there first, correct?"

I nod. I'd explained the basics on the boat ride back.

"Are you . . . okay?" he asks.

"No." Better to keep my mind busy with practicalities, so I change the subject. "Who could have given them the knowledge to create a false Sire?" I'd filled Rafe in on Kor's illness and his surgery, and I'm more curious than ever who Prometheus might be.

"I honestly have no idea who would do such a thing. But we'll need to find a way to neutralize the knowledge. Sire abilities are too dangerous in provincial hands."

Neutralize the knowledge. That can't mean anything good for my family. Despite everything I witnessed tonight, I don't want any harm coming to them.

"I don't understand," I say to Rafe. "Maker inventions are one thing, but why can't we teach provincial Sires how to wield Ha'i? They haven't all been recruited. There are many untrained Sires out there who have no idea what they are or what they could be doing for society. There's no one forbidding it any longer, so why can't the knowledge of Sires be reintroduced so the rest of the world can have some advantage?"

"Are you kidding me? Look at what your family did as soon as they learned about Sires. Abducting them and draining their blood—you think that's the first time something like this has happened? This is what that provincial world does, Ada. Wake up. They can't accept people being different, and they steal any power there for the taking. They weaponize anything that can be weaponized."

There's nothing I can say to this. I look down at my hands, rubbing my scars. My best friend, one of the most benevolent people I have ever known, has done unspeakable things for this power. What if it were in the hands of even less scrupulous people?

I had been so sure that there was someone else involved in all of this, but if the Families abducted me and they now have another informant at Genesis, it's possible that everything has been them all along. I'm not sure I can stomach that.

"What do you know about Nora Montaigne?" I ask Rafe, still unconvinced that she's not somehow involved.

"The traitor Leonora de Montaigne? She's Leonardo's older sister, a Blood Sci and Cipher master and cousin to the Crown. I despise that family."

"Is it possible Bram and Leo have been working for her and could be behind some of the information leaks and the thefts?"

"What? No. Leonora would never do anything like that."

"But you said she's a traitor?"

"She's a traitor for choosing to forsake her heritage and live among the philistines. But she's in constant touch with the Guard and only shares knowledge that they approve for her to share."

That . . . is not what I expected. And I find it surprisingly uplifting. "That's amazing, that there are actually Makers making an effort to help the rest of the world."

Rafe scoffs. "Her intentions are not so noble, I assure you. She's driven purely by self-interest and the desire for wealth. Which makes her a perfect fit for the people she's chosen over her own."

I stand, ready to stalk away in annoyance. I've had quite enough of Rafe's bigotry.

He reaches up and pulls me back down next to him. "I'm sorry," he says. It doesn't sound like something he is used to saying. He lightly tilts my chin so I'm looking at him. "I shouldn't have said that about the people you grew up with."

I scoot farther away from him, shaking off his hand. "I don't need your apologies. We've done what we came to do. Now we can move on." It's true. I don't care. I feel so empty inside. An emptiness that began when I found Rafe covered in blood earlier, and it has only grown bigger with everything else I have seen. Kor's betrayal hurts worse than anything Rafe has done.

"I *want* to apologize," Rafe insists. His gaze is vulnerable instead of the frozen indifference I'm used to. "I don't want you to be angry with me." He swallows. "I don't know why that matters." He looks genuinely confused.

I don't respond.

Rafe clears his throat. "So, you understand now that Hypatia's different— why I had to prioritize her rescue above all else?"

I nod and look up at him. I wasn't sure he'd be willing to explain. "What exactly . . . ?" I point to my teeth.

"Her Vanguard genetics are more concentrated. She doesn't use blood for doping; she needs it to survive. Genesis doesn't allow blood consumption, but they've allowed her to take transfusions. It's enough for her to function well, but the effects wear off more quickly, leaving her weak." He looks over at her, watching her sleep with adoration. "Hypatia is an extremely rare case, having strong Vanguard genetics and also being a Sire. When her abilities fully develop, she may be one of the most intrinsically powerful humans in Maker society. But the Inquisitors can't know that her unique Vanguard genetics have survived. Most Makers don't even know."

The Inquisitors can't know, yet he's telling me, so he must truly believe I won't tell them anything.

I don't even yet know what I will or won't tell them.

Hypatia looks so serene sleeping. It's hard to imagine that she's as powerful as he says. Rafe gazes at her with such love. . . . Then he looks up at me with that same gaze, which for the first time seems to be inviting me in instead of shutting me out.

"Ada." He grasps my hand. Warmth flows into my fingers as his eyes claim mine, so matter-of-factly that I can't possibly look away. "I can never thank you enough. You've saved my cousin. . . ." He pauses, processing his emotion. "I could never have helped her without you." The gentleness in his voice makes his accent more pronounced. His intensity has my heart beating fast. "I know your reasons for being at Genesis are complex, but if you tell me that you're not planning to endanger my people, I trust you. And I swear to you, on my mother's Ha'i, that I won't tell anyone."

He's sitting so close to me, in all his fierce and perfect beauty. But I know better now.

I respond flatly, "You'll keep quiet so I don't tell anyone about your family's big secret?"

"No, that's not—" He presses his lips together in frustration, then tries again. "I trust you without any threat. And I want you to know you can trust me, too."

"Rafe, let's just get Hypatia home, and then we can go our separate ways." I try to pull my hand away, but he squeezes tighter, the thrum of our unique chemistry pulsing beneath our skin.

"Ada . . ." His voice is raspy, the heat from his grip on my hand spreading slowly to other parts of my body. "Do our ways have to be so separate?" His question is loaded with something that I'm not ready to think about.

Though my mind is made up, my voice betrays me with the sound of hesitation as I answer, "I think that's for the best."

"Ada," he whispers again. He lifts my hand and gently brushes his lips against my palm. It's the gentlest of kisses. A gentleness that, once again, is so unfamiliar from him. "I like that you care. Even though I disagree with the lies you've been told, I like that you try to be *good*."

The electricity that always seems to be buzzing between us comes to life, as if my Ha'i is sparking through my skin, begging to be closer to his. I swallow a gasp.

Rafe says, "This kind of connection between two Sires who have Ha'i that is uniquely compatible . . . It's so rare. I've only ever heard about it in legends. Maybe we shouldn't be so quick to dismiss . . . whatever this is."

He trails more kisses down my hand and along my wrist in a way that makes my pulse thrum erratically in my veins. I feel something awakening inside me, something I'm not interested in dealing with right now. Especially when the placement of his kisses reminds me of another wrist at his mouth, a wrist that was not mine, painted ruby red.

Jerking my hand away from him and taking a deep breath to calm my body, I stand up. "I can never forgive you for violating that girl."

"I didn't *violate* her."

"You drugged her and used her body without consent." I know what it's like to find out I've had my blood stolen. To be lied to and used as a pawn.

"She is completely unharmed and will never know or care."

I shake my head. "And that's just it—you're not even sorry."

He closes his eyes and exhales deeply but doesn't respond.

I go to the bathroom to wash up and change into pajamas. When I come out, I look to where Hypatia's sleeping soundly in the center of one bed. Rafe is stretched out in an undershirt and silk pajama pants on one side of the second bed, watching me, his eyes holding a challenge. I silently walk to the other side of the bed, tuck myself in, and stare at the ceiling.

"I'm not the villain here," Rafe says softly from next to me.

"Well, you're definitely not the good guy."

"Neither are you." The mattress moves beneath me as he shifts his body to face mine. I turn my face toward him and find him much closer than I realized. He adds in a velvet whisper, "And maybe that's why we work so well together."

The spicy scent of his nearness invades my senses. I swallow tightly. "There's no 'we.' You and I don't work together anymore."

He blinks. And it's like a curtain comes down. All vulnerability replaced with the familiar chill, all traces of emotion gone. "If that's the way you want it," he says with a sneer. His voice is hard and mean.

I turn my back on him and try to sleep.

★　★　★　★　★

I don't sleep well. But staying up all night with a racing mind has its benefits. I've sorted things out, and I know what my next step has to be.

Rafe is back to his normal self, no trace of the vulnerable boy from last night. Hypatia takes the whole I-was-a-spy-all-along thing in stride, and she seems to be feeling much better.

She's entranced by the television, and she regales me with awed descriptions of various cartoons and the wonders of the Weather Channel. I try not to let my eyes linger on the scar that circles her delicate neck. Or the small fangs that she's now not bothering to hide from me when she smiles wide.

"Have you seen this one before, Ada?" she asks me excitedly about some high school drama. "It appears to be some kind of dystopia where everyone is cosmetically modified, and they need to fight to the death to be crowned queen of the kingdom of Homecoming."

Lovely to know that the unrealistic beauty standards of our society look like dystopian modifications to an outsider. It is kind of weird to see the airbrushed version of reality presented on TV after being away from all that messaging for so long. I don't think I've bemoaned having pores in months. Yesterday I ate a second slice of pizza with zero guilt.

It's hard to tear Hypatia away when it's time to go. "We are wrong about provincials," she says as she solemnly hands me the remote. "Television is an amazing invention."

As the three of us make our way down the elevator, I ask Rafe, "Are you worried?"

"No. It's my brother, not my father."

Prince Alex is in the lobby, attracting a lot of attention with his long hair and large physique. He looks handsome and intimidating but very unprincely in a lot of leather and denim. My heart skips a beat when I realize that Michael is with him. He looks worried and exhausted and adorably mussed.

Sweet, non-blood-drinking, non-life-threatening Michael. Well, perhaps life-threatening; when he looks up and our eyes lock, the pace of my heart certainly feels heart attack–inducing. As he takes me in, I watch the anxiety drain out of him. I want to run to him. Hug him. Tell him everything that's happened. But neither of us moves.

Alex rushes over and clutches Hypatia to him. "Thank the Conductor," he breathes. Then he quickly turns on Rafe. "What were you thinking? I told you I had it in hand! Do you not trust Chorus? There is a very delicate balance—"

"I'm sure Chorus told you we'd all come back safe and alive. And see, we have, thanks to me. And Ada."

Alex's furious eyes turn on me.

"Oh, don't blame her for anything," Rafe drawls. "You know it was all my idea. I needed help from someone who didn't know better." Then his smile turns devilish as he continues. "And I wasn't about to spend a night in a fancy hotel all alone."

I'm dying to roll my eyes.

Alex skeptically eyes Rafe's jacket, which I'm wearing again.

Whatever. I was cold

"Are you okay?" Michael asks me, approaching cautiously. "I didn't know where you were—if you went voluntarily or were taken or—"

I lay my hand on his arm. "I'm fine. I'm sorry for worrying you." I hate that I'm about to lie to him again, but there's no way I can tell the truth. "I was just so worried about Hypatia, and when Rafe suggested it, I got excited to see New York again. I didn't realize it would be a big deal." Look, if Rafe's willing to take the fall for me, I'll let him. He definitely deserves it.

Prince Alexander eyes me skeptically as I speak. But Rafe corroborates my story, and in their minds, he has no reason to lie.

"Okay, let's go," Prince Alex says. "We'll escort you back to Genesis."

They all begin to move toward the exit, but I stay put.

"I . . . I'm not going to go back with you," I say.

Now that I know what my family's been up to, it's clear to me that Genesis is not where I need to be. I need to be at home, convincing Kor and the others that there's a better way to accomplish our goal. Mom may think I'll be safer at Genesis, but I'm done being anyone's pawn, and since all of this began, that's all I've been. It's time to start doing what *I* think is right.

"Being here reminds me of how much I miss my home, my family." It kills something inside me to say it, to pretend that anything about this world speaks to me more than Genesis. Rafe and Michael look completely dumbstruck, but Prince Alex doesn't look particularly surprised. "I just came this morning to say goodbye."

Rafe glares at me, then storms out of the hotel without a word.

Hypatia gives me a long hug and insists I send her pigeons, and then she and Alex follow after Rafe.

Michael hangs back. "Are you sure this is what you want?" His warm brown eyes search mine.

"I've given it a lot of thought. I'm sure. I'll be in touch with Georgie to arrange getting the rest of my stuff." I look down at my hands, something inside me fracturing.

He steps closer. "You can change your mind."

"I won't."

I hadn't expected to say anything more, but it's Michael, and I'm upset and need to hear his reassurance.

I look up and say, "I . . . learned about blood doping."

His expression turns stormy. "It sickens me," Michael says, "that anyone could indiscriminately steal blood. Especially when our people have been libeled over false blood theft."

Our people. He's not talking about the Makers. He's identifying with me as something other than a Maker. As a fellow Jew. I've heard of the blood libels. Lies about Jewish people stealing children's blood told to rationalize generations of atrocities committed against us.

"Both sides of my family have experienced hatred for being Jewish at different times in different countries," Michael says. "Joining the Makers was a haven for them from hate and religious discrimination. The idea that the antisemitic tales of vampires could have been given any credence by the actions of Makers turns my stomach. I can't believe the practice is still allowed at Avant. But if that's why you're leaving—"

"It's not. I just needed to know how you felt about it."

"Ada . . . please . . ." He grabs my hand, and there's a desperation to his voice that I can't afford to interpret. There's too much at stake for me to be swayed by feelings that once I acknowledge, I won't be able to ignore.

I refuse to look up; there's a lump in my throat. "Goodbye, Michael. Thank you for everything."

I pull my hand free and leave the hotel without looking back.

As I make my way through the streets, I let the sounds and smells of the city whip past me. Tears are torn from my eyes by the wind as I give myself the journey home to mourn my choice. But once I get there, there can be no more doubt. No more tears.

I gave the Families a lot of sensitive information. And now Genesis is at risk. Because of me.

I have to fix it.

37

"Do you like it?" Kor asks me. Referring to the new song he just played, which he wrote for me as my eighteenth birthday present. If I didn't know him so well, his ongoing attempts to win me back into his good graces would have me charmed into a quivering puddle of hormones.

Of course I like the song. It's gorgeous, poignant, maybe the best thing he's ever written. But it's hard to care anymore.

I smile stiffly, and Kor shifts closer while he lazily strums "Happy Birthday," and I try to find stars in the cloudy city sky.

We're on the roof of Grandfather's house, a small, flat spot that can be reached through a window in one of the rarely used guest rooms. Both Kor and I have been so busy—and maybe I've also been avoiding him a little—so we haven't had much opportunity for alone time, but tonight he came over for my birthday dinner, and afterward we migrated up here with a six-pack and a guitar like old times.

But it's nothing like old times.

I've been back for two weeks. Most of which I've spent being interrogated by the Inner Chamber. Kor and my mother managed to explain away my actions at the hospital—which wasn't too difficult, since many from the

Inner Chamber don't even know what's really going on there—and now my full-time job is gaining their trust while also trying to withhold any information that could be used to harm the Makers. Today involved a lot of questions specifically about the Avant Guard and the mists surrounding the island.

Despite my mission supposedly having been one of the most important in the history of the Families, the Oculus and the Grand Master have remained completely out of everything. I need to find out more about who they are and what they're up to, but I am the last person likely to get ahold of that information at the moment.

"You seem so different," Kor says, propping the guitar against the window.

Do I? Maybe being betrayed and abducted by my best friend has something to do with that. But, based on the appreciative way he's checking me out, he's referring to my appearance.

I know I look good. Georgie packed up all my stuff and had it sent to me, and she snuck in a few of her custom designs made specifically to my measurements, so I haven't yet reverted to my old hoodies. And while I used to wear my hair wild and loose or up in a messy bun, tonight it's in an elaborate braid crown like the styles worn at Genesis. I spent hours following a video tutorial to get it just right. When Sal had seen it, she'd pruned a length of ivy and woven it through the braid.

I'm not the only one who's changed. Kor's thinner and paler, and his hair is longer. It all lends him a harshly delicate beauty. But his eyes are as soulful as ever, and I can't quite reconcile that with what I now know about him.

Kor offers me some of his beer, and I'm tempted to sip. I need the buzz to get through this pseudo-intimacy. But I hate the bitter taste of hops, and dulling my discomfort won't fix any of this, so I push the bottle away and force myself to sit with my feelings.

I can't get over what Kor's done, but I'm profoundly lonely. I don't have Izzy, I don't have any of my Maker friends, and it's really sinking in how much I left behind at Genesis. I didn't even have a chance to say goodbye. Since I've been back, I tried to reach out to some of my friends from high school, but I was never that close to them to begin with, and after months spent among the Makers, the chasm between us felt far too wide to bridge. I wish I had Georgie, Hypatia, Mbali, even my hoverjoust team. When Georgie sent my stuff back, she also gifted me her hoverboard. I cried when I saw it. I hope my team doesn't resent me too much for not returning for the rest of the tournament.

I miss Michael, too, but I try not to think about him. It hurts too much. I feel like I let him down. And while I'll be able to stay in touch with Georgie, and some of the others through her, he feels off-limits.

I toy with the folded loam pigeon in my pocket. It's the same one Michael gave me all those months ago on the day we met. The Families took it apart and ran all kinds of tests on it, then they asked me to put it back together. I was able to replace the sense and fold it into shape, but I couldn't reanimate it. Animation isn't a skill I came anywhere close to learning during my time at Genesis. So it's just a lifeless origami pigeon now. Useless enough that hopefully the Families won't notice I stole it back.

Though I don't know why I even bothered. It's just a reminder of everything I can't do. That I can't go back. That although Michael may have said that if I ever need his help he would come for me, I've severed that connection as well.

Dumb dead bird.

I pull my hand out of my pocket before I crush the loam between my fingers.

"I can't tell you how good it is to have you back," Kor says. "Once you know how much more is out there, it's so hard to connect with everyone else."

I was just thinking the same thing a few moments ago, but when he says it, it sounds so elitist. It reminds me of the way Rafe talks about provincial people. But if I'm going to influence Kor, that's not the approach to take.

"I know what you mean," I say. "Everything here feels two-dimensional in comparison."

"I want to know what it was like," he says.

So I tell him.

Not the stuff I shared over our video calls and with the Inner Chamber. But all the best parts. Everything I loved.

He takes another sip of his beer, and I'm hit with a strong image from my strange dream weeks ago—that I still haven't managed to shake—of him drinking a glass of wine. The echoing memory of a crack of thunder sends chills down my spine, and I visibly shiver. Kor puts his arm around me, and the feel and scent of him drive away the dream and conjure up years of longing instead. I let him pull me close, and I rest my head on his shoulder as I keep talking. I tell him about hoverjousting and about watching the animation of a golem I made with my own hands. I feel his breath quicken with excitement when I describe the Valkyries flying.

"You would love it, Kor."

"I know I would."

"And yet you want to tear it down?"

"Not at all," he says softly. So softly. "I just want to share their wonders with our world."

"Me too." I feel like I'm so close. That with more time, I'll be able to make him see. Despite everything he's done, I can't help but still believe his heart is good.

Kor takes my hand in his, stroking my scar with his thumb, and even without the beer, I start to feel tipsy.

"Being a Sire has really amped up my creativity," he says. "Have you always had this constant artistic urge?"

"I guess." I hear the unspoken part of the question. *If you have, then why have you done so little with it?*

"That's not the only constant urge, if you know what I mean." He laughs.

My face goes red hot. He's talking about his libido. Because, apparently, Sires are all a bunch of floozies. I had the absolute most embarrassing conversation with Hypatia about it.

"Sires tend to be quite amorous," she'd said. "Our bodies, like our minds, are primed for creativity."

Learning about the birds and bees from a fourteen-year-old was . . . an experience.

"I guess I don't really have a basis for comparison" is what I say to Kor now, suddenly wishing New York was on a fault line so the chances of an earthquake interrupting this conversation would be higher.

Our cozy sitting arrangement takes on a whole new meaning now that the spill-my-guts-about-how-horny-I-get line has been crossed. I pull my hand away, which backfires when Kor moves his hand to my thigh.

"Isn't it a rush?" Kor asks, his other hand flaring with the glow of Ha'i. "Knowing your own power?"

But I can't help thinking about what he's done to get that power. I wonder whose blood it was this time. Even knowing he needs it to keep himself alive and that it might have been given to him willingly, bile rises in my throat.

He feels me stiffen and sighs. "Ada, I know you're still mad at me, but can't you see that it was all worth it? We're going to change the world. Together."

Together.

I remember the years of watching him and Izzy go off to train without me. Of watching his concerts and his interviews and the way he leveraged his platform to make other people care. I was never more than a bystander, wishing I could have a fraction of his talents. Now he's telling me I can have everything I've ever wanted. I can make a *difference* in this world *with* him.

But I'm starting to realize that I can make a difference on my own.

He's looking at me like the two of us are the only people in the world in that way that used to make me feel so special and so confused. He does this sexy half-bite, half-lick thing with his lip that definitely has me starting to feel *amorous*. Classic Kor, trying to play mind games with me. Or maybe this time he actually thinks he wants this to go somewhere. The way his eyes are fixated on my mouth sure makes it seem like he does. Suddenly my heart is pounding, and Kor's hand is moving higher on my thigh as he leans in.

I'd wanted this for so long.

But I don't want it anymore.

I push his hand off my leg and shift away from him.

His face falls. "Ada, don't shut me out. You're my best friend."

"You were mine."

He flinches.

"Sorry, I . . . That's not what I meant."

"It's fine. I get it." He stands up. "I have to go and prepare for tomorrow anyway." His eyes, so intent on me a moment ago, could not be more distant.

"What's tomorrow?" I ask as he zips the guitar into its case.

"We're moving forward with the next phase of Operation Genesis."

"What?" All my muscles tense. I knew that my recent interviews were in preparation for sending a small team to Arcadia. But not yet. Not before I had time to make sure the plan *changed*. "I thought you said that was scheduled for the fall?" This is bad. Really bad. I rise cautiously.

"Prometheus was pleased with the return of the girl and reciprocated with information that means we no longer have to wait," Kor explains.

"But this all so fast, and the military is on alert—"

"This may seem fast to you, but I've been working with Prometheus for two years. The Oculus has been waiting for a chance like this for generations.

We're hoping to avoid a confrontation, but we're prepared to deal with the military if we must."

"You mean, like, fight them?" I can't keep the horror from my voice.

"Ada, your handful of school friends and whatever pretty face you have a crush on today are not representative of these people. Not all of them are so innocent. Do you understand what's at stake for our world here? We need access to the scrolls you told us about, and we need to get the Ha'i stone, or at least instructions for how to make one."

He's right that I'm unfamiliar with the majority of Maker society. I know things run differently in Avant, and I've seen how resistant even the most caring of the Makers are to sharing their knowledge. Access to a Ha'i stone would mean Kor could stop drinking blood and still be well. We could help so many others to be well. Are the millions of people on this planet worth sacrificing a few?

These are not the kinds of decisions I'm equipped to make.

"Besides"—Kor reaches up to grip the silver crucifix at his neck—"we've found another universal blood donor, but, let's be honest, I don't know how much longer I'll be around. This has to happen sooner rather than later."

"Kor, we'll find a way to—"

"My health isn't what's important. I'm just one person. Operation Genesis's success is what's important now. If all goes to plan, we'll arrive undetected and go straight for the scrolls."

Kor climbs through the window and jumps to the floor, then reaches up to help me through.

"The scrolls are in a very public place. It's a school. There are teachers and children—" I say as I shimmy down. The guest room is dark and crowded and smells of mothballs.

"We'll be cautious to avoid casualties. But this is too important. Too many years of history have been waiting for this moment." He turns and makes his way through the obstacles in the room and out into the hall.

Casualties. As I follow Kor down the grand staircase, I feel sick with dread. Who might those casualties be? Simon, on guard at the Ark stairs? Xander at the desk—only a few weeks from giving birth? A bookish Sophist master in the library at the wrong time, sure to get involved because he's too selfless for his own good?

Would Kor harm them for the sake of his mission? This can't be the way. These can't be the right hands to heal the world.

I think of my middle name, Isabella, named for Queen Isabella of Castile. She is still a revered figure in history; there are monuments of her all over the globe. It's a common name in the Families—who all have a historical connection to her rule—and it always surprised me just how much my Jewish father despised it, how he spit at the statue of Isabella when we passed it in DC. Why had I ever been surprised by that? Her goal of a unified Spain cost tens of thousands of lives and hundreds of thousands of exiles.

The Families claim to have moved beyond their gruesome origin, but how can they not feel the echoes of the past in these choices?

At the bottom of the stairs, I grab Kor's hand. "I should be part of this. You won't be able to navigate the island without me."

"Our new Genesis informant will help us with that."

"Who is this new spy?" I've asked Kor this question numerous times, but he won't tell me. Even with me no longer leaking information, between Prometheus and this new informant, if I can't intervene, the Maker world is truly in danger.

"Ada, I told you I'd tell you everything when the time is right." He kisses my hand and then pulls away, making for the door.

None of this would be happening if it weren't for me. It's all my fault. But I can't stop it without knowing more details.

There's only one person I can think of who may be willing and able to help me learn more.

38

Once Kor is gone, I rush up to my room. I try a few internet searches and browse multiple social media sites, but it's all useless. I don't know how to locate a random person on the internet who doesn't want to be found.

But Georgie can. I email her asking her to call me when she's available.

As I wait for her response, I take out my pastels and add some shadows to a portrait of Grandfather that I've been working on. I try not to think about how many creative pursuits I took part in on a given day at Genesis compared to the past few weeks of almost nothing. But this picture is good. Grandfather has been sitting for me in the sunroom every morning when the lighting is just right.

I bawled my eyes out when I first saw him after I got back, knowing he was going to be okay after so many months of worrying. And he really does look okay. Much more energetic and vibrant than the last time I saw him. We did some gardening in the backyard together earlier today, and he had no problem with the more strenuous pulling and digging. And yesterday, both he and Sal came down to breakfast with wet hair. Like maybe they'd both been showering. At the same time. She has been living with him in this house for a long time, so anything's possible. . . .

I'd questioned Grandfather about his surgeries, and he'd only insisted that I have nothing to worry about.

"It may be the nature of bodies to degrade, but I've spent my life as a scientist learning that we can reverse nature, that we can *improve* upon it. I can honestly say that I've never been better. And I promise you, mi reinita, that I'll be around for a long time yet."

It's not like Grandfather to make promises he can't keep, but this is something that is out of his control. Certainly out of mine.

Right now everything feels out of my control.

I abandon my pastels to check if Georgie's gotten back to me yet. I mean, I know there's no way she has, but it's hard for me to think about anything else. I refresh my screen just in case. Then again.

I pick up a pastel to keep working, but then change my mind and drop it. I can't help but think that while I sit here enhancing smile lines, Kor is about to invade Arcadia, and I'm doing nothing about it.

Instead I pace. And then pace some more.

Eventually I flop onto my bed and pick up my father's music box from the bedside table. Dad's another person I haven't had any luck reaching. I've been trying to call him every single day, but nothing so far. I twist the key, and it begins to play the familiar song. "Yosef HaLevi's Nocturne." The very same one Rafe had assured me I could never have heard in the provincial world. The notes immediately calm me. I take deep breaths and just try to clear my head. When the song ends, I twist the key to play it again and close my eyes.

A ping from my laptop wakes me. I blink a few times, then jump up when I see light streaming through my window. It's past 7:00 a.m., and I have the horrible jabby feeling of having slept a whole night in a bra.

My laptop pings again.

Incoming call from PURPLEBOOTS.

I run over to click accept, and the moment I see Georgie's wonky smile and hair—that's now bubblegum pink—I want to cry and laugh at the same time.

"You!" she says with exuberant tenderness. "I miss your face!" I can see from the video that said face is quite blotchy and smeared with makeup, though my braid crown has held up surprisingly well. The ivy hasn't even wilted yet.

"I miss you too, and I'm still so sorry—"

"Ada, we're past that. Your email said you need help?"

"Right. I need you to put me in contact with Cicero," I say.

"Okay . . . ?"

"I think she has information I can use to stop something bad from happening."

"Not a problem. I have a chat window open with her already."

"You've been chatting with her? Georgie, that's not safe. I told you who she's connected to. I don't know if she's trustworthy!"

"Relax. She doesn't know who I am. We mostly just talk about code and stuff. Plus, she's . . . really cute."

"So you can put us in touch?"

"Already done."

A new window opens, and CICERO joins our call.

Izzy's face is suddenly there, enlarged on my monitor. Thick geeky-chic glasses, spiky short hair. She does look really cute, and not the slightest bit surprised to see me.

"Hello, Ada Castle."

"Hello, Izzy King."

"Long time no see."

"I wish it hadn't been so long," I say, words full of hurt I don't have time to feel right now. I'm unsure where to begin. But nothing is worse than an empty page, so I splatter paint on it. "I need to know everything you know about Operation Genesis."

She doesn't look particularly surprised. "From what I hear, it's only happening because of the information you provided."

In the other window, Georgie's eyes widen, and she sucks her cheeks into a ridiculous fish face, but she doesn't say anything.

"Well, now I want to stop it."

"And how do you know *I* want to stop it?"

"Well, don't you?"

"Hell yeah."

I smile. And Izzy smiles back.

Georgie's face relaxes.

"So, Purple Boots," Izzy says to Georgie, "you're actually one of the Hidden?"

Georgie smiles sheepishly. "Kind of? And you can call me Georgie."

"Yes, ma'am." Izzy looks as if she would like to call her many things, but I've got a crisis on my hands.

"So, what's with the radio silence?" I ask. "And the big middle finger to everything our families believe in?"

"Yeah, right. None of this extremist stuff the Oculus is up to has anything to do with our families' beliefs."

I'm so relieved to hear her say this. It's been hard to rely on my gut that all of this is wrong when the people I trust the most think it's okay. Knowing Izzy feels the same confirms that I'm not overreacting. And it means that the Oculus is diverging from the Families' values, as opposed to the other explanation that I was starting to dread might be true, that this is who they have been all along, and everything I grew up knowing was a lie.

Now that she'll finally speak to me about it, I've been squeezing Mom for as much information about the Families as I can. It seems the Oculus has always had grander plans than the mere stewardship of the rest of the Families. Kor's father, Aragon, had dedicated his life to finding the exiles so their innovations could be shared and had passed this passion on to Kor. But now, as more of the Inner Chamber are being brought into the new operation, there are many who don't agree with the radical changes.

Izzy is surprised that I'm choosing to act against Kor.

"I tried to warn you, but you were never going to listen to me over him."

"You didn't *warn* me. You just told me not to go to Italy without any explanation. I thought it was a drunk text!"

"I'm sorry for how I handled things. I didn't know who I could trust."

I want to be hurt that Izzy didn't have faith in me, but considering how many people I've mistakenly trusted recently, I can't blame her for taking the wiser approach.

Izzy explains that as soon as I told her about my abilities and she'd begun to research Sires, it uncovered a lot that concerned her about the Oculus and their methods. Once she found out about the abductions, she knew she couldn't be a part of it, but she wasn't sure if the Families would let her walk away. Luckily, Georgie wasn't the only one to identify her from the Hidden forum. Nora Montaigne had as well, and she'd used her influence to keep Izzy safely away from the Families' demands.

But Izzy is still in touch with her brother, Roman, who keeps her updated. "And I still have access to all their databases," she adds slyly. So she has a lot of useful information.

She can't answer all my questions, but she shares enough that I can put the pieces together to get a sense of what Kor has in mind.

And it ain't good.

"I have to talk to Kor and try to stop him."

Izzy crinkles her brow. "How? They've already left."

"What do you mean?"

"I mean they're already headed to Arcadia. Roman called to say goodbye around dawn."

I freeze in panic. How is all of this happening so fast? I close my eyes and breathe deeply. I need to think. "Do you know how many others are with him?"

"Kor, Roman, and Alfie are the only Inner Circle members. Roman mentioned a few others, but they're not Inner Circle, so my guess is they could be medics or engineers for tech or transportation?"

"We need to warn Genesis," I say to Georgie, who flicks her eyes to Izzy nervously.

"I get it," Izzy says. "Time to talk about the big secrets. I'll bounce. I miss you, Ada. Catch you soon, Boots!"

As soon as Izzy's window closes, Georgie asks, "Should I get Master Loew?"

"Um, no, he doesn't know about . . . my connections."

"Ugh, fine. I'll get the blond jerk. Hang on." She scrawls a pigeon.

A few minutes later, Rafe's too-pretty face appears on my screen.

"How's New York?" he asks, not looking remotely excited to see me. Guess he got over whatever we had pretty quick. I shouldn't be surprised.

"It's not great, but we have bigger problems."

"I assume so if you've bothered to reach out to me after so long without a word."

Georgie raises her brows to the heavens.

"Be pissy all you want later, but at this moment Kor is on his way to Arcadia."

"Impossible."

I tell him everything Izzy just told us. "They've disabled the Atlas, and I think they're coming through the tunnels."

"And how do they even know about the Atlas?"

I bite my lip and avoid answering that particular question. I told the

Families so much before I understood the danger. "The point is that the vacuums and doors have been opened and disabled, and they're on their way with an aerosolized version of antimatter." Or so says Izzy, and she sounded pretty confident about it all.

Rafe pinches the bridge of his nose and, after a few breaths, says, "How many of them are coming? And do you know their intentions?"

"Probably around five or six. And I think they're after the Testament scrolls."

"Well, if it's the scrolls, I can take care of having them better protected. There aren't that many Guard on Arcadia, but there should be enough to handle a small group," Rafe says.

"Are you sure?" I ask. "They have this new airborne antimatter."

"What can you tell me about it?"

I'd grilled one of the Families' scientists all about antimatter. As a concept, it's something that modern scientists have a basic understanding of, but only on a theoretical level. The knowledge of how to cultivate and use antimatter was stolen from the Makers during the original Inquisition and was passed down only among the Oculus. Until recently.

Roman is apparently on the team that synthesized the gas, so Izzy had a lot of details.

"It's a gas that, when inhaled, temporarily suspends Sire abilities without doing any permanent harm."

"That sounds like it would do a tremendous amount of damage to Sires," Rafe says in his I-am-being-very-stern voice.

"There's only a small trace of antimatter in it. Supposedly it's been tested extensively and hasn't done any long-term damage to Sires. It's just meant to—of course!" I slap my forehead.

They both stare at me expectantly. "Do explain," Rafe prompts.

"Would it be possible," I ask, "to spread an aerosol through whatever pumps the mists around the island?"

"It's not a pump. It's a forced temperature contrast created between the hot springs and the—" He stops and goes as still and as white as marble.

"What's wrong?"

"I think it's possible. Do you know for certain that they have a way to contaminate the mist?"

"I . . . I don't know. They asked me a lot of questions about it." I had thought they were just asking because of their interest in sustainable geo-thermal energy. "I didn't tell them much, but they have multiple informants."

Georgie has started typing intensely.

Rafe pulls both hands through his hair, sending his hair tie flying across the room. "If they can do it, it would be truly devastating."

"I mean, I know it's not great," I say, "but it should only temporarily suspend Sire abilities."

"No. You don't understand. For a regular Sire, it may only prevent their ability to conduct, but that's not the only conductive Ha'i that would be affected. Do you know how many people might be in the medical wing at this very moment, being kept alive by Sire healing until their conditions stabilize? Or people who are now well but rely on conductive technologies due to injuries or illness? Anyone with enhanced biology, like Valkyries, rely on conductive Ha'i. Who knows how breathing in antimatter might affect them? Not to mention that antimatter is extremely volatile. If there's any chance it hasn't been stabilized properly, it will explode as soon as it interacts with regular matter. If this plan succeeds, many could die."

My stomach sinks, and my blood feels as if it is pumping twice as fast as usual. Kor may be lost on the path of his ideals, but he would never want what Rafe is describing. I'm sure of it.

"I've reached out to Cicero," Georgie interjects. "No full confirmation on the mists as the vector, but she says the team seemed confident that they have a way to temporarily pollute the air of the island."

"Who in perdition is Cicero?" Rafe looks as if he wants to tantrum all over the room.

"Irrelevant right now," I say.

Georgie asks him, "Is there any way you can . . . turn off the mist?"

He shakes his head. "It doesn't work like that, and we don't even know if they'll be using the mist. What we have to do is be prepared for their arrival and stop them immediately."

"Don't forget, Kor is a Sire now. And they'll have provincial weapons—guns."

"The Avant Guard have been preparing for a provincial threat since their inception."

I don't like the sounds of that. "If the Guard succeed in overpowering Kor and whoever is with him, what will they do?" I ask.

"Muddling won't work for anything beyond a matter of hours. These intruders know where we live and plan to poison our air and steal our holiest and most important texts? I don't think the Guard will have much of a choice."

"There's always a choice."

"Answer me this, Ada. What will your family do if they're not stopped?"

"They're not coming to harm you, just to take information. They have good intentions."

"No matter their intentions, we need to defend ourselves. Is that not why you felt the need to warn me about all of this?"

Yes. But was warning him a mistake? Is he even right about the gas? Would letting Kor go in and out with possible minor casualties be better than causing a face-off with the Guard where there is guaranteed to be losses on both sides?

Horrible visions of the beautiful island smoking from the destruction of battle flash in my mind. Valkyries falling from the sky as they breathe in antimatter.

I don't want any harm to come to Genesis. Or to Kor or Izzy's brother.

Alfie can burn; I don't care about him.

"We need to warn the Guard, but we can't let them kill anyone," I say.

"I can't promise you that."

"Rafe, I helped you save your cousin. Now help me save mine." He doesn't respond. "I can reason with Kor. I'm sure of it," I plead. "I just need to stop them before they get there. He wants the scrolls, but he doesn't want to cause unnecessary deaths."

"But they're already on their way. It's too late," Georgie says.

An idea, born of desperation, is forming in my mind. "Why does it have to be too late? We know they're probably traveling through the Atlas tunnel, and we know where they're headed."

Her brows furrow. "And they have a significant head start."

"But no maglev technology."

"Neither do y—*oh*. Uh-uh. No way." She shakes her head emphatically. "It's way too far. And too dangerous."

Rafe grits his teeth, and I know he's caught on. "Ada, stop and think for a moment. What you're considering is impossible. Do you know how long the journey is? How fast you would have to go to catch up to them?"

Fast, I can handle.

"It is the same technology, isn't it?" I press.

He rakes a hand through his hair. "I mean, technically the hoverjoust pit uses the same form of maglev as the Atlas tunnels, but—"

"Great! Then I've made up my mind."

"We can't rely on your success. I'll need to alert the Guard to be ready. The risk to our home is too great if you fail."

"I agree. You should have a backup plan, but it's not so simple. Kor is working directly with someone on the inside, and I don't know who it is." I'd asked Izzy if she knew anything about the new informant, but she didn't. "I don't know who we can trust."

Rafe's face is a storm. "How is that even possible? How are we hemorrhaging—" He looks skeptically at Georgie sitting next to him.

But I'm done with ever letting him doubt or speak ill of her.

"I trust her with my life," I say.

Georgie sits a little straighter, and Rafe nods. Then, to my surprise, he sticks out his hand to her. When she tentatively shakes it, he says earnestly, "I don't doubt your loyalty. I know we could never have rescued Hypatia without your assistance, and I am forever in your debt."

Georgie's cheeks flush pink, and I swallow as something inside me turns to mush.

Once I'm sure my guts are again fully solid, I say to Rafe, "We need help. Who do you trust absolutely?"

"My brothers. I'll contact Alex, but he's in Avant. We need people at Genesis."

"I trust Master Loew," I say.

"Well, I do not," Rafe responds decisively.

"What about Kaylie?" I try.

"Yes," he says. "And Hypatia, Simon, and Mbali."

The three of us talk through the details of the plan. In addition to somehow warning the Guard without tipping off the spy, Rafe will figure out how to best protect the mists. Georgie is going to get the Artisans to make and distribute protective masks, just in case. Look at them collaborating so nicely. And Rafe hasn't sneered even once.

Sheesh, my bar is set so low. When did I start congratulating boys for basic human decency? But he does deserve a pat on the back. Perhaps on the butt.

Soon we say our goodbyes, and this time there's no need for tears. I'll be seeing my friends again soon.

"Be careful, Ada!" Georgie begs.

Rafe says nothing.

They don't think I can do it. But I don't have a choice. They're preparing for an invasion. One that's all my fault. But I'm going to stop it. And I'm going to help the Families see a better way.

My slept-in birthday outfit won't do. I need to dress for speed and cold. I change into a sports bra and turtleneck, and I layer a pair of leggings under the jeans I wore for farm work on the island. I'm thankful I have Rafe's leather jacket, which is sturdy enough to protect from the wind of what is looking to be a treacherous ride. There's a leftover bag of homemade trail mix (thoughtfully prepared by Sal) in the pocket. Perfect. Who knows the next time I'll have a chance to eat. I don't have the time to redo my hair, so I leave the slightly mussed braided crown with the pretty ivy running through it. I sling the hoverboard—camouflaged in my snowboarding bag—over my shoulder and take a deep breath.

What am I even doing? This is a terrible idea. I am the last person to be able to pull this off. Even Georgie and Rafe don't think I can do it.

I push aside all my fears and inadequacies. If fixing my mistakes means being irresponsible and dumb, then that's what it takes.

I don't want to have to explain where I'm going, so I decide to sneak out through the kitchen.

"Ada?"

My plan to avoid my family has apparently failed as my mom is leaning against the counter eating leftover birthday cake. It's odd that she's not in her work clothes yet, and it's even more odd that she's voluntarily eating something that contains both butter and sugar.

"Where are you going?"

Well, I can't just tell her, can I? But I'm all out of lies today.

"I'm going back. To Genesis."

"You weren't going to say goodbye?"

I had wanted to say goodbye, but I'd been worried that facing my family would make me change my mind. I'm still not sure I won't change my mind, considering my conviction is about as stable as a soap bubble.

My mom abandons her cake and strides over to me, wraps me in a hug. "Good," she says. "It's better for you there."

Her hug is warm, but it doesn't feel nice that she's so eager to be rid of me again.

"I wish it didn't have to be this way," she continues. "I would much rather have you close. I missed you so much while you were gone."

Oh. I squeeze her tighter.

"I kept you out of everything for as long as I could, but if you have to be involved, it's safer for you there than here."

"Wait. What do you mean you kept me out of it?" I mumble into her shoulder.

"I didn't let the Families initiate you when you came of age. I didn't want them to know about your abilities and make you their constant test subject."

What?

I pull away from the hug and play her words over again in my head.

I didn't let the Families initiate you.

"I thought I wasn't initiated because I wasn't good enough?" Even thinking about it has familiar shame resurfacing.

My mother takes my face in her hands, looks me in the eyes, and says, "Ada, you have *always* been good enough."

I can barely breathe.

My mother keeps speaking, softly stroking my cheek. "The reason I finally allowed them to initiate you is so that you would be recruited to the institute. I wanted you there for your own safety. The moment the Families learned about your gift, I knew I needed to keep you away from them."

My *gift*. Is that what she thinks of my abilities? Then how could she have made me think of them as a curse?

My pulse echoes in my ears, and my voice quavers when I say, "I thought you were scared of me."

"I was never scared of you. I was only ever scared *for* you. Terrified. Of what the Families might do if they understood what you are."

There's a stinging behind my eyes and in the back of my throat as my mind rearranges my view of reality once again.

Mom leans back against the counter with a sigh. "Ada, your abilities, they're genetic; they run in our family. Your grandmother didn't have them, but she thought I might. When I was young, they were constantly testing me. I spent half of my middle school years being analyzed in a lab until they finally determined I wasn't what they were hoping for. I didn't want that for you."

I don't even know what to say. This is the last thing I expected to hear. I mean, I knew being a Sire was genetic. It probably should have occurred to me that it might run in the family.

"All my life," my mother continues, "I've felt like I needed to work harder than everyone else to make up for the fact that I had failed to be born exceptional. It became a challenge. If I could perfect everything within my control, then maybe what was out of my control would matter less. But I never wanted *you* to feel that way. I couldn't bear for you to have the weight of the Families' scrutiny on you the way I did. And you didn't need them pushing you. You have always managed to be exceptional based on your own standards, not anyone else's." She takes both of my hands in hers. "And I'm so proud of you for it."

I pull my hand away, but just so I can wipe my wet cheeks. And my nose.

"Why couldn't you have told me all of this sooner? I thought I was such a failure."

"I'm so sorry. Your grandmother . . . She would try to motivate me by telling me about her difficulties growing up. But it always felt like she was trying to manipulate my emotions to bend me into what she wanted me to be. I didn't want to do that to you, but clearly I overcorrected." She hands me her napkin to help deal with my snot fountain. "But even though I've been distant and busy and not as forthcoming as you needed me to be, it's because I was working to keep you safe. Everything I have done has been to protect you."

Were all those years of feeling inadequate worth that protection?

The anger over the possible answer to that question is overshadowed by a bone-deep sense of relief. And an extra boost of confidence that the ridiculous thing I'm about to do is the right thing. If my own mother, who has been deeply involved with the Families her whole life, thinks they're so dangerous she had to keep her daughter away from them, what does that say about what they're capable of? But now that my mother is being up front with me, maybe she can help.

"Mom, Kor started the next stage of Operation Genesis early, and I need to stop him. Do you know anything about it?"

"I wish I did, but the Oculus gave Kor free rein to act without the Inner Chamber's approval, and he hasn't shared his plans with any of us. And the Inner Chamber members are annoyed with me because I accidentally"—she puts the word in air quotes—"deleted footage of you from North Brother Island, so they're stonewalling me on everything."

Wow, she really has been working for me behind the scenes, and I had no idea.

"I don't know how to make Kor listen to me, if I can even get to him in time."

She strokes my hair. "Ada, I have no doubt that you can do this." There's a pride in her voice that seeps through me and fills in the cracks of so many old wounds. "You are so brave and so resourceful, and if that boy listens to anyone besides the Grand Master, it's you."

She pulls me into a last hug and kisses the top of my head.

It's time to do this.

And I *can*. Because I'm a Sire and a Maker, and I'm gravdamn fast on a hoverboard.

And I *will* do what has to be done.

39

I don't have the codes for the City Hall station, so I have to take the "fun route." Unfortunately, it's a lot harder without an escort. I get particularly stalled trying to open the subway car doors at the abandoned station. After two failures and a momentary fear that I'll be taking this subway line back and forth all night, I instead open the door connecting the train cars—the door that is covered in signs warning not to do just that—and I ride between cars. It's terrifying, very loud, and definitely involves rats. Do not recommend. As the train shrieks through the City Hall station, I hold my breath and somehow manage not to die or piss my pants while making the jump.

When I arrive at the Atlas platform, it's abandoned, and the air locks are indeed open.

I sit on the edge of the track, my legs dangling. Then I scooch down till my toes touch the metal below. It's a tube, no flat surface to stand on.

I unzip my snowboard bag, plop down my hoverboard—which engages with the magnetic levitation of the track—and I hop on and glide toward the air lock.

An endless tunnel of shining metal stretches ahead of me. There are

low-lit lamps set into the ceiling, and the light reflects off the polished surface, giving the whole space an eerie glow.

Let's do this.

The maglev is much stronger than I'm used to from the hoverjoust pit,
and I shoot forward so unexpectedly fast that I fall. Hard. My ankle twists
with a sickening crunch. No time for pain. I pulse Ha'i down my leg to
soothe the injury as I limp after my board and clamber back onto it.

This is good. I'm going to be able to go even faster than I thought. But
realistically, I don't think even I'll be able to stay on my board at the speed
I need to sustain to intercept Kor. I wish I had a binding to strap into like
on my snowboard.

I take inventory of everything I have with me, but I don't have any rope
or anything to help secure myself to the board.

Find anything you can use. That's what Rafe would say.

Think.

I'm already sweating. I push the flyaways out of my face, and my hand
catches on the vine that Sal wove into my braid. Yes.

I unwind the vine, grasp it in my hands, and take a deep breath.

Please grow, I request.

The vine lengthens and winds around my arms.

Yes! *Stronger. Thicker.*

Soon I have a thick vine twice the length of my body. I use it to lash my
feet to my board.

And then I *go.*

I bend my knees to find my center of gravity, and I'm a bullet. I lose
sense of what is up and down. I'm just a girl being sucked through a straw.

Which, apparently, is not a sustainable existence for all that long.

I've lost track of time and distance, and I'm utterly exhausted from doing
nothing but standing. I slow to no faster than a walk and take the time to

snack on Sal's trail mix. As I crunch on peanuts and pumpkin seeds, I hold back tears. How am I supposed to do this? It's dark, and I'm alone and tired. I ache all over. My calf muscles are killing me from involuntarily clenching them the whole way. I wish I could sit.

And then I have the most bizarre idea . . . that just might work.

I slow to a complete stop. Which is terrifying in the echoing tunnel somewhere deep under the Atlantic Ocean. I refuse to think about what could happen if the train were reactivated.

I retrieve another pumpkin seed from the bag and use my spoon to pry off the seed shell, then cup my hands in shiin around the inner seed. I am an Alchemist Sire, and I've learned how to do this. I know I can do this. *There.* I can feel a tiny thread of Ha'i still inside.

Please, grow.

And it does. I conduct until the plant is too big for me to hold, then put it down on my board and keep pulsing Ha'i into it. Soon there's a beautiful pumpkin just the right size to sit on, with a thick vine growing up between my legs, long and strong enough to strap myself to the pumpkin and the pumpkin to the board.

And that's how I continue my journey. On a pumpkin throne with a vine seat belt, trying to breathe easy as I gust through the tunnel, losing track of what could be minutes or hours.

I talk to myself. I sing. I yell at the top of my lungs.

I am a shooting star, a meteorite, an avalanche.

I am a girl riding many miles an hour on a pumpkin.

A girl approaching an air lock.

I shriek with relief as I recognize the platform. By the time I slow and pass through the air lock, I'm crying. I've made it to Arcadia. To Genesis. Home.

The station is empty and dark. No sign of anyone. No sign of Kor.

I should have intercepted them in the tunnel. There's a large hourglass on the station wall, and the accumulation of sand indicates it's around early evening. I've made good time. I can't imagine they got here before me.

Unless they traveled some other way . . .

Automatic lights blink on as someone moves in the shadows.

"Hello?" I call out.

"Ada?" a boy's voice asks.

"Simon? Is that you?"

It is. The young Valkyrie hops down onto the track. He's wearing his Guard uniform, and I'm suddenly dizzy with a strong sense of déjà vu.

"Are you okay?" he asks me.

"Oh. Yes." I'd momentarily forgotten how I must look, a sweaty crying mess sitting on a pumpkin bound to a hoverboard in the middle of a train track. "But could you help me cut these vines?"

He's quickly at my side with his spoon out, cutting me free. "Did you by any chance come through the Atlas tunnel just now?"

"I did."

"That's odd."

I don't really know how to respond. But Simon seems to be taking the whole thing in stride.

"What are you doing here?" I ask.

"I was sent down to check that the emergency exit out to the cove is secure and to disable the elevator. But once it's disabled, it can't be reenabled without a council member's key, so I have to wait down here. You'll have to wait now too; there's no way to get up."

"You were sent alone?" Why would Rafe have risked that? What if Kor had made it here before me?

"I think Rafe was hoping I would . . ." He shrugs his wings so they ruffle out slightly.

Of course, technically Simon could have flown back up, but he's scared of flying and not very good at it.

A loud grinding sound shakes the station. Simon scrambles up from the track to the platform and runs over to the emergency door, which leads to the cove outside. I stumble after him on shaky legs.

"Hide," he says to me. "I'll guard the door."

"No. I need to go out there. Once I do, you secure the exit behind me and stay out of sight."

"I am a soldier of the Avant Guard," Simon says with shaky resolve. "And if there is danger outside that door, I will protect you, Journey Castle!"

"Listen to me, Simon. I'm going out there, and you're staying in here. No matter what happens, you stay hidden. Do you understand?" My urgency must convince him because he doesn't prevent me from unlocking the door and pushing it open.

The sea wind slaps my face, salt and sand and hair blowing into my eyes. But nothing can stop me from seeing the sleek black submarine rising from the cove, Kor emerging from a hatch on top as it docks among the rocks.

40

"I wish you hadn't come," Kor calls as he finds his footing on the slick rocks, approaching the shore.

"And I wish you had consulted me so I could have prevented this mistake!" I raise my voice to be heard over the wind and waves. There's only a few feet of sand and water between us, but it feels like an impossible distance.

"Yes, I guess convincing the whole order you were trustworthy was a mistake," he replies.

His words hurt my heart.

"You *can* trust me. And you should trust me about the fact that if you use the gas, the results will be devastating. Our goals are the same, but you can't use that gas, or people will die. They'll be murdered. By *you*." With the elevators disabled, there's no way for Kor to get up to the island. But there's also no way for any help to get to me. I need to convince him to abandon his plan, and I'll have to do it alone.

He looks sad but not swayed. "We truly came hoping not to hurt anyone, but now that we're here, we'll make the necessary sacrifices."

"You can't mean that."

"My Ada." Kor shakes his head. "Who will do it if not me?" He gestures at his abdomen. "I've already damned my soul by drinking the lifeblood of others. And despite that, I'm still probably not long for this world. But before I'm gone, I'll make a difference." He raises his arms and looks up at the sky, his long hair whipping in the wind. "The Grand Master chose me for this, and God prepared me for it. I am ready to do what I have to do to save the world—" He stops talking and grasps for his cross, his eyes glowing in rapture.

But when I follow his gaze, I realize it's not his words that have excited him. Rather, it is two sets of beautiful wings. One belonging to a Valkyrie with copper hair—looking like Kor's angel painting come to life—and one to a wind horse with a statuesque rider.

Kaylie, Peggy, and Rafe are flying down the cliffside. I'm not alone after all.

Kaylie touches down on the beach, her wings spread wide, her face fierce and beautiful. Kor stares at her with awe and raw adoration.

Rafe dismounts from Peggy a few yards away. He has a magneto gun in one hand and a blade in the other. The heat of Ha'i rises off him like a boiling pot.

Kor looks back and forth between Rafe and Kaylie, then calls toward the hatch, "Backup!"

Rafe speaks. "If you turn over your weapons and allow me to restrain you and your comrades, I will protect you from harm and escort you to speak to the Council."

"I didn't come here to be arrested," Kor says, coolly raising a gun and pointing it at Rafe.

"That isn't necessary!" I step forward, panic in my voice.

Alfie and Roman make their way out of the hatch and onto the beach. Roman is armed but looks nervous. He stares wide-eyed at the sight of a Valkyrie and a wind horse, and he crosses himself. Alfie is holding a canister with a spray hose that must be the antimatter gas. He aims the nozzle like a weapon. There may not be mist down here, but if he sprays the gas and it does what we expect, it could seriously harm Kaylie and Peggy, and Rafe and I would lose our Sire advantages.

"Don't—" I start to say at the same time as Rafe moves to intercept Alfie.

Kor cocks his gun.

"No! Kor, can't we—"

And then he shoots.

I hear the crack of the bullet. Then silence.

Someone far away starts screaming.

No, not far away. It's me. I'm screaming.

But the rest of my body is frozen. All I can do is stare as a red flower unfurls its petals on the left side of Rafe's chest. Like a boutonniere.

He looks so dashing, ready for a dance.

Crack. The memory of the sound echoes over and over in my ears.

And then Rafe is crumpling to the ground. I didn't know Rafe Vanguard could crumple.

Time resumes as I see Kaylie running toward him.

And then I'm running too.

Kaylie is trying to stem the flow of blood, but it's no longer a boutonniere. It's now a bouquet, and spreading fast. Becoming a field before my eyes.

Rafe is breathing hard, eyes glassy. He manages to grin at me. "I'll be fine." I see his mouth form the words. But I can't hear them. All I can hear is the echo of the crack and the sound of my own pulse in my head.

Kaylie is speaking to me urgently, but I'm in a daze.

Kor just shot Rafe.

He *shot* him. Why didn't I let Rafe bring the Guard? This is my fault. This is *my fault*.

"Ada!" Kaylie's yell breaks through my fog. "His Sire abilities are not healing him; he needs your help."

Yes. I can help.

I crouch down and make *shiin* with both hands and align the triangle made by my fingers over the sticky flowers. I conduct, pulsing Ha'i over and over.

Please, please, please. I beg the source within me.

But he's not healing.

"Why isn't he healing?" I scream, panicked, knowing I'm exhausting my own Ha'i but not willing to stop trying.

"It's an antimatter bullet," Kor says. I turn and see him standing, staring at his trembling hand that is still clenching the gun, face pale.

Peggy is agitated, and she starts bucking and flapping her wings. Alfie turns the nozzle of the gas in her direction.

"Don't hurt it!" Kor demands.

"We have to remove the bullet," Kaylie says, ignoring the threat of the gas tank, which Alfie has swung back in her direction at the sound of her voice. She tears open Rafe's shirt. "It missed his heart, but antimatter in his body for too long, close to such vital organs . . ." She trails off as she uses a blade from her spoon to cut into his marble chest, through his dragon tattoo. Rafe is so far gone that he doesn't even flinch.

"The bullet punctured his lung," she says steadily. "I need to drain the air and fluid, so I need you to remove the bullet."

I don't know how I do it, but as Kaylie makes a separate incision, I reach into Rafe's chest. I focus on the sound of her voice giving me careful instructions. My hand is coated in blood as I pull out the bullet, the antimatter scalding my fingers until I drop it, like a shiny red ruby, onto the wet sand.

I immediately begin pulsing Ha'i into Rafe's chest, and this time it works. The blood slows. The tissue begins to mend. But Rafe has lost so much blood. He's not healing fast enough, and I feel my own strength flagging.

"Help me," I scream to Kor, who's looking on, horror-stricken.

"I . . . I've never—" He looks to Roman, who looks just as panicked and unsure, tears in his eyes.

"Do you want to have his death on your conscience?" I shriek. I see the indecision in his eyes, the war of pride and guilt.

"Kor, I need you to help me save his life!" I'm choking on my own sobs. "Help me!" I demand again. He *has* to help me. No matter what he's said about being okay with collateral damage, I *know* he's not a killer.

He drops the gun and comes running.

I show Kor how to align his *shiin* next to mine, and as soon as our hands harmonize, a powerful flow of Ha'i pulses through the triangle made by our fingers. Rafe's body jerks erratically.

"Again!" I yell, and with the next push of Ha'i, Rafe gasps in a deep breath, then seems to breathe more easily.

The flow of Ha'i was astounding, more than I've ever felt from myself or another person. But now Kor looks shaky and weakened. I remember Rafe explaining how blood doping will give a Sire tremendous power but also cause them to exhaust more quickly. Kor doesn't look like he has the strength to conduct anymore. But Rafe isn't fully healed yet.

Kaylie's face is a mask of horror. She presses her knuckles to her lips in Avant's royal salute. She doesn't think their prince will live.

I know what I have to do.

I grab Kaylie's blade, and without letting myself think too hard about it, I slice into my forearm.

Blood wells up through the cut, and I aim its drip directly into Rafe's mouth. Adrenaline and Ha'i are rushing through me with such strong force that I see the bleeding slow and the skin around the wound tighten as my body tries to heal itself. I jab at the cut with the point of the knife to keep the blood flowing. Somehow, my mind drowns out the pain. I feel like an outside observer, watching as the warm life inside me spurts out of the messy wound onto Rafe's lips.

Kor shifts away from us, and I catch an expression on his face that can't be described as anything other than hunger.

"Should we retreat?" I hear Roman ask Kor.

But I don't hear Kor's response as Rafe blinks and swallows my blood spilling into his mouth. So much blood. Until, in a ragged voice, he says, "Enough." He grips my arm. "Sing me your strength."

I don't understand, but in this moment, I'll do whatever he asks. If he wants me to sing, I'll sing. So I discard the blade and begin to hum "Yosef HaLevi's Nocturne." The cut in my arm knits together as I watch the effect of my blood slowly helping Rafe. He grasps my hands with his as I hum.

And then something in the air changes. I feel Rafe's Ha'i doubling, tripling, amplifying to levels I would have never thought possible. His body trembles as his Sire healing kicks into overdrive.

Rafe gasps and sits up sharply, his wounds already sealing shut.

The sound of a trumpet forces my gaze up the cliff, where I see the Avant Guard assembled with what looks like a large crossbow the size of a truck. A figure breaks away from the rest, spreads their wings, and flies down to us. It's Grey. He lands in front of Rafe, blocking him from any potential threat.

"Your Highness, I know you instructed the Guard to hold, but Simon flew up the cliff to alert us that you had been attacked," Grey explains.

Simon? Flew all the way up the cliff? Good for him.

Grey draws a long sword, turning to glare at Kor, who is scrambling toward the submarine, Alfie and Roman right behind him. "Go ahead," Grey yells after them, "board your vessel. The ballista will make quick work of it, and you." We all look up to the cliff, where the Guard have aimed the giant crossbow—or rather, the ballista, another one of da Vinci's original designs—straight at the sub. The three young men stop running, and Grey relieves them of their weapons.

Rafe stands confidently. Blood coats his chest from a wound that is now nothing more than a ragged scar through the eye of the dragon tattoo that guarded his heart.

He says to Grey, "You and all the Guard witnessed that despite what this man did, he also helped to save my life. Let that be considered when their fate is decided."

Grey bows his head. "We will inform the Council."

Rafe turns to Kor. "Are you willing to cooperate now?"

Kor looks up at the Guard and then at me.

"You don't have a choice," I say, trying to communicate with my eyes that he should trust me.

Kor nods.

Rafe asks, "Do you have any more of the antimatter bullets and weaponized gas?"

"Yes."

"What about more men?"

"Two more men. I can retrieve them and the remaining antimatter weapons." Kor steps toward the water's edge, where the submarine waits, partially submerged. I'm surprised he's agreed. He seems a little too eager to get into the submarine, which makes me nervous.

"Not without supervision," Grey growls. He restrains Alfie and Roman with spidersilk ties and then moves to accompany Kor into the sub. "I warn you, philistine"—he again motions to the Guard standing in wait at the top of the cliff—"if you try anything while inside the vessel, they will not hesitate to obliterate it."

Soon after they enter, the sub powers down, and then Kor is coming back out, followed by two terrified men. One looks like he is probably the captain of the submarine, and the other one I recognize as the security guard Rafe incapacitated on North Brother Island. Grey is close behind them carrying a large black duffel, presumably containing their weapons.

As Kor allows Kaylie to bind his hands, I can't help but notice that his cheeks are once again suffused with color, and his strength seems to have been restored.

Grey and Kaylie lead the five men into the station.

With all concerned onlookers gone, Rafe staggers, and I guide him to sit on a rock.

A shadow falls over us as a cloud blocks the setting sun. Rafe looks up and smiles, and my eyes follow his.

No, not a cloud.

Massive wings and shining black scales eclipse the sky. I see a whipping tail, sharp claws, and fierce, intelligent eyes. And then the majestic creature lands in front of us, Prince Alexander riding astride its back.

He pulls Rafe and me up with him, and we fly into the bruised orange of the sunset sky.

On a gravdamn *dragon*.

41

Riding a dragon is the most breathtaking, wondrous, terrifying experience of my lifetime. But I don't have long to appreciate it. In what feels like mere moments, we land on the institute's ornithopter pad. Prince Alex immediately heads to the council room as Bioscience masters check Rafe's vitals. Everyone is too busy to question how and why I'm back on the island.

I duck into the first bathroom I pass to wash the blood off my hands. I scrub them till they're raw, but there are still brown traces under my nails, so I keep scrubbing.

Everyone's alive. Everyone's alive.

I keep repeating it over and over. I left New York this morning with that goal in mind, and it's been fueling me for this entire endless day.

I look at myself in the mirror. Yep. I look like someone who hoverboarded through a tunnel for hours and then did impromptu surgery on the beach. My adrenaline is still pumping, every heartbeat communicating urgency, but I'm not sure what I should do next.

I could go to my room, find Georgie, get some sleep. But my feet don't lead me to the Winter wing. Despite successfully managing to avert tragedy, I feel so empty. So lost. And there's only one person I want to see.

When I reach the door I was instinctively drawn to, I feel foolish. He's probably not even here now. But I knock anyway.

"Come in."

Michael straightens, startled when I step into his office. "Ada?" He's standing at his desk surrounded by a larger-than-usual mountain of files and books.

His hair is a tempest, his jacket and cravat long gone; a light dusting of curling brown hair peeks through the V of his unbuttoned collar.

"Hi," I say.

"How . . . ? Hi?" He's not wearing shoes, and his socks don't match.

He blinks, and then the papers in his hand fall to his desk and he rushes to me, enveloping me in a hug. He smells like tea and chocolate, and even as my pulse quickens from his nearness, I feel calm for the first time in hours. Maybe days.

"I thought you weren't coming back."

"I had to," I say into his chest. "I'm not sure there's a place for me in the provincial world anymore."

He pulls away, holding me at arm's length. "Don't say that." His brows knit. "Your world is amazing. You've done so much to remind me of that. Don't forget it yourself."

Your world. Is he saying he thinks I should have stayed there?

When it comes to Michael, it's always been this same endless carousel of doubt.

He smirks at me as if I've said something funny.

"What?"

"It's just . . . that look on your face. The one you always make when you take an intended compliment as an insult."

"Well, I did warn you that I'm a chronic cynic."

"You're not a cynic." He shakes his head knowingly. "You're way too hopeful to be a cynic. A cynic would anticipate everyone letting them down instead of expecting them to do better."

His eyes have turned so serious, and I realize he's never stopped touching me, his hands warm and firm on my shoulders.

"You can't take a compliment because you're too humble to see your own worth—"

I cut him off. "Trust me, Michael, I've never been the girl you thought I was. I'm not humble, I'm just a total mess."

"No," he insists, squeezing my shoulders. "I won't let you put yourself down anymore. You have all this insecurity, but underneath there's this steel resolve of wanting to understand what's right and true, and you're so open to questioning what you think you know." He steps closer. "Meanwhile, I'm the one everyone thinks has it all figured out, when inside I'm actually just a ball of noisy, conflicting ideals that I can't make sense of. Except when you challenge my beliefs, and suddenly everything that really matters comes into sharper focus."

My breathing is unsteady as I look into his eyes. His guard is down, and I see the boy I met in Italy. Not the prodigy master who's younger than all his colleagues and working twice as hard to prove himself, but the passionate boy with a sweet tooth who craves connection, sees the wonder in everything, and is willing to open his mind to different perspectives.

I *know* him. And he knows me. We have always understood each other.

"Michael . . ." But I don't have the words to express any of my jumbled thoughts.

"I missed you," he says, voice tight. He strokes my cheek, and my breath catches. His eyelids are heavy, his pupils wide, and when instinct has me tilting my face up to his, he leans to meet me. Our noses brush, then hesitantly our lips. Michael cups my face in his hands as he kisses me, soft and sweet and tender.

I'm kissing Michael. Michael is kissing me.

"I've thought about this so many times," he breathes between kisses. My lips part, and his tongue slides against mine.

Me too, I want to say, but I've lost my ability to form words, so I say it with my kisses instead. *I think about you all the time. You mean so much to me. The thought of not seeing you again was tearing me apart.*

I grasp his shirt as the kiss deepens and grows more urgent. And then he's pushing me up against his desk, his body pressing into me. He buries his hands in my hair, the remains of my braid crown coming undone.

There's a twisting inside me that pulls everything tight like tuned guitar strings.

Scratch the dragon ride; this is the most breathtaking, wondrous, and terrifying experience of my life.

Michael hoists me onto his desk, papers scattering. His kisses travel to my neck, and he murmurs my name against my skin. I slide my hands into his hair and pull his face back to mine, my teeth nipping and sucking at his bottom lip.

His hands move down my back, lower, his fingers press into my curves through my jeans, and I swallow his strangled moan. My legs wrap around his waist, and as I press against him, I can feel how much he wants me.

Everything about this feels so right.

But how can it ever work while I'm lying to him? And if I tell him the truth, I'll surely lose him.

My momentary hesitation causes Michael to still. His breath is ragged as he slides his hands up to my waist and gruffly whispers into my ear, "We shouldn't be doing this." His breath hits my neck in hot gasps as I feel him trying to get control over his body.

"Yes, we definitely should," I say, pulling him close and resting my cheek in the hollow of his throat. I feel his Adam's apple bob as he swallows, and I turn just enough to be able to press my lips against it, then my tongue. I feel the vibrations of his groan.

Please stop not kissing me.

But he gently pushes my legs from his waist and peels away from me. A rush of cool air steals the warmth of his now absent touch.

"Ada—" But Michael's words are swallowed by a gasp of pain as he clutches his stomach. He lifts his shirt, and we both watch mesmerized as letters form on the bare skin of his abdomen.

"Gravdammit, Ari!" he chokes. Michael's skin is reddened and swollen as the letters continue to form. His teeth clench with obvious agony.

When it's clear what the inverted letters say, all the color drains from his face.

They have Hilde.

What? My blood chills.

Of course. Kor told me that they'd found another universal blood donor. I slide off the desk to my feet. How is that people I love keep harming other people I love? I take a deep breath. No, they won't harm her.

Michael looks up at me with complete and utter hopelessness. "I warned her. I . . . I can't help her." He runs both hands through his hair and clutches his scalp.

But maybe I can help her. The Atlas is down, and Kor is detained here on the island, but I can use Georgie's computer to call Mom.

"Ada, I'm so sorry. I know the timing . . . I have to go."

"I understand."

He gives me an awkward hug, rushes to his desk to retrieve something from the center drawer, and then hastens out of the room.

I take a moment to fix my hair, straighten my clothes, and have a total mental freakout about the fact that I just made out with Michael. Then I follow him out and head to my apartment.

It's too late at night to have any chance of reaching Mom, but I assure myself that I have no reason to think that Hilde is in any immediate danger. I'd met some of the other Sires when I was home, and Kor had been truthful when he said they were well treated. The ones I spoke with—including the renowned scientist who had been a missing person in the news for months—were cooperating voluntarily, excited to be a part of groundbreaking experimentation. Plus, with Kor here, Hilde's blood is safe for now.

When I get to my apartment, Georgie shrieks and jumps up, overturning a pile of spidersilk masks she's been sewing with the help of Mbali and Hypatia.

The next few seconds involve a lot of hugging.

Mbali asks, "If you're back, does that mean the air contamination was prevented?" Her being here and knowing what's going on means she knows what I've done. Yet she seems just as happy to see me as Georgie and Hypatia.

"Yes," I say, my throat tight with emotion. "It's over."

There's more hugging.

"How dare you not tell me that dragons exist!" I say into Georgie's neck as she squeezes me tight.

"Wait. Dragons exist?" she asks, pulling away, her brows cocked skeptically.

"You didn't know? But I saw dragons on the television in New York," Hypatia says.

"Those are pretend ones!"

"How did you think they know how the pretend ones should look if there were no real ones to base them on?" Hypatia asks, as if this logic should be completely obvious.

This leads into a discussion of how I learned about dragons, and I tell them a very protracted version of what took place at the cove.

"Simon flew all the way up the cliff?" Hypatia asks incredulously.

"He sure did." I don't mention it was because her cousin had been shot in the chest.

That feeling of déjà vu returns. The imagery of Simon flying up the cliff as Rafe bled below jostles something in my memory.

A long hoverboard ride. A crack of thunder. Simon flying over Rafe, who is lying in a field of red flowers . . .

That incessant dream I'd been having.

An unknown beautiful girl pouring wine for Kor.

Oh. *Ohhh.*

That was why Hilde looked so familiar when we met. I had *dreamed* about her.

I don't understand how or why, but I dreamed about everything that happened tonight.

And now I understand how Kor went from weak and exhausted to reinvigorated after he went back into that submarine.

I don't need to call Mom. I know exactly where Hilde is.

42

I wait to act until it's late enough that I know most of the institute will be asleep and the village empty. As I make my way down the reenabled elevator, the view through the glass is dark with only an eerie glow from the bioluminescent lichen clinging to the cave formations.

I don't know why I'm so sure of my dream, but I am. I'm sure of something else as well: My goals *are* different from the Families'.

Kor may have helped heal Rafe, but he was willing to shoot him and take Hilde captive. The Grand Master has backed all his decisions.

It's time for me to admit that I belong at Genesis. With the person who does share my goals. We may have had different paths to the same conclusion, but we both want Maker society and provincial society safely learning from each other. After I take care of this Hilde situation, I'm going to tell him everything.

And then I'm going to kiss him again.

Together Michael and I will come up with a plan to make both the Makers and the Families start doing things differently. But I'm done being a pawn for the Families. I'll let them think I still am, but it's time I trust myself to do things my way.

The elevator doors slide open, and the train platform is abandoned and silent as I make my way out to the submarine. I use my Sire glow to illuminate the inky black cove. There's no sign of the events of a few hours ago. The footprints have been washed away by the sea. So has all the blood. The submarine appears untouched. I suppose the Guard is planning to deal with it later.

The waves are so loud that they drown out all other sound. Which is why I don't hear the other elevator or the door.

But a reflection in the water alerts me that I'm no longer alone on the beach.

I turn, and Kor is standing behind me with his own Sire glow. Alfie and Roman and the other two men move quickly toward the submarine.

"I thought you were locked up," I say, my stomach sinking. I'm happy to see that none of them have been harmed, but something's not right.

"Our other operative did what you failed to do and released us." A motor growls as the submarine powers up.

"I had a plan. I would have freed you."

"I believe you," he says. He steps toward me and takes both my hands in his, our Sire glows blinking out. But we're close enough that I can see the pleading in his eyes. "I should have believed you earlier. Now that I understand the risks associated with the gas, I see why you had to interfere. I was arrogant and overconfident and should have listened to you when you were in a position to know better than me."

Dissonant emotions clash within me. I'm tuned to assume Kor is well intentioned, and here he is, apologizing.

But I know that if he has Hilde, none of his words matter.

"You had said you'd found another universal donor Sire. You drank her blood to get your strength back earlier." When they were in the sub, Grey's attention couldn't have stayed focused on Kor the whole time he was rounding up the other men and all the weapons.

Kor nods.

"Is she in the submarine?"

"No, just refrigerated blood pouches."

Ah. So the dream was more . . . metaphorical.

"Is she safe? Is she being treated well?"

"Yes, Ada, I swear. She's agreed to donate willingly and has been very helpful in assisting me with my treatment."

A small percentage of the tension in my shoulders releases. I don't like it, but at least I know Hilde is safe for now.

Kor continues. "We need to leave before anyone notices we've been released. Are you coming with us?" His hands squeeze mine tightly, possessively. But I'm not his sidekick anymore.

I shake my head.

"Please come." His voice cracks. "I won't let anything like this happen again. I trust you; I'll make sure the Inner Chamber and the Oculus trust you."

He's looking at me with the same sad smile that's broken a million hearts. He fully believes his own performance, but I don't.

However, if he's ready to trust me, I can use that trust to get what *I* need.

"No. I think I can be more useful to you here for now." It's actually he who will be useful to me. Good thing I've had a lot of practice lying.

Movement by the station draws my eye. Someone's there, but night cloaks them in darkness. A shrieking wind ghosts the shore, and I shudder against the chill.

The shadowy figure steps forward. "Ada?" an all-too-familiar voice asks. I pull my hands from Kor's, my heart in my stomach.

A torchlight flicks on, revealing Michael's horror-stricken face. "What are you doing here?" he asks, voice hollow.

He knows what I'm doing. He heard what Kor said. I know he heard; I can tell from the look in his eyes. Disbelief, fear, anger.

Heartbreak.

"Ah," Kor continues. "You two seem well acquainted."

"What's going on?" Michael whispers, shadows playing over his face. The face I was just holding between my hands.

"I can explain—" I choke on a sob.

Why did this have to happen now? Right when I've finally decided where I want to be. Because of him. Because of the beautiful world he's shown me.

He'll never forgive me.

Kor is still speaking, but nothing could make me care about what he's saying. I stare into Michael's torch-lit eyes, and seeing all that betrayal aimed at me, I feel actual, physical pain in my chest.

"Aren't we lucky for recruiting him?" Kor is beaming at Michael.

Wait.

What?

"Prometheus arranged our introduction."

His words don't sink in. It's like he's speaking another language. Like my brain isn't receiving enough oxygen to think, to be able to put the pieces together.

How could Michael be a spy? He's the most honest person I know.

He's also the person most likely to want to help provincial people.

Kor is looking back and forth between us with confusion. Then realization dawns. "Oh, I see. I was under the impression you liked the blond one?"

Michael still hasn't said anything. He hasn't tried to deny it. Why isn't he denying it? My throat is tight, and I feel lightheaded. I need him to deny it.

In the darkness, I can't tell if the crashing in my ears is the waves or my rushing pulse. I can't tell if it's sea salt on my tongue or my own tears.

"Ada," Kor says. "We have to go now. Last chance."

I want to stay right here, where it's too dark to see the truth. Where the wind and water can steal reality and drown it with the tide. But that's not an option. The options are to go back to the Families with Kor. Or to stay with the Makers but without Michael as my ally . . . or as anything else.

Only a few moments ago I was so sure that I knew where my allegiances lie. But now? Everyone I choose seems to be on the wrong side.

But my decision isn't dependent on Michael. My beliefs haven't changed. The plan isn't ruined, only altered.

I'm too raw to do more than shake my head.

"If that's what you want." Kor leans down and kisses me on the cheek. Then he relights his Sire glow, which illuminates his face like an angelic halo. "Goodbye, Ada." After one last fervent glance, he heads to the sub.

Michael and I stand in silence. The hull of the submarine creaks as it begins to submerge, spraying water in our direction.

"You're a great actor," Michael finally says, droplets of water glistening on his hair in the dark. "I thought it was real."

But he's the actor. I see it now. How I have indeed been too young for him all along. A naive girl, so easily manipulated into thinking I knew who he was, when I really had no idea. The memory of his kiss that had been warming me now feels like ice. I want to claw through my stomach and pull out the feelings that have taken root.

I rekindle my Sire glow so we can talk face-to-face. "I'm surprised you agreed to betray your home," I say.

"The provincial world is a beautiful place, and it deserves to share our knowledge," he replies stiffly. "You successfully convinced me of that." His jaw twitches.

"But . . . you know they're the ones who took Hilde? That they're going to use her for her blood?"

"How do you feel about that?" he challenges.

This question feels like a trap. I can't jeopardize my plan by making the Families, or their spy, doubt my commitment.

"I'm just surprised that you're okay with their methods."

"I understand doing what has to be done for a worthy goal," Michael says.

There had been a spark of hope inside me that maybe Michael's involvement was some kind of farce. But with this response, the spark flickers and dies. If Michael is willing to abandon Hilde to the Families, then he's not the person I thought I knew.

"Were you doing the same to Vanguard?" he asks. "Using him like you used me, as a means to an end? A prince sure is a powerful tool to have in your pocket."

I feel sick. "It wasn't like that. With either of you."

I shouldn't have said that. I should make him think it was all strategy. But despite what he now believes, Michael's the one person I've never been good at lying to.

He lets out a humorless laugh. "Sure. You just happened to be in Florence the same time we were tipped off to a Sire in danger." He throws up his hands. "I was so stupid! As if I would just coincidentally run into my perfect girl!" He turns and starts walking toward the station.

His perfect girl. I can't tell, even now, if this is part of some act. I can't tell if his hurt is real or just another manipulation. I can't trust anything about the version of him I thought I knew.

Either way, I now need to pretend to be his ally. I walk after him, practically running to keep up with his long gait.

"Michael, I did all of this for my world, which is hurting and needs a better chance." I blink as we enter the station, adjusting to the light. "I never meant to hurt you. I lied about why I first came to Genesis, but not about anything else. Our relationship—"

He cuts me off. "Ada, you can't expect me to believe anything you say now that I know the way you operate." He says it as if I sicken him.

I didn't know that I had any heart left to break, but something inside me is cracking and leaking, slowly poisoning my insides.

"The way *I* operate?" I follow him into the elevator. "How could you think my actions are worse than what you've done? I've known you—this place, these people—for a few *months*, but this is your *home*. Bloche has been your mentor for years. You're the only one he trusts with his council key. And that thing is a master key for the whole institute. I bet that's what you just used to help them escape. Am I right?"

The elevator doors slide closed, trapping us together in the confined space.

"And how did Korach even know I have a council key?" Michael snaps accusingly. "A fact that he was fully aware of when he approached me to work together. How did he also know that I have files, in my *private* office, containing the location of provincial Sires?"

I feel a wave of shame.

Michael looms beside me, and his eyes flash as he continues. "I had wondered, and now I know that he only knew because *you* seduced me to spy on me."

Anger quickly replaces my shame, and I almost slap him. "I never seduced you. If anything, it was the opposite."

"That's ridiculous. I worked hard to maintain appropriate boundaries."

"So did I!"

"It doesn't matter." Michael's impassioned gaze moves from my face to the wall. "We have a job to do. From what Korach said, it sounds like you attempted to dissuade them from coming here?"

I nod, staring at our matching closed-off expressions in the reflection of the dark glass, the passing flicker of glowing fungi a sinister parody of romantic candlelight.

"Me too," he says, all businesslike. "I only agreed to free them if they committed to never dismiss my concerns for my people's safety again."

That may be so, but he still let them keep Hilde.

The ride seems endless as we silently fidget next to each other.

When Michael speaks again, it's practically a whisper. "When Prometheus put me in touch with Korach, I accepted his offer because of you. You're the one who told me to stop making excuses and do something. And you were right."

I did tell him that. But I would never have wanted him to betray his friends and family or willingly be part of activities that I can't stomach the thought of being a part of myself. The fact that he had that in him at all means that his kind and loyal persona was all a mask.

He lifts his hand to chew his thumbnail, and I instinctively reach to stop him. We both still as our hands touch.

I speak before I can stop myself. "Why does this hurt so much?"

He releases a long breath and says, "Because we lied to each other, and trust is lost."

I turn my face so he doesn't see me cry.

"Don't cry," he says softly. He steps closer and tilts my chin back toward him, then swipes his thumb across my wet cheek. "Part of me thinks this is all an act, yet I can't bear to see you cry."

My body reacts to him as someone familiar, something it wants. It hasn't caught up with what my mind and heart know to be true. He steps even closer, and I don't push him away, not when he cups my face in his hand, not when he skims his thumb across my bottom lip. Not when he leans into my ear and breathes, "Maybe being on the same side isn't such a bad thing."

For a second I almost believe him. Almost forget that we aren't actually on the same side. My lips tingle with the memory of his mouth, my body primed to slip right back to where we left off.

I could rise on my toes and kiss him now. I could do the very thing he's just accused me of doing and use our connection to secure his trust.

But I don't want this version of him.

I don't.

His gaze smolders with anger and want, as if he could punish me with a kiss, vent his anger with our bodies.

It would be hot.

And heartbreaking.

I look away.

Michael steps back and clears his throat.

When we exit the elevator, he says, "We'll go straight to Bloche. I have a plan to explain how they escaped."

"I have one too," I say. Because I do. But it doesn't involve him. "It's better if you seem unconnected to any of this. Your cover is more important than mine. Let me take care of it alone."

He raises his brow, but there's no dimple to be seen. "Okay, we'll do it your way. Your manipulations have gotten you this far."

It's like a knife through my heart. And with each step we take toward the institute, I feel it twist deeper.

43

"Are you sure you're okay?" Rafe asks me for at least the third time. He's escorting me to meet with the headmaster and the Crown Prince, with whom he has called a meeting at my request after the events of last night. "You . . . don't look well." I've told him about Kor's escape, but I neglected to mention the part about my heart being ripped from my chest. Or anything at all about Michael.

"I'm fine," I assure him.

I want to come clean to Genesis, but how can I do that without telling them about Michael? Not telling them leaves them so exposed, yet there's a part of me that still can't imagine that whatever choice he's made could be wrong. And to be able to help both sides, I'm going to need to utilize Michael as an ally.

I resolve to tell them if it becomes necessary, but not yet.

However, I'm ready to confess my own involvement and help to make sure the Makers are protected for whatever the Inquisitors may plan next.

"You do realize," Rafe says to me, "that I've always known."

"Known what?"

"Who your family is. Why you were here."

I stop in my tracks. "What do you mean?"

"Why do you think I mistrusted you so much? Do you think the Guard managed to keep the Makers hidden for all these years without checking the background of all recruits? You think we didn't immediately realize that you are a direct descendant of the Castile line?"

My skull throbs. "Then why did Genesis accept me?"

"Chorus told them to, and they trust her visions implicitly. No one other than the Council knew, but I found out from Alex."

"I don't understand. If you knew, then why did you agree to work with me?"

He shrugs. "I thought you could be useful to me. More asset than enemy . . . and then—"

I jerk my gaze from his and start walking again, not wanting him to finish that thought. He chuckles bitterly and follows.

When we arrive at the council room, Rafe knocks, and we wait to be admitted.

He comes to stand facing me, a little too close, so I step back and hit the wall behind me.

I say words that I know will push him away. "That time on the Atlas, the power outage? It was because of me."

"I gathered."

"I provided the location of the station in New York and alerted the Families of our arrival so they could use a magnetic pulse to stop the train and plant a tracker." And I've been consumed with guilt ever since, assuming that leading the Families to Carnevale must have aided in Hypatia's abduction. But now I wonder if Michael helped them. How long has he been working with Kor?

Rafe hasn't said a word in response to my admission.

I break first. "I'll admit, I expected a little more of a call-for-blood reaction to that information."

"I believe I promised to avoid any more death threats," he teases with the quirk of a smile that makes my mouth go dry.

He steps closer, and my breath hitches as I press into the wall, no space left to retreat. We're both gazing intensely at each other, and it feels different. For the first time, both of our masks are off. He has seen the worst of me, and I of him. We know each other's values without pretense. I feel naked; I'd become so used to wearing my mask.

Rafe lifts his hand to push the hair away from my neck and then he strokes an electric finger down my throat. "I can still taste you," he whispers, leaning in, his nose brushing against my skin. He breathes in deeply, but I have lost my own ability to breathe at all.

I feel barely there wet warmth as his tongue traces the column of my throat, making my entire body shiver and tighten. Then his teeth teasingly press into my skin, and my eyes flutter closed as I arch into him. I didn't know that a heart so recently broken could race this fast. I didn't know that the promise of a bite could make me want—

The door to the council room opens, and we jump apart.

Prince Alex's soft gravel says, "Come in."

The council room is large, and the walls are covered in colorful frescoes from ceiling to floor. Bloche sits in one of the chairs around a grand round table in the center of the room. Carved on the table in front of him is the Genesis emblem. Prince Alex takes a seat at a spot marked with a dragon. At a glance around the table, I see almost every seat is marked with an emblem. Each of the guild symbols are represented as well as the emblem of the Avant Guard, the Viper I recognize as the emblem of the Matriarchy of the Isles, and the Eye that represents the Prophets of Naiot. Rafe and I are not invited to sit.

"I assume we have you to thank for the escaped criminals?" Bloche asks me calmly.

"Yes," I respond.

"And for them coming here in the first place?"

I nod. "But I hope to help lessen the threat they pose by learning their plans and warning you of them."

"You have been working on their behalf but want to change allegiances?" Bloche asks. Prince Alexander looks on, brows drawn, fingers steepled, but he doesn't speak.

"Yes."

"And why should we trust you?"

Rafe interjects, "For what it's worth, I trust her."

I'm surprised by how much it means to me to hear him say that.

"But there's something else you should know. Something more important." All our eyes focus on Rafe as he continues. "Last night, I dreamed of her."

I feel a slow burn creep up my neck. "Rafe, I don't think—"

He quiets me with a hand to my arm, but he's not looking at me. He's looking at Alex. "Yesterday she fed me her blood to heal me."

Bloche says angrily, "Prince Alexander, the Council assured us that if we accepted Avant students onto this campus, there would be no blood consumption—"

The prince holds up his hand. "With respect, Headmaster, I think we need to hear what Raphael is trying to say."

"After I drank Ada's blood," Rafe continues, "I dreamed of her all night. Of her . . . in the future."

"What did you see?" Alex asks.

"I didn't understand most of it."

Alex shakes his head. "Blood prophecies are always cryptic. Record every detail you can remember. You'll need to speak with Chorus."

"Are you suggesting that Journey Castle has the Sight?" Bloche asks.

"If by consuming her blood, Raphael experienced prophecy, then it would seem so."

Bloche turns to me and asks, "Have you ever had premonitions or visions?"

My mind is a whirl. Of course I haven't had visions!

Except I have. *The dream.*

"Once," I say.

Alex glares at me intently, and with a note of accusation he says, "Receiving prophecy involves a ritual that requires extensive training. But unreliable and cryptic premonitions can be induced with Kishuf—the corruption of nature with dark arts, like blood magic. Did you consume blood before your vision?"

"Of course not." Except . . . "Oh. Simon—he fell on me, and his cheek cut on my teeth." I cringe at the memory of blood filling my mouth. "But it was totally an accident."

Alex stands and stalks over to me. He looks down, straight into my eyes. His gaze is cold, regal, commanding. "Who are you?" he asks.

For a moment I don't answer. Then I say the name that once brought me pride. "My name is Ada Isabella Castle, from the Daughters of Castile, steward to the histories of the Families of the Holy Inquisition." I swallow and continue. "I was sent here to gather information for the Families. But I now renounce that task." Well, at least partially. "From now on I want to help protect the Makers of Genesis."

Prince Alex shakes his head. "But who *are* you?" he presses. He's asking a question that I have been unconsciously asking myself for some time now.

While I've been finally getting to know my *self*—my heart, my beliefs, my values—I've had doubt cast on everything I thought I knew about my upbringing and who I'd always thought my family was.

"I'm not sure how to answer your question," I say sincerely. "But I can tell you this. My father is a musician named Joseph Levi."

Alex's eyes go wide, and I hear sharp intakes of breath from Bloche and

Rafe. The room seems to go still for a silent moment, and then everything is moving faster than my heartbeat.

Alex grabs Rafe by the shoulders and says intently, "You must tell no one. Not even Father."

"We have to inform Chorus," Bloche says, standing.

Alex shakes his head in frustration. "She probably already knows. She hasn't wanted to meet the girl. She's been saying it's not yet time." He shakes his head again, his long hair shifting like a living thing. "I wish she would . . ." He trails off and looks at me again. "Yosef was not a Prophet himself, but his grandmother was." His grandmother, meaning my great-grandmother. Was a Prophet. "It would make sense that his child would inherit the Sight." Alex advances on me. The intensity has not left his eyes. "You must never ingest blood to induce a blood prophecy. You were lucky this time, but I cannot stress how dangerous Kishuf is. When the time is right, Chorus will train you to develop your Sight properly using the ritual stones. Kishuf will never be necessary." He strokes his beard. "By the Conductor, the child of Yosef HaLevi . . . How old are you?" he asks me.

"Eighteen."

"And your father is still alive?"

When I nod, Alex silently mutters what I assume to be a prayer as he runs his hands through his long hair. I remember what Michael had said about how it was unknown whether Yosef HaLevi had perished during the Fall of Naiot.

No one in the Families has ever heard of Naiot. My mother was married to my father for ten years, and even she had never heard of it.

I'd reread the *Testament of Chorus* countless times since my conversation with Michael that made me realize my father had some kind of connection to the village. But as I take in what they're saying about him having been from a family of prophets, I start to understand that the people who died in

Naiot were my *family*. A lot about my father makes more sense now—his emotional distance and moodiness. I can't imagine how it must have been for him to have learned what happened to his home and family, to have lived when they had not, and to not have even be able to talk about their existence and properly mourn. My heart breaks for him.

Suddenly Alex's eyes widen as he assesses me. He takes note of my long hair, which hasn't been properly cut in months, and in a soft voice he asks, "Have you taken the vow?"

I shake my head. I know what he's asking. I'd been suspecting it about myself ever since I'd learned that my father was a Nazir and what that meant, and I'd remembered the way Dad always insisted on keeping my hair trimmed.

"I will train you myself," Alex says.

Bloche sits back down. His voice is choked as he asks, "She is also a Nazir?"

"I think she amplified me twice," Rafe answers.

Of course, the fire when we were training. And yesterday, when he asked me to sing to help him heal. . . .

Bloche is staring at me, his one visible eye wet. "A Sire, a Nazir, and a Prophet?"

"The Child of Three," Alex declares.

"What? No—" I try to interject, but Rafe grips my hand tightly, silencing me.

"Isn't the Child of Three prophesied to be Chorus's child?" Rafe asks.

"No." Alex shakes his head. "The prophecy says only that the child will be of her blood—which could mean any direct relation—and that she will teach them. After the Fall of Naiot and her whole family's death, it made sense for many to assume it would be her child, but"—he is gazing at me with an awe that makes me uncomfortable—"Chorus's mother, Psalm, was Yosef's sister, so perhaps *his* child is the one that was foretold."

"When did you turn eighteen?" Alex presses me.

My head is spinning. "Uh, three days ago."

"Eighteen years ago, one day after she buried her village, Chorus had a vision of hope coming into the world. That was the same day you were born. It all aligns."

I feel shaky and, honestly, horrified. Everyone is so quiet and just staring at me with misplaced reverence, as if I have something to give them. I have *nothing* to give them.

Their long-awaited messiah who will bring them out of exile—*me?* That can't be. I'm just a mediocre Sire. I don't even know if I believe in prophecies. I'm not even telling them the whole truth about anything. Any prophecy relying on me is destined for a whole lot of disappointment.

Bewildered, I look at the intricate murals on the walls surrounding me. Robed figures who look lifelike enough to walk off the walls. Valkyries, unicorns, wind horses, dragons. I'm an impostor in this world. A jack-of-all-trades among masters.

No. I close my eyes and chastise myself. I don't believe that anymore. What is a jack-of-all-trades if not a Renaissance man in training? I'm more than I've given myself credit for. But there's still no way that I am who they're suggesting. The one prophesied to reunite them with the world.

Except, hasn't that always been my goal? To join the wonders of this world with my own? My heart feels trapped in my throat.

There is a quiet knock at the door, and at Bloche's barked invitation, Michael walks in.

"Oh, I didn't mean to interrupt—" He takes in the shocked faces. "Is everything okay?" His eyes lock with mine. I pull my hand free from Rafe's grip. A muscle in Michael's jaw twitches, and he turns to Bloche.

"All is well, my boy," the headmaster says, his voice heavy with emotion. "All is exactly as it should be."

I look from the headmaster, who thinks I will be the salvation of his people, to Michael, who thinks I will contribute to their betrayal. I gaze down at my hands, at my fingers. I take in the crescent scars, the lines of my palms, the web of the blue veins.

What are these hands of mine capable of?

ACKNOWLEDGMENTS

To my agent, Ali Lake, no amount of thank-yous will ever be sufficient. You were not only the first person to take a chance on me and my book, but you also grasped the layers of this story in a way that none of my other readers ever have. You have shown me that with the right agent, even the hardest parts of publishing aren't so hard. I'm so excited that we have been given the chance to grow our careers together.

Thank you to my editor, Sarah McCabe. Working with you has been a dream. You helped bring out the best in this book, and you did so in a way that always made me feel supported and heard. I adore your attention to detail and respect for the process of getting everything just right.

Thank you so much to everyone at Simon & Schuster who has made this book possible. I know that as I write this, I haven't met all of you yet, but I am endlessly thankful for everything you are doing behind the scenes to create my book and to get it into the hands of readers. My deepest gratitude to Justin Chanda, Karen Wojtyla, Anne Zafian, Anum Shafqat, Emma Saska, and Tatyana Rosalia, and also to Penina Lopez, Cecilia Gray, and Kayley Hoffman. And to Chrissy Noh, Caitlin Sweeny, Alissa Rashid, Lisa Quach, Bezi Yohannes, Perla Gil, Remi Moon, Amelia Johnson, James Akinaka, Saleena Nival, Elizabeth Huang, Trey Glickman, Shannon Pender, Amy Lavigne, Julia Ashley Romero, Lisa Moraleda, Nicole Russo, and Maryam Ahmad. A million thank-yous also to Christina Pecorale and her sales team and Michelle Leo and her education/library team.

Thank you to the incredibly talented Dominique Mayer and Michael McCartney for the gorgeous cover illustration and design that will be the reason many people pick up this book. Also to Robert Lazzarreti and

Michael McCartney for the map illustration and design, and to Aleksandra Simonović for the emblem illustrations. Sarah and Michael, I truly appreciated our collaboration on all the visual elements of the book; thank you both for your incredible vision and for being so flexible with my pickiness and changes in direction.

Thank you to my sister, Devorah. Over the long journey of writing this book, you have been on your own journey, from your graduation and the start of your career to a cancer diagnosis, treatment, and remission. And through it all, you have been my best and most constant source of support and feedback. You were still a toddler when I moved out of the house, and I am so thankful that so many years later, this book helped bring us closer as sisters. (And Azzie, I love you, too.)

Thank you to Michal Schick, Jenn Levine, and A.C. Huntley, the best writing buddies/hype team/group chat an author could ask for. Had we not started our accountability write-ins during lockdown, I don't think this book would exist. You were there every step of the way through the ups and downs, and you truly are my writing sisters—and the best book aunts ever!

Thank you to the Salon: Rachel Rose, Genoveva Dimova, Katy Hays, Joel Dane, Meredith Adamo, Sandra Salsbury, Ahana Virdi, Amy Jackson, Cee Jordan, Jill Grun, Brooke Johnson, Mitchell Logue, Anna Makowska, and also Egg, Amber, and Ren. You folks have seriously midwifed me through the entire process of submission and debut. I have learned so much from every single one of you, and your friendship has been as much of a boon as your writing and publishing support.

Thank you to The Doctors, Ariel and Jill, for fielding all my random medical questions over the years with patience and enthusiasm. So many of those theoretical conversations have been woven into the fabric of this story.

Thank you to the many friends and fellow authors who have done things large and small that made all the difference. I cannot possibly list you all here, but know that I deeply appreciate every one of you. To name only a few: Thank you to Katy Hays, Brigid Kemmerer, Genoveva Dimova, Shea Ernshaw, and Ashley Shuttleworth for your gorgeous blurbs! And to Crystal Seitz, in you having done this all right before me, you truly acted as my headlights, helping me navigate this process with the wisdom of your experience. To my many beta readers who gave of their time and helped me polish this book at varying stages, I could never have gotten to this point without you. Special thanks to Madison Story—your enthusiasm for my plot and characters fueled me through many bouts of impostor syndrome. I can't wait to see your stories on shelves one day soon. (I tried to find the right Taylor Swift reference for this occasion, but it's probably best that I couldn't as this is getting too long, and this time I don't have you to show me what to chop.) Thank you also to Leah Enowitz for coming with me to research the Cloisters, helping me with structural sketches, and also for being a hype-woman extraordinaire. (It brings me so much joy that one of your designs made it onto my map.)

Thank you to all of the writers on the internet who selflessly provide valuable resources for writers like me, and to all the various online communities and discord servers I've benefited from over the years. Special shoutout to OLUF, authortube, and r/pubtips. Also to the random girl on YouTube who said if you don't sit down and write, it won't get written. You were right.

Thank you to the inhabitants of the many teachers' rooms I have graced over the course of my different jobs. I was so lucky to be surrounded by scholars in all the topics that I am no expert in who I could pepper with esoteric questions that helped me craft this world and bring in relevant aspects of real history. And a special thank you to Milana Korchman because I never would have kept writing this story if it weren't for your early enthusiasm and gossiping about my characters between our classes. Thank you also to Adina

Kastner who went from being an English teacher buddy to a writing buddy and a constant source of encouragement.

Thank you to my parents (and stepparents), for raising me to have the drive and belief in myself to start and finish this project, and for doing so with a love for art and music that helped inspire the themes of this book. I promise none of the parents in this book are based on you!

Thank you, Moshe. You may be sick of hearing me talk about anything to do with publishing, but you only have yourself to blame since you are the one who encouraged me to take my writing seriously. All these years, you have been the person keeping our home—and my sanity—running even when book deadlines left you feeling like a single father. Thank you for being such a loving partner who helps bring out my best self. If anyone ever thinks I am good at writing love interests, they have you to thank for being the perfect muse. And thank you to our little bear, who taught me the true potential of what a human can create and the truest meaning of love.

Last but not least, thank you to every single reader, bookseller, librarian, and influencer who ever recommends this story to someone new and helps it find its audience.

Lamnatzeach b'niginot mizmor shir. For the Conductor, a song.